Books by John Rose
3303 Ward Court N.E.
Salem, Oregon 97305
alioregon@aol.com
www.amazon.com/author/johnrrose

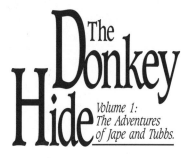

The Donkey Hide

Volume 1:
The Adventures
of Jape and Tubbs.

BY
JOHN R. ROSE

Rose Publishing / Salem, Oregon

Library of Congress Catalog Card Number 93-93653
ISBN 1-881170-04-7

Printed in the United States of America

First printing . . . . . October 1994

Rose Publishing
3303 Ward Drive NE
Salem, Oregon 97305
1-800-842-7421
(503) 393-8488

Table of Contents

Introduction

A combination of many things produced the writings in this book. While watching the Oprah Winfrey show, something about "Children's Rights," the idea behind "The Donkey Hide" was conceived. The life style of Tom Sawyer and Jape, the hero of "The Donkey Hide" is similar. In an effort to produce a story line that would hold the interest of both young and old, while making a point regarding the lack of change in laws protecting children in the last half century, this book was born.

The setting for the adventures of Jape and Tubbs is in rural America, Crossroads, Oklahoma in 1939. The story is fiction; however, the author grew up in that area. Although, the book is fiction, some of the adventures were from memories of his childhood. All the characters named in the book are fictitious. If the book portrays any character either living or dead it is truly an accident.

This book is written without sex or filthy language. In spite of that you will find that it will provide a few hours of interesting reading. The story is about the daily life of two nine year old country boys which creates the adventures of Jape and Tubbs. This book will allow those of that era to rekindle some of the fond memories of days gone by, while providing the younger generation with some insight as to what life was like only a few years ago.

In 1939 there were only a few cars on the roads in that part of America. The rural folks, for the most part, went to town in a horse-drawn wagon. Some of the well to do owned a horse and buggy; however, most of those parked the buggy and purchased an automobile. Children could see good clean movies for a dime; Gene Autry, Roy Rogers, Tom Mix etc.

Children were spanked at home and at school. Very few children ever graduated from the eighth grade without getting spanked. It was a common every day occurrence at school. On the other hand it was very uncommon to hear any student "talk back" to the teacher. Respect, was instilled in every student. Along with the academics, the report card provided a grade in: thrift, obedience, dependableness, courtesy and cleanliness. Oh my, oh my, hasn't time changed.

The words,"junk food," had not yet been added to the American vocabulary. People ate what they could get, survival was their main concern. Both husband and wife worked from before daylight until after sundown to survive. In many homes a hot bath was a luxury. Some could take a day off now and then to attend church on the Sabbath but during harvest and farming season most worked seven days a week until the crops were in or the farming complete. A day of rest was a luxury most could ill afford. Those living the rural life were hard and lean from consistant daily toil. Obesity was so uncommon that many children paid a dime at the county fair to see the "Fat Lady."

In 1939 the penitentiarys treated the prisoners differently, prisoners had to wear clothing with broad stripes and their food by today's standards would have been called garbage. The prisoners were tied down and whipped as punishment. The leather strap they were whipped with was called "The Donkey Hide." The wide strap of leather was much more humane than the old "Cat of Nine Tails" which brutally cut the flesh. Those providing punishment felt the six-inch wide leather strap was a step in the right direction and, of course, a few years later the whipping of prisoners was abandoned entirely.

Children's rights have not changed much since 1939. Without getting into the plot of the book by changing a few items, the setting of this story could just as well be in the 1990s as during the 1930s.

That period of American history is known as The Great Depression and, in general, times were extremely hard. On looking back it could be the last of the real good times. Jape and Tubbs could roam the hills, walk to town or go to the county fair by themselves without any thought of being molested. Everyone left their possessions outside without fear of losing anything to a thief. Most of the rural homes were built without locks. Children were taught respect while discipline and punishment were part of the learning process. If a child was promoted from the third to the fourth grade, that child could read and write.

Surviving the elements truly was an adventure by today's standard of living. Nothing was easy, but that is why it was an adventure. Life during that period was not easy but that was the way it was for those two nine year olds every morning when they jumped out of bed to face the world. Come and join Jape and Tubbs, drift back in time and enjoy the relaxed world of two country boys as they try to survive . . . the Donkey Hide!

Chapter 1
Blood Brothers

There was a light breeze from the southeast but not enough to keep the blistering hot sun from burning the red-dirt road. Jape plodded along, his bare feet getting hotter with each step. He wasn't in any hurry as he carefully picked his steps in an effort to stay off the hard, hot clay. Buggy and wagon wheels had beaten the road into a fine, velvety dust. In 1939 there were a few cars around but one was seldom seen traversing that old road. On the rare occasion when a car did drive through the countryside, everyone working in the fields would gawk until it disappeared around a curve or into the horizon, out of sight. It then became the topic of conversation for the next week.

Most of the ruts made after the last rain had long since been pounded into dust but a few clods and short, jagged edges of ruts remained. Jape tried to avoid these by sliding his bare feet through the hot dust to feel the cooler ground two inches below the surface. It wasn't ten o'clock yet and by mid-afternoon the sun, along with a steady southeast wind, would cook that red dirt all the way to China, then Jape would have to walk on the cool grass at the edge of the road.

The summers in the south were hot but Jape was dressed for comfort. His old straw hat did a great job of keeping the sun from cooking his brain while providing shade for his eyes. He was wearing only the straw hat and a pair of striped overalls, the regular attire for most country boys in that community. His overalls had two good suspenders, all of the buttons worked but there were a few neat patches. His mother gave strict instructions to take care of them because they had to last all summer. This meant he would not get a new pair until school began next fall when the old ones would be converted to work clothing and worn while doing the farm chores before and after school. The straw hat was two years old already and he would wear it until it was too small and then it would be passed on to someone else, as it had been given to him. The hat would cost twenty-five cents if purchased at the store and money was extremely scarce around Crossroads.

Crossroads, a little farming community three miles east of Paoli, Oklahoma, had a two-room schoolhouse on one corner, one room housing the first through the fourth grade and the adjoining room the fifth through the eighth. Two stores and an electric sub-station occupied the other three corners. There was electricity to the sub-station but only two or three houses, the school and the two stores had electric lights but no other electrical conveniences. The toilets at the school were of the four-holer variety, one for the boys on one corner of the schoolyard and another for the girls across the yard.

Since school was out Jape spent his time working on the farm, getting into trouble or working hard to keep out of trouble. The broomcorn thrasher was coming by the school house about ten. Several boys were needed to work on the crew and any boy wanting to earn a little money would be there. The farmers always allowed every boy in the community the opportunity to work. Jape and his friends were exactly the right age to help out. This thrashing crew consumed all of the men, women and kids in the community. The men usually traded work, you help me and I'll help you; however, the boys were paid fifteen cents per hour. The average time for thrashing was about two hours and the boys did not get paid for waiting around or traveling to the next farm. They usually got to work three or four jobs in a day and, on a good day, could possibly earn a dollar. This was the way most had to earn money for new shoes for school. All of the boys from eight to twelve were doing a pretty good day's work on the farm; the work on the thrashing crew was a lesser task than the work they would be doing if they remained home.

What Jape and most of the boys looked forward to was the harvest dinner and the swim in the river to get the stinging dust off at the end of the day. All of the farmers worked in a cooperative effort, with several families uniting in an effort to get the broomcorn thrashed and stored. The men and some of the women worked in the field, while other women cooked and prepared the food. The thrashing crew went from one farm to the next, arriving at the one with the dinner ready about noon. Usually the food was served outside, like a giant picnic, on temporary tables with white sheets for tablecloths.

The meals were always the same — a home-grown feast — with almost nothing purchased from a store. The bread was hot and home-made, either large dinner rolls or biscuits and always lots of cornbread with several large bowls of fresh butter. The choice of beverages was generally iced tea, Kool Aid, milk and water. The women took great pride in providing many kinds of pickles including several kinds of regular cucumber pickles, then each lady brought her specialty such as pickled green tomatoes, peppers, peaches and, of course, various kinds of delicious relish like chowchow. Every meat dish that could be produced from a steer, hog or fowl was available — roast beef, pork, baked ham, sausage, chicken — along with potatoes and gravy, potato salad, fried potatoes, okra, green beans, large platters of corn-on-the-cob, hominy and on and on. The dessert was always a large variety of cakes, pies and giant cobblers. Everyone in that community lived out of the garden in the summer and canned their food for the winter, or else lived on beans, potatoes and cornbread. If given the opportunity, Jape and his friends would have worked free just to be able to eat dinner at the harvest table.

Just the thought of all this food caused the saliva to accumulate in Jape's mouth. He spit into the hot sand as he looked toward the schoolhouse to see if anyone else was there yet. Nope, no one in sight. He ran around the building to check. He was the first one to arrive. Jape stopped at the pump to get a drink of water. The well with an iron pump was located under an open arbor next to the schoolhouse. The spout of the pump had a one-inch pipe about four-feet long welded onto it, with small holes drilled on top of the pipe. Water squirted out of these holes for the children to drink when the handle was pumped up and down. Jape made a few pumps on the long, iron handle which brought cool, fresh, well water. By the time he ran around the pump to get to the spurting water it was down to a trickle. It took two people to get a good drink but Jape did manage to catch a few dribbles. He threw his straw hat under the spout and pumped several hard strokes, causing the water to splash over the hat. The water, naturally, ran right through the straw but left the hat wet and cool. Jape flopped the hat onto his head allowing the water to run down his neck and back, skipping and twirling his body in a circle as he ran away from the pump, then swinging the hat in a large circle which caused the water to fly as when a wet dog shakes himself.

Jape was always the first one to arrive at any meeting and it was his dad who was the real driving force, telling him he should always be prompt. In his effort to miss out on as much of the work at home as possible, Jape usually left much, much too early. He was smart enough to know he would rather be waiting at the school than working at home. His friend "Tubbs" was exactly the opposite, always late, generally tardy at school, but, not unlike Jape, usually in trouble at school and at home. When they weren't in school or required to work, the two boys were together somewhere, doing something. Looking down the road, Jape saw Tubbs trudging toward him, but he was nearly half mile away. He knew it was Tubbs by the waddle. Tubbs sure didn't get his name because of being skinny. But Jape was shocked to see Tubbs arriving so early, because usually he was last.

The distance didn't mean anything to Jape, who took off in a run to meet his companion whom he had not seen in over a week. Only when work prohibited it were they not together. The lads stayed all night at each other's house at every opportunity. Some nights they slept out on a creek bank while each boy's parents thought that their son was at the other parents' home. The hot sun quickly dried the water from Jape's straw hat and the cool water was replaced with sweat. In spite of the heat he continued to trot toward Tubbs. A quarter of a mile down the road the two boys met. There were very few rural telephones in that part of the world in 1939. Word-of-mouth was the main means of communication and this morning neither boy had known for sure that the other would be there. However, each had a solid understanding of the other's habits and since the thrasher was coming by each knew the other would be there without anything being said.

They were both smiling as they came into sight of each other. Boys didn't hug and they were too young to shake hands, so . . . Jape ran right on by Tubbs knocking his hat off, then ran in a circle laughing at him. Tubbs picked up a rock and threw it in the general direction of Jape who laughed and ran back to push Tubbs. The two boys shoved each other a few times, their way of hugging and telling the other, "I love you" without a kind word being said.

"How come you're early?" Jape asked.

"I'm not, could be I'm late and the thrasher has already gone by. How long you been here?"

"Not long, no fresh tracks since the mail man's buggy. They will be by in good time. Don't fret, the longer we wait, the less time to work."

"We miss the thrasher and we miss dinner!" Tubbs grimaced.

"You know where we're going for dinner?"

"Nope, don't matter it's always good."

"Good hell, it's Christmas and Thanksgiving all rolled into one."

"You better watch your mouth, Jape. You have said that naughty word several times lately. You're going to get into a bad habit this summer and when school starts Mrs. Auld will take you into the closet or, worse, wash your mouth out with soap."

"I watch my mouth at school and all I said was hell. All the big boys say more that that and —"

Tubbs interrupted, "You're not a big boy until you get promoted to the big room. It will be one more year."

"Don't hurt to practice cursing a little. The big boys chew Days Work. I think I have the cursing down pretty good. I can say DAMN and HELL about as good as those smart-aleck sixth graders in the big room. If I had a nickel to get a plug of Days Work."

"You'd what?" Tubbs challenged. "Become a smart-aleck fourth grader instead of waiting a couple years? And if Mrs. Auld finds out you are chewing tobacco, you will not only get it in the closet but she'll tell your dad."

"For chewing? Yep, I guess you're right but I could practice when we're out on the creek. You know, when we're alone and no one would ever know. Then when I get into the big room, well, they wouldn't have anything on me."

"Well I'm not going to spend any of my thrashing money on tobacco. You can waste yours if you want. Besides, Brownmule is a lot stronger than Days Work. I heard one of the ball players say that anyone with a hair on his chest would chew Brownmule. You got hair on your chest, Jape?"

"Nope, and you don't either. I'm not old enough but you're a sissy and never will have hair on your chest."

He took off running while Tubbs trotted along behind as Jape was much faster. Jape disappeared around the corner of the schoolhouse, running toward the well. He had ten little water fountains spurting from the pump when Tubbs arrived. Jape quit pumping at the exact moment that Tubbs leaned down to drink. Tubbs looked up, put his hands on his hips and glared at Jape who started pumping again. Tubbs stood there as the water gushed into the air. He turned and leaned down to drink and Jape quit pumping again. Jape burst out laughing as Tubbs said "It won't be so damned funny if I get my hands on you."

"Naughty, naughty you said a bad word. I'm going to tell on you."

"So tell on me but let me drink, I'm hot and tired." Tubbs complained.

Jape started pumping as Tubbs drank his fill of water then turned to ask, "Want me to pump for you?"

"Yep, if you would please."

"Oh, aren't you the polite one, now that you want some water."

"I can do without but I could also use a drink. I tried to pump my own before you got here but it didn't work," Jape explained.

Tubbs started pumping but Jape didn't trust him he stood and watched for a few seconds then asked, "I know you're pumping but are you going to get even or let me drink?"

"No, go ahead and drink. I'll be nice to you. But hurry here comes the thrasher."

Jape gulped down a few swallows of the cold water and they ran toward the road.

The farmer slowed the tractor down but didn't stop as the boys jumped on. The rest of the boys were already on the thrasher. Jape started talking with one of the boys immediately, learning that the thrasher had gone by the school at six that morning and already had been to two farms. They were headed for one more before going to the Johnson farm where they would eat. Most of the boys knew each other but some of the crew were from other neighborhoods, strangers to Jape and Tubbs. There were too many on the crew to get introduced all around but the two boys learned where they were going and where they would have dinner.

On this two-mile ride they drove past the Webster farm. The orchard wasn't far from the road and several trees of red ripe peaches could be seen. Tubbs turned his head slowly toward Jape and the boys' eyes rolled back into their sockets with a perfect understanding of their thoughts. Each knew they would be eating peaches before the summer was over.

The farmer had a one-lung "Popping Johnnie" (John Deere) with a large flywheel which drove a twenty-foot belt that ran the thrasher. The broomcorn was hauled from the field in horse-drawn wagons. The beds on the wagons tilted to let the broomcorn slide out the back onto the ground in neat piles. The broomcorn straw all pointed in the same direction. Broomcorn grew tall like sugar cane, with a single head about eighteen inches long containing twenty to thirty straws holding seeds. These seeds had to be knocked out and that was the purpose of the thrashing crew. Then the fiber had to be cured before the remaining straw could be made into brooms. This was accomplished by shelving the straw in an open building immediately after thrashing so that the hot, dry air could cure and harden the straw. This area of Oklahoma was the broomcorn capital of the world.

After the tractor and the thrasher were set-up, the work started with two lines of workers on each end of the thrasher. One line carried the unthrashed corn to the thrasher. This started with a worker picking up a workable arm load of the unthrashed corn which he carried to the thrasher table. This table contained a moving conveyer belt with a butting board. The corn was butted up against the board to make sure the stalk ends were straight as they moved along on the conveyer belt. This allowed the heads to travel through the teeth of the thrasher equally. Inside the thrasher short metal wires or teeth were flopping around in a circle to knock the seeds from the broom or straw part of the head. These seeds were blown out the back of the thrasher by a giant fan causing a lot of broomcorn dust to fly around in the air. This dust had a very unpopular quality; it caused the flesh to sting and burn. Not many people looked forward to working on the broomcorn thrasher and those who did also looked forward to going for a swim afterward.

This first job for Jape and Tubbs took less that two hours but they were paid for two anyway, a total of thirty cents each. The boys were well pleased and ready to head for the next job and the dinner table. The farmer sometimes didn't make as much as thirty cents after paying all of his harvest expenses.

Jape and Tubbs had their own agenda. As the thrasher headed for dinner the tractor seemed to go a lot slower. As they rolled along the dirt road the two boys talked about many things including what they were going to spend their money on. Tubbs had kept a secret from Jape for a few days and it was burning a hole in his tongue. He blurted out, "I'm getting a 22-rifle!"

"You're not either. Where you going to get a 22?"

"A friend of Mom's has one, said I could have it if I chopped cotton for a week and that's what I have been doing. In two more days, it will be mine."

"Oh, good, good, man-oh-man, we can go huntin' with a real gun. We can throw the slingshots away." Jape was elated.

But Tubbs challenged, "No we can't. Shells cost 20-cents a box and they don't have any at Crossroads."

"I'll spend twenty cents on a box of shells. You know my uncle owns the store and —"

"I don't know why you say that. He isn't your uncle, he's your grandpaw's brother. Your uncle is your mother's brother," Tubbs pointed out.

"Okay, so he's my mother's uncle. He's something to —"

"Yep, you're their poor relatives and you can't buy anything if they don't have it and can't get it."

"We'll see about that!" Japes said. "Hey, let's jump off at the school and go get some candy-beads. I'm out and it is hard to shoot any other rock and hit anything. What'a ya say?" Japes was eager to change the subject and gather candy-bead rocks that the boys used for ammunition for their slingshots.

"Yeah, I could use a pocketful too, but if we leave the thrasher we might not be recognized as part of the crew and miss out on dinner. We can get some candy-bead rocks on the way back tonight. We'll be going back by the school to get to your "uncle's" place. You know we are going over there this afternoon?" Tubbs asked.

"I didn't hear that. Are you sure?"

"Yep, I'm sure."

Jape started to say something but the thrasher pulled into the driveway hitting a bump and half of the boys were bounced off. The tractor didn't slow down until it got to the barn with a dozen boys running along behind. The farmer and a crew of Johnnies were waiting. Johnnies were the men who worked in the field, breaking, cutting and hauling broomcorn. The gals who worked with them were called Sallies. The crew of men began getting the thrasher ready. Several wagonloads of unthrashed corn lay around the barn yard, they were ready to thrash. One man shouted to the thrashing crew, "You young fellows better go get washed and get to the table. We'll be along before you get started good." Then he raised his voice for the ladies, "Get these guys started eating so they will be finished and ready to go to work in about half an hour." From those instructions an old woman about thirty came around the corner of the house telling the boys to wash up and shouting, "Dinner is on the table!"

The boys didn't usually get a head start on the men but the thrasher seldom arrived at exactly noon either. The men wanted to be ready to start thrashing immediately after dinner. All of the boys dug into the food but no one appreciated the fried chicken as much as Jape and Tubbs because they rarely had fried chicken at home — only occasionally on Sunday when the preacher said he was coming to dinner and then the best parts had better be left for him. Occasionally the preacher wouldn't show up and on those Sundays the boys got to eat some of the good meat. Both boys were good hunters and killed a rabbit now and then — certainly more frequently than they had fried chicken. The boys dug into the meat and the corn-on-the-cob, then topped their dinners off with very hearty portions of peach cobbler. After dinner they pushed back from the table and waddled out toward the thrashing machine. They were too full to work but so was everyone else but they worked anyway!

After the thrasher got going it was a good job. The south breeze had picked up but the thrasher was stationed so that the wind would blow the dust away from the crew of workers. Everyone was full and content and no one made a remark when paid for two hours after working two hours and twelve minutes. The boys were back on the thrasher headed for the next job, Uncle John's. Only now they had sixty cents in their pockets. Jape had one large half-dollar and a dime. That half-dollar sure did feel big dangling in his right front pocket. Tubbs had six dimes, said they were lighter and easier to carry.

Jape and Tubbs were not hard to spot even among that motley group of thrasher hands. Without exception every boy was barefooted and some were limping. Nearly every boy had something wrong — a stone bruise, half a toe nail missing, broken toes and cuts, tears and abrasions — but they were all smiling. All Uncle John had to do to find Jape and Tubbs was spot the two with the most dirt. The other boys had worked two more jobs but still were not as dirty. These two kids could walk through a church on Easter Sunday morning and get dirty. On greeting the thrashing crew he saw Jape and immediately shouted and waved for him to come over. Jape and Tubbs ran to meet him.

"Jape, I'm going to fill two sheds at the same time. This way the crew will not have to stand in line or wait. The thrasher can keep on working. You two boys will punch slats. Go over there," he said, pointing to two long broomcorn sheds built about sixteen feet apart, "and get those slats ready. You boys make sure you have slats ready every time the shelver needs them, you understand?" Both boys in unison, "Yes, sir, and thanks." They turned to run toward the sheds. This was what every boy dreamed about, the best job of all. While all the other boys carried that stinging corn, all they had to do was place two boards into one of the slits on the side of the building and when the shelver filled the last shelf with corn, push the two boards through so he could make another shelf and start laying corn again.

This was their lucky afternoon, although it was at least 110 degrees in the shade, the boys were pleased with their new-found position in life. The other boys on the crew could only look on with envy. Usually each had a turn at being king of the hill as relatives seem to always take care of their own. Uncle John had a much larger broomcorn crop than most and the thrashing took much longer, a couple minutes over three hours. Both sheds were nearly full when the end came in sight. Uncle John came around to pay the boys while they were still working. The thrasher driver wanted to get a running start to the next job as John's had taken longer than expected and another farmer was waiting. Uncle John winked as he gave each boy a half dollar. The boys later learned that all the other boys had been paid only forty-five cents.

Uncle John turned to walk away then turned back to ask, "Jape, you boys coming back this way to go home tonight, aren't you?"

Jape looked at Tubbs, shrugged his shoulders to answer his question with one of his own, "I guess so, why?"

"Stop by and see me. I may have a surprise for you!"

Jape grinned, "Okay, Uncle John."

The man turned to go about his business of paying the remainder of the crew. They finished the job in about five minutes and by the time everyone got a drink of water the thrasher was headed out to the next job.

The heat was blistering hot, and sweat was running off of everyone. Not a complaint was heard; the boys wiped sweat while grinning broadly. Each had his own hate for the heat and the hard work but what the money would buy kept them working and smiling. Tubbs had to run a little extra hard to catch the thrasher. Jape gave him a hand as he was the last boy on. They were on their way to another job. Punching slats was a real break for Jape and Tubbs. The other boys had to carry the corn and they were rubbing, scratching and griping a little about the rash it caused some of the boys. Everyone agreed a swim would be nice later but it was too far to go to the river. If the next farmer didn't have a pond, Jake knew of several on his way home but he kept his mouth shut. Many of the farmers didn't want anyone swimming in their ponds.

After a short rest, Tubbs mused, "Wouldn't it be great if we could do this every day all summer?"

"Yeah, we would be rich when school started."

"Wonder what a car would cost?"

"Wouldn't matter, Tubbs, we would be rich and could buy anything we wanted."

"We wouldn't be rich on a dollar a day. We would only have fifty or sixty bucks and that ain't rich."

"Twenty bucks is rich to me. I never had more 'n a dollar, ever," Jape said.

"You got a dollar and a dime now."

"Yeah, and I'm borderline rich too. I can get a new pair of shoes for three dollars and forty-seven cents."

"Don't your dad buy your shoes?" Tubbs asked.

"Yeah, but then my mother picks 'em out. If I can pay for 'em I get to buy what I want, as long as my wants aren't too far out. Wonder what Uncle John wants?"

"He said a surprise, does he have a watermelon patch?"

"Don't know but we should find one on the way home tonight. Wonder what time we'll get to quit?"

"Last year we worked until after ten, they had lights on the tractor."

"For fifteen cents an hour I'd work all night," Jape told his friend.

The boys rode in silence; the heat was terrible but the work had to be done. It was four miles to the next place.

When the thrasher pulled into the barn all of the boys jumped off and waited like a herd of ducks, to be told what to do. The owner of the thrasher went right to work getting set up. His crew knew what to do but those waiting to assist could not work until the thrasher started. The boys knew this farmer by name and nothing more. Jape walked around the thrasher to get a drink of water from a gallon jug hanging on the fence.

He heard the owner telling the thrasher operator, "Yes, I did tell you to bring a crew but I didn't tell you to bring a bastard. If God won't do business with a bastard, you can bet your sweet ass I'm not either. All the boys can work but those two."

The thrasher operator lowered his voice and answered, "Keep you voice down; one is right behind you and his relatives own half the county. Let me handle it, there's no need to cause major hard feelings. After all the boy can't help it."

"I don't give a damn, no one is going to say I hired a bastard," the farmer insisted.

"Okay, okay, I'll tell the boys. It's too hot to argue, I'll take care of it."

"I want the bastard off the place, not hanging around to get a ride back. Send him down the road. Is that clear?"

The more the man talked the more angry he became. The thrasher driver finally walked off and Jape ran back to Tubbs. He didn't know who they were talking about. He had heard the word "bastard" a few times but only when his father was very, very angry. He knew it to be a swear word but he did not know the true meaning.

The thrasher operator approached the group of boys walking directly over to Jape and Tubbs. He put his arm around the two boys pulling them along with him as he walked and talked, ''Well boys, I need to talk with you and I guess give you a very sincere apology. This farmer told me to bring twelve boys and I forgot to count; we have fourteen and since you were the last two boys to arrive, well, I have good news for you. You don't have to work in this inferno of heat. Sorry for the walk back, boys, but you can cut across the pasture. Thanks for coming, you are both good workers.'' He patted both boys on the back and returned to his work. Jape knew what he really meant but Tubbs stood there with his mouth open. Both boys looked back at the crew, when Jape said, ''Lets go see what Uncle John's surprise is.'' He hit Tubbs on the arm and the two boys took off in a run. It was too hot to cut across the pasture, the boys walked down the road. It was farther but that's all they had to do.

The road was hot and the dirt burned their feet. The grass was a little better but there were goat-heads and sand-burrs mixed in with the grass. They could not walk relaxed on the grass; as quickly as they relaxed up jumped some goat-heads. It was too hot to work at walking in the grass. The hot dirt was soft and the boys slid their feet along playing as they talked. Some of the broomcorn dust was still clinging to their sweaty bodies and there would never be a better time to go swimming. If they cut across the pasture in the wrong direction, it would be a little farther but the Yoakum's had a big pond. This would be an excellent time to swim, Mr. Yoakum would be working. They crawled through the four-wire fence and ran across the pasture. It was two miles to the pond.

Tubbs spotted a small grove of persimmon trees. Persimmon trees grew very rapidly and were somewhat of a problem. The boys were looking for small trees not more than twenty feet tall and from six to ten inches in diameter at the bottom. Most farmers cut them for firewood but they grew right back. The boys played cowboy in the tall, straight trees. They climbed up as high as they could then started the top of the tree swaying back and forth. The other boy was doing the same thing in a tree close by. Each would try to make his tree bend close enough to the other one so he could push the other boy out of the tree or ''off his horse.'' Now and then one of the boys could stop the other boy from running his horse (swaying) but it was nearly impossible to get thrown from the horse. The green trees had a lot of spring and the boys were able to get them to bend ten or more feet. Once in a great while the tree broke and the lad went flying through the air to the ground. The six to ten foot fall never hurt either boy. They laughed and played for over an hour. They road several good horses to death and never got thrown. They were good riders but those trees were hard on overalls. Both boys would need a patch in the seat before long. They headed toward the pond in a run but Tubbs soon ended that. He was too fat to be running on such a hot day and he screamed those exact words at Jape who usually ran every where he went.

The boys knew the location of Yoakum's pond but had never swum there before. This was a water reservoir made by filling up a gorge with dirt which was one way farmers had of trapping rain water and holding it on the land for the farm animals to drink. This was cheaper than drilling a well or putting up a windmill. The consistency of dirt was good for making dirt dams. The water held good; however, there was no way of telling how deep the water was by looking at the slope of the hillside on each side of the dam. Sometimes when making the dam the farmer bulldozed the bottom out very deep and once in awhile a canyon was dammed up and it could be twenty- or thirty-feet deep. Most of the ''tanks,'' as they were called, were shallow from six to ten feet deep and the slope was very gentle making them a very safe place to go swimming.

The boys dropped their overalls and in the same motion threw their straw hats on top to run into the warm water. Two steps and they were in over their heads. They bobbed up and down while washing the broomcorn dust off their little two-toned bodies. Where their shirts should have been, their bodies were a dark chocolate brown, except for two white strips up the front and a cross in back where the overall straps protected the skin from the sun. They were only six feet inside the dirt dam. The boys learned to swim little by little but neither boy was close to being an accomplished swimmer. Each thought he was better than the other at anything they did, other than running and Jape was the runner.

''Isn't this great. I'm glad we didn't have to work. Just think we would be hot and stinging all over right now,'' Tubbs gloated.

''Yep,'' Jape agreed, ''we would have sweat running down our back with that stinging stuff all over us. Wonder why it stings anyway?''

''Something about the pollen on the seeds, but I don't know.''

"I thought bees did pollen. Wonder if they make broomcorn honey?" Jape asked.

"No, stupid, they don't make broomcorn honey. Speaking of honey, do you know who has a watermelon patch?"

"Only my grandpa and he does have some nice ones. It's another mile over there."

"For you but from here — right on my way home. What'a ya say?" Tubbs challenged.

"Wonder if, no, I got to go see Uncle John, anyway. Then I'll walk with you over to grandpa's watermelon patch. You can't tell anyone we did this. I'll get my hide tanned, but good."

"But he's your grandpa, Jape, he don't care. If we asked, I'll bet he would give us one."

"Sure he would and next Sunday at church he would tell my mother, who would tell my dad, who would tan my hide for being over there. We're supposed to be with the thrasher and as my dad said, NO PLACE ELSE! Let me tell you, when he says that he means it, sooooo I keep my mouth shut because what he don't know keeps my behind safe."

"You do get spanked, don't you? My mother spanked me when I was little but now she does a lot of shouting but we get along pretty good. She has it rough and I don't give her a hard time. If I had a dad like you, well I would catch it more I guess."

"Let's go see what Uncle John's surprise is," Jape said, changing the subject.

"Do you think you could swim all the way across?"

"Sure, real easy, why do you ask?"

"Bet you can't, its too far," Tubbs said.

"Do you think you can? I can if you can," Jape wasn't about to be outdone.

"I'll bet I can make it across quicker than you."

"What do ya wanta bet?"

"I don't know, we'll discuss that after we see who the winner is." Tubbs started swimming for the other side. Jape was in deep water and could not push off but he lunged forward and swam as fast as he could. The boys only knew one stroke, dog paddling. This was a slow process and the heat had taken a lot of the boys' strength. They were fifty yards from the shallow side when Jape let down to tread water and rest his arms. His feet hit bottom and he lowered himself onto his knees to rest while Tubbs kept paddling along. Jape never said a word about being in shallow water. He stopped for a minute to rest then walked along on his knees as Tubbs was swimming for dear life. Jape asked, "Are you going to make it?"

"Don't - know - I'm - getting - very - tired," Tubbs gasped.

"You know if you don't make it, you'll drown?"

"Yes - I - have - been - thinking - about - that."

"Why did you want to attempt such a thing in the first place. You want me to drown? Oh say, if you drown, can I have your money?" Jape continued to heckle.

"If - I drown - you'll - take - it - anyway."

"If you can't make it, go on and drown. You are only suffering by putting yourself through all the misery of trying to swim."

Tubbs was about to cry but Jape wasn't about to give up teasing him.

"I - may - drown - I can't - move - my arms - I'm going -"

Jape interrupted, "I don't know why you insist on swimming all the way. It's a lot easier to walk. If you rather drown than walk, go under."

Jape stood up in the water in front of Tubbs. There was a long pause then Tubbs' feet hit the bottom. He was in water only waist deep. His face seemed to light up for a moment when he knew he wasn't going to drown. Then changed again when he turned to Jape in anger.

"You idiot, you were going to let me drown in knee-deep water."

"No I wasn't, you have been swimming for the last thirty yards and I have been walking. I thought you wanted to see if you could make it swimming. I found it much easier to walk."

Jape laughed then became serious, "No, we should be more careful. We're lucky to still be alive. If we had walked up from this side, we would have been swimming into the deep water instead of into this shallow water, both of us would have, you know we would both be —"

"Okay, dead, go on say it. I hope you learned a lesson today. Don't be challenging me to beat you at swimming and stuff all the time."

"Yep, it's always Jape who gets us into trouble, isn't it. Well, mark this one up on your wall, Mr. Tubbs. Whadya say we walk around the tank instead of swimming back across to get our clothes?"

"The first good idea you ever had, Jape, and for once I do agree."

The boys walked out of the water and around the big pond to their clothes. They flopped the old hats on and started pulling their pants on when Tubbs asked, "Do you think we will get to work on the thrasher any more this year?"

"Darn it, I didn't think to ask where they would be tomorrow," Jape said. "Sure we should be able to get more work. Several farms still have broomcorn standing in the field. They will need help, someone will let us work."

"Make sure you didn't lose your money."

Jape blurted out, "I already have, it's gone. My pockets are empty and its not on the ground."

"Oh, it has to be there some place. You had it when we got here, didn't you? It's not in your tool box?" Tubbs was talking about a small metal Garrett snuff box that Jape always carried.

"Nope, the tool box is full. I don't know; I never thought about it after Uncle John paid us. Do you still have your's?"

"Yeah, I tied my dimes up in my snot-rag. I lost a quarter last year and don't take no chances. I can always find a large rag but a dime is hard to find and especially when, like now, we have to back track for miles if we ever hope to find your money."

"Well, I just lost my new shoes," Jape was sullen.

He was feeling sorry for himself, still searching the bottom of his pockets hoping to find the money, but it was not to be. The money was gone. Tubbs put his arm around Jape's shoulder as they walked away. "You can have half my money if you want. After all we are friends and if you lose, I lose, too."

Jape looked up at him and his eyes flashed. "You are one heck of a stupid jerk. You shouldn't give me your money. You worked hard for it and it's yours. I'm too stupid to take care of mine and should lose it. No, no I would never take your money, but thanks."

He put his right hand upon Tubbs's left shoulder for a couple steps. The loss of the money created tremendous mental stress for both boys. Jape was hurt for being so careless and losing his money and Tubbs was hurting because Jape was in pain.

"Shall we backtrack and try to find it?" Tubbs asked. "When we were riding the trees you could've lost it."

"No, I didn't, I never fell, not once. I can ride a tree without the money falling out."

"Okay, when did you lose it, smarty pants. You could have lost it when you were acting smart, punching slats while hanging upside down. That was just before we left and after he paid us. Did you check your money after that?"

"You know I did; I always check my pockets when I have money or did I check the money? I could have checked it, but you may be right. I don't know if I checked it or not. I know I still had the money when he paid us and we can start looking from that point."

"Do you have a hole in your pocket?"

"No, Tubbs, I'm smart enough to check for a hole."

"I'm not too sure how smart you are. You work all day in the hot sun and lose your pay. That, isn't smart, nope, not smart at all."

The two boys argued and talked until they reached Uncle John's place. They were first welcomed by the barking dogs, then Uncle John came to the door. He shouted for the dogs to shut up, then asked the boys inside.

His first comment, "You boys are a little early, the thrasher break down?" Jape looked at Tubbs and back to answer the question but before he could answer Uncle John continued, "What's wrong, you boys look like a dragon just ate your family!"

"Yes sir, and we feel about the same too." Jape explained, "We didn't get to work after going over there. They only needed twelve boys and we made fourteen."

"No big deal, you boys can work again next week. There is lots of broomcorn left to harvest."

"Tell him the rest before it gets dark," Tubbs urged Jape.

Uncle John looked at Jape with a questioning eye but didn't say anything. Jape looked at the ground and shuffled his feet.

"I lost all the money I made today."

"Oh, my goodness, Jape, that is terrible but if you didn't work, how in the world did you manage to lose your money? If you walked down the road or were you boys wrestling on the ground some place?"

"I think he lost it before he left here. Could we go check while it's still light?" Tubbs asked.

"Sure and if it gets dark, I have a flashlight. And say, Jape, we also have electric lights now."

He walked over to flip a switch on the wall. The sun was still up and the light wasn't very impressive. He added, "I'll show you again after it gets dark. You boys will eat supper with me?" He raised his voice, turning to shout through the screen door. "Two more for supper, honey."

"Electricity just like the school house. Are you rich, Uncle John?"

He laughed at Jape's statement and added, "No, not rich, Jape. In the long run it's not much more expensive than the lamp and someday you will have electric lights, too. Now let's go see if you did lose your money here."

The two boys ran on ahead of the man. Jape, of course, was first and then a scream of delight, "I found it, I found it." There in the dust were two bright and shining half dollars and a dime. The dime was in full view but the larger coins were half covered with broom-corn dust. The strong southerly wind had blown the dust off making them very easy to see. Jape could not keep his teeth from shining through his open mouth, extended in a broad grin.

Tubbs ran over and hit Jape on the shoulder as Uncle John lifted Jape's straw hat and roughed up the lad's hair. After feeling of Jape's hair he asked, "You boys been swimming?"

"Yep, we had to get that broomcorn dust off," Jape said.

"This was a scorcher, wasn't it? I'm sure glad to get my crop in the shed. Wish I had a pond to go swimming in."

Jape was afraid he was going to ask where they had gone swimming but the boys lucked out. In an effort to change the subject Jape volunteered, "Tubbs is going to get a 22."

"A 22, huh. Well that could be good. Do you know how to shoot? Have you been hunting with a gun before?"

We've been hunting lots of times but —"

Tubbs interrupted, "My uncle took me hunting a few times and I know how to shoot a 22. I shot a squirrel one day. It will be better than hunting with our slingshots. We will have squirrel for dinner every Sunday after I get the 22."

"You sure can have squirrel and rabbit for dinner," Uncle John agreed. "But you must also remember that a 22-bullet will kill anything it hits. Most farmers would rather shoot their own cows when they get ready to butcher. That gun could get you into a world of hurt. You boys are a little young for a gun but I remember getting my first gun when I was nine. You boys six or seven now?"

"No, we're both nine and in the fourth grade," Jape said. "I been hunting with our old 12-gauge for sometime now. The shells are too expensive. That may be a problem with the 22."

"You're right, when they sell what they have on the shelves, no more ammo for us. It's all going overseas for the war effort. I have two cartons of 22-shorts that would be good for you boys to get started with. I'll tell you what, when you get your 22 come by and I'll give you some tips on shooting and also trade you one 22-shell for every insulator you can find under the old telephone line."

"What is an insulator?" Jape asked.

They were walking past a little shop with the front open.

"Here, I'll show you." He walked into the shop and took out a white glass insulator and gave it to the boys. They looked at in with sincere interest.

"What's if for?"

"Now that I have electricity, I can build an electric fence. I can put up one wire as a temporary fence and utilize the grass on my cultivated land. The insulator is used to keep the electricity in the wire. See here, boys, a nail is placed in the hole in the middle and nailed to a post. The electric wire fits along this groove and is held in place by another wire. If the electric wire touches something else, like the fence post, it won't work any more. It is called shorting out. This is all good for me except one problem, exactly like the 22-shell. I can't buy insulators either. When they constructed the telephone line they built it with six wires. Now only one line is workable and they have changed insulators. They use only the larger, fancy ones. These little ones are not adequate for their use anymore but perfect for my fence. Most of the old ones are still laying where they were thrown away when they made the changeover. You boys have the time and energy to walk the line and gather up those old ones. You do that and I'll trade you, one 22-shell for one insulator."

"Is that the surprise you had for me?" Jape asked.

"Nope, I was going to wait until after supper but now that you asked. You boys do a lot of hunting, don't you."

"Yes sir, and we'll do more after Tubbs gets his 22."

"What else would help on your hunting trips?"

"A dog, a dog, you got a dog?" Jape was excited.

"Yep, we have to get rid of Mr. Tips."

"That's a good hound, are you sure you want to give him away."

"Yes, he's getting old and I don't have the time to go hunting with him anymore. It's not fair to him; he'll live a lot longer running in the woods with you two boys. There's only one problem, you know what?"

"Yes, my mother may not let me keep him."

"I've already talked with your dad. He told me to have you lock Tips in the corncrib for the first few days. Once he's been hunting with you boys a few times, he'll stay around. Your mother can't catch him and Tips is smart, he'll stay out of her way, okay? Now, you boys come on in and get washed up for supper."

Jape was shy and there had been a time when he would not eat with neighbors or friends, even when he was hungry. When visiting with family, he would be offered cookies or cake and say, "no thank you," his mouth watering. His mother explained that it was not rude to eat what was offered, but it was rude to eat like a pig. That long discussion was passed along to his good friend, Tubbs, and from that day on they never refused a meal or a treat if sincerely offered in friendship. Uncle John and Aunt Lucy were very happy to share their supper with the two boys. Jape finished about the same time as Uncle John but Aunt Lucy and Tubbs were still working on dessert.

"Could I take a look at Mr. Tips," Jape asked.

"He ain't changed any, son. Can't we wait until Tubbs finishes and we'll all go out together. You should get home before dark or your mother will start worrying."

Jape pushed his chair back and motioned with his head for Uncle John to come outside. Uncle John was shaking his head in either disgust or concern but it didn't matter to Jape, he had a burning question to ask.

When they reached the front porch Jape said, "I heard a dirty word today and I don't know what it means. Will you tell me the truth?"

A dirty word, huh? Well, my boy, I certainly will not lie to you. Tell me the word and let me see if I do know the meaning."

"Bastard, what does bastard mean?"

"Where did you hear that?"

"The first time was when the cows pushed the fence down and got into the corn. Dad called the cows, bastards. Then today the farmer would not let Tubbs and me work because he said we were bastards."

"I can believe your dad calling the cows that but what in the world did you boys do to make him angry with you."

"Nothing, we were standing with the other boys waiting for them to get the belt hooked to the thrasher."

Oh, wait a minute you were at old man Rhoar's farm. Your friend, Tubbs, doesn't have a father, does he?"

"No sir, but he has a mother."

"I don't know for sure but Rhoar is some kind of off-beat religious nut but I guess to him we're all nuts. He still reads and follows the old testament, you know the old part of the Bible."

"Okay, but what has that got to do with calling us a bad name."

"Jape, your friend Tubbs is, by the terms of the Bible, a bastard."

"No, he isn't, nothing wrong with him."

"You asked me for the truth. A bastard is a person who is born out of marriage, like Tubbs, without a father. According to the Bible all bastards and all their off-spring are doomed for eternity in hell. Of course the new testament changed all that."

"You mean Tubbs is going to hell because he don't have a father?"

"That is what Rhoar believes, not me. Forget about Rhoar and his filthy mouth; he should have it washed out with soap. Let's get Tubbs and get you started for home. I'm glad you have that walk, not me."

Uncle John walked around back to get Mr. Tips. The dog looked like any black-and-tan hound, without the tan. He was solid black except the tip of his tail and there was a six-inch tip of sparkling white. The old hound had been tied up so much that he was getting fat and lazy. He wagged his tail and tried to lick the boys all over. Jape dropped down on his knees to hug and pet the dog.

Uncle John watched them walk down the driveway but he came running when they started to cut across the pasture.

"Where you boys going?"

"We're going to cut across the pasture, it's a lot closer," Jape said.

"It's going to be dark soon. Don't you think it would be better to walk around the road. You could get lost or step on a snake in the dark."

Now Jape knew every inch of every hill and creek for miles. The only part of this world he didn't know about was McCrimmin's pasture and it was two miles away and he knew that snakes go into their dens at night. Something was bothering Uncle John about them cutting across his pasture.

"You're right Uncle John, thanks."

He grabbed Tubbs by the arm, jerking him back and they continued to walk down the road. Uncle John stood in the driveway for a few minutes then walked back inside the house. The boys looked back as Uncle John blinked the porch light a few times just to show-off a little for the boys. He was proud of his new electric lights. He was an old man, probably 35 but he still had a little boy left inside.

Jape was leading Mr. Tips with Tubbs plodding along beside. They walked for some distance in silence, when Jape said, "Are you too full to eat a good ripe watermelon?"

"I'm never too full for watermelon. But we don't have time to get to your grandpa's patch and get home at any reasonable time."

"Right again, Mr. Tubbs, but I'll bet Uncle John has a watermelon patch right over the hill in that draw. They did have an old barn over there and after it was torn down Aunt Lucy made a garden. I haven't been up that draw this summer. And he didn't want us cutting across because we would have to walk right through his watermelon patch. What else? He ain't worried about us walking across the pasture. Get lost? I could find my way home blindfolded. He don't want me to find his watermelon patch."

Jape was laughing now, he had a good story to tell next winter when the snow fell. Everyone tried to keep their watermelon patch a secret. Then, after the melons were all gone, they would brag about it. This time it would be Jape's turn to brag!

"He was real good to us. We going to get a melon anyway?" Tubbs asked.

"Sure, just because, just because, I don't know what because — could be we are just mean little bastards."

"Don't use that word, Jape, it's not nice."

"I said damn and hell and I can say bastard if I want."

"No, you can't, not and be my friend." There was a tone to Tubbs voice that caused Jape to look at him. His eyes were moist and his voice was trembling. That was the answer Jape was looking for.

"What have my words got to do with us being friends?"

"You know what bastard means?"

"Yes, do you?"

"Yes, I'm a bastard, Jape, but I don't like being called one," Tubbs told his friend.

"I didn't mean to call you a bastard. I was repeating what — !"

"Go ahead, someone called me a bastard, didn't they?"

"Yes, but I thought they were talking about me too. That's why we didn't get to work today. That old man is crazy but we can be just as crazy."

Jape stopped to give Tubbs the rope attached to the dog and pulled out his toolbox, the metal snuff box. He always kept his top-cord, a fish hook along with a variety of other small doodads in there. He took the fish hook and pricked his right thumb causing a large drop of blood to drip. He took Tubbs' right hand, Tubbs looked away as Jape stuck the rusty hook into his thumb. They looked into each others eyes with total sincerity. The intent of their purpose could not be more holy. Jape and Tubbs pressed their bleeding thumbs together.

"Now my blood and your blood runs together." A line from a movie he saw at the Sun Theatre last year. He continued, "We are both brothers of the same flesh and blood. If you are a bastard, my brother, I am also a bastard and you and only you can call me a bastard any time your little fat heart so desires."

Tubbs stopped him, pointing to a figure of a man outlined in the shadows nearly half mile away. It was Uncle John walking over the hill to see if the boys had remained on the road or doubled back to get into his watermelon patch. The boys giggled and went on down the road. Their summer was not going to be without plenty of delicious watermelon!

Chapter 2
The Adventure

A week later it rained which was unusual for that time of year. The creeks were all full but nothing flooded. With that rain the corn crop was laid by and provided enough moisture to make a fair crop of cotton. One more late summer rain would sure help all the cotton farmers. Now the tanks had enough water to last until fall. Jape was told to take his new dog and go hunting. It was too muddy to do any field work and more than likely it was a way of getting Jape out of the way so his dad could get something accomplished. When Jape saw the opening he was quick to ask, "May I stay all night with Tubbs?" His dad's attitude was that the only thing better than one day without Jape around was two days. Permission was granted and for once dad didn't give a million "Do Not's" as he ran to the corn crib to release the dog.

Jape took Mr. Tips and headed for Crossroads, with plans to fill his pockets with candybead rocks, then cut across to find Tubbs. He was lost without his buddy. Jape could do things by himself but it was much more fun when Tubbs was there to share with. The weather was cooler but very humid. The sun was sucking the water out of the ground very fast. The road had ruts made by the mailman's horse and buggy. Only one other wagon had been on the road. Jape cut across the school yard to the little creek bank where the rocks were found. There were candybeads in a couple other spots but this was closer. The round rocks were pitted like a golf ball and nearly as round and a little heavier than most rocks. When one was broken open it had a straight grain all running to the center of the rock. All these rocks were the same only some were larger than others. He never found any as large as a golf ball. Most were the right size to shoot in a slingshot. With this excellent ammo for their slingshots they would have a better chance of killing a rabbit. Both boys were fair shots; however, it took a great shot to kill a rabbit but every now and then one of the boys would get lucky. That luck always meant that they would have fried rabbit with hot biscuits and gravy for supper instead of beans and potatoes. That was their reason for hunting.

Jape finished filling his pocket with rocks while trying to decide what to do. He wanted to go get Tubbs but it was two miles to his house and the same two miles back. He could go over to the Webster farm and get some peaches but that wouldn't be any fun by himself. He could check out Uncle John's watermelon patch and hope Tubbs would come along later. He stood up to drop the last handful of rocks into his pocket to hear a strange noise. He turned to look all around, then he heard it again. He ran a few steps up the hill to see four boys lying in the grass, giggling and watching him, all four jumped up laughing. Tubbs shouted, "I got the .22." Jape ran toward the boys asking "Where's it at?"

"Home, I don't have any shells."

Jape ran over to push Tubbs as he spoke, "We'll get some later. You got plenty of candybeads? What are you guys up to, anyway?" The other boy spoke up, "I don't have a slingshot. Tubbs said you were good at making one. Would you help me make one right quick this morning?"

"Sure, if you have some rubber."

The boy pulled out two long strips of red rubber he had cut from a tube out of a car tire. He held them out for Jape to examine, "Will this do?" Jape was proud to be the expert, "Yep, perfect, now let's find a good forked stick." The boys walked around the brush for a few minutes. It wasn't difficult to find a perfect fork for a slingshot. Jape pulled out his Barlow knife and cut the green limb about a foot below the fork. After pulling the limb out of the brush he cut each fork off a little too long. With his pocket knife he made a measurement up one side and then the other. Each fork had to be exactly the same length. He made smooth pretty cuts as a craftsman carving a rifle stock. He took out his tool box, the Garrett Snuff can, and cut about ten inches off his top cord. By unraveling the short piece, he had a string to tie the strips of rubber to the top of each fork. The tool box also contained two leathers for slingshots. Jape was about to put his leather on the new weapon when the boy spoke up, "I got my own leather." Jape put his leather back in the "tool box" and again used the string from the top cord to tie the boys leather onto the red rubber straps, making the slingshot complete. Jape was quick to accept the role of slingshot expert. After finishing the weapon he took out a candybead. Telling the boys to, "Stand clear." He fired the rock at a stump a few yards away. The solid round rock flew straight to the mark. Jape grinned as he gave the boy his new sling-shot, "Nobody has one any better."

Remembering what Uncle John said about the .22, Jape repeated, "This is a dangerous weapon it can kill anything you hit. The farmers around here want to shoot their own cows when it comes time to butcher. So watch where you are shooting. Now, if everyone has a slingshot, let's go hunting."

Tubbs was grinning from ear to ear and shaking his head.

"You are full of it today, aren't you?"

Another boy spoke up, "Tubbs told us you knew where we could get some peaches. We didn't come all this way to go hunting. We can hunt closer to home." Jape looked at Tubbs who shrugged his shoulders. Jape and Tubbs usually did those things alone.

"Yep, I guess so. The orchard did seem to have plenty of peaches, if they hadn't been picked. All you guys want to go?" Every last one of the boys nodded his head in full approval.

"We can go up the road for about a mile and cut across the pasture and go in from the back." Tubbs explained.

"Yea, there is a little gully that runs up there and we can't be seen until we get close to the orchard." Jape added.

"There's tall Johnson grass along the back fence. We can hide in that to get into the orchard from the gully. What do you think, General Jape?"

"I think we'll be eating peaches in a little while, Chief Tubbs."

The boys took off in a run with Jape out in front. At the road they stopped to crawl through the fence, then walked up the road. It was easy walking, other than the mud squished up between their toes. The sun was out and by tomorrow the road would be dry. It didn't take long for them to walk the mile on the road. They cut across the pasture and found the gully. A few yards down the ditch one of the boys made a comment about how high the banks were on each side. The canyon walls were a little over their head.

"It's not so deep. I've seen much deeper." One boy declared.

The other boy answered, "So have I but I wouldn't want to fall into this on a dark night."

"Oh, it wouldn't be bad with the sandy bottom."

"I suppose you'd jump off, would'ya, would'ya?"

"Yea, I would and it wouldn't hurt me neither."

"Okay, let's see you jump."

"Okay, I will if you will." All the boys stopped to listen to their argument. They finally agreed to climb out of the ditch and jump off the highest part. The little cliff was about ten feet high and the bottom was heavy mud. The first boy, the smaller of the two went first. He grabbed his nose like jumping into water feet first.

Tubbs pointed and yelled, "Look, he's holding his nose."

The kid hit the mud and fell sideways laughing. The second boy was about forty pounds heavier. His feet were driven into the mud up to his knees. He stood there laughing as all the boys slapped their legs and roared with laughter. He was in the mud so deep he couldn't get his feet free. Tubbs jokingly suggested they go ask Mr. Webster for a pail of water to soften the mud around his feet.

"I've seen a wagon stuck, a tractor stuck and nearly every piece of farm equipment stuck, Grandpa even had a cow that got bogged down but never thought I would see you guys get bogged down. Just stay in the mud and wait, we'll bring you a peach on the way back." Jape said as he winked at Tubbs.

The boys sat down on rocks and different hard spots and waited for the lad to wiggle and work loose, inch by inch he pulled and pushed while the others laughed. No one would offer a helping hand. When he got tired he stopped to talk and then continued the task of getting out. After about ten minutes of flopping around he got loose from the mud.

Webster's orchard was about two hundred yards from their house. He was from old German stock, a hard worker and no one ever had a better neighbor. In his middle fifties, Webster had been around long enough to know about boys. Anyone who happened by got something from his orchard. Those who could afford to spend a little money bought canning peaches for fifty cents a bushel or whatever they could afford to spend. Jape knew if he walked up the road and knocked on the door Mr. Webster would tell them to help themselves to all the peaches they could eat. If he did that, all the fun would be gone from the adventure.

The boys crawled out of the gully and ran in a low crouch, using a fence row of tall Johnson grass to hide behind. The going got a little rougher as they approached the fence. A large patch of goatheads (large thorns growing like a mat on the ground) separated them and the fence.

They could not run through the goatheads. Each boy tip-toed through the goatheads and yelps of pain could be heard from time to time. Old man Webster was probably in the house asleep or so the boys were hoping. After crossing the moat of goatheads, getting through the three-wire fence was easy.

Of course, Jape was already in the top of the largest peach tree by the time the other boys got through the fence. Mr. Tips trotted over to the thick shade of the tree and flopped down. He wasn't used to so much activity on a hot day. Jape tossed Tubbs a giant red peach from the top of the tree and took a bite from a really juicy one, boy, it was sweet and delicious. He was about to toss the other boys some when out of the Johnson grass stepped Mr. Webster. A yell that changed into a scream came from one of the boys, "Run, Run" The three other boys ran and dived through the barbed wire fence and right through the goatheads which must have torn their feet to shreds. In seconds, all three boys had disappeared into the gully from which they came.

Mr. Webster had Tubbs by the back of his overall suspenders. Tubbs spun his wheels in an effort to run but Webster was about six foot four and grown men would have difficulty getting loose from that grip. He looked up into the tree at Jape,

"Shuckins-a-tall, oh my, shuckins-a-tall, Jape, are you eating these hot peaches right off the tree. I thought you were a lot smarter than that. We have some cold peaches at the house and they are much better sliced with ice cream. You boys are in luck, we just made a freezer of ice cream."

Webster turned to look toward the fence where the three boys had disappeared, "Too bad about your friends, we do have plenty of peaches for everyone but I'll give you some to take home."

He looked over at Mr Tips who was lying comfortably in the shade of the peach tree panting. "Your dog is the only smart one in the bunch, he knows how to enjoy a good shade."

Jape was trying to get out on the other side of the tree but Webster's long arm reached into the tree and pulled the 85 pound lad out of the tree like Jape would pick a peach. Webster continued in his slow southern drawl with a heavy German accent,

"Shuckins, boys, the wife will be so proud to have you young fellows drop by. I do wish you would have came by the house. Only a few minutes ago we finished off an ice cold watermelon and was wondering what to do with part of it. I'll bet you boys could get rid of some cold melon. How about some melon, too?"

He looked down at the two lads who weren't talking. He had a firm grip on each one and wasn't about to let go, at least for the moment.

"How's your dad's corn this year, Jape?"

This direct question forced Jape to look up and answer, "It does look good, I heard him tell my mom, this morning, that this rain would put the corn over the top. Whatever that meant?"

"That's good news, mine too. How is your mother?"

"Okay, I guess, she felt good enough to give me a thrashing last night."

The old gent laughed and released his hold on Jape but kept a firm hand on Tubbs while making small talk all the way to the front porch. He pointed to a porch swing on the front porch, telling the boys, "Take a soft seat in the shade and I'll have some peaches and cream coming right up."

Jape watched Mr. Tips who flopped down in the shade of the porch. For once he would like to change places with that stinking old dog.

Webster opened the screen door and raised his voice, "Maw, bring us three more helpings of sliced peaches and ice cream."

She must have known what was coming because as he turned around to sit down she appeared, all smiles, with three large bowls of sliced peaches and ice cream. The ice cream was homemade with real peaches and heavy cream from their Jersey cow. This was a first-class dish. Mrs. Webster provided all the ladies in the neighborhood with her recipe for homemade ice cream. That rich and delicious ice cream could never be purchased in any store. Any other time and under most any other set of circumstances that would have been the best tasting dish those boys ever had. At that moment, both Jape and Tubbs had difficulty swallowing and there wasn't any flavor in the entire bowl. The boys ate in silence as Mr. Webster talked.

At a break in his babbling, Mrs. Webster appeared with two peck sacks of peaches. She set them down in a chair next to the boys, "Now here is a sack for each of you. You boys tell your mother that we have plenty of peaches, they are falling off on the ground. If they want some to can, they are welcome to come help themselves."

Mr. Webster cut her off to add, "If your watermelons aren't ripe yet come back and I'll give you a cold one. I would send one home with you but I think Maw has given you a load to pack now. You boys ready for another bowl?"

"No sir, this one is plenty for me."

Webster looking at Tubbs, "How about you, young man. I don't believe I know your name?"

"Tubbs, I'm a friend of Jape's. We go to school together."

"If you are a friend of Jape's you are a friend of mine. Shuckins-a-tall boys, when you are up this way be sure and drop by. We get lonely here, maw and me. We love company and boys your age are a big kick in the pants for us. Maw loves to cook and we would love to have you come by for dinner some day or supper in the evening. Anytime you boys are around on a hot day and want to go for a swim, my big pond is right across the draw. You boys are welcome to swim any time you want to. If you're going to drown in there come by and let me know first so I can notify your parents."

He laughed as Mrs. Webster corrected him, "Now, pop, you shouldn't talk like that, these boys are good swimmers and they aren't going to drown. But he is right, we would love to have you boys stop by and eat with us. I love to cook and now that our kids have moved to town, I don't get a chance to show off my skills very often."

Tubbs reached over to set his empty bowl down on a little table. Mrs. Webster continued, "Would you like another bowl?"

"No thank you, that was very good."

Jape stood up as he contributed to the conversation, "I have to be home early, we really should be going home now." He was attempting to make a statement and get permission to leave at the same time.

Both boys would have felt much better if Webster had shouted at them or kicked their behind. A blast of buckshot in the seat of their pants would have been much better than all this kindness. Jape had had his butt beat on more than several occasions and was screamed at frequently, that attitude along with the usual criticism he could handle. The Webster treatment was something new for both boys. The most difficult part, it was real. The Websters were truly nice people. Those two boys never wanted to get away from a place so much in all their young lives. Their hearts beat for joy when Webster said, "Yes, if you boys ain't gonna eat another bowl you better get headed home. You make sure your mother puts them in the ice box so they'll be better eating."

Jape took a couple steps as a test to see if Webster was really going to let him leave. After two steps, Tubbs stood up to join him.

Webster wasn't looking at the boys but at the dog, "Isn't that John's dog, Mr. Tips, or one of his pups?"

"Yes, he is Mr. Tips, but Uncle John gave him to me."

Webster helped the boys get the large sack of peaches in their arms. "You boys don't try running, those sacks will break or you'll fall and bruise every peach in there."

The boys walked off the porch and out toward the main road. Mr. and Mrs. Webster were still standing on the front porch waving to the boys until they went over the hill out of view.

The boys walked in silence for awhile. First one then the other would cut their eye over to steal a glance at the other one. Finally Tubbs said, "I rather be horse whipped."

"Nope, you haven't seen my dad whip a horse or for that matter whip me. I'll take the Webster treatment anytime." He stopped to laugh and push Tubbs with his free hand. "I was so scared I could hardly taste that ice cream, was it good?"

"What do you mean? Taste it, I could hardly swallow. I don't know if we were eating peach or banana ice cream. If he would've cursed a little or told us we did something wrong. That old man is pretty darn smart?"

"How's that? You think he's smart because he caught us?"

"No, not because he caught us, the way he handled us."

"Why don't you say it right, stealing, we were stealing, I guess."

"Guess, come on Jape, you know we were stealing but that was the only reason we didn't go to the front door and ask in the first place. Stealing is the right word but when you say it Jape, it sounds so dirty."

"The sound of dad's strap across my butt would be much worse if he finds out. Cause Webster caught us don't make him smart."

"Not that he caught us but think about it, I won't ever take any more of his peaches, will you?"

"Nope, or watermelons or anything. It's real hard to be naughty when people are so nice."

"Yep, thank goodness for people like old man Rhoar", Tubbs added.

"Does he have any fruit trees?" The boys laughed but each knew the real meaning of Jape's question.

"These peaches are heavy."

"We should walk all the way to Paoli picking up insulators. Mine is getting heavy, too. What you going to do with yours?" Jape asked.

"You got any money? My mother could make a cobbler but I'm going to stay all night with you. I can't take them home. It's a long walk to Paoli."

Jape stopped and set his sack on the ground then whistled for Mr. Tips. The dog was trotting ahead of the boys. He came running at the whistle. Jape took out a peach offering it to the dog. Mr. Tips sniffed the peach but wouldn't eat it. Jape broke it open and tried again but again the dog stuck his nose out but refused to eat.

"Dogs don't eat fruit, they are carnivorous." Tubbs explained
"What are you talking about?"

"Dogs don't eat fruit, they eat meat."

"Yeh, and so do I when I can get it but I like a peach now and then, too, and I'm not a carnival."

"Carnivore not carnival and you are too, any animal that eats meat."

Jape changed his voice into a base tone to mimic Webster, "Okay, okay, shuckins-a-tall, my boy, you do know a big word, now let's get on with the little problem of two peck sacks of peaches, shuckins-a-tall."

"We can't eat'em because I saw you pass up seconds on peaches and ice cream. I'll bet that was good stuff, wish I could've tasted it."

"What are we going to do with these peaches? I can't go home either, I'm staying all night with you." Jape tossed half the broken peach to Tubbs, who caught it with one hand. Each boy ate half the peach Mr. Tips had refused.

"Wonder what happened to the boys?" Tubbs asked.

Jape laughed and sat down on a clump of grass along the barditch, leaving his sack of peaches sitting in the road. "They are home trying to pick the goatheads out of their feet. You know they won't believe our story about the Webster treatment, will they?"

"We could kill two birds with one stone. Walk all the way to Paoli looking for insulators and when we get there sell the peaches."

"Where we going to sell peaches?" Jape asked as he leaned back on his elbows to stare into the clear blue sky.

"Go door to door." Tubbs explained, "And ask every lady in town . . ."

"If she wants to buy some peaches." Jape interrupted, "Not a bad idea, but since it's not mine, it probably won't work. You know anyone in town?"

"A few kids and some of my mom's friends. We could stop at the store at Crossroads, they might buy the peaches."

"And they might tell my Dad too, then my butt won't hold shucks and I won't be able to go hunting for the rest of the summer. I'm not going to walk by there with these peaches. When we get to the creek, we'll cut across to the road to Paoli." Jape gave firm instructions.

"Why not, I haven't been to town all summer. Do you think we can get twenty cents for the peaches?" Tubbs questioned.

"You are wanting to buy a full box of shells. I don't think you can find a box to buy. We better pick up insulators and trade with Uncle John. That's a sure thing."

"Okay, but if we can buy a box, that would be a sure thing, too. We may not find a single insulator." Tubbs was providing practical advise.

"We can look, there are a lot of poles between here and Paoli."
The boys cut across the pasture to avoid being seen in Crossroads. At each telephone pole they put the sacks of peaches down. The rest felt good to their arms. The few moments it took to search the grass under the poles was about right to give them renewed energy to walk to the next pole. They looked under and around several poles before finding anything, then under one pole they found three insulators. One insulator was hanging loose and by standing on Tubbs shoulders he was able to knock it off with a stick. Their pockets were already full of candybead rocks with very little room left for insulators. They agreed to hide the four insulators along with their slingshots and the rocks, then pick them up when they came back by. They were getting tired of looking for insulators and carrying the peaches. They force marched the last mile into town.

On walking across the railroad tracks at the edge of town Jape asked,

"You ever ride on a train?"

"Nope, but my mother did. She went to Ardmore once."

"We should go for a ride someday. The bums ride all the time, for free. Wonder how they catch the train without being seen?" Jape pondered.

"The same way you get peaches without getting caught?"

"Guess we can forget going for a train ride. I'll bet the engineer don't know about the Webster treatment." Jape promptly responded.

"Let's go to the blacksmith shop. Mr. Beal has bees and I watched him put a swarm of bees into a hive last summer. He's a nice man, he might buy some peaches."

"Where's the blacksmith shop?" Jape asked.

Tubbs pointed to some old buildings about a block away, "Right around there."

They walked around to the blacksmith shop, the fire was going in the forge but no one was around. Upon approaching the front door Mrs. Beal came around the house to greet the boys, "Hello boys, how are you today?"

"We're hot and tired. We were hoping you liked peaches as much as we do. We want to sell some peaches." Jape told Mrs. Beal who walked over to talk with the boys across the yard gate. "They look like nice peaches. We are planning on driving out to the Webster farm and get some in a few days. I sure could make dad a nice cobbler with those. What are you asking?"

"We don't know what to ask, would you —"

Mrs. Beal, "I have a quarter, would you take twenty-five cents for a sack."

Jape jumped on that statement, "Yes, ma'am, that is fair."

Tubbs was also shaking his head up and down in quick agreement. They would have sold both sacks for a dime as they were tired of carrying them.

Mrs. Beal continued, "If you boys will come in the house for a moment, I'll call my friend and she will give you a quarter for the other sack. Or do you have someone special to sell it to."

"No ma'am, your friend can have it." Jape spoke as he winked at Tubbs when she turned to walk into the house. Mrs. Beal called her friend who agreed to take the peaches but the boys would have to walk about five blocks to deliver them and collect the money. They left with a new inspiration on life.

After traveling less than a block Jape said, "We aren't out of the woods yet."

"What you talking about?"

"When she goes out to see Webster, he will know it was us who sold her the peaches. She already knows these are Webster's peaches."

"Oh no, she don't, a peach is a peach and coulda come from anywhere." Tubbs argued.

"Yep, but how many peach trees you got or for that matter you even know about? Not many around, are there?"

Tubbs looked all around and pointed, "Yep, there's one right over there."

"Okay, I hope you're right because my butt's the one in the sling."

Paoli had both a grade school and a high school. These boys were getting a kick out of seeing all the buildings. Once or twice a year they made a trip to town and this was the first time they had been in town together. They were feeling real grown up. Their feeling of independence was magnified by the fact that in a few minutes they would each have a quarter in their pocket.

On walking past the grade school several boys were playing marbles on a high sandy spot in the school yard. Mr. Tips ran over to the boys who waved and shouted at Jape and Tubbs.

"Like your dog's tail," was one boy's comment.

"Thanks, can anyone get into the game?" Jape shouted back at the boy.

Another boy stood up and shouted, "Anyone with marbles, we play keeps."

Jape winked at Tubbs, "We got to deliver some peaches. We'll be back in a few minutes. We have enough marbles to stake up for a couple games."

"We'll still be here, waiting." The boy answered as several others laughed.

They delivered the fruit. The elderly lady was pleased to get the peaches and glad to pay the boys the quarter. Each boy felt much better with twenty-five cents burning a hole in his pocket.

"I have thirty-five cents. I brought a dime with me." Tubbs told Jape.

"I gave mom my thrashing money to keep for my shoes but we could spend this quarter for shells. Do you have any marbles with you? I have three and my taw." Jape responded.

"I have four, I think." Tubbs answered

"Let's go get into the game, then we'll have a pocket full."

"Yep, they play for keeps. If I pick them up for you can I have half what you win?" Tubbs asked.

"If you loan me your four marbles to stake up I will."

"You better be careful, you know these city boys love to take us country hicks," Tubbs shot back at Jape as both boys laughed.

Jape grinned as he answered, "I don't care, its your marbles anyway."

When they got back to the school the boys were waiting. A new ring was drawn about five feet in diameter. Six boys, including Jape, staked up for the first game. They asked Tubbs to play but Jape told them he didn't have any marbles. The fact was, Tubbs wasn't any good but Jape was something else. Those city boys were about to get a lesson in shooting marbles. Jape wasn't lacking in self-confidence and his hand to eye coordination with a marble was fantastic. Each of the six boys put five marbles in the ring. One of the larger boys used the forefinger and the thumb to push the thirty marbles into a large "V", not unlike racking a set of pool balls. Then the boys lagged or tossed their taw at a line to see who would shoot first. Jape pulled the snuffbox out of his pocket and took out a marble just a little larger than all the others. This marble, his taw, was a little heavier. He didn't get the first shot but he did get to shoot second. The boy shooting first hit the rack of marbles but didn't hit them hard enough to knock one out of the large ring. Jape laid his right knuckle flat on the ground and fired, the marbles scattered in several directions. Several went flying out of the ring and Tubbs went to work picking up the marbles. Jape's taw stuck inside the ring, right in the middle of all the marbles. The rules; the shooter can keep shooting as long as he knocks a marble out of the ring and the taw remains inside. Jape's taw seemed to have eyes. He would shoot one marble and the taw would spin over to stop very close to the one he would shoot next. This pattern of shooting continued until Jape had about twenty of the thirty marbles. He made an easy shot, knocking the marble out of the ring and the taw also rolled out of the ring. He said, "Darn it," looked up and winked at Tubbs. The next boy took his turn. Jape got one more shot before the ring was cleaned out but he missed. Tubbs knew he missed on purpose, but it looked good.

This game of marbles went on for about two hours. Jape never took all the marbles in any one game, although he could have several times. One of the boys was a fair shot but didn't know how to control his taw. He would get a few marbles then his taw would go flying out of the ring. One of the boys said he was going to the store to buy more marbles.

Jape asked, "How many marbles do you get for a nickel?"

"Twenty five, I think."

"I'll sell you forty for a nickel and you won't have to walk all the way to the store," Jape offered.

The boy gave him a nickel, "Okay, but not any chippies."

Jape turned to Tubbs, "Give him 20 of yours and I'll give him 20 of mine."

Another boy, "How many can I get for a penny."

"Ten, if you promise to join in the game, if not, only five."

Tubbs took the penny and gave the boy ten marbles. Jape would have them back after two or three games, anyway.

Another boy piped up, "I'll take 40 for a nickel, too." With that sale they were back to their seed.

In the next game one of the boys brought out a steelie. Jape never saw a steel marble before. The kid wasn't that good but the steel ball was so heavy it stopped by sheer weight and the shooter didn't have to have any talent to win. It was so heavy when it hit the rack of marbles it knocked several out exactly like Jape was doing. That steel ball promoted a fair player into an excellent player. Jape had to take a look at the steelie. He asked about buying one. The kid explained that it was a steel bearing from the axle of a car. Jape didn't understand but the kid agreed to show him where he could get a bearing with several steel balls inside. The boy made Jape pay him a nickel for the information.

Jape gave him the nickel and they left the game to go find the steel balls. The rest of the boys were glad to see Jape go. Without him there, they could win a few marbles. Some of the boys never won but for some reason they kept playing. They would lose all their marbles, go get more and lose them. Tubbs was better than some of the boys but he never played keeps.

Mr. Tips had been lying quietly in the shade while the boys were playing marbles but was quick to jump up and follow once the boys started to walk off. He didn't wander around or get into trouble. The boys never had to shout at him for barking. He followed along behind when a house dog ran out yelping and making a lot of noise. Uncle John had trained him well. Three city boys walked with Jape and Tubbs to find this bearing thing. They walked several blocks then went into an alley behind a store. From the alley the kid pointed across the street. There was a car sitting on blocks of wood. All four wheels were gone, the hood off, and appeared to be a wreck.

The boy pointed to the car, "The bearing is that round thing on the front axle."

"Well, let's go get it?" Jape responded as he started across the street.

"Nope, I can't cross the street." The boy lied to Jape. "My parents told me never to go over on that side of town. I'll wait here while you go get it."

The lad had taken his steelie out of the bearing taken off the axle on the other side and nearly gotten caught. He didn't want to have to outrun the banker again.

"Will anyone care if we get the bearing?" Jape asked, looking from one city boy to the next. Each boy shrugged their shoulders and shook their head.

"The steel balls do make fine taws." Tubbs spoke up.

"I don't care if you go get it. No one is around and it is apparently a worthless old car. If you get it, I'll help you hammer out the steel marbles." The boy who had taken the nickel replied.

"Okay, I'm not sure what you are talking about. I'll go over there and put my hand on what I think is the bearing and you shake your head when I touch the bearing, okay?"

The lad agreed and Jape ran across the street with Tubbs and Mr. Tips close behind. Jape found the bearing right off. On looking across the street all the kids were shaking their head up and down. The bearing would not come off because of a large nut on the end but it was loose. Jape could turn it with his hands but with great difficulty. The nut was heavy with black grease, exactly like the kind his dad used on wagon axle's. After a few moments of hard work, the nut was off and the bearing slid off the axle into Jape's hands. He felt of the bearing which was a lot heavier than it looked. About that time a large fat man with city clothes on came running around the corner of the next block screaming, "What are you stealing now, you dirty little bastards."

Jape looked across the street for his new friends but those boys were long gone. From the word the man used he had to be shouting at Jape and Tubbs. This was an attitude they could deal with and they did. They made the fat man some tracks, then circled the block in their effort to get back to the marble game.

When they got within a block of the game, they saw a police car parked there and the cop was talking with the other boys. Jape and Tubbs sneaked behind the house across the street from the school and listened to what the boys were saying. One was telling the cop that they never saw Jape and Tubbs before. He thought they were from Wayne or out in the sticks some place.

Then he shouted, "No, they didn't run off there's their dog. They're still some place around here."

Mr. Tips didn't know to hide, he was trotting around out in front of the house as if he lived there. The boys all ran at the dog who ran toward Jape and Tubbs. Once more Jape was out in front as they made more tracks.

The cop car drove around the block but Jape grabbed Mr. Tips and waved for Tubbs to hide with him behind a hedge next to the road. The police car went racing by and a short time later several of the boys from the marble game ran through the yard obviously looking for Jape and Tubbs.

Jape told Tubbs, "Okay for now, but we better wait here for a few minutes. That cop will be back and then he'll go farther down the road. Let's head up the highway, if they see us going that way they'll think we live in Wayne."

Wayne is a small town to the north and the boys lived east out of Paoli.

"Then we can cut back across the field later."

"Yep, and if they don't see us we can cut back anyway."

Before they could move a female voice right behind them asked, "What in the world are you boys up to?"

She nearly scared them to death but Jape didn't turn around or get up, "We're playing hide-and-seek with some of our friends. Please don't tell them where we're at. I have been "it" all afternoon and this is my first time to hide."

The lady was not impressed with these two dirty little boys with greasy hands and she told them, "Okay this time, but next time find another yard to hide in. Don't you dare touch any of the clothes hanging on the line with those greasy hands of yours either. You hear that, young man?"

"Yes ma'am, and thank you. We'll find a different place next time."

The lady went into the house and Tubbs said, "You've been in town for about two hours and already you're lying exactly like a city boy."

"I did not lie, we are hiding and they are seeking us, oh my, here comes that cop again and he's going slow." He held Tips a little tighter. The cop cruised by and this time the fat man was in the car with him.

Immediately after the cop turned the corner the boys ran back to the school and cut across the yard to hit the highway about half mile north. They were really wanting to go east. The highway was straight for a long ways going north out of Paoli and they had only walked about a hundred yards when they saw a car coming and then they saw the red light.

Tubbs stopped and said, "Wait a minute, I love to hear the police siren. Let's see if they turn it on."

"Run, you fool, or you'll be on your way to jail." Jape scolded.

They crawled through the fence and ran across the pasture but they had been spotted. The boys and Mr. Tips was a good two hundred yards out into the pasture when the car stopped, without having used the siren.

The fat man started shouting. He added "rats" to the other names he had been shouting at the boys.

To that Jape jibed, "When he was calling us bastards, I knew he was after us, but "rats". The man must be a friend or relative of your family."

Tubbs couldn't talk for huffing and puffing, "We're going to get into trouble crossing Owl creek."

"What do you mean trouble? Would appear we're already in trouble or we wouldn't be running. Anyway, we could stop and talk to the policeman. Remember what Mrs. Auld always said, "the policeman is our friend."

"I mean from the water, we'll have to wade and get wet."

"I've been wet before."

"Mrs. Auld forgot to tell you that policemen aren't too friendly when you've been naughty. You didn't steal that bearing, you purchased it for a nickel."

"I don't believe I paid the right fellow. The fat guy may not be willing to sell it to me for a nickel or any price, what do you think? Should I run back and ask him? They're still standing there watching us. So let's turn here and go north for a ways. This should keep'em searching north or as that kid said "Wayne". When we get into the brush we can cut back and go south and east."

"Wonder why they don't chase us?" Tubbs asked.

"They don't want to get their good clothes dirty."

Jape was right, the fat fellow and the cop stood on the highway watching. The boys walked north up the fence then out of view still going north. Once out of view they walked across a small creek, through some grass and started over the railroad tracks when they heard a train coming. They grabbed Mr. Tips and dropped down in the grass. It was a long north bound freight. The train pulled onto the siding to let a passenger train go by. The empty car right in front of the boys had the door open.

"Lets go through the box car and jump out the other side. That way we won't have to wait, this train may set here until dark." Jape told Tubbs.

Tubbs would follow Jape through a den of alligators. Jape ran out of the grass and climbed into the box car then helped pull Tubbs inside. He whistled and slapped his legs and here came Mr. Tips, he was old but he made it inside that box car with one leap.

The boys ran across to the other side of the box car when Jape said, "No, no, don't jump out now here comes a train on the other track."

No more than the words were out of his mouth and a southbound passenger train let out a blast on the steam whistle and went screaming by. The wind from the train rocked the car they were standing in. The noise and the speed were a little frightening. The feel of fear was mixed with a little adventure in both boys minds. Jape put his hand on Tubbs shoulder as they stood in the door watching the train go past. Would they have something to talk about at school next fall!

Immediately the train jerked and the box car started rolling forward. The passenger train was still going by on the other track. The box car started off slowly but it was rolling right along when the caboose on the passenger zipped past. The boys could jump off but this was their first experience with trains. Jape always wanted to ride on a train and unless he jumped quickly his wish was going to come true. The boys looked at each other with a question mark in their eyes and both received the same mischievious grin that broke into a broad smile. They knew they were going on their first train ride. Jape walked to the door on the west side and sat down with his feet hanging out like riding in the back of his dad's horse drawn wagon. He patted the floor for Tubbs to come sit beside him but Mr. Tips beat Tubbs to the spot. Tubbs dropped down on the other side. They watched the sun set in the west in a sea of red and purple, it was a terrific train ride.

"Wonder where we're going?" Tubbs asked.

"I was wondering if we will ever be able to get back." Jape answered.

"Trains run both ways. We can climb on one headed south tomorrow and we should make it back."

"Yea, the train will go through Paoli at about this speed too. How fast are we going? You don't know, either, but it would kill us to jump."

"We got money, we can buy a ticket back. When someone is on the train or buys a ticket the passenger train stops at Paoli."

"Get a ticket with a quarter. And I thought you were smart. A ticket will cost a lot of money." Jape told Tubbs.

"I got forty-one cents. Oh, I'm getting hungry do you —"

"You sold the peaches and Mr. Webster asked you about another bowl. Don't you wish you had a chance for seconds now? We can't complain, my dog hasn't had anything to eat either and he isn't griping."

"If we can get off in a town let's go get a milkshake. I know a milkshake only cost a nickel."

"What is a milkshake?" Jape inquired

"You haven't had a milkshake?" Tubbs blurted.

"Guess not, I don't know what it is. Unless you put some milk in a glass and shake it up. That wouldn't be so great. Right now I'd love some cornbread and milk."

"A milkshake is made with ice cream milk and different fruits and other good stuff we don't have out on the farm."

"Where did you learn about that?"

"We went to the drug store last winter to get some Black Draught. This guy, you know a big boy, working there was making something in a large shiny metal-type glass. Mom said he was making a milkshake. They poured this thick soft ice cream like stuff into a tall glass and then sucked it out with a straw." Tubbs explained to Jape.

"They put straw in ice cream. What kind of straw, broomstraw but it's not hollow. They must —" Jape couldn't believe what he was hearing.

"No, you idiot, a paper straw. Even I've had a coke with a straw."
Tubbs was getting put out with his buddy.

"You mean like a reed that I make whistles out of or like you can swim under water and breathe through. It's round and hollow on the inside?"

"Yes, but a lot smaller and made out of paper."

"See, I'm not so dumb. Just because I never saw one —"

"You missed the point all together. I want to buy a milkshake. Mom said that was the best drink any town has to offer."

"And they only cost a — Oh my, look up there. The cop is parked at the next crossing!" They grabbed Mr. Tips and ran to the back of the box car. The boys couldn't contain themselves. Both were peeping around the door when they went whistling past the cop car. The fat man and the cop were looking in all the wrong places. With any luck, they would give up and the boys would be home free.

The train continued traveling north, through Purcell, Norman, Oklahoma City, and Wichita, Kansas. The boys were sound asleep curled up in one corner of the box car with Mr. Tips when the train squeeked, banged and jerked to a stop in Wichita, Kansas. They had been rolling all night, it was black dark outside and they didn't have the foggiest idea where they were; however, there was nothing wrong with their appetite. They pushed the dog off and all three stretched. The boys yawned and stood up in an effort to get the aches and pains from their young muscles. Sleeping for hours in a slouched sitting position didn't provide total relaxation and comfort even for two nine year olds. Mr. Tips stretched his legs and swayed his back in his effort to get the kinks out of his old dog tired body. His flanks were also caved in from the lack of food but he could miss a few meals and sustain life from the internal fat; however, the first topic of conversation was;

"Is breakfast ready, Mom?" Tubbs mumbled as he yawned.

"Yes, yes, right now would be a good time to find out that we have been dreaming and wake up to the smell of mama's cooking." Jape replied.

"But we would be missing out on all this fun. I'm so hungry, I could eat your dog. You know some Indian tribes do eat fat dog."

"Yep, but look at Mr. Tips, he's hungry, too. Let's get out of here and find something to eat. We got money, we can buy something, someplace." The boys walked up to the door and looked out across row after row of box cars. There was a sea of railroad tracks, trains and more box cars. They stood in the doorway for a few moments in awe at the sight. The lights of a city, street lights and switch engines illuminated the area providing adequate lighting to determine that they were in a large railroad switching yard; however, neither boy ever dreamed that such a place existed.

Jape jumped out of the box car and Mr. Tips followed and Tubbs complained that the jump was too far but he finally jumped but when he did he fell and hurt his arm. He rolled over on large rocks, getting his clothes even dirtier. Jape was already walking down the tracks with Mr. Tips a few yards out front. Tubbs ran up complaining about his arm but Jape wasn't giving him any sympathy. They didn't know where they were going but with every step they were seeing something new.

First Jape and then Tubbs would shout, "Would you look at that or what in the heck is that?"

The boys were getting a very expensive lesson in the true value of travel.

About half mile down the tracks they met a man that was carrying a lantern, something like the one Jape used on the farm. The man looked at the boys and held the lantern up so he could get a better look.

The two boys kept on walking as they said, "Good morning." The man returned the greeting, "Good morning, boys." He shook his head and started to walk away, then turned to ask, "Where are you fellows going?"

The boys stopped and looked at each other. They didn't know what to say and, for once, Jape didn't have a glib answer. The man turned to walk back, "I thought so, run away from home didn't you?"

Jape and Tubbs at the same time, "No, we didn't, we are going home now."

"Where is home?" The railroad man asked.

"Crossroads." Jape answered, in his world, everyone knew were Crossroads was.

"How far out of town is Crossroads?"

"Oh, its about —"

"Exactly three miles." Tubbs informed them.

"Three miles to Crossroads, nope. I've lived here for thirty four years and there ain't no Crossroads three miles from here."

"We live three miles out of Paoli." Tubbs corrected.

"Paoli, what is a Paoli?" The man asked.

"It's a town." Jape answered, "You never been to Paoli?"

"I never heard of a town by that name." You boys by any chance come in here on a box car?"

"Would that be a bad thing?" Jape asked.

"Hell, yes." As if catching himself just in time he changed his attitude to say, "Well, yes and no. If you try to ride in a box car there are so many bad things that can happen to you. You can get locked inside the car and starve to death, slip and fall under the train and the wheels cut you in half. That is to name only a few of the bad things and there are no good things."

"We didn't get locked in a box car but we are starving to death." The railroad man held up the light to see a chubby fat lad who's entire body was covered with carbon black. He added, "You boys rode up from the south in a empty carbon black car, didn't you?"

"What is carbon black?"

Railroad man, "Like soot from the chimney. It's very fine and gets all over everything. You boys are covered with it. Do you know where you're at?"

Jape looked around at how big the place was and the lights in the distance. "Oklahoma City?"

Railroad man, "What state do you live in?"

"Oklahoma, why, where we at?"

Railraod man, "You, son, are in Wichita, Kansas!"

Both boys grimaced at the thought of never seeing their family again. They looked up through the faint glow of the lantern light with a blank stare of helplessness and fear that worked like magic on the heart strings of that old railroad man. The boys were still looking for adventure but they were lost in a strange new world. The fear of being alone, lost and hungry never before crossed their mind. That look was only too obvious to the railroad man. The man looked at the boys with understanding and compassion when he said, "I must admire you guys. I always wanted to catch a freight when I was a lad. Guess that's one reason I got this job." He turned to look up and down the track, "I guess you boys could use some food? How long has it been since you ate?"

"I had breakfast." Tubbs informed the man.

"You had breakfast this morning?"

Jape was quick to respond to that statement. "No sir, yesterday morning."

"Yesterday morning, then you are ready to eat." He turned to walk across the tracks toward the big lights. "You boys follow me and I'll see if I can't get you something to eat."

They walked across several railroad tracks, around engines and box cars for several minutes. The man stopped to ask, "That dog keeps following us. By any chance does it belong to you?"

"Yes sir, Mr. Tips is my dog."

"You are telling me that you boys jumped a freight with your dog?"

"Yes sir, he's a good dog too."

"Oh my, you boys jumped a freight in Oklahoma, with your dog and rode all the way up here. Where were you going?"

"We were wanting to ride a train. We didn't care where it was going."

"We thought it would stop in Purcell and we could get off and then catch the next one back to Paoli." Tubbs added.

"Where is Kansas anyway?" Jape asked.

Tubbs punched Jape, "It's the next state north of Oklahoma. You should know that, we studied that in —"

"Okay boys, but my geography ain't all that good either. Paoli must be on the main line, but where? Is it south or north of Oklahoma City?"

"It's south." Tubbs informed.

"What is the name of the county seat, you know where the court-house is located?"

"The courthouse is in Pauls Valley and Paoli is seven miles north."

"Okay, I can help you get back home. You boys relax and enjoy the adventure." He stopped and once more held the lantern up to look at the boys, "I want a promise out of the two of you. If I help you get some food and a ride home. I want a promise that you will never, never catch another train unless you have a ticket, is that a promise?"

"Yeh, I promise, do you want it in blood?" The man laughed as Tubbs punched Jape, "You idiot, adults don't make promises in blood." The man laughed, adding, "You may be right, son, but you may change your mind about adults, if you ever go to a bank to borrow money!"

They continued to walk across the big yard. They finally reached a large building with several men working inside. The railroad man told the boys to wait on a bench just inside the door.

Jape pointed to a large copper spittoon sitting next to the counter. "All I need is some Brown Mule and I could hit that thing from here."

"I thought you wanted Days Work, and no way, it's too far, you can't spit that far." Tubbs challenged.

"Bet I can come close, if I stand up."

He stood up and rolled his tongue around in his mouth gathering spit. He leaned forward and spurted saliva about twelve feet across the floor, missing the copper container by at least four feet. Tubbs grabbed his stomach laughing. Jape took a couple steps closer and tried again and this time a few drops hit the mark. A woman stepped around a small counter, looked over her spectacles and glared at the boys then exclaimed,

"Oh my goodness, you boys have carbon black all over the place." She turned to scream at someone named George. "George, get out here. These boys are getting carbon black all over the waiting room. Do you hear me, George?"

For the first time the boys looked at each other. Each boy had a white ring around both eyes, the nose and mouth and the rest of their body was black. Both boys started laughing and pointing at the other one. They were black all over. Jape reached over and rubbed Tubbs bare shoulder, then looked at his hand. His hand was black from the fine particles of dust. Tubbs pulled Jape's straw hat off and continued to laugh and point to the contrasting color where the hat had shielded the boy's head from the black dust.

"We need to find a pond to go swimming." Tubbs remarked.

The lady overheard what he said and answered, "What you need, young man, is a good spanking, then a hot bath and in that order. If you continue to spit on the floor I may take the liberty of contributing to the first half of your needs. Now, sit down and be quiet until George gets back."

Both boys shrugged their shoulders and sat back down.

Tubbs whispered, "She must be the boss."

Jape answered in another whisper, "Could be she's his wife."

The lady shot back, "I am neither, but I will be the one to put you two outside if you don't keep quiet."

Before they could get into any more trouble the railroad man returned. He was smiling and greeted the boys, "Let's go get something to eat. I haven't had breakfast myself, follow me."

The three walked outside to find Mr. Tips waiting to greet them. The man said, "Uh-oh, I forgot about the dog. Just a minute."

He left them standing just outside the station house door and went back inside. A short minute later he returned with three sandwiches made with store bought bread and meat. They looked good and either boy would have been pleased to eat those sandwiches for their breakfast.

The man asked, "We have a chain here for dogs. There is an old rug he can lay on and I'll give him this. Be okay to tie your dog up here while we're gone?"

"If Mr. Tips is as hungry as I am he won't mind being tied up for awhile. But you better let me do it."

Jape slapped his leg and the dog came trotting over. Jape snapped the chain into the ring on the dog's collar as the man put the food into a pan next to the old rug. Jape pointed to the food and told Mr. Tips to eat. The hound gulped down the food before they turned around to walk away.

Tubbs laughed, "He does eat like a dog."

"I was right, he is as hungry as I am. I'll probably eat the same way."

Tubbs laughed and pushed Jape as he responded to Jape's remark. "Unless you've changed, you always have."

Jape ran at Tubbs saying, "Why, you little jerk, I'll." Tubbs ran around the man laughing and holding on to the railroad man for protection, shouting, "I was joking, I was joking."

The man said, "Now, now, boys, let's straighten up and fly right. We have to get a little of that black off you guys."

He pointed to a door marked, "Employees Only" and said, "You boys go in there and get washed up."

Looking at Jape, he added, "You have more than carbon black on your hands. You'll find some good soap in there that will take that off. You drop those clothes, overalls, hat and all into the large tub in there. Wash all the carbon out and the hats too."

Tubbs interrupted, "We don't have anything else, they'll be wet!"

Man continuing, "Your choice is wet or dead, put them back on wet, they'll dry in a few minutes after the sun comes up. Don't tell me you boys haven't been wet before. Now go wash your body clean, and I MEAN clean. You will be riding back in style but they will not let you on the train that filthy. I'll meet you back inside when you finish. Tell the lady in there to get me and I'll take you to breakfast, now hurry."

"You're George?" Jape asked.

"Yes, that's right, I'm George."

"George sir, what if we need to go to the toilet?"

"You're in the right place. Go on in and help yourself."

"Go inside the building? You got toilets like at the courthouse?"

George saw a problem coming and turned to walk into the room with the boys. "You fellows never used a flush toilet before?"

He looked at the boys and could tell by their negative look that they hadn't. He walked over to a flush toilet and pointed to the seat.

"You sit there and when you finish you use this paper. Toss the paper into the water."

He pulled off a handful of paper and tossed it into the toilet. "Then you stand up and pull down on this wooden handle attached to the chain." Pointing toward a white box near the ceiling and six feet above the commode. "That thing is full of water and when I pull down on the chain the water will flush the paper down and away, like this."

He pulled on the chain and both boys jumped back as there was a very loud gushing of water into the commode and the paper was washed away.

"Hey, Tubbs, we seen a flush toilet. Wait until I get home."

"You boys use that tub of hot water if you want a bath or you can take a shower. Don't take all day your train will be leaving shortly."

People come in all kinds and types. These boys truly lucked out, some in the position of authority with that same railraod was known to lock bums, hobo's and runaway kids in box cars and leave them to suffer. Others endured terrible beatings at the hands of railroad cops. Thousands of men were traveling back and forth across the nation during the great depression in their search for employment. Those charged with the task of keeping these men from traveling free were given an impossible job. Right in the middle of all this conflict two little boys show up in one of the largest railroad yards in the mid-west.

Twenty minutes after leaving the two boys in the wash room they showed up in the waiting room squeaky clean. They told the lady to tell George they were back. She walked over to the counter, lowered her head to look over her specs at the boys. Her demeanor hadn't changed toward the boys, her eyes searched them up and down. She turned to talk in a raised tone to George who was apparently in the adjoining room. "George, your little urchins are here. What can I say, but they appear to be clean."

She turned to look back at the boys. "Take your hats off and sit down." The boys did as told. After they were seated, she lowered her head and looked at the boys again as if conducting a final visual inspection, then returned to her work.

Jape put his hand up to Tubbs's ear to whisper very low. "Don't she remind you of Mrs. Auld?"

Tubbs wasn't taking any chances, he didn't answer. He turned to frown and look Jape in the eye, then put his finger over his lips for silence. A moment later out came George in a rush. He was looking at a pocketwatch as he walked around the corner. "Okay, boys, let's go get something to eat." They walked across several sets of railroad tracks to a brick street and two blocks down the street they entered a small cafe. This was a new and exciting time for the two boys. The place was empty except for two men sitting on stools drinking coffee. They were dressed exactly like George. They turned to look and speak to George as the three of them sat down in a booth across and in back of the two men.

"Your boys, George?"

"Yep, until after breakfast, anyway."

Man at counter, "They look like future engineers to me."

"It's a small world, they may own the line by the time they are our age. With their spunk and energy it could happen."

The waitress walked over to put three glasses of water on the table, "Coffee George? And what'll your friends have?"

Knowing the boys didn't know how to order at a cafe he answered for them. "Yes, Marge, I'll have my usual coffee but we're eating a hearty breakfast this morning. Bring us three orders edof ham and eggs."

He turned to the boys, "You rather have bacon or is ham alright?"

The smell of bacon inside the kitchen had their saliva juices flowing. Both boys nodded their heads and said, "Yes." George looked at them with a question as they looked at each other.

"Is that yes for ham and eggs or yes for bacon and eggs?"

Again both boys, "Don't matter."

The waitress asked, "You boys don't look like Wichita to me. Where ya from?"

Again George answered for them, "They're visiting from Oklahoma. They're on their way home. I'll tell you about it later, right now bring on the food. We have a train to catch."

"Okay, okay; do you want toast or hot buscuits and gravy?"

Before George could say a word Jape answered, "Hot biscuits and gravy for both of us."

She looked at Tubbs and he was smiling in full approval. She shouted their order to the cook as she walked back to get a cup of coffee for George. Jape leaned forward, lowering his voice to George, "We may not have enough money to pay for ham and eggs. I wasn't going to tell her what I wanted until I found out what it cost."

"You do have money?" George was shocked and didn't know if he was making a statement or asking a question.

"I got more than him. He's only got a quarter. I got forty-one cents."

"This is your lucky day. You do have money enough. Ham and eggs does cost twenty five cents." He pointed to a blackboard over the counter that had a sign,

{"Today's Breakfast Special" Ham and eggs 25 Cents.}

He continued, "I'm buying today, you boys can keep your money." The waitress placed the cup of coffee on the table and George told her, "Please bring the boys a large glass of milk."

Tubbs asked, "What are we to do with our hats?"

"Wear them or hang them on that hat rack." He pointed toward the door. Jape pulled his hat off and Tubbs took both hats and put them on the rack.

"Our mom won't let us eat with our hat's on." Jape told George.

"Mine either." George answered as he pulled his cap off and laid it in the next chair.

A few minutes later, the boys were wolfing down breakfast.

"I was wondering if there was some special reason you fellows hopped that freight?" The boys looked startled and glanced back and forth at each other. The picture of that police car was branded in both their minds. They both lied in unison, "No sir, we just wanted to ride the train."

The bearing, heavy with black grease, was in Jape's back pocket. He had it wrapped in pretty white toilet paper. It was not an easy item to sit on. Reaching back, he moved the bearing into a more comfortable position and said, "Well, there was one kinda special reason."

"What was that?"

"Well, it was about a milkshake."

"A milkshake. A milkshake like you get at a drug store?"

"Yes sir, I guess. I never had one and Tubbs said they had them in big towns. We were going to a big town, get a milkshake and go back home. Only we ended up here."

George burst out laughing, "That makes sense, hell, I remember when I was your age. You are nine years old and never had a milkshake? Yep, I'll bet there are hundreds of kids around the country in the same boat. And I'll also bet most of them would not have the grit to catch a freight train with their dog to get one. Excuse me for a moment, boys." He walked over to a telephone hanging on the wall. He gave the crank a couple turns and said, "Helen, this is George, connect me with the shop."

He looked back at the two boys and winked, then turned back to the telephone. "Sheila, forget about that wire. These boys aren't runaways. I'll handle it from this end. I'll tell you about it later."

Jape looked at Tubbs and both boys shrugged their shoulders. George returned to finish his breakfast. All three finished about the same time. George wiped his mouth on his sleeve. Tubbs stuck his elbow in Jape's ribs and pointed to the napkin. Both boys picked up their napkins and wiped their mouths but George never noticed.

He looked at them to ask, "So you came all this way to get a milkshake?"

"Not really, we wanted to go to Purcell and get a milkshake. It was an accident that we came here, strictly by mistake." Tubbs told him.

"The railroad made a mistake and didn't stop in Purcell." He laughed and continued, "The way I see this, the railroad made a mistake and they should make it right. Here is how the railraod will correct that error. I have already made arrangements for your return. You will ride in the caboose of another freight that does stop in Paoli and that, my boys, is pure luck because we only stop there about twice a month. You cannot return from this adventure without succeeding in your quest for a milkshake. I could get one here but you are too full to truly enjoy a big cold shake. I will arrange for three shakes to be delivered to the caboose someplace along the way. Before you fellows get home you will have accomplished your purpose, okay?"

Both boys smiled and shook their head in the affirmative. They left to walk back to the station house.

Jape spoke up, "You didn't forget about my dog? I'll NOT leave without Mr. Tips."

The man put his arm around Jape's shoulders, "Nope, never for a moment. He will ride right in the caboose with you boys. And that will answer another question for me. You boys can take your dog into the washroom and give him a bath too. If you don't, he'll get carbon black all over the caboose. Hey, between you fellows and the gate post, I'm not supposed to do this. The man in the caboose is a good friend. Don't tell anyone else or both that man and old George here will get into very hot water. Jobs at our age are hard to find and at this day and time nearly impossible, okay?"

Once more the boys agreed.

The sun was peeping up over the flat Kansas skyline as the long freight rolled along with the usually klicky-klat, klicky-klat. The only other sound was the loud pounding of the happy hearts of two boys riding in a caboose holding their straw hats in their hands with their heads poked out of the window.

Jape turned to the man, "When will we get to Paoli?"

"We're supposed to get there at 4: 17 P M but sometime we get there at three and sometimes five. One thing for sure, we do get there." The boys looked at each other with full understanding. They would have plenty of time to get home. If they made it home before dark, they would be in great shape.

The ride home was a great experience. The man had the patience of Job answering all their questions with a smile. This would be a ride they would live to tell their grandchildren about, if they were lucky enough to live so long. The flowing green hills and the bronze waving fields of wheat flew by as the wind whipped the boys hair around. The engineer made the steam whistle scream into a lonesome tune as he approached every crossing. If the little tune wasn't complete he continued on the horn, sometimes for a mile past the crossing. Picking cotton was accomplished by crawling or bending down, a back breaking task. Only last year, Jape remembered standing to stretch and rest his back for a moment in the cotton field as did everyone straining to hear the train make that same music when sounding for the Paoli crossing. Workers for miles would stand and listen to that tune, smile and go back to work. That lonesome tune from a steam whistle on a freight train was the only friendly sound some farm workers heard. A friendly gesture during a very unfriendly time in the history of America. This fall Jape and Tubbs would have a brand new vision when listening from the cotton patch.

The boys were so engrossed in their ride and talking with the man they forgot about the milkshake but George didn't let them down. The long train stopped in Oklahoma City to drop off a few cars and pick up a few more. During this period, half the train was abandoned on a siding. The boys didn't have anything to do so they let Mr. Tips out for a little exercise and continued to point and ask questions. Only a few minutes after stopping, a young man came on board with a large white box. He opened the box and, guess what; the boys were about to drink their first milkshake. The delivery boy gave the man a note, then stuck a paper straw into a large paper cup and turned to hand the first shake to Tubbs. He repeated the same steps for Jape and the railroad man got his own. The man put his shake down as the boys sucked on their straw at the same time. Both boys looked at the other with a pleasant surprised expression and burst out laughing.

The man spoke as the boys continued to gulp down the delicious shake. "This is a note from George. He says, "I forgot to ask the boys what flavor they liked. I got strawberry, don't forget to let the dog out or you may have MORE than carbon black to clean out of the caboose. Tell the boys to have a safe trip home and good luck. George."

"So this is strawberry?" Jape pondered.

"Its great, I like strawberry now that I have tasted it." Tubbs said.

"You boys never had a strawberry . . . anything . . . no strawberry?"

"Nope, only saw pictures in books at school. We have wild blackberries but never found a strawberry." Jape answered seriously.

"You boys are going to enjoy life. You may not have tasted a strawberry but I'll bet before the grim reaper gets your old bones there won't be much of life's little treats you haven't tasted."

Chapter 3
The Catfish

After the train ride the two boys said their farewell and walked slowly and silently down the railroad tracks. At their crossing, the boys stopped to wait for the train to pull out. A few moments later they were waving to a man in the caboose, who only yesterday was a total stranger and now he would be forever branded a friend in their young minds. They ran back on the track to watch and wave as the train disappeared from view. That crossing would be one of their special spots for the remainder of their lives. Everytime they crossed a railroad track, they would remember their first train ride and smiles would creep across their faces. When the opportunity was right they returned to hide in the grass and wait for the chance to wave at the man in the caboose of the 4:17 P.M. freight going through Paoli.

For those two little boys had just completed a lifetime of excitement. Each one knowing the remainder of the summer would be uphill and boring. The dread of getting back into the dull routine of their regular life was all laid out in front of them. Prior to yesterday, they had found excitement in just watching the train go by and riding on one was a dream come true. They wanted to run home and tell their parents about the adventure. Only one problem, they would get spanked for doing such a stupid thing. They could talk and laugh with each other and that made it all worth while. Each boy walking along watching the little puff of dust form when their barefoot hit the hot dust. In only two days the mud had dried and the traffic had beat it back into dust.

"What you doing tomar?" Jape wanted to know.

Tubbs didn't answer the question but asked one of his own, "Am I asleep? Am I going to wake up or did we ride all day on a train?"

"Let's sleep on it and see. Don't tell anybody or I'll get it." There wasn't a need to explain what "it" was as both knew the meaning very well.

"I don't know, more than likely work," Tubbs finally answering Jape's question.

"Yea, me too, if not, let's go hunting with your .22. We can get four shells from Uncle John by trading the insulators."

"You going by to trade the insulators today or not?"

"Nope, think I'll cut across the pasture and get home."

"Me, too, Mom works and we could go hunting."

"Why don't we plan on day after tomar."

"We can hide the insulators on the road. The first one back trades the insulators and leaves a note, okay?" Tubbs was thinking out loud.

"And to think I'm going to be able to use my education already. Mrs. Auld said learnin to read and write would be necessary. But I don't have a pencil and neither do you." Jape explained why his plan wouldn't work.

"Day after tomar and we can meet at the insulators by ten."

"Can you tell when it's ten? You don't have a watch."

"I can get close with the sticks. I'll be here when you get here."

The boys had been taught how to tell time by looking at shadows made by sticks they poked in the ground. It wasn't as accurate as looking at the face of a railroad watch but they could get close. They never failed to make it to the dinner table on time.

The boys were smart to wait a day for planning their hunting trip. The next day found both boys working at home. Jape had to shell fifty pounds of corn, hoe the garden, fill up the washtubs with water and carry firewood for the wash pot. The water was pulled out of the well by the use of a rope and pulley, then carried in a bucket to the wash pot. The tubs for washing and rinsing were stationed close to the well to avoid carrying the water. Jape cut the fire wood with an ax from limbs his dad had hauled to the house in a wagon. After cutting the wood, he had to carry the short pieces to the wash pot. His mother would stack it around the pot because she liked to start the fire herself. The next day was wash day and the water was heated in a large iron pot, the only way they had to heat the water. Jape had to make sure there was plenty of wood stacked near the pot for his mom. He would catch it if she ran out of wood before all the washing was done. While his mother did the weekly wash, his dad went to town. The eggs and cream had to be sold once a week or it would spoil. This money was their only source of income. Then once a month he took the corn to the mill to have it ground into cornmeal. They ate cornbread every day, a big ticket item in their daily diet.

Jape was hoeing in the garden when his dad walked by to ask, "When are you boys going to take Mr. Tips out and get us a mess of squirrels?" Now this was a switch. His dad asking him to go hunting. Usually, he had to put up a plea for hours to get out of the house.

"If I can get all this work done. I was hoping to go."

"I hear Tubbs has a .22, you boys should be able to bring in a mess of squirrels every now and then. Or can you shoot?"

Jape had not told him about the .22 for fear he would not let him go hunting with a real gun. His dad had the attitude that one boy with a gun was okay but two boys with a gun would be hazardous to their health. He must have talked to Uncle John. Jape was praying he had not learned about the peaches. Dad's have a way of learning about nearly everything but every now and again Jape could pull one off without getting caught. This could be one of those times.

"We can shoot." Jape advised in a matter of fact statement.

"A tip to the wise. Unless you want to be laughed at every time we go to town or you get caught in a crowd at Crossroads, you boys better not let anyone see a squirrel shot any place but through the head."

"What if we accidently hit one someplace else?"

"Those guys don't care, you either hit the squirrel in the head or suffer the teasing for the rest of your life. They remember being teased when they were boys and now they want to pass it on. You two boys are the right age to become the butt of some good old fashioned 'hoorahing'. If you happen to miss and hit one someplace else run home and let your mother cook it. You may make hundreds of perfect shots and nothing will be said but miss once and they will bring that up for the rest of your life."

"Okay, thanks, is it okay to go hunting tomar?"

"Yea, we got the crops all laid by and I'm going to take it easy for a few days myself. You can go, but be careful with the .22. It's a good idea to wait until Mr. Tips has one treed to load the gun. That way you are less likely to shoot each other. Four squirrels will be a mess for us and Tubbs can stay all night. I'll be looking forward to a mess of squirrel tomorrow night." He turned to walk away then turned back to repeat, "You boys be real careful with that gun."

The next morning each boy left early in an effort to beat the other one to the insulators. Each had the bright idea of trading for the .22 shells before the other one got there. Jape wanted to be first to make sure Tubbs didn't shoot all four shots at something other than a squirrel. Tubbs wanted to be first so he could say he beat Jape at something. Each boy arrived at about the same time running towards each other in greeting.

"What you got a shirt on for?" Jape asked.

"My mother said the sun was cooking me. I had to wear it or stay home. It don't matter, I can take it off."

"Did you tell anyone about the train?" Jape knew the answer but had to ask anyway. It was his seat he was looking out for, Tubbs didn't get spanked.

"No, I'm not a total idiot. Thanks for asking because now I know it wasn't a dream. It would be nice to tell someone about it." Tubbs answered.

"We could go to Crossroads and brag. I bet most of those old guys never rode on a real train." Jape liked talking about his adventures.

"Yea, and we could fly to the moon if we had wings. If my mom finds out we'll never be together again. She thinks you're a bad influence on me the way it is." Tubbs didn't get spanked but he was equally afraid of getting grounded as Jape was from getting the thrashing. This parental influence worked on both boys, most of the time.

"Don't feel bad both my parents believe I'm a bad influence on myself." Jape replied and slapped Tubbs on the shoulder then laughed.

The two boys sat on the little bank created by erosion over the years as the road cut down into the hillside, leaving a short cliff for the boys to sit on. Mr. Tips was right there to lie first on one boy then the other, giving them a lick across the face every chance he got. It was a beautiful day, no wind at all but the boys could look forward to a hot, hot day but excellent for swimming.

"It's a good morning for squirrels, they will be lying out on a limb enjoying this sunshine. Let's go get the shells." After that remark from Jape they were off in a long trot with Mr. Tips running in circles barking with excitement. He knew a gun was for hunting and hunting meant the same thing to him as to the boys, fresh meat! It was less than a mile to Uncle John's place. Uncle John had his crop laid by too but there was always work to be done on the farm. The boys found him resetting a post in the corral fence.

"How are you boys this morning?" Uncle John shouted greetings.

"Great, we're going hunting with Mr. Tips. We have some insulators to trade," Jape replied in a loud cheerful voice.

"Good, how many you got?"

"We only have four. They aren't that easy to find," Tubbs answered.

"You're right about that but if you will kick the grass around a little you can find some that the grass has grown over. This should be enough to get you a good mess of squirrels." Jape was thinking, Uncle John sure knows an awful lot about finding insulators.

"We sure hope so, we haven't had any this year."

"We do get a rabbit occasionally but with a gun, now we can have meat any time we wa . . ." Tubbs wrinkled his brow and glared at Jape for butting in. Jape didn't pay any attention to Tubbs as he burst in again,

"Every time we can find some insulators."

"Let's go to the house and I'll get the shells for you. Where is your trading material?" Uncle John dropped the posthole diggers in the hole and turned to walk toward the house with the two boys following.

The boys grabbed for their back pockets, each taking out two white insulators. He took the insulators to roll them around in his hand for a good inspection. Once they passed his critical visual inspection he tossed them into a large metal bucket with two gallons of similar insulators. Yep, Jape was talking to himself, after seeing all the insulators in the bucket, his thoughts were right, Uncle John had already picked up all the easy ones.

"You have a watermelon patch this year, Uncle John?"

"A watermelon patch isn't worth the bother. Too many people with good patches to waste the time. What about you, you guys got a patch?"

"Nope, dad planted some in the cotton patch. We found them when we were hoeing but they won't be ripe for sometime yet."

"It will be a pleasant treat to find one while picking cotton."

"You used to raise the best yellow meated melon in the country."

"Yep, they sure were good. I gave your dad some seed."

"We have a patch, when they get ripe I'll bring you one," Tubbs said.

"Oh no, that would be too far to pack a melon. Several of the fellows around the store have large patches."

The boys got the four shells and left walking toward the creek. Mr. Tips ran in circles barking with excitement. The dog was ready to go hunting. Tubbs stopped to load the gun but Jape stopped him.

"Guns can be dangerous and we don't want to get into trouble on our first hunting trip. What d'ya say we don't load it until we want to shoot."

Tubbs wanted to carry a real loaded gun but he agreed to wait. The excitement was welling up inside both boys. Their first squirrel hunt with a .22. "Then you carry it for awhile, it's heavy." Tubbs grumbled.

The rifle was short compared to other models. This was a little Stephen's single shot. To load the rifle, the hammer had to be cocked, then a rolling block containing the firing pin could be pulled down, the shell could then be inserted. Once the shell was inserted directly into the barrel the block was pushed back into place and the hammer lowered into a safety position on the block. When ready to fire, the hammer had to be cocked, then by pulling the trigger the weapon fired. The rifle was very accurate. This was an excellent rifle for the two boys to learn with. Being a single shot, it limited their inability to one mistake at a time. With their limited supply of shells, they would be exceptionally careful not to waste a single shot.

They went up the creek through a neighbors pecan grove. All the little bottom land farms contained pecan trees. With the creek close by and the pecan trees supplying the food, the squirrels remained fat all year long. The weather was nice and with fat young squirrels in nearly every tree the boys should have meat for supper. They hadn't gone two hundred yards when Mr. Tips treed. The boys ran to the dog only to find him barking up a giant cottonwood. After a few minutes Jape found the squirrel lying flat on a limb high in the tall tree.

Jape explained the situation about shooting the squirrel in the head. Tubbs was pleased to walk away from the tree because it was a long shot and they could not afford to miss with only four shells.

Mr. Tips was barking, treed again within a few hundred yards. The boys ran to the tree, their adrenal glands were in high gear. Mr. Tips was telling the boys that dinner for everyone was up that tree. This was a pecan tree with millions of leaves. Finding a squirrel in a green tree with plenty of leaves wasn't an easy task but the boys went about their chore as a general would prepare for battle.

Jape pulled Tubbs head over to his ear and whispered as if the squirrel could understand their childhood slang, "You sit down right here." Pointing to a spot out a ways from the tree. "I'll walk around the other side and make noise and shoot into the leaves with my sling shot. You should see him move. If you don't see him, move over a few feet and wait again. If we circle the tree a coupla times and don't see him, I'll climb the tree, we'll get him."

Tubbs sat on the ground in his effort to be very still and not make any noise. On the other side of the tree, Jape was talking to Mr. Tips, shooting into the tree and making all kinds of noise.

Tubbs made it half way around the tree, sitting first in one spot then the next until he screamed, "I see'um, I see'um, I see'um."

Jape came running while Mr. Tips continued to bark at the base of the tree. Tubbs pointed to a thick clump of green leaves near the top of the tree, "See there he is right in the middle of those leaves."

Jape saw a glimmer of red hair as the gentle breeze turned the leaves.

"Okay, let's load the gun." Their eyes met in excitement and each noted the other was grinning from ear to ear.

"It's your gun. You take the first shot. You do know how to shoot? Make sure you don't miss. Does it have a hair trigger? Do you take a fine or full bead?"

"Crap, this isn't the time to ask me all that. I never shot it before. Your guess is as good as mine." Tubbs pulled the block down and continued, "Put one of your shells in there. I can't get into my pocket and load this thing too."

Jape got a shell out and pushed it into the barrel, "Aim for its head."

"Head, head, I can't even see the squirrel," Tubbs exclaimed.

"Back up a little and let's wait. He will move and then you can get a clean, clear shot. I'll go around to the other side and make him move again."

Tubbs was pointing the gun and trying to aim. "I can't hold the thing still."

Jape shouted right back, "Be quiet, I'm to make the noise over here." He shot a rock right through the bunch of leaves next to the squirrel with the slingshot. The animal turned and Tubbs could see the squirrel very well. He waved for Jape to come back.

This time Tubbs whispered, "See him, see him, stand right there and I'll brace on your shoulder. I don't want to miss."

Jape stood still but not still enough for Tubbs, "Hold your breath, every time I start to squeeze the trigger you breathe and the barrel moves." Jape held his breath for nearly a minute and just before he passed out he gasped for air then shouted, "You idiot, are you going to shoot or not."

"I wanted to see how long you could hold your breath. You were turning blue and the darn squirrel moved. You do want me to shoot him in the head, don't you?"

Jape looked up to see the squirrel looking at them, "He's right there shoot it this time and don't make me turn blue."

"Okay, when I say 'now' you start holding your breath. I'll shoot or I'll tell you to go ahead and breathe," Tubbs instructed.

"That's better." Jape answered as Tubbs took careful aim, "Now" and Jape held his breath. "Bang" The squirrel came tumbling out of the tree. The boys ran to get their first squirrel. The sound of the shot spooked another squirrel that jumped from the tree in an effort to escape on the ground. This was an open dinner invitation for Mr. Tips. The dog ran like a great infielder for a ground ball. Mr. Tips scooped the squirrel up and two chomps later he swallowed it, hair, hide, tail and all. The boys looked at each other in amazement.

"You better start feeding Mr. Tips a little better," Tubbs spoke up.

"Can you believe that, he ate the whole thing!," Jape commented.

"Well, after all, he is a dog, you know," was Tubbs reply.

They continued to hunt up the creek, mile after mile, tree after tree. Time or distance was not their concern. They wanted four squirrels for dinner. Mr. Tips treed several squirrels but some of trees, like the cottonwood, were too tall and they had to go on to the next. Some of the larger trees had hollow limbs with holes for the squirrels to hide in. There were lots of squirrels and with their natural ability to hide, there would always be plenty of squirrels; however, before ten the boys had each shot two squirrels.

They took their game to the creek and field dressed the meat and Mr. Tips got another good meal. Jape's Barlow had one blade that was razor sharp. This blade was used for this purpose and this only. His dad explained the facts of life to him. He would be in a world of hurt if the blade came up dull, it was good metal and very hard to get sharp and nearly impossible to get that sharp. His dad spend two hours one cold evening last winter sharpening that one blade. Jape was very careful never to use it when making a slingshot or any other small chore that required the use of a knife.

After cleaning the squirrels they put one in each of their back pockets and headed back home. They walked out of the creek bottom right into the persimmon thicket where they were playing cowboy last week. They could not resist the temptation, the trees were tall, limber and made excellent horses. The boys shouted, screamed, laughed while riding the trees back and forth and up and down. Mr. Tips found the thickest shade and laid down to pant.

Equally as quick as they started, they stopped, when Jape asked, "Want to sample one of Rhoar's watermelons?"

"It's early enough they will still be cold. Yep, I could go for some." [Night temperature is lower and the melons cool off during the night. Once the sun comes out the melons get hot — hot and aren't very good to eat.]

Jape took off in a run with Mr. Tips running along behind. Tubbs screamed at him, "If you're so full of energy you can carry the rifle." Jape stopped running to wait for Tubbs to catch up. While hunting with the gun loaded they would fight over who was to carry the gun, without ammo, it was only a load to pack. The boys knew exactly how to get to Rhoars melon patch. They weren't terribly concerned about getting caught; however, they would rather not. Those boys were NOT going to work at avoiding a conflict with Old Man Rhoar. This was apparently their lucky day. They were half mile away when Tubbs first saw the dust coming from Rhoar's field. He was discing the newly harvested broomcorn field. He would not be close to the melon patch.

This field, like most good watermelon patches, was located in a small sandy draw. The rich bottom land produced large sweet melons. The boys could tell they were walking on good soil because the Johnson grass was much taller than they were. They walked in a circle until they found a trail. A common mistake most farmers made. Rhoar and his family walked to the patch everyday, leaving a path that was easy for the boys to follow to a beautiful field of melons. It was only about half an acre but contained several very large melons and hundreds of smaller ones.

"Find the ones he has covered up, we want those," Jape informed.

"What do you mean covered up," Tubbs wanted to know?

"My grandpaw always pulls Johnson Grass and lays it over the top of his prize melons. They ripen in the shade better without getting sunburned."

Tubbs found a large melon, "Jape, come here and look at this thing?"

Jape ran over to see a melon much too large to be carried out. "Man, oh, man, will old man Rhoar be disappointed to know we ate this one?"

"We can't carry that thing. I don't want to eat it here in the hot sun. We can break it in half and carry it to that tree and eat it," Tubbs told Jape.

"Pull the vine off and let's roll it, roll it, my boy. Whoow, that is a whopper. Wonder how much it weighs," Jape asked, as the two boys stood starring at the hugh melon.

The boys took turns rolling the giant melon into the shade. They stopped when the melon was resting right next to Mr. Tips, who as usual was lying there panting.

"We can't lift it to drop it. How we going to get it open?" Jape grinned as he pulled out his Barlow. The kid stuck the knife into the melon, it was so ripe it split on it's own. A little more help and the boys had the giant open. The heart was red ripe and delicious. They grabbed large handfuls of heart and stuffed their face until their tummy's were bursting. The melon was hot and would have been better with salt. What made it extra sweet and delicious was the conditions under which they got it.

"Only one problem, Rhoar may not be smart enough to know who ate his prize melon. Wish there was some way to leave my mark."

"There is, give me your Barlow," Tubbs said as he reached for the knife.

He pulled out the knife and laid back in the shade, "Loan − loan, not a gift. What are you going to do? Don't waste any of the melons. Even us bastard brothers are above that," Jape spoke as Tubbs ran into the patch.

Tubbs was squatting down next to one of the larger melons, when he asked, "How do you spell bastard?"

"Mrs. Auld never included that word in our spelling class. As she said, sound it out and spell it . . . B a s t u r d . . . What are you doing?"

Jape jumped up and ran over to see what Tubbs was up to. In letters four inches tall and half an inch wide he was scraping the word on top of the melon exactly as Jape quoted. The boys worked at this task until every large melon was marked with the same word and spelled the same way.

They backed up to survey their craftsmanship and actually jumped up and down for joy. Tubbs was laughing so hard he fell over on his back to kick his feet and tears came to his eyes.

He jumped up as Jape said, "Brother, that is a job well done."

He stuck out his hand to shake, then stopped to say, "We should have a secret handshake."

Jape raised his knee up to his chin and poked his right hand under the knee. "Raise your leg and lets call this our melonshake."

Tubbs tried to raise his knee up to his chin but fell over when trying to hop close enough to shake hands. Once again the boys fell over laughing. Jape stood up telling Tubbs to put his head against his. With the boys facing each other and using their heads as a balancing point Tubbs was able to raise his leg and get his right hand under to shake hands. Their secret handshake was established.

Jape whistled for Mr. Tips and they headed for home. Tubbs stopped and asked, "Wouldn't it be a good idea to take your Uncle John a melon. Especially since he don't have any?" Both boys burst out laughing again.

"Great idea, especially since he don't have any. One thing, it's too far to carry a big melon and we wouldn't want to give Uncle John a −."

"It's not noon yet. The mailman would give us a ride if we gave him a melon, too," Tubbs informed Jape with a gleam in his eye.

"You're a genius, Tubbs. The road is just over the hill. I'll pack one and you get another one. Darn, they are all marked or all the big ones are."

"I can scrape that off, while we wait for the mailman at the road."

Each boy gathered up a large melon but there was a problem. They couldn't carry the rifle and the melon too. Jape reached into his pocket for the tool box. By tying one end of the top cord to the trigger guard and the other end to the barrel he made a top cord version of a gun sling. The gun hanging around his neck and the melon in his arms was a load. If their parents had asked them to work this hard they would bitch forever about slave labor. The boys stopped to rest often but their goal was worth the effort or they thought so.

The melons reached the road in good shape, and Tubbs scraped the word "BASTURD" off the melons leaving a wide white streak on a very green melon. Jape took the four squirrels out of their pockets and shook them back into shape. Being curled up in their pockets didn't help their general appearance. The boys wanted to stop by Crossroads to show off their game. They didn't have a long wait, down the road came the mailman. He was using his horse and buggy. He had a good car but only used it from time to time. The horse and buggy could get him around the route during any kind of weather. On nice summer days like this he took the buggy just to enjoy the weather and give the horse some exercise.

Jape and Tubbs had talked about what they were going to say to the mailman. They arrived at a decision not to lie but in case either one did have to lie it was understood they would cross their fingers behind their back and it would be all right.

The mailman pulled the horse up, "Whoooa."

"Hi, how are you today," Jape shouted.

"You boys lost?" Then as if answering himself, "Oh, I know, you heard about the chewing gum. Ok, I saved a little back for boys like you."

Jape and Tubbs looked at each other and shrugged their shoulders. He reached into his bag pulling out two sticks of chewing gum. "Wrigley has come out with a new stick of gum. They are giving a sample stick to every person on some rural routes and I made sure we were on his list of routes."

He smiled and winked at the boys, then continued, "As if you didn't know. Are the melons for me?"

The tone and manner of his voice let the boys know he was joking but the look in his eye told them he was sincerely interested. The boys were peeling the paper off the gum. While still trying to get the gum stuffed into his mouth, Jape told him, "Yes sir, one of the melons is for you and the other one is for Uncle John. If you will give the melon a ride to Crossroads."

"Certainly, boys, which one is mine? I'll put it up here and the other one will sit here in my empty mail seat. You boys can ride on the rack in back."

"Take your choice, which melon do you want," Tubbs asked?

"They are about the same size, oh, give me that one." He pointed to the one in Jape's arms. Jape had difficulty getting it up high enough to load. Tubbs ran over and together the two boys pushed the melon up into the buggy. The next one was loaded the same way.

A few minutes later the buggy stopped at Crossroads and the boys jumped off. Jape ran over to an empty bench, where he laid the four squirrels and the .22 rifle. Then Jape and Tubbs took the melon from the mailman. He thanked them and was off to finish his route.

Jape whispered, "He didn't ask, we're home free."

"Melonshake", the boys were in the middle of their shake when four men came out of the store.

One guy said, "You boys lost your mind?"

"Yep, we're crazier than a bed bug but we're going to have squirrel for supper, what're you eatin," Jape gave him a smart mouth answer, which was something he didn't do when his dad was around.

"Where did you steal the melon?", the fellow returned the comment.

"From your patch and it's for Uncle John. He don't have a patch this year, you know! We want to leave it here. It's too heavy to carry all the way."

"Sure put it over there in the shade. He'll be in after while and I'll tell him you left it. Where'd you get it, anyway?," the store operator asked.

Tubbs was standing directly behind Jape who put his hands behind his back with fingers crossed on both hands. "The mailman gave it to us for hoeing his garden."

"Why would you want to give it away?," the man asked.

"We need shells for my .22 and he gave us four this morning so we could go squirrel hunting," Tubbs gave a sincere reply.

Jape turned to grin, Tubbs was a poor liar. Jape would not have believed him for a moment but the man did.

"Oh, I see. John did buy a carton of shorts sometime back, a good trade," the man had bought the boys story.

"You boys need .22 shells?," a second man asked.

"Yes sir, we do," Jape answered.

"I'll trade you a box of .22 shells for two full grown cats."

"What kind of cats?," Tubbs asked.

"Regular cats, you know, house cats."

Jape thinking he wanted them for pets asked, "Do they have to be good mousers?" All four men laughed, because they knew what he wanted with the cats. He was going to use them to train his tree dogs.

"Nope, just full grown cats. Can you boys find a couple?"

"For a box of .22 shells, yep, we'll find-em," Jape answered.

"I left an orange crate here. It'll hold two cats. The box of shells is here, too. Whoever brings two cats first gets the shells. Good luck, boys."

Another man examining their squirrels, "Who shot'm fer'ye?"

"We shot all four. I shot two and Tubbs shot two."

"Look close, when we shoot, we shoot their eyes out," Tubbs told him.

"Did your dog chase'em up a little persimmon tree."

Jape crossed his fingers again, "No, we shot all four out of that old cottonwood across the draw from Yoakums barn." Knowing that was the tallest tree around, it was full of squirrels but too tall for anyone to kill a squirrel with a .22 short.

The man knowing he was being had laughed and said, "Okay, Jape, you're as full of hot air as your dad. You boys better get on your way before those squirrels spoil."

A second man, "Good shooting, boys." He smiled and winked before going back inside the store.

A few minutes later the boys were home skinning the squirrels so his mother could cook them for supper. His mom wasn't finished with the washing, she said, "If you boys want those squirrels cooked before dark you could help me wring out this tub of clothes."

This wasn't anything new for those two. They jumped in to twist the clothing until all the water was squeezed out. Then the article of clothing was shaken back onto shape and hung out to dry. After hanging the last two tubs of clothing on the line to dry, his mom said, "You boys should go swimming, it's going to be a scorcher this afternoon. The water in the creek would be cool."

She wiped her forearm across her brow to knock the perspiration from her face.

"Thanks, Mom, we'll help you finish and if it's okay, we'll do that."

"It's all done, you can dump out the water, rinse out the pot then get out of here. Supper will be ready about dark." She glanced over the boys to add, "Chicken fried squirrel, hot biscuits with cream gravy. If your dad gets back in time, coconut cream pie for dessert. Speaking of eating, what are you boys chewing on?"

"Chewing gum. The mailman gave it to us," Jape answered.

"He said the factory, Wrigley, furnished enough so he could give everyone on the route a stick. One should be in your mail box," Tubbs said.

"It does smell good, now you boys get gone."

They left the .22 at the house, no need to carry a rifle without ammo to go swimming. They got to the creek just in time to see a cottonmouth trying to swallow a frog. The snake was trying to swallow but the frog was a little too big. The snake was working it's jaws loose in an effort to get it down.The frog was still alive, working its front feet in an effort to pull free. A struggle which it could not win.

"Would you look at that? Get a stick, that cottonmouth is a terrible snake. Not only deadly poison but it's eating up the bull frogs. I didn't know they ate frogs," Jape prompted as he ran to get a stick.

"Yea, and they would eat us too if they could," Tubbs answered as both boys hit the snake at the same time with a dead limb which broke from the blow. It didn't help the physical condition of the snake either. Jape grabbed a large rock and hit the snake on the head with it.

To hear Tubbs shout, "Be careful and don't hit the frog."

To that Jape laughed, "Don't you think the frog'll die anyway. The snake already has his fangs hooked into the frog. That frog is already full of poison."

"Yea, but animals aren't like people. They can recover, that frog will make it if we can get it out of the snake's mouth," Tubbs explained.

About that time in came the cavalry, Mr. Tips nearly ran over the boys to grab the snake and shake it from side to side with such tremendous force it not only threw the frog from the snake's mouth but the head was snapped off the snake. The boys both jumped back in awe of Mr. Tips actions. The dog didn't turn loose of the snake but threw it about ten feet away from the boys then approached it very carefully sniffing to see if it was still able to strike. The snake moved a little and the dog jumped back, then jumped back in again for another violent shaking. This was not the first snake that old dog had come in contact with.

After the snake was dead the boys looked for the frog and found it lying near the swimming hole. It was dead, too. Jape, "Ok, we'll have a funeral for the frog." They dug a hole in the sand and buried the frog. Tubbs ran up the creek bank and grabbed a handful of sun-flowers and pushed them into the sand where the headstone should be.

"I'm not in a mood to go swimming with the cottonmouths. Let's do something else," Jape suggested as he splashed his feet in the cool water.

Tubbs was sitting on a small log with his bare feet nearly knee deep in the cool water. Mr. Tips was lying sprawled out in it looking pleased and content with himself for killing the snake.

Tubbs asked, "What do you recommend we do on such a hot afternoon?"

Jape jumped up as if the idea bulb just went off in his head, "Let's go exploring. Let's check out part of McCrimmin's pasture?" Jape was mak-ing a suggestion but it was presented more in the form of a question.

McCrimmin's pasture had always been off limits. They never knew why, once someone said they had a mean bull in there. The fence around the pasture was the best one in the whole county. The post were all solid oak and the barbed wire was extremely tight and it had six wires while most everyone else could only afford three or four wires and they were not nearly so tight. No one knew how big the place was. It could go all the way to the river for all they knew. Since it was off limits, it had always been something of a challenge. This appeared to be the right time and place to cross the line.

"Yea, but we can't go far. We don't want to get lost in there with your mother frying squirrel," Tubbs wanted to refresh Jape's memory of dinner.

They splattered water on each other for a few seconds as the dog barked and ran up stream also splashing around. It was hot, about 120 in the shade.

The boys took their time and walked the half mile to McCrimmins line fence. They looked up and down the barbed wire fence as if it were the border to a prison compound. Each boy climbing over in his own way while Mr. Tips laid over on his side and scooted under. They were excited, this was new territory. For years, this land was forbid-den to everyone. Not even the adults in the community went hunting over here. The boys didn't know why nor did they care. They were headed into another adventure come what may. The sun was too hot to be walking across an open pasture when they could walk up a draw in the shade. After cutting across two ridges they hit a nice little draw and within a hundred yards came upon an old dam or pond. Water was seeping from the ground like a spring. They continued up the draw to find two more small ponds and then the big one. They looked in awe and excited wonderment and each knew how Balboa must have felt when finding the Pacific Ocean. This pond was deep enough to swim in, at least ten feet deep. Old willow trees lined the banks on part of each side. Three old trees provided shade for the dam. Grass was knee high all over the dam, no cow or horse tracks anywhere. Bull frogs the size of Mr. Tips were jumping into the water creating huge waves across the pond. The frogs were so big the boys burst out laughing.

"This is as bad as that train ride we didn't take. Can you believe the size of those frogs. Did you ever eat frog legs," Tubbs asked?

"No, never did, but we won't be able to say that tomorrow."

"Okay, how we going to catch those giant things. They didn't get that big by being stupid," Tubbs explained.

"Nope, they got that big because — no one has been to this pond since Sam Houston was Governor of Texas," Jape shot back.

"So you remember a history lesson. We still can't catch a frog."

"Sure we can and I didn't learn about Houston in a history book. I read a book called, "Six foot Six", he was, you know."

"You're so smart, did you know he was also Governor of Tennessee?"

"Yes, and he was also the president of a country before he was the Governor of Texas! Did you know that?"

"No, I didn't know he was six foot six. I went to the same school you did. Yes, Texas was a country before it became a state. What has that got to do with eating frog legs," Tubbs wanted to know.

"He was a tall guy and it don't have anything to do with eating frog legs. You got anything red in your pocket," Jape asked?

Jape took the fish hook and the top cord from the tool box. He tied the hook on the end of the cord. Tubbs had done the same thing many times to go fishing but not to catch a frog.

"What are you doing," Tubbs asked?

"Grandpaw said frogs would bite anything red if you dangled it in front of them on a hook. We can catch those big frogs like catching fish. Only we can see the frog, instead of having to wait for hours for a fish to come along we dangle the hook right in front of the frog and bam, we got a delicious meal on a hook. See if you can find something red while I cut a long willow pole."

Tubbs checked his pockets both front and back, nothing red.

"I ain't got nothing red. What you got in your pockets?"

Jape shouting from across the lake, causing several more frogs to jumped in. "I don't have anything red. Wonder if another color would do?"

'I don't know, why didn't you ask your grandpaw?"

Jape ran back around the pond with a long willow pole. It was at least ten feet long and appeared to be exactly right for the purpose intended. He tied the other end of the top cord onto the pole and made a few practice maneuvers with the pole. It was perfect, he could drop down to hide in the tall grass and hold the red object right in front of the frog. Only one problem, he didn't have anything red.

In disgust, they sat down on the dam in the shade of the willow. Jape remarked, "This is a perfect spot. These frogs have been here for years growing up waiting for us, now we don't have anything red."

"Wonder if they would grab a grasshopper," Tubbs pondered. The grass was full of grasshoppers of all sizes.

Jape jumped up to chase after one, "I don't know but let's try."

They caught a large grasshopper and put it on the hook. A little breeze was blowing and the hopper didn't want to drift down to the frog. Jape tied an old nut to the line about two feet up from the hopper. The weight of the nut would hold the line tight in the wind and allow the grasshopper to flutter in front of the unsuspecting frog. They tried this on three or four frogs without the desired results. The grasshopper, the cord or a combination of all three only caused the frogs to hop back in. Once more, in disgust, the boys stopped to do some heavy thinking. Jape just dropped the pole down leaving the grass hopper in the water.

"We can catch a couple cats and trade for that box of .22 shells then come back and with the .22, we can get a real mess of frog legs," Tubbs told Jape as they looked at each other in total disgust with their failure.

"Bright idea, where we going to get two cats," Jape shot back?

"In town, lots of people in town want to get rid of cats."

"Yea, I guess so. With nine lives they probably live forever. Wonder if we can get two for free or will they . . ."

Tubbs didn't let Jape finish, he shouted at Jape, "For free, you dummy."

They were interrupted by a large splashing noise as their pole went flying out into the pond.

Tubbs screamed, "Your pole, your pole, you have a fish on. That darn grasshopper caught a fish."

"Look at that thing go. How we going to get the pole," Jape shouted?

"Well, your mother told us to go swimming. Go on, dive in, after all it's your pole," Tubbs shouted as he slapped his legs laughing.

"The pole is going under, no, it's coming back this way. Watch it." Jape was so excited he ran across the dam and flew threw the air to land on the willow pole about ten feet from the bank. He succeeded in getting the pole but the fish had control. Jape tried to pull the pole but instead the fish took him out into deep water. The boy and fish drifted along slowly as the fish pulled him out into the middle of the pond. He had a death grip on the big end of that willow pole. When the fish stopped, the entire pole would float to the top.

Tubbs was screaming, ''It's pulling you all over the pond. It may be an alligator,'' while running in circles yelling and laughing.

Jape was too busy to laugh, he wanted to get that fish but the fish was equally as strong as the boy and a much stronger swimmer. The fish continued to circle around in the deep water. Jape could not pull the fish up and the fish could not pull him down. The pond may not have been deep enough for the fish to pull him under. Jape tried to swim but with only one hand he didn't make any progress toward the bank, the fish wanted to go the other way, guess which way they went? The struggle continued with the boy treading water while screaming for Tubbs to do something.

''What can I do?,'' Tubbs shouted back.

''Get a long pole and pull me in.''

Tubbs ran to find another pole. Suddenly the fish swam into shallow water. That was a mistake, once Jape got his feet on the muddy bottom the contest was over. Jape didn't make any attempt to ''play'' the fish or worry about it getting off the hook. He ran ashore pulling that catfish like a horse does a plow. The lad left the water in a run and the fish came sliding and flopping out. Mr. Tips must have thought the monster was chasing Jape. The dog came racing over with bristles raised to attack the fish as he had the snake. The dog barked while jumping back and forth at the flopping fish. After the fish was several yards from the water Jape stopped to look back. Both boys stood looking at the giant fish with their mouths wide open. They never dreamed of seeing such a fish and certainly never catching one that size and especially out of that old hillside pond.

Tubbs's eyes were the size of saucers, ''How big is it?''

Jape was excited, ''No one will ever believe this. I don't even believe this. This is even bigger than the train ride. Tubbs can you believe this?''

''Yep, but only because I see it. This calls for a melonshake.''

Jape jumped up to butt heads with Tubbs as each boy cocked his leg and did a down under shake and they didn't come close to falling over.

''We may have to develop a catfish shake after this,'' Jape added.

''Wonder if that is the son or the daddy fish. I'll bet that is one of the little ones. There may be fish in there so big I could use you for bait. It's a wonder this little one's mom didn't come up and swallow you for trying to catch her little baby fish," Tubbs exclaimed.

Both boys rolled around on the carpet of bermuda grass laughing.

"There could be some big ones in here," Jape spoke hopefully.

"Big ones, big ones, what do you call that thing." Tubbs sat up to point at the four foot fish laying on the bank.

Jape grinned at his buddy, "I guess a fishing story never gets so big that there isn't a bigger story in the pond."

"What we going to do with that thing?", Tubbs asked.

"Eat it, you idiot."

"We can feed the entire county for a year with that one fish."

"No question about that. We can certainly have all the catfish we want to eat once mama gets that thing in the skillet." Jape promised.

"What, you know, we can't tell anyone where we caught it," Tubbs explained.

"You're right, oh no, I forgot about that. What'll we tell this time?"

"A few fish do come up the creek when it rains and we did have a rain the other day. We'll tell'em we caught it in the swimming hole," Tubbs prompted.

"That will work, if they check, the snake is there for proof. No, no, a good fisherman never tells where they catch the big one. We'll keep it a secret and they'll believe we caught it at the swimming hole," Jape said.

"Good idea, are we going to take the fish to the store?"

"Sure, they will be talking about us for years to come. Those old men go fishing all the time and they never caught one that big before. This may be the largest fish in the world," Jape wasn't about to pass up the chance to take that fish to the store.

"They have larger fish in the ocean but not many this big."

Jape was trying to lift the fish, "Oh no, it's too heavy to carry."

Tubbs jumped up to check out that statement. Neither boy could lift it up high enough to get it off the ground. They sat down looking at the fish in disgust.

Suddenly both boys started laughing, whooping and hollering with laughter. Neither knew what the other was laughing about and as abruptly as they started, they stopped and each boy asked, as he wiped the tears from his eyes, "What you laughing about?"

"You first," offered Jape.

"No, you first."

Jape held his hands behind his back. "Guess how many fingers I have extended on my hands."

"Both hands or one?", Tubbs inquired.

"Both hands."

"Seven."

Jape jerked his hands out from behind his back. Two, I win you go first.

"You must think I'm a real dummy. You are lying, you had your fingers crossed. You never had any fingers extended that wasn't crossed. I win because you cheated and who told you that crossing your fingers eliminates a lie in the first place?" Tubbs scolded him for cheating.

"Everyone knows that, crossing your fingers, is like time out or nothing counts, you know. Okay, I was laughing at us. We have been fishing many times and I always wanted to catch a big fish. If someone asked me what a big fish was, well, I would have held my hands about two feet apart or even less. We catch a giant and, well, this is funny."

"Me too, I was laughing because this fish is so big it's unreal." The boys sat back down once more looking at the fish; however, Mr. Tips was watching it very carefully walking back and forth in a half circle.

The boys sat flat down on the grass with their chin resting in their hands, disgusted. They had to do something and do it quick. The afternoon was going fast and they were looking forward to a special supper. This wasn't the day to get home after dark.

Jape jumped up shouting, "I got it, I got it."

"You got what?"

Jape ran over to pick up the fishing pole. "Get the hook out of its mouth. I don't want to lose my lucky hook."

Tubbs was trying to get the hook out, "You can say that again, this is one lucky hook. "Now, what are we doing?"

"Remember the movie scene last year when we watched 'Nyoka, The Jungle Girl'. They captured the crocodile, remember how the natives carried it off tied to a pole. Well, here is the pole for our fish," Jape told him.

Once more the top cord came in handy. They wrapped the cord around the fish and the pole all the way from it's gills to the tail. Jape cut the pole off after the fish was tied on, making sure they had enough pole left on each end of the fish for easy carrying. They left the pond walking with a tad bit more pride in their gait than when they arrived. Nothing quite like catching a big fish to boost a boy's ego.

The two boys cut back across McCrimmins pasture, forgetting about the boiling hot sun. With a boy on each end of the pole packing the heavy fish, they headed straight for the road but once again it was a labor of love. They were looking forward to the reception at the Crossroads store. At the fence, they dropped the fish on the ground and rolled it under the wire. After climbing over the fence they sat down to rest for a moment,

Jape shouted, "The thing is breathing, look at the gills move in and out. It ain't even dead yet."

"Hope it ain't a witch changed into a fish."

"Don't be silly, witches don't make themselves into fish. They only change into ghosts and things like that," Jape told him like he knew.

"Don't either, a witch can do anything," Tubbs corrected.

"If I was a witch, right now I would change you into a horse so I could carry this fish out of here real easy."

"If I was a witch, I would snap my fingers and we would already be at the store eating some of Webster's icecream."

"Where is your chewing gum?", Jape pointed to Tubbs mouth laughing.

"I swallowed mine when you ran out with the fish. Where's yours?"

"Swallowed mine, too, get hold of that pole and let's go."

The boys walked out to the road and the two miles to the store.

Jape opened the door, sticking his head in, "You fellows want to see a fish?" He returned to help Tubbs take the cord off. In the fall, the store bought pecans from anyone who brought them to the store. They weighed them on a large set of scales. Knowing the store had that set of scales he wanted to see how much the fish weighed.

One of the men poked his head out of the door. He gasped, then whistled, turning back to shout, "My God!, come look what these boys have now, it's a whopper!"

Several men followed him out to take a look at the fish. Uncle John was in the group. Everyone was talking at the same time and asking the same thing, "Where did you catch the fish?"

Jape pulled the large mouth open and pointed inside, "I hooked him about one foot down there."

Everybody laughed. Uncle John spoke, "I don't blame you boys. If you have found a good fishing hole, keep it to yourselves. These guys can make it to the river a lot easier than you can. I don't want to know the spot on the river but how did you get there and back?"

"They were here earlier. They went squirrel hunting this morning." One of the men informed the crowd as he was there when the boys came by with the squirrels.

"That's right, they didn't have time to walk to the river. That fish had to come from the river. Nothing that big in any of the creeks around here," the operator of the store explained.

"No pond fish ever gets that big," someone stated.

"It rained the other day. The creeks were up, a big one does come up here now and then."

Uncle John, "Hey, that fish is still alive. Throw it into the horse trough."

Jape tried to pick up the fish. Uncle John, realizing his dilemma, grabbed the catfish and by the use of both hands tossed the fish into the horse trough. The fish splashed from the fall and drifted lifelessly to the bottom. Everyone walked over to look into the watering trough at the fish. The debris from the splashing water settled down and away from the fish. The gills moved a little, then a little more as the men watched and waited. A minute went by without much action but the gills were working back and forth. One of the men said, "Reach in there and touch him, Jape." Jape reached into the water and touched the fish, which came to life splashing water all over everyone. Everyone shouted and laughed at the commotion this stirred up, glad that the fish was still alive.

"We'll only have to kill it anyway. I want to eat it," Jape commented.

Uncle John, "From what I hear you boys will be eating squirrel tonight. Oh, by the way, thanks for the melon."

"That's okay, knowing you didn't have a patch this year and we have a large patch," Tubbs told him.

"What's this you been telling these boys, no watermelon patch?"

Jape couldn't see it because Uncle John turned his head but Jape knew he winked at the crowd of men. Uncle John immediately changed the subject, "Your dad was in earlier, Jape. He says you and Mr. Tips are getting along fine. He is a good squirrel dog, isn't he?"

"Yep, he did good today. We got to get the fish and go home. I have to be there before dark."

"Supper'll be ready about dark and we're having chicken fried squirrel, hot biscuits and cream gravy," Tubbs didn't want to be late for supper.

"Jape, how about leaving the fish in the trough for a few days so everyone can see your big catch?", the store operator asked.

Jape looked at Tubbs and both boys looked back at him as they shrugged their shoulders, "I don't know."

"Someone will get our fish," Tubbs added in a concerned tone.

"No, they won't, Jape. It will be fine there but your fish will be a big attraction and those coming to look at the fish will spend," Uncle John said.

The store operator offered, "Okay, okay, I'll give you a candy bar if you will leave him here for a week?"

Jape looked at Tubbs and asked, "How about two candy bars and two pops a week and we leave him here for two weeks."

The man laughed, "The kid IS your nephew, John. Okay, do I understand you right, a candy bar and a pop for each of you once a week for as long as the fish is here."

"Yep, that's right," Jape answered.

"And you take care of the fish for the boys. Make sure it doesn't disappear, okay?", Uncle John prompted.

"No problem, I'll tie the dog to the trough at night."

Uncle John turned to look at the boys, "I'm down here every day anyway. I'll keep a close watch out for your fish."

"You boys want a candy bar and a pop right now?", the operator volunteered.

"Yea," was Tubbs quick reply but Jape butted in,

"No, we don't, we're going home to eat supper. We'll be back tomar when it's hot for a cold pop. We may catch an elephant tomar for you to tie next to the fish."

Chapter 4
The Pot of Gold

The squirrel dinner was topped off with a piece of coconut cream pie. The pie was made with real cream, rich, thick and delicious. Mom cut the big pie into four pieces, serving each person one fourth of the pie. This wasn't unusual, every pie was always cut into four pieces, anything smaller was totally unacceptable. Dad couldn't wait to see the catfish. Immediately after dinner he saddled up a horse and rode up to Crossroads. The boys were exhausted, they went to bed almost immediately after eating dinner. The fishermen were sound asleep when Jape's dad came in all excited about the fish. He was very proud of his son.

The family was awakened the next morning at 6:00 AM by the unusual sound of a car horn coming down the road to the house. "Ugga-ugga-ugga —ugga-ugga-ugga". Jape's father jumped out of bed, jerked on his trousers to run outside barefooted.

"Oh, my God, something terrible has happened." Jape's mom moaned.

A few minutes later, dad returned to verify her thoughts. Her grandfather had died in his sleep, he was seventy six. In 1939, that was considered old but he had been feeling well a few days before even running a foot race with Jape nearly beating him.

The boys dressed and helped get the chores done early. Dad harnessed and fed the horses while Jape milked three cows. Then Tubbs turned the cream separator which was usually Jape's job, the cream was taken from the milk so it could be sold and the skimmed milk was fed to the pigs. They were finished with all the chores before daylight.

The entire family or Jape's mother's clan was to meet at grandpaw's house. They would feast, gossip and pay their respects today and the funeral would be tomorrow. Jape's parents had two ways of getting there, walking or by riding in a horse drawn wagon; needless to say they chose to ride. Dad and mom sat up front in a spring seat while the two boys sat in back of the wagon with their feet dangling and Mr. Tips ran along behind. Tubbs was holding his .22 across his legs. There wasn't much to talk about on that ride. Death wasn't something the boys knew much about. It was something they made every effort not to talk about.

Tubbs whispered, "Who died?"

"My mother's grandfather, my great-grandfather."

"He must have been old?"

"No, not really, he's the one that had the Greyhound races at Crossroads, the one who drove the big black car, he liked me."

"Too bad, too bad. Somehow it don't seem right me totin' this rifle, going to a funeral and all." They rode in silence for a ways.

Then Tubbs continued, "Now we won't be able to get any frogs!"

Jape lowered his voice to another whisper, "Dad is planning to take you home in the wagon. If I can stay all night with you we can go to Paoli and get two cats. They don't need me at this family get-together anyway."

A mile down the road Dad spoke, "Son, we're going to stop and view the body. I realize you have not seen a dead person, but it is considered disrespectful not to go by and say your last good-by. You and Tubbs can both go in with mom and tell him ''by." He was the best, so don't do anything stupid. Go in with your mother, and bow your head in case they're praying. It's in his home but act like you're in church."

"The boys will be fine. I'll hold their hands," Jape's mom told him.

Only a few of the family members were present. The house was not filled with laughter as Jape always remembered it. There was the quietness of death about the place. Mom entered the house with a boy by each hand. Nothing was said, they were directed by hand signal to go into the master bedroom. There was grandpaw laid out on the bed, white as a ghost. Jape was shaking all over and didn't want to look at him; however, nothing he tried to do succeeded. He wanted to close his eyes but his curiosity didn't allow him that luxury. In life, the old gentleman was a man of class. From Jape's short boyhood memories, death didn't fit the man because he was one of Jape's favorite people. Jape had rather remember the last time they had a foot race, now the ghost of his death was branded in Jape's mind.

They left great-grandpaw's place and traveled the rest of the way in silence. The wagon turned in at grandpaw's place and dad spoke again. "Whooa" He stopped the team at the gate, "Jape, there ain't no need for you boys to have to suffer through all this boredom. You can either jump out here," looking at Tubbs, "or after awhile I'll take you home. It would be nice if Jape could stay all night with you tonight. I'd appreciate it if your mother would let you spend the day with Jape tomorrow. He won't be going to the funeral and he shouldn't be alone."

He turned to talk to Jape, "Please come back over here in the morning and do the chores for grandpaw. They will have so much food, you boys may as well have a good dinner. Your mother and I must go to the funeral."

Dad was both frustrated and embarrassed about what he was about to say. He looked at Jape and for one split second there was the glimmer of a little moisture in his dad's eye.

"Sorry son, you don't have nothing fittin' to wear to a funeral and we just don't have the money right now."

"That's okay, I don't want to go. What about our chores at home?", Jape asked as the boys jumped off the wagon.

"Your mother and I will go home tonight and be back tomar. I'll see you back here early in the morning. Now Jape, you get over here in the morning before daylight and do the chores. This is a trying time for your grandpaw. They think you're special, give them reason for continuing to feel that way. I'm sure your fish will be most of the conversation all day anyway. You boys try to stay out of trouble!"

Mr. Tips was going crazy, barking and running in circles. Tubbs had the .22 cradled in his arms and of course the dog thought they were going hunting. They started walking down the road. It was early, the sun was sifting through the pecan trees warming a gentle southern breeze, God in all his wisdom could never paint a more beautiful morning. Jape knew every squirrel in the county was out taking advantage of the morning sun and they didn't have a single .22 shell.

The dirt was cool to their bare feet. Everything seemed perfect, but "death" has a way of disrupting the mental process of everyone and especially those two boys. They didn't realize what the problem was, but this was the first time they could remember that they didn't want to go hunting. While the family was getting ready to attend a funeral; well, they just didn't want to go kill anything, nope, not even a frog!

"Let's sit down and rest," Jape commented.

"Rest, rest, you sick? We haven't walked a hundred yards and it isn't even hot yet. What's wrong? Did you want to go to the funeral?", asked Tubbs.

"No, I don't want to go. I never been, have you?"

"Nope, the only one I want to attend is my own. That way I will be sure I don't have to see any more dead people."

"Wasn't that spooky?", Jape shot back.

"Yes, I was scared to death. I closed my eyes," Tubbs admitted.

"I wanted to but couldn't. Did you hear my knees banging together?"

"Nope, I wasn't listening for your knees, my heart was in my throat."

"Yep, me too, I'm not in the mood to go hunting," Jape confessed.

"Yea, I know how you feel. On a day like this, we should think of something good to do, like go to Paoli and get two cats," Tubbs suggested.

"Yea, but that won't take all day, we can walk and think about something to do after we get the cats."

"After we get the cats we will have a whole box of .22 shells. It won't be hard to think of something to do then," Tubbs reminded him.

"We may as well look for insulators on the way." He ran up the little bank to kick the grass around under a telephone pole. Tubbs and Mr. Tips followed as Jape continued, "What are we going to carry the cats in?"

"I can carry one and you can carry one."

"In our hands?", Jape asked.

"After all they aren't wild cats, tigers or something."

"My aunt had a cat that was very gentle but when I tried to pet it, the thing went crazy. She said it didn't like strangers."

"Did you ever see a dog with a running fit?", Tubbs changed the subject.

"No, what's that?"

"Here's one, I found one. I beat you finding one. Oh, the dog yelp's and runs like crazy in a circle and just goes crazy."

"Something like a mad-dog, I guess?", Jape questioned.

"I don't know I never saw a mad-dog," Tubbs admitted.

"You ever smoke a cigarette?"

"Not really, I found a cigar butt and tried to light it one day."

"Where did you find a cigar butt?", Jape wanted to know.

"In town, a few years ago. I brought the cigar home and later got a match. I was too little to think of getting more than one match. The match went out. I ran to get another one with the cigar in my mouth, Mom saw me. Boy, did I catch it for that."

"But you didn't get a whipping?"

"No, but I thought she was going to kill me. I never did that again."

"We must get something to carry those cats in, a gunny sack, a box or something," Jape was concerned about how to carry the cats.

"Okay, we'll get it 'something' in town. They have more of 'something' in there than we do out here. Whoever we get the cats from will give us something," Tubbs said, but he thought carrying them would not be a problem.

Uncle John was right, by kicking around in the grass they found more insulators. They also noticed several insulators still on the poles that could be pulled out easily with a hammer. Once more they stashed their booty in the same place as they did before, prompting Tubbs to ask,

"What did you do with the bearings?"

Jape took out the tool box and produced one steel ball just a little smaller than the average marble. "I hit the thing with a hammer until I was blue in the face. I finally used dad's big sledge hammer and knocked it apart. The steel balls went flying but I found most of 'em."

"Where's mine?"

Jape stuck the steel marble into Tubbs out stretched hand. "This is the only one I have with me. Take it and when we get home I'll half the others."

Tubbs looked at the steelie and grinned, "With this I may be able to win some of your marbles."

Jape grinned, crossed his eyes and stuck out his tongue at Tubbs, "Don't bet the homestead or your cattle ranch on it."

"Okay, smarty pants, I'll bet there is some kid in the City that can beat you."

"Yep, and there are fish in the ocean bigger than ours, too."

The boys didn't know how to go about getting the cats. They walked around town, it was early and most town folks aren't early risers as those living on the farm. Nearly every house had one or more cats lying or sitting in a chair on the porch. Then the boys thought they had struck pay dirt when they saw a hand-painted sign on a piece of cardboard, "Free Kittens." The boys went up to the door and knocked. The lady answering the door was very friendly, she asked, "Good morning, boys, you want a kitten?"

"No, ma'am, our cat died. We need a good mouser," Tubbs told her.

"Oh, no, we only have three little kittens left. Their mother is a good mouser but I'd never part with her."

"My mom sure does miss the cat. It's her birthday and I don't have any money for a present," Tubbs was hoping to get her assistance.

Lady, "You dear boy." She opened the door and continued, "Come on in."

"Do you know anyone who would like to find a good home for a full grown cat that is a good mouser?", Jape asked the lady.

"If not a good mouser, we can train it," Tubbs added.

"Well, how sweet, you boys are so nice. Let me call around town."

Jape winked at Tubbs and both displayed crossed fingers. The lady went to a telephone hanging on the wall in the front room. The boys looked at each other as their eyes got wide. This was a lady of means, she had a phone. She cranked on the handle a couple turns, then spoke into the mouthpiece. "Sara, connect me with Tilly, please."

She turned to the boys and pointed to a large sofa located across the room. "You boys have a seat, please." They took off their straw hats and sat down. They were across the room and could not hear the conversation. The lady made several telephone calls before stopping to talk with the boys.

She smiled at the boys, "Nothing positive, but Rachael has several cats and she was wanting to find a good home for one or two. She don't have a phone. Betty is going over to see her now. I told her I would send you boys by to talk with her. You'll love Rachael, she is so nice and makes the best cake. If she invites you in, don't say no. She has the best cookies in town."

"Where does she live?"

"I'll walk out on the porch with you. If I can point, I give better directions."

She told the boys how to find Rachael's house and wished them luck.

Mr. Tips jumped up from the shade of the house and followed them down the street. Within half a block, a man shouted at them, "Hey, fellows." The boys stopped and looked back.

The man shouted, "You boys wanting a cat?"

"Yes sir, we do. We need two cats," was Jape reply.

"I only got one, you can have it if you take it now, right now.

"Sure, where's it at?", Tubbs asked as he turned and walked back.

"Right there on the porch. Not an original name but that's "Tom". Just pick him up and go."

Tubbs ran up the steps and picked "Tom" up from his nap in the chair.

Jape asked, "Do you have a box to carry him in?"

"Nope, just get him out of here. I'm too attached to'im, I may start crying. Take'im and go, boy, take'im and go."

Tubbs walked down the street with the cat lying on his shoulder, stroking the fur and talking with the cat. "Nice kitty, good kitty, pretty kitty."

They were only a few steps from the corner when two ladies walked around the corner to meet them face to face.

One lady screamed, "My God! what are you doing with my cat! Put my cat down now and I mean NOW."

The boys were shocked, their mouths fell open, the cat was scared stiff. It's claws dug into Tubbs bare shoulders on hearing the fear in it's master's voice. Mr. Tips thought the cat was doing harm to Tubbs and ran up growling. The cat suddenly panicked, screamed like a wild panther, then ran across Tubbs shoulder and down his back to come face to face with Mr. Tips. The cat's hair and tail was standing straight up, old Tom was scared to death. He screamed again and ran back up the front of Tubbs. Every time the cat's feet touched Tubbs, it's claws penetrated flesh, with each step the cat's claws jerked out flesh and blood.

Tubbs was screaming, "Oh awaha, oh awaha, oh awaho."

When the cat got to the middle of Tubbs' overalls, he developed diarrhea. This thin liquid spurted three feet covering the front of Tubbs trousers. The cat leaped off Tubbs, flying through the air to hit the ground running for home with Mr. Tips right behind him, bawling like the hound that he was. Jape took off after Mr. Tips screaming at the top of his lungs. The two women were also running to save the cat. Tom ran to the porch and climbed up one of the support posts. Mr. Tips stopped with his head cocked sideways looking up at the cat. He didn't bark treed because he knew house cats were off limits. Uncle John had raised him with cats. The dog knew something wasn't right, he stopped and waited for Jape to give instructions.

Jape ran up screaming at the dog, "Get out of here." Pointing to a shade in the street, "Go lay down, now get out of here."

The dog walked out to the shade and laid down. The two ladies ran up panting more than the dog.

One lady screamed at Jape, "Why were you trying to steal my cat?"

"I didn't have your cat. That boy down there did."

He turned to point at Tubbs who was still halfway down the block. Tubbs was standing in the middle of the street with his arms held out in a helpless gesture. He had liquid cat dung all over the front of his trousers.

"Don't be sassy with me, young man. You are with him."

They were interrupted by a noise from next door. The man that had given the boys the cat was rolling on the floor of the porch laughing.

He rolled over to sit up on the first step of the porch. He could hardly talk through tears of laughter but he managed to shout, "Jake, did you see that?"

Those words were the invitation for everyone to come out of hiding. Five old men seemed to appear from nowhere and they were all laughing.

The picture became clear to the lady and she turned to Jape, "Did that old man give you my cat?"

Jape shrugged his shoulders, "The cat ain't hurt."

"Answer my question, young man, or I'll have your hide. I was a school teacher for thirty-five years and I've tanned more boy's keisters than a few and you're right in line to be next if you try to lie to me, young man."

Jape could see a little of Mrs. Auld in her eyes, "Yes, ma'am, he gave us the cat."

She turned her wrath from Jape to the old man. "You think you are so darn cute. You can get your own ride to the funeral tomorrow. You will not ride in my car." She stomped up the steps and disappeared into the house with the other woman right behind her.

Jape turned to walk back toward Tubbs not knowing if he should laugh or cry. He wanted to laugh, it was funny, but he was hurting for Tubbs. The cat had clawed him something terrible. The old men were still laughing as each one said something to the effect that the incident was the most comical event to happen in Paoli since the last tornado.

The lady poked her head back out the door to shout at the man again, "You men are all alike, you have a warped brain and sense of humor. Now, go help that poor boy get cleaned up. You should not be laughing, you should be ashamed of yourself."

The old man winked at Jape still laughing, "Son, I am ashamed of myself." He turned to put his hand on Jape's shoulder. "The devil made me do it. Why it's Jape. I didn't recognize you. What you boys doing in town?"

"We need two house cats."

"Yes, how silly of me to ask. You boys do need two cats. Well, I did try to give you one."

He burst out laughing again. Then stopped to get serious. "Jape, your great grandpappy and I have had many good laughs. We are going to plant one hell of a good man, hell no, a great man. You have his blood in your veins, Jape, and for that you should stand tall and proud. He was a friend to everyone and never had an enemy. Not many men can say that and not have their fingers crossed."

Jape looked up at the man in a shocked way because he knew that crossing the fingers would eliminate a lie. The man continued, "Let's go see how we can help Tubbs."

Jape was wondering how he knew them.

Tubbs was still standing in the street with his arms extended but he was grinning. The stench of the cat fecus was so strong Jape didn't want to get within ten feet of him.

The man smiled to say, "Hold your nose, boys. Looks like that cat made mincemeat out of your hide. You will have to be cleaned up before we can doctor those cat scratches. We better get some alcohol or iodine on those or they could become infected. Well, let's see, since I did get you boys into this — uh-mess," he pointed to the front of Tubbs pants, "I should at least try to get you out of it, follow me." In back of his house the man had made a shower using a fifty gallon barrel and the water was heated by the sun. A hose ran into a small can with holes in the bottom that sprinkled the water out for a shower.

He told Tubbs, "Drop your pants and get under this. It may be a little cool this early but anything will be better than that odor."

Tubbs looked around to see who was watching but that spot was secluded. He stepped under the leaking can as the man said,

"There is a bar of soap on the."

"Thanks, I found it."

"How we going to get the stuff out of his pants?", Jape asked.

"That isn't a problem either, with a little soap and water. I washed yesterday and for some unknown reason I didn't pour out the water. They walked back to a wash pot, he dropped the filthy trousers into the cold but soapy water. The man walked back to a shed, got a hoe and returned to use it to slosh the trousers up and down in the water. "If this don't get the smell out nothing will. I have lots of lye soap in there."

He worked the trousers up and down until Tubbs was out of the shower. He shouted, "Did you get the water turned off."

"Yes, sir," Tubbs answered.

"Good, your trousers will be ready in a few minutes. We have to rinse them before you put them on." He walked over to the clothes line and got a pair of his overalls and gave them to Tubbs.

"Put these on, until your's gets dry."

He rinsed and hung Tubbs trousers on the clothes line, then put iodine on the cat scratches. Tubbs looked like a spotted Hyena.

Turning to the boys, "Ok, that's that, but we still have one big problem."

"What problem? Getting his trousers dry?"

"Nope, the sun will take care of that. You boys still need a cat."

"Two cats," Tubbs corrected.

"Two cats, okay, we need two cats. Your trousers will be dry in a little while, just about time for me to find you two cats."

"This time with the owner's permission," Jape suggested as all three laughed.

Tubbs asked, "Could we put them in a box this time?"

"A great idea, how far you got to go?", the man wanted to know.

"Nearly to Crossroads," Tubbs advised.

"That is a fer piece to pack a couple cats. We better fix you a box." He got an apple box, nailed a divider in the middle and tied two pieces of rope in a circle on each end for handles. On walking outside he said, "I know a lady who will be happy to get rid of two cats. You boys let me do the talking, okay. This lady is a little different."

They walked about ten blocks, then up a long driveway to a house secluded by trees, vines and bushes of all kinds. At least five cats jumped to run out of the way as the man walked up to knock on the screen door.

A tall thin woman came to the door, opened it, looked up at the man, turned to spit tobacco juice about ten feet, "What the hell you want, Charley?"

"Nothing, Maud, I am going to town this afternoon and thought I would see if there was anything you need?"

"The store here has most everything I need."

"Yep, but Garrett Snuff and Brown Mule is cheaper in town, just thought."

"That's what you get for thinking." She looked at the boys and back to the man, "You're young'uns?"

"Nope, never seen'em before in my life."

"You're a liar, Charley, but one hell of a good one. Now, what do you want?"

She spit again hitting a rock about ten feet across the walkway, "Don't make me put a knot on your head right here in front of your grandkids."

"Nope, never wanted anything, just to show off my young'uns and see if you needed anything from town. If you don't, then we'll be going."

He turned as if to walk away then turned back, and as if it was an afterthought, "You should feed these cats, Maud, they are looking terrible."

"If you were worth a damn you would haul some of them off for me or find them a new home. Why don't you take a half dozen with you to town today."

"Well, I guess we could take a couple."

He turned and walked back. She spit again, "You're not joshing me?"

"Nope, catch me two and I'll give them a new home."

She lowered her voice to a sweet tone, "Kitty, kitty, here, kitty, kitty."
Seven cats showed up looking for something to eat. She pointed to
the box, "The box for the cats?"

Jape and Tubbs looked at the man who laughed as she said, "Charley,
you old liar, you came all the way over here to get two of my cats
and then didn't have the guts to ask for'em. Okay, boys, grab two,
any two."

They returned to get Tubbs' own trousers and walked back by the
school. The man was going to the store for something and agreed
to walk with them. Some of the same group of boys were playing marbles. They recognized the dog and then the boys.

One boy shouted, "Did you guys get into trouble?"

"Yea, but we took care of it," Jape shouted back.

"What did they do to you?"

"Tied us to a railroad track with a train coming," Tubbs joked.

"How did you get loose?"

"We didn't, the train cut us in half," Jape continued the joke.

"No, we can't play marbles with you guys, anymore, that's all."

"The cop told us not to play with you anyway, you're a shark."
They walked on by and Charley asked, "What's he talking about?"

"Nothing, I won some marbles, playing keeps and they called the cops."

"That is a good story. Now uncross your fingers and tell the story."

Tubbs butted in,"We best turn off here it's much closer. Thanks a
lot, mister."

Jape had a double purpose for the next question, change the subject
and make some money, "Would you or any of your friends be interested
in buying some nice yellow meated watermelons?"

Charley jumped on that, "Yes, I would and I have friends who would
too. You have a big patch?"

"Not very big but we have a few to spare."

"How big are the melons and what are you going to ask?"

"Don't know, what will you pay?"

"Oh, from a dime to a quarter . . . . . . .for a large one."

"Okay, I'll bring three in tomar in a wheelbarrow."

"Nope, can't do that tomar. Everyone will be at the funeral, but the
next day would be fine. When you get in town, you know how to find me."

The sun was about midway in the sky, it was hot and the cats were heavy. Their bare feet plodded along in the hot dust hill after hill, mile after mile. At grandpaw's place they stopped to get a cool drink from the creek and then sat in the shade of the bridge. There was only one mile left to pack the cats. Sweat was running down their faces and Tubbs was complaining about the cat scratches hurting. They certainly weren't in any hurry to get the cats to Crossroads. They sat in the shade of the bridge for a few minutes then Tubbs walked out into the water.

Suddenly he jumped out shouting, "Come here quick, there's an alligator or something in here."

Jape and Mr. Tips both came running. Tubb's feet had stirred the mud into the water causing it to become murky and they couldn't see anything.

Jape asked, "What was it? And don't tell me it was an alligator either."

"I don't know, it was big and it was in here and there it goes, see it, see it." He pointed up stream about three feet. A large dark object disappeared back into the muddy water and once more Tubbs screamed and jumped out of the water. "It hit my feet, it hit my feet."

About that time a giant snapping turtle stuck his head out of the muddy water to breathe. Both boys screamed with excitement as Mr. Tips jumped into the water trying to catch the turtle. The turtle was eighteen inches across and weighed thirty pounds. When they recognized what it was they got a long stick and pushed it out of the deep water. Once in shallow water they could hold on to its shell without worrying about getting bit.

"Don't let it bite you. It won't turn loose until it thunders."

Tubbs looked up at the clear blue sky, "That could be weeks."

"A very good reason not to get bit. Put a stick in his mouth and see what he will do." Jape was holding the turtle with both hands. The head and feet were half way inside the shell. Tubbs pushed a long piece of old sunflower stalk at his mouth. Just as it passed the turtle's mouth the head popped out about six inches and snapped off the flower stem. The boys laughed as Tubbs said, "He could certainly bite your finger off."

"Probably hurt a little but he couldn't bite it off. Get a pecan limb and see what he does to that." Tubbs pulled out a dead limb from a pile of debris under the bridge. The dead limb was about half inch in diameter and the turtle snapped it right off.

"How was that? Want to stick your finger in his mouth?"

"He's not fast enough to catch my finger. I can touch his head and he can't bite me," Jape bragged.

"You better not, he will bite your finger smooth off. Then you'll catch it for sure when you go home. Your dad don't have time to take you to the doctor today of all days."

"Ok, I'll tie a stick onto my hand and show you." He used the top cord and tied a green stick a little larger than his finger to his hand, running it up the back of his forefinger. This way the turtle could bite the limb and his finger at the same time. The limb being larger would keep the jaws of the turtle off his finger, should the turtle accidently be faster than the boy, or that was Jape's plan.

Tubbs continued to hold the Turtle as Jape waved the stick in front of the turtle's mouth. The turtle was getting tired of biting sticks.

"You're not touching his head and your finger isn't close enough, even if he wanted to snap at it."

Jape looked up to scream back at Tubbs and the turtle snapped catching the stick and Jape's finger right in the middle of the second joint. The green limb was larger than the finger but the turtle's jaws were strong enough to cut half way into both the limb and the finger.

"Oh, my God, start praying for rain. We need thunder in a hurry."

Tubbs fell off the turtle laughing, "You're so damn fast, how did that slow old turtle ever catch Mr. Speedy, Speedy, Speedy, ain't so fast anymore."

Jape was grimacing, "You said another dirty word and you know you will go to hell for cursing like that. Quit laughing, it's not funny, this thing may not let go until it thunders."

The turtle was holding on like it had lockjaw. Tubbs continued to laugh, "Now who's going to hell? Even a moron wouldn't stick his finger in a snapping turtle's mouth. And remember this morning when I had cat stuff all over me. I seem to remember some guy laughing. Wonder who that was?"

Jape was talking through clenched teeth, "Hold it with one hand and get my knife out of my right pocket for me."

Tubbs reached over and got the Barlow out of his pocket then asked, "You going to cut his head off?"

"Not yet, here open the big blade for me."

Tubbs opened the blade and Jape took the knife in his left hand. He pushed the blade into the turtle's mouth behind the stick and used it as a lever to pry the turtle's mouth open. A little effort and he was able to jerk his finger free.

He had to untie the stick from his hand to lick the wound. Tubbs let the turtle go back into the water as he watched Jape suck on his wounded finger, "You do know that Turtle saliva will cause leprosy in people? That turtle will get your finger one way or the other. Now it'll just fall off."

"I would have been in a world of hurt if I didn't tie that stick on. That was a great idea, huh?"

Tubbs shook his head, "No, not really, sticking your finger down there in the first place was a dumb idea."

Jape wanted to change the topic, "That is the biggest turtle I ever saw."

"We gotta get those cats on down the road."

"Remember we can get a cold pop and candy bar at Crossroads."

"Yea, I had forgotten about that and I could use some food."

Suddenly Jape stopped to lower his end of the cat box, then Tubbs followed but asked, "Now what's wrong?"

"My mom don't get to eat watermelon very often. Does your's?"

"Never thought about it but I don't guess she does, why?"

"Let's borrow grandpaw's wheelbarrow and take melons to both our mom's. And that would be our good deed for today, okay?"

"How we going to do that?"

A few minutes later the boys were running across the pasture. The barn was slightly over the hill from the house and the boys could get the wheelbarrow without being seen by all the people. Once they started back they had to stay on the trail. The wheel was too difficult to roll through the grass, sand or soft dirt. The cats were much easier transported by rolling than carrying. At the store, they left the cats and picked up the box of .22 shells. On looking at the fish, they burst out laughing and produced a melon-shake right in front of several men causing them to roar with laughter. Then they headed back down the road with the wheelbarrow.

They stopped at Uncle John's place, parked the wheelbarrow out front and went to the door to knock. There was a note on the door, "I'm going a little early. Dinner is on the table, eat and come on over." The boys knew the note was left for Uncle John whom they missed by only seconds. It was less than a half mile to grandpaw's place from there.

"Well, I guess we're in luck, come on in," Jape asked Tubbs inside.

The boys went inside and ate leftovers but they were good. They made a biscuit and sausage sandwich to eat on the way which created a problem when they tried to roll the wheelbarrow. Jape ate with his right and Tubbs ate with his left using their other hand to push the empty wheelbarrow.

They went directly to Uncle John's watermelon patch and it was a beauty. There were at least thirty large melons ready to harvest. He had enough nice ripe ones to take a load to town. The only problem they may be too ripe and would split open bouncing along on the rough road. The boys made three trips taking four melons each trip. The last trip, Tubbs pushed the melons out of the patch. Jape tied some thick limbs together with his top cord and brushed out the wheelbarrow tracks. Once they got on hard soil the barrow didn't leave any tracks but Jape did a little camouflage work anyway. The first load they took down the trail to the creek and across to Jape's place. Then they stashed a load along the road but over the hill so they could pick them up in a couple days to haul to town. They hid the melons in Johnson grass several feet off the trail. Before leaving Uncle Johns, Jape walked around and across the yard making sure they didn't leave any wheelbarrow tracks. This last load of four nice melons was hauled right out past the house and down the road to Grandpaw's house.

They stopped about a hundred yards up the road and Tubbs pushed the cart as Jape brushed out the tracks. They rolled on past the gate another hundred yards where Jape took over. He pushed the cart into soft dirt making tracks very easy to read coming from the direction of Tubbs' house.

"With all the funeral traffic today our tracks will be wiped out by tonight," Jape was speaking more hopefully than knowledge of fact.

They rolled right up into the yard with the melons while twenty people stood around watching. Everyone was there, the entire family, including Uncle John. Grandpaw was the first one to walk out to meet the boys.

He smiled to greet them, "Hi, Jape, what you boys got there?"

At that point, several of the men broke away from the crowd to see what the boys were up to. Grandpaw hugged Jape, "You're getting bigger every time I see you. Growing like a weed. You boys had dinner?"

Tubbs looked at Jape and Jape answered, "Yes sir, we ate at his house before leaving with the melons."

Dad a little suspecting, "Where did you get those melons?"

Both boys had their hands behind their back as Jape answered, "You should be proud of us. Every time I go see Tubbs we eat our fill of good yellowmeated melons. I asked Tubbs If we could take some to mom and Grandmaw. So you can thank Tubbs here."

Jape's dad realized he didn't get the answer he was looking for. Any other date, time and place he would have followed up but today he let it go. Then Uncle John spoke up, "Those look like mine."

Someone in back, "But you don't have a patch this year, John?"

John, "Last year, sure look like the melons I raised last year, last year!" John winked at a couple family members but the boys didn't see him.

Jape ran toward the house, "These melons are for grandmaw and she will decide when and who gets to eat'em."

After unloading the melons and putting the wheelbarrow away the boys headed back towards Tubbs' place with the family shouting thanks all around. Everyone was eating a big slice of sweet yellow melon.

"How does that one compare with those you raised last year?", Jape shouted back at Uncle John as he ran back to put the wheelbarrow away.

"This is good but mine was sweeter," Uncle John shot back.

"Yea, you have much better soil. We have six more insulators!"

Uncle John didn't answer but nodding his understanding as he was still mumbling something about his being the only yellowmeated melons in the country. Next winter when it snowed, Jape would catch him at Crossroads and admit to stealing the melons, from a patch he didn't have!

The next morning the boys were up early. They arrived at Grandpaw's house before daylight but not before the old folks were up. Jape knocked on the door and when Grandmaw opened it, the entire countryside was flooded with the aroma of frying bacon and coffee perking. Jape and Tubbs had not been thinking about eating but their eyes met and instantly each knew what the other was thinking, breakfast at Grandmaw's house.

"Come on in, boys, breakfast will be ready in a few minutes. The chores will wait until you have had something to eat."

Grandpaw shouted from the other room, "You boys wash up then come on in, I'm getting my shoes on. I'll eat with you boys and we can do the chores together. Your dad told me you would come over and do my chores but I'm so used to doing them, well, no one else can do them the way I do."

The boys put their straw hats on a nail over the wash basin, washed their hands and face, dried with a towel then walked into the living room to sit down and wait for breakfast, within five minutes grandmaw called,

"You men come get it, it's on the table."

Grandpaw sat on one end of the long table and Grandmaw on the other with Jape and Tubbs facing each other.

Without a word being said everyone bowed their heads with their hands placed palms together over their large china plate. Grandpaw said the blessing.

Immediately after "Amen" Grandmaw said, "Get those biscuits while they're hot and there is plenty of fresh butter today. We were out and I had to churn yesterday of all days. You boys dig in."

They had three kinds of meat; bacon, ham and sausage and a large platter of fried eggs. The sausage was homemade with a lot of spice and a hot flavor that made it delicious.

Grandpaw spoke up, "You fellow's rake off a half dozen eggs and get a pound of that meat. You may get hungry before noon."

Jape opened two hot biscuits then sliced off a half pound of that fresh butter to stash inside the biscuit. The next two biscuits were covered with rich white cream gravy. Next, he took his grandpaw's advice, by taking six eggs. The old folks had coffee and the boys a large glass of milk. The meal was cooked on a woodstove but the biscuits were perfect, each one exactly the same, brown on both top and bottom. The boys topped off their breakfast with the hot biscuits, butter and homemade plum jam. On completing the meal, their plates were as clean as when they sat down. It was a custom, at home or anywhere else, if you take food out, you eat it. A guest could eat two or three full plates of food and be welcome to come back. On the other hand if a guest left one small spoon full on the plate, waste. The waste was taken as a slap in the face — an insult to the host and that person would not be asked back to break bread again.

Jape could milk a cow a lot faster than his grandpaw and for that reason he was appointed to that chore. Tubbs carried hay to the mules and corn to the pigs. The boys did most of the work with grandpaw giving instructions. This made everyone feel good. Grandpaw carried the bucket of milk to the house and the boys carried a load of kindling wood for the cook stove.

"What you boys going to do while we're at the funeral."

"Don't know, it don't seem fittin' to go huntin'. We may go swimming. What do you think, would going swimming be okay?", Jape asked.

"It's going to be a hot one today. Sure, no reason you boys can't go swimming. Don't go in my little pond, go down on the creek."

"We'll spend the day relaxing in the shade b gy the swimming hole."

At the house Grandmaw told the boys, "There will be lots of food in here for everyone and that includes you boys. I know everyone will be dressed up for the funeral but you boys are just as welcome as those with their fancy duds. Don't go hungry because you're not dressed up, too."

Grandpaw provided the boys with their schedule for the day. "Everyone will be leaving early. We have to attend a ten o'clock service at crossroads and then the graveside service at two P.M. If we're not here, just help yourself."

Grandmaw interrupted, "Be sure and cover the food up when you leave so the flies can't get at it."

"Yes ma'am, thanks for the good breakfast," Jape answered seriously.

"Yes, thanks, you sure are a good cook," Tubbs added his appreciation.

Later that morning the boys climbed a little hill and sat on a flat rock watching all the cars coming and going. From the high ridge they could see both directions, in back of them, they could see the fence line to McCrimmins pasture while out in front was Grandpaw's bottom land and pecan trees with the creek running down the middle.

Tubbs broke the silence, "This old rock has been here a long time."

"Sure, as long as the world. Indians sat in this same spot and even buffalo grazed here. I'll even bet outlaws and bad men have been here."

"Wonder if Jessie James or the Daltons were ever here?"

"Those old guys at Crossroads are always talking about how outlaws used to come through here after robbing a train. Someone dug up some treasure some time back. They say outlaws have been here many times."

"Do you think outlaws really did bury their loot?"

"I don't know, if they had too much to carry they might."

"Wonder how they would remember where they buried it?"

Jape pointed to a big pecan tree in the bottom, "See that big limb sticking out from that old tree. They would bury a pot of gold under a limb like that, then when they came back, it would be real easy to find."

"Why not an oak tree or . . . ?"

Jape stopped him, "Oak trees are cut down for firewood. No one would ever cut down a pecan tree, they're a real money maker. It'll be there forever or until it quits producing nuts."

The boys lay on the flat rock soaking up the warm morning sun for a few moments in silence.

Jape rolled over smiling, "You want to have some fun?"

"Does a rooster crow? . . . We don't need any trouble . . . What?"

"Buried treasure, buried treasure, they will be talking about the buried treasure for a long time, . . . longer than my fish."

"What are you talking about?", Tubbs wanted to know.

"This would be a great day to rob a bank or dig up buried treasure because everyone for miles around will be at the funeral. We don't have a bank to rob but we can dig up some buried treasure."

"You didn't answer my question, what are you talking about?"

"Not real treasure, we'll make everyone think that while they were at the funeral some outlaws came in here and dug up a pot of gold." Jape jumped up, he was getting excited about his idea, "Come on, come on."

"What are we going to do?", Tubbs asked.

"The first thing to do is dig a hole."

They ran to the barn and got two shovels. At the pecan tree, Jape backed up against the tree then took ten giant steps and stopped.

He grinned back at Tubbs, "Right here is the center of the buried treasure." Jape used his heel to draw a large rectangle in the soft red soil.

Tubbs asked, "We dig here?"

"Yep, we dig and toss the dirt out anyway you can. Dig like you think an outlaw would dig," Jape was laughing, the plan might work.

"Why would an outlaw dig any different than anyone else?"

"I don't know. I thought you might know something about outlaws."

"I'll help you dig but this seems crazy to me. How deep do we have to go. The dirt will get hard after while," Tubbs reminded him.

"Not deep, outlaws don't like to work or they wouldn't be outlaws, but down deep enough that grandpaws plow didn't hit it. So you see it don't have to be very deep. Just deep enough to get us some laughs."

"YOU dig for awhile and see how much YOU laugh," Tubbs commented as he stepped out of the hole and pushed the shovel at Jape.

Jape started digging. The soft dirt shoveled out very fast and easy or the boys would have given it up as a bad idea. The hole was shaped so the sides were straight, providing the appearance it was dug by adults. The boys paid attention to detail, making sure the hole was directly under the big limb and all the dirt tossed out on the side away from the trail.

They left the shovels leaning against the pecan tree and ran back to the barn for the wheelbarrow. By standing in the wheelbarrow, Jape could reach the well pulley which he unhooked to take down. The chain attaching the pulley could be used to attach the pulley to the pecan tree. The rope was untied from the well bucket. Everything but the bucket was loaded into the wheelbarrow. Next, the two boys picked up grandmaw's iron washpot with great difficulty as it was heavy, putting it into the wheelbarrow.

"Now we need some rust," Jape informed his mining partner.

"What do you mean, rust?", Tubbs wanted to know.

"Anytime a metal pot is buried in the ground for any length of time it'll rust. We have to give'em some rust. Everyone will be down in that hole looking for clues. They need something to verify what they want to believe. Let's go out back to that old car body."

They ran around the lilac bush, into the pasture where an old model "T" Ford body had been left years before. Brush and weeds had grown over it and it could not be seen from the house anymore.

Upon their approach a hen flew out cackling. The boys stopped and looked at each other knowing they were about to find a nest of eggs. Hens will hide their nest out from time to time in an effort to hatch off a batch of little chickens. Most of the hens lay their eggs in the chicken house but this old girl and a couple of her lady friends were laying in the old car. The boys found a nest of thirteen eggs and would have taken them but Jape was very superstitious about the number thirteen.

Jape didn't want any part of stealing thirteen eggs, "Nope, let's wait for a few days and then there'll be more. Anyways, we don't have time to sell'em today."

"Can we use this old bucket to carry the rust in?", Tubbs asked.

"Sure that's perfect. You hold the bucket under the fender." Tubbs held the bucket and Jape hit the fender with a rock. Large chunks of rust flaked off and some of it hit the bucket. The boys continued to knock rust from the old car until they had nearly half a bucket. Jape pointed out that some of the larger pieces were curved, the shape of the fender would be about the same as the curve off a pot-of-gold.

They took turns pushing the wheelbarrow as it was very heavy. They made it without any great difficulty. Jape climbed the tree and hooked the well pulley to the big limb. Once the pulley was in place it wasn't difficult to hoist the iron washpot over the hole. The hole was only about four feet deep. Jape lowered the pot into the hole allowing it to drop as naturally as it could straight down. Then he raised it and let it fall hard into the moist red dirt. On pulling it back up they could see the perfect imprint of the three legs and the bottom of the pot. Tubbs held the rope while Jape jumped down in the hole and placed handfuls of rust around the legs and on the bottom of the pot. Some of the larger curved pieces of rust was placed a few inchs outside the area of the pot. Jape crawled out and the two boys pulled on the rope to drop the pot many times onto the rust. When they had the rust pounded into the dirt with a clear impression of the pot they quit.

The well pulley and the washpot were replaced exactly as before. The bottom of the washpot was rubbed with the ash from its original location. No one could tell that the pot had ever been moved. The boys were proud of their genius. When the wheelbarrow was returned to the barn, each boy turned to the other and a 'melonshake' was made without a word. Then they burst out laughing. They skipped out to the road and stopped. Wheelbarrow tracks, uh-oh, Jape ran to the horse manger and grabbed a large double handful of straw tieing it into a bundle as he ran down the trail dragging it to erase the wheelbarrow tracks. This worked but the trail still didn't look right. He put his top cord back in the tool box.

Jape shouted for Tubbs, "Come on." He caught the mules which were as gentle as Mr. Tips. He tied a lead rope to the halter of each mule. Tubbs took one and Jape the other. They made ten or more trips with the mules up and down the trail from the pot of gold to the hard packed yard.

"It's getting late we better get this finished. Someone will be coming home soon," Tubbs informed Jape who was acting as construction foreman.

"You know what we forgot to do?", Jape admitted.

"Nope, what?"

"Grandpaw told us to turn the mules out after they finished eating this morning. We didn't do that, so turn your's loose. They will think the mules made these tracks going or coming from the creek for water."

The mules ran for the creek once turned loose and the boys made a dash for the big rock on top of the hill.

It wasn't as late as they thought. They were waiting for everyone to return from the cemetery when the funeral procession went by going to the cemetery. Each boy lay on the rock watching. The big long black hearse came over the hill driving slowly with two more long black vehicles right behind that one. Neither boy said a word, each boy was counting "103" cars, including the hearse.

"You know it's bad luck to count the cars in a funeral prossession."

"Yep, I know. If you count the cars in a funeral procession you'll burn forever in a pit of brimstone. How many did you count?", Jape asked.

"You tell me first. Wonder what brimstone is? You didn't count, did you? This big rock could be brimstone".

"Sure I did but you were afraid to".

"Yes sir, I did, too, count. There was over a hundred, now you tell me how many more than."

"Three, one hundred and three, with the hearse."

"You did count. It will be a long time before there will ever be that many cars on this old road again."

"Yep, probably never, unless they are driving out from town to look for buried treasure." Both boys burst out laughing.

"Let's run down and eat." Tubbs jumped up to face off with Jape for a melonshake before running down the hill to eat. The boys found a feast of desserts waiting on Grandmaw's table. They ate their fill and complied with her request to cover the food when they left. When the boys ran out the door each boy had a piece of pecan pie which they ate while walking back to the rock. They were waiting for the people to return, to find the 'pot-o-gold' missing. That thought kept running across Jape's mind, find the gold missing. Then he asked Tubbs, "How are they going to find the gold missing?"

Tubbs shrugged his shoulders in a helpless gesture, "I don't know, this was your idea. Why ask me?"

"Grandpaw may not walk down to the creek for a week." He rolled over on the hot rock looking into the cloudless sky.

Tubbs sat up looking at Jape in disgust, "You mean we did all that work for nothing, no one'll ever find that hole until it rains and caves in?"

"Well, I didn't think about that. We'll have to think of a reason for someone to walk down that trail and find the hole."

"We could find it. You know by accident," Tubbs suggested.

"No, no, no, we have to have someone else find it. But who."

They remained on the rock talking about the misfortune of poor planning. Each boy blaming the other one for most of the failure and trying to think of a way to have the pot of gold discovered. Cars were driving into the yard and most of the family had returned. The boys were lost as to exactly what to do next. They sat on the rock with their feet hanging over the edge.

Jape pointed toward the creek, "Who's that?"

"Can't tell but they're walking toward the creek."

"Looks like those two men that were at Crossroads yesterday."

"They know there'll be lots of food here after the funeral. They'll earn their supper if they keep walking up that trail."

"Those two are so brain dead they may walk right by and never see it."

"No one can be that blind."

"Just the same, cross your fingers."

He spit over his left shoulder, looked over at Tubbs who turned to spit over his left shouder. They sat there with fingers crossed on each hand watching every move the two men made.

The boys thought the men had walked on past the hole when suddenly they turned to look and walked over to the spot. One of the men jumped down into the hole and disappeared from their view, then the second man gave him a hand up out of the hole. The two shouted to each other but the boys could not distinquish what was said. As the two grown men took off running toward the house the boys jumped up and did a 'melonshake' on the big rock.

The boys took off in a run, they wanted to hide and listen to what was being said before returning from their swim. They waited in a clump of Johnson grass about a hundred yards from the hole, barely managing to get into their hiding place in time to see a large group of family and friends coming over the hill. Jape's dad wasn't there but grandpaw was right up front with the two men. Several of the men were talking at the same time. Everyone agreed a pot of some kind had been pulled from that hole. Instantly, the mark made by the chain and pulley on the limb was pointed out.

One man pointed to two shovels leaning against the tree, "They left their tools."

Jape punched Tubbs, "Oh, I forget the shovels, we're in trouble now."

Grandpaw walked over to inspect them, "Nope, these are mine."

Uncle John, "They used your shovels. This was a planned thing."

"Who do you think it was?", someone asked.

"Someone who buried this a few years ago waiting for the right time to dig it up. This was the perfect time with everyone away at the funeral. They had all day to get it out and get away," was Uncle John's statement.

"Maw and I don't go to town that much any more. Seldom are we both gone at the same time. It could have been a problem for them."

"No one else around today?"

"My grandson and his friend Tubbs, but they were off swimming and."

"We should call the sheriff, it may be part of some outlaw gang."

Jape whispered, "We may as well get out of this hot grass and enjoy the fun. Remember one thing, we been swimming all day."

"But we did eat dinner here?", Tubbs reminded him.

"Yea, we came across the hill, ate and went back swimming again."

"Okay, this is our first trip up the trail."

"Yea, let's run out and act surprised." The two boys jumped up and ran out of the grass and were fifty yards up the trail before any of the men took their eyes off the treasure hole to look at the two boys. Even then, they didn't pay that much attention to them. Grandpaw asked how the swim was and if they had seen anyone around. They boys walked around and looked in the hole like all the men were doing. Their questions were pushed aside as only those of a kid. The boys listened and from time to time gave each other a wink.

Jape's dad arrived later and gave him permission to stay all night with grandpaw. Tubbs arrived in time for breakfast the next morning. The two boys were to help do the chores and be of any assistance. The sheriff would be there early and the boys wouldn't miss out on anything. The sheriff arrived about ten oclock with three other men, one of whom was a news reporter who brought a camera. One man was a scientist of some kind and the other was a metallurgical engineer. The sheriff was all decked out in his suit and big white Texas hat. The three other men were wearing funeral type suits. All three men shook hands with Grandpaw and acted as if the two boys didn't exist until they asked for help to carry tools, kits and a tripod for the camera. The two boys winked at each other and jumped right in to help.

At the site, everyone but the boys posed for their picture with the hole. They would have, too, but they weren't asked. In those days, kids were to be seen and not heard. From the gist of their conversation, the boys concluded that someone had taken a booty of treasure from that hole. The sheriff was confident that it was one of the band of famous outlaw gangs along with the help of some of the local folks. The scientist asked the engineer to hand him samples of the soil under the pot. There wasn't any doubt in his mind the soil was positive proof. Moisture from the pot indicated to him that there had been gold in the pot. Water that ran off the gold had discolored the soil. This the man said was a fact. At that statement the newspaper man did some writing in his little pad and the boys winked at each other. The engineer took samples of the metal, including one large curved piece which he examined with extreme care. He placed the metal on a big white piece of paper with a large pair of tweezers, pointing to the fact the rust had formed in a curve. It had fallen from a large oval object, like the side of an iron pot. He explained that the rust was from heavy iron and his expert opinion was the same as the scientist. An iron pot of some type had been extracted from that hole. And once more the boys nearly fell over laughing but contained theyselves to only a wink.

The educated fellows nearly broke their arms patting each other on the back but they finally left. After they were gone, grandpaw asked the boys to get a fresh bucket of water for Grandmaw. Tubbs ran to the house for the bucket while Jape and Grandpaw walked out to the well.

Grandpaw said, "Oh my, look at that. The pulley is hooked backward. He reached up to unhook the pulley and gave it to Jape, "Hold this for me."

He turned the chain around and put the pulley back. Looking over his glasses he winked, "Wonder how that happened?"

Chapter 5
The Revival

If Grandpaw knew anything, he kept it to himself. He never once let on that he suspected anything other than a gang of outlaws had dug up some buried treasure. The newspaper came out with several articles about the sheriff's investigation. After those articles came out, at least seven men turned themselves in to the sheriff admitting to riding with the Daltons, Jessie and the Wild Bunch. Each man told his own version of how he helped the gang dig up the buried treasure. Someone's thoughts on the story is probably still being told around the Crossroads store today.

Jape and Tubbs had a box of .22 shells and they wanted a mess of frog legs. They were drawn between taking the melons to town or going hunting for frog legs. The debate wasn't that long or difficult, they went hunting. They left Tubb's house shortly after daylight. Their destination was the McCrimmins pasture pond. Grandpaw's house was on the direct route to get there. They accidently, just happened to get to grandmaw's house in time for breakfast.

These boys were not dumb by any sense of the word. They stopped off at the woodpile. Jape was exceptionally good with an ax, he usually cut on an average of one cord a week at home. With that much experience he should be good with an ax. Jape cut and split small kindling wood for the cook stove.

The sound of the ax brought grandpaw to the door, "What are you boys up to this early in the morning."

Tubbs was approaching the house with an arm load of kindling wood. Grandpaw pointed to the wood box, "Toss it in there."

Jape shouted from the woodpile, "Knew you were getting low, Grandpaw."

Grandpaw smiled, "Yep, the wood box is getting low," he lowered his voice to add, "and it's time for breakfast."

Grandmaw poked her head out the door, "When you boys get the box full, come on in and eat. I got oodles fixed."

Tubbs looked up at Jape, "What's oodles, I never ate oodles before?"

"She means lots or plenty. You know what she means. If you're going to be a smartass, you can sit out here while I eat the oodles."

The boys filled the woodbox and went inside to wash up for breakfast. Grandpaw gave Jape a page torn from some eastern magazine. "Jape, I see by this ad that Taylor Fur Company will be buying fur again this winter. You boys should be able to sell enough opossum hides to buy your school clothes. You should write to them now and ask for shipping tags and a price list. Then you'll know if hides will be worth the skinning."

"Yessir, I sold several last year in Paoli but didn't get much."

"What do you think, will they be a good price this year?"

"Don't know, that's why I'd like to see you boys write, okay."

After breakfast the boys thanked grandmaw and started out the door. She pushed several cold biscuits into Jape's hand, lowering her head to look over her glasses at Jape, "Your dog, sweetheart, hasn't had breakfast yet." Mr. Tips smacked his mouth and took care of his breakfast in short order. The boys took off in a run but stopped when they saw the old Model "T" body with the hen's nest. They couldn't resist taking another look. This time two hens flew out. There was a new nest with seven eggs in it but the old one still only had 13.

"You ever smoke any Bull Durham?", Jape asked Tubbs.

"You know better."

"Want to?"

"I will if you will."

They took the seven eggs from the new nest and one out of the old nest to eliminate the number "13". They headed to Crossroads with eight eggs to sell. Who knows why they didn't take a dozen?

The mile to the store was covered very quickly. The boys ran around to the horse trough to check on the fish. A wagon and team were tied to the hitching post and a family with five small children was enjoying the fish. The boys walked around to look at the fish from the back side. The little boys were watching in awe as the fish swam from one end to the other. The trough was only three feet wide causing the fish to bump his tail when turning around.

Tubbs spoke up real proud, "We caught it, it's our fish."

One of the larger kids smiled and said, "Yea, sure it is. An' the moon is green cheese."

Jape grabbed Tubbs pushing him toward the store, looking back to smile at the kids he pointed his forefinger at his own ear, making a circling motion, then shrugged his shoulders. This got a laugh from all the kids.

Inside the store the owner smiled, "What can I help you boys with today?"

Jape and Tubbs walked up to the counter, each boy laid down four eggs. The man opened the cash register.

"You selling these all together or four each?"

"What difference does it make?", Jape wanted to know.

"Anything less than one dozen is a nickel. Less than six is two cents."

"I thought they sold for ten cents a dozen?", Jape argued.

"They do, but you have four or together you have only eight."

"We've been to school, too, you know," Tubbs reminded him.

"Did you boys see the morning paper? A big article about your grand-daddy losing some buried treasure. The sheriff has caught one of the gang that helped dig it up." He pointed to a newspaper lying on the counter. A picture on the front page showed the sheriff and his crew at the hole.

Tubbs burst out laughing, "So they caught one of the gang, huh?"

"What did you say, Jape?", the store operator asked.

"What difference does it make, a dozen should be a dime. Six should be a nickel and eight — a little more. You trying to cheat us?"

The owner was looking the eggs over very carefully, "Oops, one egg is cracked. Did you boys find a nest of rotten eggs?"

Wife from other room, "Bring me the cracked egg, I'm baking a cake. I have to have one anyway, if it's rotten, better me than a customer."

The man walked into the back room out of view and gave his wife the egg. He returned to hear Tubbs tell him, "Those are fresh eggs."

His wife shouted, "The boy's right, this egg was laid this morning."

"Were you boys wanting to buy something?", the operator asked.

"Yea, a sack of Bull Durham and a plug of Brown Mule," Jape advised.

"A sack of Bull Durham is six cents and a plug . . ."

"Okay, trade us a sack of tobacco for the eggs," Tubbs interrupted.

"And you're getting one egg for the cake free with that deal," Jape informed him as he walked over to look into the glass case at the tobacco.

"I'll save you boys a piece of the cake. Thanks for the egg," the lady shouted from the other room. She wanted to keep the boys happy.

The store keeper reached over to take a sack of tobacco off the shelf, tossed it to the boys, "You boys better enjoy your pop and candy now. After you smoke that stuff you'll be sicker than a horse." The boys weren't listening, they ran out the door and down the road. Each desperately wanted the opportunity to roll their own cigarette, . . . like the real men do.

They couldn't wait to give it a try; however, smoking their first one walking down a public road didn't seem wise. They ran past Uncle John's house which was the first house, then hid in the creek. The sack was broken open and the thin package of cigarette papers removed. Jape took one paper and Tubbs another, they looked both ways up and down the creek. No one was around, they filled the paper, first one then the other. The Bull Durham sack had a draw string top and the string was yellow. There was a round white tag on the end of the yellow string with the words "Bull Durham" printed on it. Most of the men let this string and the tag hang out of the top pocket of their overalls. Jape couldn't wait to get the sack closed so he could put it in his pocket and let the little tag dangle. With the cigarette paper full of tobacco in one hand, Jape caught the string in his teeth and pulled the sack closed exactly like he had seen the big boys do. Once the sack of tobacco was closed he stuffed it into the top pocket of his overalls, making certain the little round tag was hanging outside. The boys worked at rolling the tobacco up in the thin tender paper. One problem, they had too much tobacco and too much saliva, the paper wasn't big enough for the tobacco and the paper was too soggy to roll into a cigarette. If a person with a broad knowledge of smoking and a full understanding of all phases of construction had viewed their workmanship it could be said that they finally got something that resembled a cigarette made. Each boy put the white paper stuffed with tobacco in his mouth, looked across to the other boy as their eyes got wide, no matches!

They laughed at each other as they sat back and simulated smoking, puffing on the unlit cigarette. Jape even laid back, crossed his legs and blew make believe smoke rings into the air.

Tubbs took a couple deep drags exactly like the big boys did out behind the old four-holer at school then said, "Mine's a Camel, look, it's got a big hump on it's back."

"We've got to get a box of matches," Jape instructed.

"We can't get any at the store. A small box cost a penny and that guy is so tight he wouldn't give us a drink of water," Tubbs complained.

"Uncle John would have some."

"We better not go over there for a few days, huh?"

"Damn, we gotta," Jape replied.

"You don't have to use that word. Now that you have a Bull Durham tag hanging out of your overalls you're tough, huh?"

"Why didn't you think, everyone needs a match to light up."

"As always, this was your idea and once more it didn't work. There's no law against you thinking about something once in awhile," Tubbs said.

"Not so, my ideas always work. Yesterday, that was a great idea."

"I'll admit it worked out. You're just plain lucky, yesterday that was dumb luck. Those two old boys came stumbling down the trail or that hole would still be exactly that, a hole, a dumb hole in the ground."

"Better not let you have a match. You go bonkers just sucking on one that ain't burnin'," Jape wisecracked.

"Let's go ask your aunt for a few matches. Your Uncle John will be out doing something this time of day, anyway."

"I'll stay here and you go ask. He won't be angry with you even if he does miss a melon or two."

"No grit, you're pathetic, you are. I'll go get some," Tubbs said as he walked off toward the road.

"Okay, I'll wait here for you and hurry."

Jape sat down on the creek bank to wait. Tubbs ran up the creek to the road then sat down on the bridge to wait. He had figured Jape out pretty good, two minutes later here came Jape in a long trot.

Tubbs hid in a clump of grass and jumped out at Jape, shouting, "Boo" Jape didn't pay any attention to Tubbs's effort to scare him as Tubbs complained, "I thought you were going to wait."

"Oh, if you go up there without me you'll screw it up so bad that my aunt will tell my dad and I'll get it again. I don't feel so bad getting my hieney busted for my mistakes but it bothers me to catch it for yours."

"Yea, I get you in so much trouble, don't I. Well, right now I'm going to save you some more. Unsnap that overall pocket and hide that Bull Durham tag or you'll be in more hot water."

Jape stopped to follow Tubb's suggestion as Tubbs continued, "Now, don't tell me I don't think."

"Okay, thanks, that's why I keep you around."

At the door Jape knocked and his aunt came smiling. She opened the screen door to talk. "Come in, boys."

"We don't want to come in. We were by here yesterday and you weren't home. We saw the note you left for Uncle John and helped ourselves to a glass of milk and a sandwich. I wanted to thank you."

"The door is always open, you boys are welcome to help yourself any time you want. Dinner isn't ready but come on in and I'll get you a sausage and biscuit. I know you boys are going hunting and won't get to eat until after dark tonight."

The boys stepped inside. She went into the kitchen.

"You're right, we are hunting. In fact, we have a rabbit in a hollow tree and want to borrow a few matches to smoke'im out," Jape lied.

"Sure, right there on the wall. Help yourself to a handful." Both boys stepped around the corner to take a handful of matches from the match holder on the kitchen wall near the wood cook stove. She turned to hand Jape two biscuits with a large sausage in each one and the same to Tubbs.

"The sausage is old, John likes fresh cooking, anyway. I was wondering what I was going to do with those. Thanks for coming by, boys."

The boys thanked her and left.

They ran down the road again and cut across the pasture to avoid the possibility of coming in contact with Uncle John. They never said a word, while stuffing their face with biscuit and sausage as Mr. Tips watched with his head cocked to one side. Jape finally tossed him half the biscuit from the second one, then Tubbs did the same thing.

The dog wagged his tail in appreciation. Once the food had been devoured, Tubbs, "I saw you, you lied to your aunt without your fingers crossed."

"You want I should tell her we need matches to smoke Bull Durham."

"No, I want you to cross your fingers when you lie like that."

"That's a white lie, we don't need to cross our fingers for that."

"Now that school's out and Mrs. Auld isn't around, we're lying all the time, using bad words and now we're smoking. We're on our way to hell."

"We're not smoking yet but wait until we get to the creek."

He took off in a run leaving Tubbs to poke along.

Under the shade of a large wild mulberry tree, they rolled another cigarette. Their second attempt was even worse than the first. The paper broke and they wasted half a dozen papers before getting the hang of rolling tobacco into cigarettes. They did finally get fire to the tobacco and puffed on their first cigarette. In their effort to enjoy a smoke, each boy lied to the other one. The tobacco taste was terrible and the smoke burned their mouth; however, each boy told the other one how good it tasted and felt. They were trying to do all the things with the smoke they had seen the big boys do at school. Jape tried to blow smoke out through his nose. He succeeded in doing so but it burned his nose causing him to cough and strangle by accidently inhaling smoke into his lungs. The boys continued to puff on one cigarette after another. They didn't smoke one and go on about their frog hunting, they smoked one right after the other until they were inhaling, laughing and coughing. Shortly before they finished off the tobacco and right after they used up the last cigarette paper, both boys turned green and puked up the biscuits and sausage. They puked for half an hour and washed their face in the creek several times.

The cool creek water felt good. While crawling to find a place to lie down, Jape said, "Now, I know how a sick horse feels."

They sprawled out in the shade and went to sleep. Mr. Tips flopped down beside them to pant and keep a watchful eye out, for a biscuit!

Two hours later the boys woke up with Mr. Tips licking their face. He had gotten bored trying to sleep in the sun. The shade had moved and the boys were out in the sun. Each boy sat up looking silly at the other one. Neither boy gave the outward appearance of being the picture of health. Jape returned to the creek to wash his face once more.

Tubbs asked, "Does that help any?

"It's cool and that feels good." Tubbs stumbled down to the creek and washed his face. They laid back down in the shade to watch the clouds.

Suddenly Jape whispered, "Look at that, look at that", he pointed to a crow hopping into a nest right above them in the next tree.

"It's a crow's nest." Any other time those words would have been shouted out with excitement, but the tobacco had taken all the excitement away from both boys. That weak statement was all Tubbs could manage.

"Yea, now we can get one of the little ones and raise a pet crow."

"You feeling that good already?", Tubbs asked.

"Nope, but someday I'll get to feeling better and we can do that."

"Makes me tired just thinking about climbing the tree."

"Me, too, but we can't stay here all day. Let's get a drink of cool water and go get those frogs. We'll feel better after a little walk."

"Little walk, it's a mile over there."

"Yea, just about a mile, but that ain't far. We can rest."

Tubbs got up to get a drink of water. "A drink does help. Whatta ya say we get some more eggs and smoke Bull Durham every day?"

"Not me, that nickel would be much better spent on a milkshake. I never been so sick, I was sick as a horse. I'll just watch you next time."

"You're thinking now, keep on thinking like that. I'm never going to smoke anything but grapevine again."

The two boys headed for McCrimmins pasture but they were not walking as fast as usual.

Behind the big dam the boys loaded the .22 and slowly crawled over the dam in their effort to sneak up on the big ones before they jumped into the water. They were about in position to get their first shot when around the corner came Mr. Tips running across their line of fire to chase first one frog then the next. He thought it was fun to hear the big splash they made when landing in the water. The dog went around the pond barking and jumping at the frogs. The boys didn't say a word and they certainly didn't chase and scream at him like they usually did. Both boys simply sat flat down on the dam and waited patiently. A few minutes later Mr. Tips returned to see what was keeping the boys. At that point, Jape took out his top cord and tied the dog to a tree.

Although the boys had a full box of .22 shells, they continued to shoot frogs the same as the squirrels, neither boy missed. Two frogs jumped at the same moment the shot was fired giving the appearance that the shot missed the mark; however, Jape wasn't buying that. He walked out into the mud and felt around on the bottom of the pond and found the frog. The frog had been hit right between the eyes but still jumped into the water. Several of the frogs jumped after being shot. Each time Jape searched and found the frog in the mud where it landed. After shooting twelve of the largest frogs either boy had ever seen, they headed for home to find a cook. The frogs were over 18 inches long and weighed four pounds each. This would be a rare meal for those country bumpkins, now all they had to do was get home.

Mr. Tips was untied and the big game hunters headed for the house. They were elated with their hunt. Their first experience with smoking was in the distant past, over two hours ago. They were feeling great; however, the hot afternoon sun slowed the boys down. With all that weight to pack they should take it easy. They found a shade to park and rest before reaching McCrimmins line fence. Mr. Tips was bawling on the trail of something but the boys didn't pay any attention to him. He ran in circles for a few minutes, bawling on trail all through the thicket, then treed only two trees over from where the boys were sitting. At that point, the boys knew they were a little more tired than usual, because they only looked at each other instead of running to the tree.

"You go check it out," Jape instructed Tubbs.

"You go, its nothing, anyway," Tubbs answered but neither boy moved.

Both boys grinned knowing each one was as tired and sick as the other. Mr. Tips wasn't going to quit, he kept on barking treed. He was talking to those boys, he knew something was up there and he was telling them about it. Slowly, both boys got up and walked toward the tree. As they approached the tree something flew out the top.

"What's that?", Tubbs did manage to get a little surprise in his voice.

"Look at it go! look at it go! It's a flying squirrel!", Jape screamed.

Before that one hit the ground another one sailed out of the same tree, gliding across a fifty foot opening to land right behind the first squirrel and run up another tree. Mr. Tips was fooled by their flight but he saw the second one and gave chase but they were safely up the tree long before he got there. The boys were not tired any more, their adrenal glands were working overtime again. Both boys took off in a run screaming for Mr. Tips to stop. The squirrels went up a big tree into what appeared to be a squirrel hole near the top.

Without hesitation, Jape grabbed a limb and was climbing the tree before Tubbs got there.

Tubbs shouted, "What are you doing?"

"I want to catch one. Did you ever see one before?"

"No, never did, did you?"

"Never did either, we'll take it to Crossroads. I'll bet we can sell it."

"Don't hurt it, they're too little to eat and they were cute."

"I won't hurt'em." Tubbs watched him climb. He could go up a tree like a monkey. He was small, strong for his size and had been climbing trees for years. This was a large tree with big spreading limbs. The hole was in the main trunk of the tree but about twenty feet from the ground. Jape would have to hug the trunk and scoot up the tree or stand on a limb to be able to look into the hole. Some holes go up and some go down. The holes going up are usually used only for temporary hiding places. The den tree always has a hole that goes down into the nest.

Jape was nearly in position to check out the hole but he was too short to see into the hole while standing on the last large branch. He had to hug the tree trunk and shinny up the tree to peep into the hole. His face was directly against the tree as he poked his face and eye directly over the hole. He was looking directly into the deadly eyes of a cottonmouth coiled and striking. Jape didn't have time to think. The snake's fangs were only inches from his face. His toes and his hands pushed his small frame away from the tree. Gravity and his pushoff propelled him downward and backward as the snake's fangs snapped out hitting only air where the boy's face had been. Jape screamed as he fell, about six feet down, his back hit a large limb breaking his fall to some degree, his limber body flopped off the limb to travel upside down into more limbs about ten feet farther down. His rapid descent was slowed by the branches when suddenly he was jerked to a full stop when his right ankle and foot caught in a fork. He was hanging upside down with his head in such a position that he could look Tubbs directly in the eye.

"Well, that was cute, BUT a flying squirrel you're NOT."

Jape was in pain. He thought his back was broken and knew his ankle and foot had been jerked clean off. His bare skin was scraped and scratched all over. The wind was knocked out and for a few moments he couldn't talk. Tubbs wanted to laugh, but for fear Jape was hurt, he didn't. He continued to talk, "I've watched you climb a lot of trees. I must admit, you came out of that one much faster than all the rest. Did you see the squirrel?"

All Jape could muster was, "Nooooo."

"What did you jump out for?"

"I didn't jump, I fell."

"No, you didn't. I saw you, you jumped backward and flew straight out about five feet, then you fell. I thought you had gone crazy or had a suicide wish. Are you hurt?"

Jape was hurting so badly, he forgot about the snake and through clenched teeth he managed, "I'm not hurt. I always hang around like this."

"Get down out of the tree," Tubbs instructed.

"There's a snake in that hole, a big cottonmouth . . . I can't get down."

"No, there isn't, cottonmouths don't climb trees."

"THEY don't? There's a cottonmouth in that hole."

"If you're going to live, get down out of there."

"I can't get down. My leg may be broken. I can't move my right leg, it's hung. Give me a boost and meby I can get loose."

It wasn't easy, but Jape managed to get down from the tree. His leg wasn't broken but he was bruised, battered and his ankle was seriously sprained. The pain could not have been worse if it had been broken.

He told Tubbs, "Forget about the flying squirrels, leave the frogs and throw the .22 away, I'm not carrying nothin'."

Jape wasn't in any condition to walk or be of assistance. Tubbs knew Jape was hurting or he wouldn't be talking like that. Tubbs carried all the frogs and the .22 while Jape limped along. At the fence, Tubbs pulled up the bottom wire and Jape rolled under like Mr. Tips always did. When they reached the creek Jape sat on a log, putting both feet in the water. The water felt warm to his left foot and cold to his swollen right one. Before reaching the house the pain was so bad Jape couldn't put pressure on his foot at all. Tubbs found a long stick, which Jape used as a walking stick. He could hop and use the stick for balance, keeping the weight off his right foot. This was a slow pace but they finally get to the house.

His mom got a small washtub, filled it half full of warm water that felt hot to Jape. She poured two pounds of Epsom Salts in the water and made him keep his foot in that for four hours. Tubbs had the privilege of cleaning all twelve frogs. Before he finished cleaning frogs, he promised the frog God, the rain God, the sun God and every living thing that he would never again shoot anything that he had to clean. The frogs were so large that Jape's mom cooked all four legs and the back. There was enough meat for two good meals.

While Jape was soaking his foot and Tubbs was cleaning frogs, Jape's dad rode over to grandpaws and brought back a pair of crutches. They were old but in good condition. One of Jape's uncles had broken his leg several years ago. The crutches had been hanging in the smoke house all this time. Jape had played with the crutches many times, trying to walk with then without falling over.

After soaking his foot, Jape was put to bed. His mom put a box on the bed with a pillow on top to keep his foot elevated. Once when no one was looking he took it down and found out why it was being elevated, the pain was much worse when the leg was lowered.

When his dad returned with the crutches, Jape asked, "How long will I be in bed?"

"Nice try, son. You can have one night of lazy time. Tomorrow morning I will milk and do the chores. Tomorrow night, you WILL be back in the swing of everything. You can do anything we have to do around here on crutches. So, relax and enjoy your frog leg dinner. You may not enjoy working on those things." pointing to the crutches, he continued, "You shouldn't be killing a flying squirrel, anyway. They're too small to eat and there aren't many of them left. Serves you right for bothering those cute little fellows."

"We wasn't going to kill'em. We wanted to capture one."

Jape's mother spoke while still working in the kitchen, "Yea, I never seen one. Do they really fly?"

"No, not really, they sail through the air and it looks like they're flying the way they go," Jape tried to answer her question.

"What do they use for sails?"

"When I was a boy we killed one and . . ."

"Naughty, naughty, naughty, Pop. You killed a flying squirrel."

"It was an accident, I thought it was a regular squirrel when I shot it. Anyway, to answer mom's question. They have loose hide all the way from one foot to the other. When they jump out they spread their feet and the hide does catch the wind to slow down the fall and as Jape says they glide or sail through the air."

"Their hide is sorta like a parachute, Oh, my these frogs are jumping around in the skillet. I can't believe this, you guys come here."

Dad didn't move but shouted, "They always do that when cooked fresh. My mother said she wasn't going to cook anything that jumped around in the skillet. That was her statement until she slapped her lips around a couple of those big legs, then she changed her mind. Those frog legs are about the best eatin' there is in these parts. I never saw such big frogs as those. Where did you boys find'em anyway?"

They were saved by perfect timing. Mom shouted, "I'll have supper on the table by the time you get washed up. Jape, you stay right there. I'll fix you a plate and you can eat in bed."

Dad washed up and forgot his question.

Dad was right. The frog legs were the most delicious thing they had ever tasted. The cream gravy and hot biscuits went very well with those large chicken-fried frog legs. The boys washed that down with a large glass of milk. Tubbs crawled into bed with Jape and the two boys were sound asleep before the supper dishes were washed and put away.

At breakfast the next morning, Dad spoke to Jape, "I intended to tell you last night but those frog legs were so good, I forgot. Grandpaw needs some ice for their icebox. He's planning on walking to Paoli to get some. You boys may as well go get the ice for him. He don't need to be packing twenty five pounds of ice in this hot weather."

"Jape can't walk to Paoli on crutches!", Jape's mom told his father.

"It's only three miles to Paoli, mark my word, if he don't go to Paoli for gramps, he'll be out hunting or doing something and he'll walk twenty five miles up and down the creek. The road is smooth and level. It won't hurt him none. The exercise will help with the healing process, anyway."

"I'll be happy to pack the ice," Tubbs volunteered.

"That's nice of you, Tubbs, I know gramps will give you boys a nickel or two extra for a candy bar, or would that make you mad?"

"We'll go, I can make it. I shouild know how to walk on these things anyway by the time I get back."

"Don't forget, be back in time to help do the chores early, your mother and I may go someplace. And leave Mr. Tips here, that dog will tree something and you'll break you neck trying to climb a tree with that ankle."

Dad caught the dog and locked him in the corn crib.

By the time they arrived at grandpaw's house, Jape had mastered the art of walking on crutches; however, they didn't fit him right. Grandpaw noticed the problem right away. He took the crutches to his shop and did a little repair work. The crutches were now six inches shorter. With the new length, Jape could really motate. Gramps was extremely pleased that he didn't have to walk to Paoli. They were asked to get another item too, snuff for grandmaw.

Grandpaw gave Jape a half dollar, "You boys take a nickel each and buy yourself something. Get a glass of snuff and 25 pounds of ice. Can you remember that?"

Both boys nodded a 'yes'.

He continued, "Get a glass of snuff, like we drink out of. Do you know what I'm talking about?"

Jape nodded his head, 'yes', because all their drinking glasses were six ounce snuff glasses.

"The snuff will cost 17 cents and the ice a dime. After you boys spend a nickel each, you'll bring back 13 cents. And don't lose the change on the way back. Do you have a hole in your pocket?"

Jape answered, "No sir, I have good pockets. We won't lose the money."

"I don't know, I heard about your thrashing money," Gramps grinned.

"But I found it again. Could we use your wheelbarrow to haul the ice back in?", Jape asked with a plea in his voice.

"We usually carry it back in a gunny sack. A wheelbarrow will be too much trouble, won't it? You'll have to push it all the way over there and all the way back. We have a sack and an old quilt to wrap the ice in."

"I was thinking that my foot might get bad and Tubbs could push me and the ice. These crutches are hard on my arms."

"Boys, boys, boys, it's your sweat. Take the wheelbarrow if you must but remember I warned you. Make sure you get it back here today!"

The boys headed down the road with Tubbs pushing the wheelbarrow and Jape hobbling along on the crutches. Neither boy said anything but each knew the real purpose of the wheelbarrow. The only problem the watermelons were half mile in the other direction. This was one more mile for them to push the wheelbarrow.

Then Tubbs brought the problem to Jape's attention, "No wonder you wanted to do this today. I'll have to push the thing all the way. Going up hill will be a real problem, doing it all by myself."

Jape complimented, "You're a lot stronger than me. You can stop and rest and we'll make it. There is only one big hill going over there, anyway."

"Yes, but there is that one long hill coming back."

"The load'll be light coming back. You'll see, we can do it."

"Yes, I can do it, is what you're trying to say," Tubbs corrected.

They loaded the four watermelons and took off. The first part was downhill and Tubbs rolled along much faster than Jape could hobble. The uphill part was not as much fun. Tubbs pushed for a short distance then stopped to rest, pushed and stopped to rest. Tubbs hung in there, sweat was running down his face as if he was in a shower. This was much harder work than any thrashing job had ever been. Jape was following along praying he wouldn't quit. They rolled to the top of the last hill from where they could look across the little valley and see the town of Paoli.

While resting, they heard voices and noise off to their left. Jape hobbled over to take a look. Three men were working on something at the edge of the woods. Apparently, a pole building of some type was under construction, they had ten-foot post in the ground, each post had a fork at the top.

Jape asked, "What are they doing ?"

"How would I know." He took his hat off to wipe water from his brow, "I'm only your slave. I don't think, I just work."

"Quit feeling sorry for yourself and take a look."

The two boys walked a few steps further to get a better look. They saw two cars, a Ford pickup and three men working. They were busy building something out in the middle of this pasture. Curiosity took control, the boys left their melons to investigate.

For the first time, Tubbs was walking out front while Jape was trying to keep up on his crutches. One of the men stopped working and walked out to meet the boys with a big smile on his face. The man was working but he was dressed in good clothing, the kind everyone the boys knew wore when they went to town or to church. They gathered that he wasn't too smart, or the man was very rich. The truth came out when he introduced himself,

"I'm Reverend Gibbs, you boys live around here?"

Tubbs answered as Jape hobbled up, "Nope, don't live around here."

"You boys going into town?", Gibbs asked.

"Yep," Tubbs answered.

"Great, could I get you boys to pass out some leaflets in the name of the Lord," Gibbs asked.

He turned to look at the boys, "You boys do love God, don't you?"

Jape spoke for the first time, "I never met God but everyone speaks well of him. I would sure love a milkshake about now. If you could see fit to buy us a milkshake."

Gibbs interrupted, "Boys, boys, we are working for the Lord and in his name, we give. We must learn to GIVE to the Lord, not take. Get in the spirit of giving. How many leaflets can you boys pass out this afternoon?"

Tubbs asked, "What are they for?"

"We are having a revival meeting here every night for the next week. We must get the word out to everyone in the community. God's work, son, must be accomplished in every village, hamlet, city or town, big or small. We are here to do his work and must ask for the help of others, both young and old. You boys will have lots of time to pass these out around town and get back home before dark. We start the meeting about dark. Be sure to tell your parents to come, we'll have some beautiful singing."

"I don't have parents," Tubbs told him.

"I can't carry those things around on crutches."

"Sure you can, son, roll a bundle up and stick them in your pocket. At each house you stop and give out one. Only one to a house, you're working for God now, my boy. In the name of the Lord, all good things are accomplished. What do you mean you don't have any parents?"

"I'm a bastard!", Tubbs tried to confess but for some reason Gibbs wasn't listening. For some strange reason Jape didn't want to be out done he volunteered. "And I'm an orphan."

Gibbs looked them over good, they looked the part. "You boys got any money?"

"We got a nickel each to spend."

"The Lord does work in mysterious ways. You boys will of course give that nickel to God now that you have the opportunity."

He pointed to a large silver pan, something like a washpan only smaller and shiny. "That is God's collection plate, you can put your money in now."

"We only have a half dollar. We have to go to town for someone. We don't have our nickel yet?", Jape explained their position to the preacher.

"No problem, my fine lad. You can drop your nickel in here on your way back from town. Now don't let the devil get hold of you and spend it on pop, candy or something foolish. Let God have his way with your money today."

"We better get going, we have a lot of work to do in town."

Gibbs gave Tubbs about 100 flyers as they walked away.

At the road, they stopped to look at each other without saying a word. Jape sat down on the front of the wheelbarrow so Tubbs couldn't push it away and his actions prompted Tubbs to ask, "What are you doing?"

"Do you believe God needs our nickel?"

"Never thought about it, why?"

"So I make God happy by giving him a nickel. I thought God was all powerful, you know. He made the earth, sun, moon and everything. If he can do all that, what does he need with MY nickel?", Jape wanted to know.

"Well, did you notice if that man had his fingers crossed when he was talking to us.? He may be a liar, some of those fancy preachers do that."

"Preachers lie, that don't sound right. A good preacher won't lie."

"Everybody tells white lies. He wants the nickel, not God. How is he going to give the money to God, anyway?", was Tubbs' question.

"Could be he'll climb on top of those poles he's putting in the ground and toss it up to God on high."

"Where is "on high" or heaven? God don't spend money, preachers do."

"I'll tell you what. We'll give God a chance to have it all."

Jape took out the half dollar and tossed it straight up into the air and shouted, "If you want any of our money, please take it, God."

The half dollar fell back down landing with a splat in the hot red dust.

"See, see, God don't want our money or he would've taken it."

"God had his chance, the preacher won't be spending my nickel either."

The boys weren't satisfied that Gibbs was all bad; however, they didn't go door to door handing out flyers. When they sold Charley a watermelon they gave him a few. Charley had more friends that wanted watermelons than the boys had melons. Seeing Jape on crutches he gave the boys a one dollar bill for the four melons. He told the boys that his friends would be happy to come by and pick up their melon. This way, the boys wouldn't have to walk around town. At the store, the boys found out that Charley was only doing them a favor. The store had melons, the same size, for fifteen and twenty cents.

They left half the flyers at the store and the other half at the ice house. Paoli didn't have a ice plant. The town was located on the main highway (77) and on the route for daily ice delivery from the plant. All the local residents went to the ice house for their ice. Very few people could afford a refrigerator in 1939 but nearly everyone had an icebox. This was their only way of keeping food from spoiling.

The man at the ice house wrapped the boys ice in some old newspapers, then in the quilt the boys had in the gunny sack. That package was then placed into the gunny sack and tossed into the wheelbarrow. On crossing the railroad tracks they smiled, remembering the wonderful train ride that already felt like a lifetime ago.

Tubbs shouted, "There it comes, there it comes."

Sure enough, their timing was perfect, the 4:17 PM was coming through. Jape ran with the crutches, just a little faster than Tubbs could push the wheelbarrow. They crossed the tracks and waited. Tubbs was jumping up and down. Both boys started waving and was still waving when the caboose went whizzing by. The moment it passed, their friend ran out back and waved the full length of his arm. The boys walked away in silence and never spoke until they reached the top of the long hill east of Paoli. Once more sweat was running off Tubbs. Jape was feeling sorry for him but there wasn't anything he could do. At the very top of the hill they stopped to let Tubbs catch his breath.

"You ever been to a revival meeting?"

"Nope, you?"

"No, wonder what they do?"

"I guess church things, like the man said sing and preach."

"I heard tell they scream and roll around a lot."

"Who rolls around, what do you mean?"

"Well, what I heard is that they preach a lot of hellfire and brimstone, then get excited, the Lord takes their tongue and they talk funny and roll around on the ground screaming."

"Sounds like a dog with a running fit. Dad says there's one thing they will never forget at church."

"What's that?", Tubbs wanted to know.

"Pass around the collection plate, like old Gibbs here, after the nickel."

"He must get a bunch of nickels, he can afford to work in good clothes. Look, they have the roof on that thing. Looks like one of those places where they sell watermelons along the highway, don't it?"

"Yea, it does, guess that's what they call a brush-arbor. Let's go talk with him again. See what he says this time."

The boys walked across the field toward the little group of workers and the preacher. Not only had they completed the arbor, they had constructed a scaffold that was holding up a fifty gallon barrel.

The preacher rushed out to meet the boys, "Did you get God's message delivered to all the God fearing folks in Paoli?"

Tubbs answered, "Yes sir, and we got several God fearing people working on it at this very moment."

"Good boy, now you can deposit God's money right over there."

Once more he pointed to the shiny collection plate.

"No, sir, we can't do that. You were right about us. The devil got into our souls and made us eat a candy bar."

"I was afraid of that. I could see the devil in your eye when you two left. One day you boys will be two of God's finer workers. The makings of two good deacons right here. Where you boys off to now?"

Tubbs shrugged his shoulders.

Jape asked, "What's the barrel for?"

"That's our water supply. It gives us drinking water and we use it to sprinkle the ground. After people walk around all day, the ground becomes very dusty."

He pointed to several old garden hoses nailed to the poles holding up the brush. "We can turn that spigot yonder for sprinkling or drinking. Kind'a like different religious denominations, one you get sprinkled, the other baptized." He laughed at his own effort to be funny. "Right now it's turned for drinking. You boys want a sip of God's cider?"

"Sure, I could use a drink."

"Me, too."

They walked over and he turned the handle so the water ran out into a large cup. Jape drank first then gave the cup to Tubbs who finished it off. They only had one large metal cup for every one to drink from.

Jape asked, "How do you make the water go out there."

The preacher turned the handle the other way, then smiled.

"But I don't see any water?", Jape stated.

"Patience, my lad, the lines have to fill up. It takes a moment."

They walked back to the arbor just in time to see the water start sprinkling all over the inside of the arbor. Gibbs walked back to stop the water.

You have church at night?"

"Certainly, and right here every night all week."

"How do you see in the dark?"

"We hang lanterns out. Where you boys from?"

Tubbs answered, "Wayne, we live at Wayne."

"You know anyone around here?"

Jape didn't know why Tubbs was telling the story, but he wasn't going to louse up his plans, "No sir, not a living soul."

"Those are old crutches, crippled from birth?"

"He can't help it, mister," Tubbs informed him.

"You take me wrong, son. God can heal your every affliction. You can toss those crutches away and walk free from the burden of pain and suffering. All you have to do is believe and you will be healed. Can you boys be here tonight?"

"Too far for me to walk," Jape told him.

"You truly don't have parents or know anyone around here?"

"No, sir, and I'm still a bastard. Let's go."

"We gotta go now," Jape agreed.

"You don't have a father. Is that your only problem?"

"Yep, that's it".

"You boys come back tonight and the Lord will take care of you."

Jape shouted as he hobbled out toward the road, "Too far to walk."

"We can help you boys earn some money tonight. And get the Holy Spirit to heal you at the same time. Wouldn't you like to throw away those crutches. How long you been crippled?"

Tubbs shouted back, "He's been a little touched all his life."

"On crutches all your life. No wonder you get around so well. Come on back tonight and you'll walk home without those crutches?"

The boys remembered the ice and put it into high gear. They didn't let any grass grow under their feet getting home. They were feeling finer than frog hair. They earned fifty cents each and were sitting on top of the world. Jape was so intoxicated with all the happenings of the day he forgot about how bad his ankle hurt. Had he been home lying in bed, he would have been complaining constantly. Neither boy had mentioned his foot all day.

The first question grandpaw asked was, "Where is my thirteen cents?", then, "How is your foot, son?"

The boys learned that God's word does travel fast. Grandpaw and grandmaw were getting ready to go to the revival meeting. Jape was to get home immediately so they could get the chores done early. Dad and mom were coming by in the wagon to pick them up. Everyone was going to join in on the singing. Nearly everyone from around Cross-roads would be there. Tubbs was to go home, get cleaned up and meet them back on the road, if his mom would let him go to the revival with them.

Jape got home at the right time. Dad was leaving the barn with Mr. Tips. He had fed and harnessed the horses but waited for Jape to do the milking. Jape milked all three cows without any problems. He hopped around, using his heel to balance on. The only difficulty was carrying the bucket of milk. Dad returned to carry the milk to the house. He hooked up the team to the wagon while Jape separated the milk. Jape could see this revival was a big thing for them. Mom was all dressed up in her funeral dress. Immediately after getting the chores done, she pulled him inside to wash his face, neck and ears.

Then pointing to the bed, she said, "There is some clean clothes and wear a shirt tonight. We are going into God's house, you make yourself presentable".

He put on a clean pair of overalls and a short-sleeved white shirt. He was hobbling out the door when his mom told him, "Go put your hat back. It'll be dark in a few minutes. You won't need that filthy thing."

His dad spoke up, "We ate, if you're hungry grab something off the table."

He hung the hat on a nail over the wash basin and grabbed two biscuits and a hand full of bacon strips from the table.

They drove around the road, past Crossroads and toward Paoli. Dad let the horses trot most of the time. They hadn't been worked for a few days and were feeling good. Mom was in a hurry, she seldom got out of the house and didn't want to be late for the singing tonight. They saw some friends coming from the north in another wagon and dad didn't want their horses to catch them; however, their friends passed when they turned in to pick up grandpaw and grandmaw.

Jape knew Tubbs would be waiting at Yoakum's corner.

Mom told Tubbs, "You sure do look nice all cleaned up."

"Thank you." He jumped in back to sit with Jape. They rode over the same ground Tubbs had labored so hard in his effort to roll the wheelbarrow. Life seemed so complicated for those two boys.

Tubbs whispered, "Wish we had this wagon today. We could have taken a load of melons."

"Nope, Uncle John would catch us if we had taken any more. In a few days we can do it again. Look at those insulators."

He pointed to three on one telephone pole that were about to fall off. "We need to bring a hammer and climb the pole."

"I'll bang on the bottom and make sure the snakes are all scared away before you start climbing," Tubbs teased.

"It'll be a few days before I'll be climbing. My foot is still bad."

"Does it hurt?"

"Sure it hurts, hurts somethin' fierce and it's all blue and purple under my sock." He had worn a sock all day on the injured ankle.

"Oh, it ain't either. Le'mme see?"

Jape pulled his foot up into his lap and pulled his sock down below the ankle. The foot and ankle were about two sizes too large and it was a deep dark blue or purple."

Tubbs stared at the foot in disbelief, then shook his head and shrugged his shoulders in sympathy. "What can I say, Jape? That does look bad."

It wasn't sundown when they arrived. The sun was a large ball of fire floating just above the western horizon. The sky appeared to have exploded around the sun blasting out streaks of blue, pink and purple. As the big ball of fire was rolling out of sight over the distant landscape, their wagon rolled to a halt between two other wagons. Dad left plenty of room between wagons. He unhooked the horses and tied one on each side of the wagon and fed them some corn. This would keep them occupied and content to stand for a few hours.

Jape looked around and counted twenty three wagons and 17 cars already there. Over at the brush-arbor the preacher was wearing a full smile, from ear to ear. Every time another vehicle, wagon or car pulled in the smile grew a little. Jape thought he was going to burst his mouth if anymore cars showed up. He was really dressed up tonight. Guess those really were his old clothes he had on earlier.

"You boys don't need to sit under the arbor, stay out here and save the chairs for the ladies and old folks. You can hear the singing just as well from out here. We'll be leaving early, right after the singing," then dad lowered his voice, "These people get a little wound up with their hellfire and Holy Ghost preaching. You boys hang around and keep an eye on the horses."

"Yes, sir."

The adults walked on over to shake hands with Reverend Gibbs and get a chair, leaving the two boys to watch the horses. Most of the chairs were already full. They found a chair but it was close to the front. One must come very early to get a seat on the back row.

The boys climbed up in the spring seat to get a bird's eye view of the show. This was something like a carnival or the Fourth of July.

Suddenly, Tubbs gave Jape a sharp elbow in the ribs. "Look at that, look at that." He pointed to the Ford pickup backing up to the arbor with a piano in back.

Jape looked but didn't see what he was talking about, "So they're going to have music."

"No, look who's going to play!", Tubbs exclaimed.

There was Maud, the tobacco spitting cat woman.

"You don't think she can play the piano?", Jape questioned.

"A little spit and polish sure does make the difference in a lady?"

"She sure don't look like the same old gal that gave us the cats."
He continued to point and say, "Look, look, there's Charley and he's
all dressed up. What these folks won't do for the Lord."

Tubbs punched him in the ribs with his elbow again, "You better
watch your mouth. The Lord just may be around here some place
tonight and hear you."

Preacher Gibbs brought the meeting to order with a loud and long
prayer, then turned the meeting over to none other than old Charley
who was to lead the singing. Charley introduced Maud, their pianist
for the evening. He went on to say she was the best in the county.

Jape whispered, "Wonder if she can spit off the truck."

"You don't have to whisper. They can't hear us way out here, but
sure, she can spit farther than most of the guys at Crossroads."

"Bet she ain't chewing tonight. God may frown on women chewing. You heard anything about that?", Jape was courious.

"From what my mom says, God don't care for tobacco at all."

"I didn't ask you if he chewed. I wanted to know if he cared if women
like Maud chewed or not," Jape told Tubbs.

"Yes, I heard you the first time. Mom says God don't like tobacco
and especially around church and this is kinda like church, I guess."

Jape was staring at Maud across the cars and people, "You know
that old gal is good looking for an old woman. She sure does look
different spruced up. I'm going to watch and see if she spits."

The singing started, and the sound of the Lord's music drifted across
the valley. Charley had a beautiful bass voice and to show it off he
tried to outsing the piano. The louder Charley sang, the louder Maud
played and the stronger the audience became. All the old Christian
gospel songs were blasted out from the hill top. The soft warm evening air carried the sound of God's music in the breeze. Several people
sitting in rocking chairs on their front porch in Paoli were able to hear
every word. Maud may have been the best pianist in the state.

The singing was going along real good when several boys from Paoli
ran by their wagon. Jape asked, "Where you guys going?"

One boy answered, "He just let the air out of the preacher's tires.
We're going to hide and listen to a preacher cuss."

"What makes you think he'll cuss?"

"He's my dad, guess I know what he'll do."

Jape turned to Tubbs, "How would they let the air out of the tires?"

"Wonder if they let it out of all four tires?"

"If my dad had a car I wouldn't let the air out of the tires. I would appreciate riding in a car more than that. They'll get it for doing that."

"No, they won't, those city boys don't get into trouble like you do."

"Let's go see if they did let the air out of the tires. We can see the horses from over there."

The two boys jumped down from the spring seat. Jape tried to keep up with Tubbs on the crutches as they walked around behind the cars. Three or four cars were parked close to the arbor and next to the pickup truck with the piano.

Tubbs asked, "Wonder which one belongs to the preacher."

"We'll look for one with the flat tires." The two boys weren't trying to hide but they were walking slow in the semi-darkness. They stopped behind one car to listen to Gibbs talking with one of his two helpers.

"You need more than two actors. Wish that boy on crutches was here. He was an orphan and didn't know anyone here. Nothing like seeing someone toss away a pair of crutches to get the spirit to move a crowd. Look around and see what you can do, then light the lanterns."

Jape whispered as the men walked away, "They were talking about me!"

"Yea, wonder what he was talking about."

They walked along behind the preacher and the other man. The preacher went behind the arbor out of view. The preachers helper pulled an old man out of the crowd as Jape and Tubbs walked up to the car where the two men were talking. The preacher's helper spoke as he gave the old gent a pair of dark colored glasses, "Here put these on."

The old man put them on as the other man asked, "How do they fit?"

"Good, but I can't see very well in the dark."

"You're supposed to be blind. When he heals you, you throw the glasses into the crowd and scream, I can see, I can see, and get out. Here is five dollars. You give a good performance and get the hell out of here."

The old man answered, "Like I did over at Rosedale, last week?"

"Yes, that was perfect or we wouldn't be using you again."

The two men walked back toward the singing.

The boys looked puzzled and turned to walk behind several cars, then stopped to watch two men lighting lanterns. First, they lit several that were hanging inside the arbor, then more along the outside perimeter. This provided adequate lighting or would after it was real dark. The two boys were watching the lighting process and didn't realize two men had walked up behind them until the preacher spoke, "God bless you, boys. It's good to see you made it back." The boys jumped as if they had been caught doing something wrong.

Jape was the first one to respond, "Yes sir, but it was a long walk."

Preacher Gibbs, "God bless, God bless, the Lord is with us here tonight. So you have been on crutches all your life."

"It does seem that way, right now."

"You boys do love God, don't you?"

The boys didn't know what to say.

Jape snapped back, "You bet, sure everyone loves God."

"You believe the Lord can heal you, don't you?"

"If he can make the world in six days, including flying squirrels, he can do nearly anything he wants to do, can't he?"

Gibbs turned to the other man. Jape saw a wink that he wasn't supposed to see. Gibbs said, "These are the two orphan boys I was telling you about. They are good Christian boys, take care of them and I'll see you later."

The man walked out of the light a few feet and turned to lower his voice as he spoke to Jape, "Would you like to walk without those things?"

"Sure."

"Okay, I'm going to give you that opportunity. God will be in this little arbor tonight. He will heal several other people, too. When the preacher calls for those that want to be healed, you get in line."

"Come on, Jape, you don't want to do that. Everyone will laugh at you and besides we're going home right after singing."

"Are you boys good actors?"

"Don't know, never acted, I guess."

"Sure you have. We are all actors. You ever do something wrong, tell the teacher it wasn't you and get away with it?"

"Sure, everyone has done that," Jape admitted.

"That's acting, I'll bet you're good too. Could you act out a role tonight for, let's say, a one dollar bill."

Even Jape knew actors made big money. Jape pulled out the one dollar bill, "I have a dollar already. How about a five and I'll give you a real show."

"That is more than we can pay. Will you scream and throw away your crutches, then run out of the arbor?

"For five dollars, I'll scream to high heaven! I can't throw away the crutches, they belong to grandpaw."

"No, no, I didn't mean that you would lose your crutches."

"He can toss them to me and I'll take care of them until he is finished with the acting. He'll need them to get home, he HAS a bad foot!"

"Okay, you boys stand in line right over behind that gentlemen."

"You mean behind the blind man, with the dark glasses?"

The man turned to take another look a Tubbs, "Yes, behind the blind man."

"Where is my five dollars?"

"We'll pay you after the show."

"Nope, you pay me now."

"We pay only after we take up collection."

Jape raised his voice, "You'll pay me now. Exactly like you did the blindman."

The man returned to take Jape by the arm, "You hold your voice down, young man, or we won't let you act at all. How do you know about the blind man?"

"He's my grandpaw," Jape lied, then asked, "Do I get paid or not?"

He turned his back on the crowd, stuck his right hand deep into his right front pocket and pulled out a large roll of folding money. He peeled off a five spot. But before giving it to Jape he placed his hand on Jape's shoulder saying, "Listen, kid, you damn well better give a good performance or I'll break both your legs."

He slapped the five dollar bill into Jape's hand and walked away. He looked back to point at the blindman standing in the shadows of the lights, meaning for Jape to go stand behind him.

"Now you've went and done it," Tubbs told Jape.

Jape pulled out the five dollar bill, smoothed it out and held it up to the light to make sure it was a five. It may have been a coincidence but old Charley and the crowd broke into the first verse of "Bringing In The Sheaves" as Jape gave the five dollar bill to Tubbs to examine. Neither boy had ever held a five dollar bill before.

Tubbs spoke again, "You're in real trouble now. You won't even be here for the acting. That guy will break both your legs."

"If I wasn't on these dang crutches, he couldn't catch me. I don't have to worry too much, that big guy is spending someone else's money and as dad says, 'Come easy-Go easy'."

"If it wasn't for the crutches, you wouldn't be in trouble. It won't work for them anyway. The preacher wants to fool the crowd and most of the crowd knows you. They will only laugh at the preacher when you walk up there to be healed. You're leaving anyway, what you going to do?''

"I don't know, we'll think of something."

"What do you mean we? This is your acting job, not mine!''

"You want half the money?"

"What I gotta do?"

"Whatever it takes to get out of here without my legs broken."

"I get half. You have six dollars. Three of that is mine."

"Sure, if you do what I tell you to do. I would do it but I can't run."

"All right, I'll do it or at least I'll try to do it. what?''

Jape told Tubbs his plan and Tubbs explained why it wouldn't work. They hashed and rehashed plan after plan until one came to surface that both boys agreed would work. They did a melonshake giggling so loud that adults turned to look at them. A look was all it took to stop their giggling. The boys stood around listening to the music for another two hours. When Charley advised the crowd they would sing one more song and turn the meeting back to Preacher Gibbs, the boys went into action.

Jape started hobbling off, the man walked over to stop him, Jape said, "I've got to go to the toilet. I'll be back in a few minutes."

While the man had his back turned talking with Jape, Tubbs walked by the water supply and turned the handle for sprinkling. He turned the handle and was back standing in line as if waiting for Jape when the man returned. Jape walked out to the wagon and climbed into the spring seat.

It took the length of the song for the water to fill the lines and start the drip method of sprinkling for watering down the crowd. Water started dripping, first one place then another. The preacher was in back getting ready to come out front, his two helpers were busy; one watching the line of actors and the other one pumping up the preacher's tires. No one showed any concern for the little drip of water here and there until a few drops hit one of the hot glass lantern globes. Of course the globe exploded, first one lantern, then two and another one. The water was coming down through the arbor dripping on everyone. Ladies jumped to avoid getting their good clothes dripped on. The water collected dirt from the brush, dripping muddy drops onto their best duds. Within seconds, the arbor was empty and all the lantern lights were broken except one. It was hanging directly over the pulpit. Not knowing what was going on, the preacher ran out to take control and restore calm. When he awakened to the problem and cut the water off it was too late. He shouted, but to no avail. Everyone was leaving.

When the old folks got to the wagon, they found Jape and Tubbs sitting in the spring seat watching the horses. Dad hitched the horses back to the wagon while the ladies talked with old friends in the moonlight. They knew half the people there and everyone was either trying to ask a question or answer a question at the same time. This was a big event in their lives. Only once or twice a year did they get the opportunity to visit with some of their old friends and neighbors. They didn't give a hoot about the preacher's lanterns being broken or the arbor getting wet. They blamed the preacher for poor planning, other than the singing. They did love Charley and Maud. Each person agreed that they would have to get together more often. Slowly, each one drifted out in their own way. The moon was out, but with only one lantern and a leaking arbor, the hellfire and brimstone sermon was postponed until tomorrow night.

The car lights were spooking some of the horses causing men to curse. Women could be heard shouting for children to get in before they got run over. The preacher was shouting for the folks to come back tomorrow night as he apologized for the problems. Several ladies were making statements of disgust about the dirty stains on their good clothes. Dad was driving toward the road when the boys heard the man shout, "Catch that kid."

The preacher could be heard to shout back, "What kid are you talking about?"

In the distance, they heard the faint answer, "The kid on crutches."

Tubbs hit Jape in the ribs with his elbow, "Okay, brother, you owe me three dollars."

"Yep, now give thanks to the Lord for his blessings. We have enough money to get a pair of shoes."

The two boys fell backward laughing to lay flat on their back and do their 'melonshake'.

The moon lit the countryside with a dim candlelight brilliance as fireflies sparkled everywhere. In the distance a whip-o-will or a bob white could be heard. The evening was beautiful as the horses followed the broad ribbon of red clay stretching to the east in front of them. The sound of their hooves seemed to echo like musical drum beats across the night. The horses knew they were on the way home and their gait was a little upbeat. The family was pleased with the evening. The women were enjoying the moonlight ride.

Mom spoke to grandmaw, "Wasn't the music just beautiful? Why don't we do this again tomorrow night?"

"I would love to, but it may be too much trouble," Grandmaw answered.

Dad stopped her, "No problem at all. That Charley sure can sing. Then we have a date again tomorrow night."

He turned to look back at the two boys, "What about it fellows, you want to go again tomorrow night?"

Chapter 6
The Fishing Trip

The week of the revival came and went without Jape's parents missing a single night. The family enjoyed the singing, but they never remained to listen to Reverend Gibbs. The two boys missed all but the first night. For some reason, those two didn't want to go back for seconds.

There was a week of very hot weather and dad allowed Jape to lounge around the house without doing much work while his foot healed. With the help of his mom, he wrote a letter to Taylor Fur Co. in St. Louis. Jape made a couple trips over to talk with his grandparents, he wanted to tell gramps about writing the letter to the fur company and to return the crutches. Grandpaw had received more mail from the Sheriff's office about the lost treasure, he looked over his bifocals at Jape, "Four more men confessed to digging up the treasure. Lying, I can understand, but lying about something like this, I don't understand. I just don't know why a man would lie about a thing like that."

"How does the sheriff know he's lying?"

"This man said they dug the hole six feet deep. That was one of the little things that tipped the sheriff off. Even the sheriff can tell the difference in four and six feet, providing he has a ruler!"

Grandpaw leaned back in his rocking chair to change the subject, "What are you boys going to do with that fish, It's a big attraction at the store? He may want to keep it until it dies of old age."

"I don't know, eat it one of these days. I'll get Grandmaw and Mom to cook it and the whole family can have all the fish we can eat. I would like to ask Tubbs and his mother to eat catfish with us, would that be okay?''

"Certainly, certainly. I still don't know where or how you boys got that big fish. I have difficulty believing it came up our little creek.''

"Don't ask, Grandpaw, it'll be good eatin' even if you don't know where it came from.''

"Yep, I'm sure it will. Everyone believes you boys went to the river and caught it a couple days before you brought it to the store. If you can catch that size fish, you should talk with your dad and get permission. He'll let you boys walk over to the river. You're big enough to spend a night away from home, especially this time of year. You boys can swim, the dog will keep the snakes off you. You can't get into much trouble at the river.''

"Do you really think he would let me go?

"Sure, I already talked with him but don't tell him I said so!''

"Which way should we go to get there?''

"Since this is your first time.'' He grinned at the lad as if the boy had been there before and he knew it! "Walk down the road toward Paoli, go left at the cemetery and keep walking until you come to the river. You'll have to jog over here and there, go down a creek or walk down the highway. When you get to the river find a hole and, what am I saying, you boys know how to fish. I never caught one as big as that one at the store.''

"One of these days, I'll take you fishing and show you exactly where and how I caught the big one, Grandpaw, and that's a promise.'' Jape had returned the crutches since his foot was almost back to normal. The swelling was gone but it was a little tender. He had to walk carefully and it was still painful to run. He attempted to trot occasionally but after a few steps, the pain discouraged anything but walking.

In his effort to get together with Tubbs he walked to the mailbox and waited for the mailman. The mailman went by Tubbs's place about eight, arriving at Jape's around ten. The postman teased Jape for a few minutes about someone stealing the fish at the store. He wanted to know what Jape was going to charge for directions to his secret fishing hole. They had a nice visit with the postman again expressing his appreciation for the big watermelon. Jape explained that his foot was getting better but he didn't feel like walking all the way to Tubbs's place. He gave the postman a folded piece of paper, asking him to deliver it to Tubbs. The boy didn't have three cents for a stamp nor did the postman ask for one. In those days, the postman would take the time to visit and be of assistance to anyone on his route. This was a "Special Delivery", not as a paid employee of the U.S. Mail Service but as a friend. The note was hand delivered the next morning and it wasn't put in the box, it was hand delivered directly to Tubbs himself. That mailman thought little boys were important.

The note to Tubbs read, "Meet me at the store at noon." Jape didn't sign his name, he didn't have to, Tubbs knew without asking who it was from. The postman told Tubbs that Jape was walking without the crutches. That was good news, they would be going hunting. Tubbs was caught up with his chores and all he had to do was leave his mother a note and he was gone.

Jape was sitting on the bench in front of the store petting a cat when he saw Tubbs coming up the road. It was too hot and his foot wasn't up to running down the road to meet him. He dropped the kitty to jump up and wave. Mr. Tips just lay in the shade of the store, continuing to pant. When Tubbs got there with the .22 the dog went crazy running in circles, barking. He, too, knew they were going hunting.

Tubbs spoke first, "I see you threw away the crutches."

"Yep, Rev Gibbs's prayers are finally coming to pass."

"Yes, the power of prayer does work miracles."

"Let's work another miracle and get a pop. We are two weeks behind, its time to collect. You haven't been up here without me, have you?"

"You know better, I didn't think about that!", Tubbs admitted.

"Put that gun down and lets treat ourselves to a cold pop."

On their entering the store, the operator shouted at his wife.

"They're back."

Female voice from the back, "Who's back?"

"The boys you saved that cake for and they didn't show up, the fishermen!"

The lady came out front carrying a large white, freshly baked cake on a cake stand. She said, "I saved you boys a couple pieces of cake for a week and finally had to eat it to keep it from spoiling. Your timing is perfect for a piece of fresh coconut cake. You boys like coconut?"

"These boys will eat anything if it's free.", her husband advised.

"It ain't free, we furnished the egg . . ."

She interrupted, "That's right, Jape furnished the egg. And I'll be right back with two pieces of cake. You want a piece now, honey?"

"Sure, I don't want to watch these two stuff their face and me be empty handed."

"We would like a pop, too, please?"

"You want one pop or each of you want one pop. I guess that's a stupid question. You boys haven't collected any of the fish rent. I put a piece of paper up on the wall to mark down your collections, time and date but so far the paper is all blank."

"You can put down two pops for today", Tubbs prompted.

"You don't want a candy bar to go with the pop?"

"Not with a big piece of cake. We'll save the candy for another time."

"Honey, don't give these boys too big of a piece of cake and I hope you know you're generous heart is costing me candy sales."

She walked in before he was finished, "You don't have to shout. I'm not deaf and I don't believe I could give these boys a piece of cake that was TOO BIG."

Jape looked at the piece of cake consisting of four layers and the large end was at least three inches wide. This was a BIG boy's size. Jape and Tubbs dug in. Tubbs grinned as he said, "Exactly right, exactly the right size. I haven't taken a bite but I know it's going to be delicious."

"Did I see you playing with a cat?", the store manager asked between bites as he looked directly at Jape.

"You mean the one outside here?"

"Yea, how in the world did you catch it? We have been trying to get it in a cage for several days. No one can get close to it."

"I was settin' on the bench, it walked up and laid down on my lap."

"Who's cat is it?", Tubbs asked.

"The same hound man you traded your two cats to. Someone else left this one here for him, he uses them to train his dogs with. This one got out of the cage. If you would catch him again, we'll put it back in the cage?"

"Sure, but could I borrow it for a couple days.", Jape asked.

"You want to borrow a cat for two days?"

"Sure, I'll bring it back."

"What you want a cat for? No, No, No, don't answer that. I don't want to know. If you will catch the cat and get it into the cage you can have it for a few days but be sure and have it back by Saturday."

Tubbs was looking funny at Jape, thinking ONE more of HIS screwball ideas.

The boys left the store stuffed with delicious coconut cake, carrying a wire cage with a housecat inside. Tubbs continued to look at Jape in a suspicious manner but didn't ask, but Jape volunteered, "We're going Crow hunting. You do have the box of .22 shells?"

"Sure, what's left of'em or I should say most of'em."

"You ever shoot a crow?", Jape asked.

"Nope, never wanted to. Why should we shoot a crow? They ain't good to eat, are they? I never heard of anyone eating one."

"They're a bad bird, they destroy everything. They eat the corn, the pecans and sometimes they peck holes in the watermelons."

"No one can get close enough to shoot'em.", Tubbs informed him.

"Today we're going to get close enough."

"What's that cat got to do with shooting crow's?"

"Everything, crows are smart, you know? They can count but only to three. Since we're only two we can't fool'em. The cat will cause'em to forget about us and we can sneak around and get some good shots."

"We don't want to waste very many shells shooting crows."

"No, not really but we should shoot a few for practice."

"Practice, practice, have you ever missed?", Tubbs shot back.

"No, but neither have you."

"Then we don't need any practice.", Tubbs voice was scolding.

"Okay, I want to see what the crows will do if I put this cat in their nest. If you want, call it a scientific experiment."

A few minutes later, the boys were under the large tree by their swimming hole. Before they got started, Mr. Tips caught a large Cottonmouth and killed it. The boys picked up the large deadly poisonous reptile to examine its fangs. By pulling the lips back the deadly teeth were exposed for their visual inspection.

"Are you sure it's dead?", Tubbs asked.

"I don't know, I'm not going to take any chances. I'll hold it by the head until we're through."

Tubbs interrupted, "Why don't we milk it? In the book, they talk about milking a snake. Do you see any way to milk that snake?"

Jape held it up looking, "Don't see anything like the cows have."

"You dummy, I saw a picture in the reptile book. The milk comes from the fangs. Look at this one, see the little hole, its hollow."

About that time the snake came to and wrapped its body around the boy's arm.

"Holy Moses, it's alive. Throw it down, throw it down."

Jape had a tight grip on the snake right behind the head. He laughed and started chasing Tubbs, "No, no, here, help me milk it first."

"You're an idiot, if it bites you, you'll be a dead idiot."

Jape looked at Mr. Tips who was sitting over to one side with his head cocked sideways thinking the same thing Tubbs was shouting. Jape tossed the snake to the ground and Mr. Tips grabbed it a second time. This time he didn't stop until the snake was in pieces.

Jape looked up the tree at the crow's nest. The old crow was gone. They couldn't see or hear her but they knew she was watching them. Tubbs didn't do much climbing so Jape knew this would be a test for his foot. He started up the tree, piece of cake. He felt good and the foot didn't hurt unless pressure was applied to a specific spot. He made sure that didn't happen. When he got to the nest he found four young crows, they were fully feathered but much to young to fly. Each bird had its mouth open expecting mom to drop a worm inside.

The problem would be getting the cat up to the nest. Jape descended to the ground where the two boys huddled for a brainstorm. Neither boy felt it was a good idea to take the cat out of the cage. Especially after the incident in Paoli, Tubb's body was still healing from his wounds. The cage was made out of chicken wire and the animal was clearly visible. If they hung the cage right beside the nest, the Crow could see the cat and think it was there to get their babies. A great idea! − but how to get the cage, cat and all up to the nest. If they had a rope, Jape could climb the tree and pull the cage up from the ground. The only thing they had was a top cord which Jape tied to the handle on top of the cage. Tubbs stood under the tree holding the cage until Jape climbed the length of the cord. Jape pulled the cage up to that limb. Jape waited at that spot for Tubbs to climb up the tree to his location. Once more Tubbs held the cage while Jape went on up the tree and then pulled the cage up. The boys continued to do this until Jape had the cage near the nest. About this time, the crows started screaming and diving at Jape and the cat. Jape used his top cord to secure the cage to the limb. Immediately, he scampered down the tree to watch the frustrated crows, swooping and diving at the cat. The crows were making lots of noise, screaming their ''CAW - CAW - CAW''. The cat could be heard fighting back. The cage separated them but the cat stuck it's paws up through the wire to hit at the diving crows.

About fifty feet away, the boys built a brush shelter to hide under. Once the brush ''arbor'' was built they left, walking in plain view across the pasture. Knowing crows are smart enough to count, they didn't try to leave one boy in the shelter. They walked about five hundred yards up the hill and cut back into a draw. They went from tree to tree down the draw until they were back in the shelter. Jape was holding Mr. Tips by his collar. The crows were so concerned about the animal in the nest they didn't pay any attention to the boys sneaking back. When the boys left there were less than a dozen crows diving and screaming at the cat. When they returned there were over a hundred. Crows and more crows were coming from everywhere. Within half hour the sky was black with crows. Those boys didn't realize there were that many crows on the face of the earth.

Tubbs's eyes were big as saucers, "Gee whiz, Geeeee Whiz, you wanted to see what would happen? You wanted to know what would happen? Did you ever dream this would happen? There is a million, zillion, trillion crows." He burst out laughing and pushed Jape out of the shelter. Both boys rolled over laughing but the crows didn't bother to notice the boys. The crows were engrossed with their own problem and continued to call in reinforcements. The boys continued to laugh and watch the excitement. Crows filled the trees for two hundred yards in every direction. The noise they were making was so loud the boys had to shout at each other to be heard. There were at least a thousand crows in the air directly above the cat at all times. The cage was the only thing that kept those crows from peeling the hide right off that cat. Jape's scientific experiment was working; however, it was working too well!!

Suddenly most of the crows flew back a hundred yards, the noise drifted away with the crows and they could talk without shouting. Then the reason was obvious, up the creek walked Dad, across the field came Uncle John and from the other direction, grandpaw. The boys remained in their shelter, each one wanting to burst out laughing but afraid, too. Jape didn't know if he was in trouble or not. Each of the adults saw the other one coming. All three arrived at about the same time.

"What's all the excitement about?", Uncle John asked.

"Don't know. Did you ever see so many crows?", Jape's dad asked.

"Nope, never did but something sure has them upset."

"There's a nest in that big tree. I saw it last week." Grandpaw said as he walked around to get a better look and broke into a little chuckle, "I see the problem." He pointed to the nest in the top of the large tree for the benefit of the other two men.

"That cat's in a cage of some kind, isn't it?", dad asked.

"Well, there may be some dumb housecats around but I don't believe you'll find any dumb enough to stay in a crow's nest without being in a cage," looking around he continued, "Wonder how a cage got up there?"

Uncle John whistled for Mr. Tips and the dog barked in response. Uncle John grinned, "Yep, the boys are having a little fun."

After the dog barked, Jape turned him loose and he ran out to greet the men. The two boys were a little slower to respond. They walked across the creek grinning with Tubbs carrying the .22.

"You boys shooting crows?", dad asked.

"No sir, we haven't fired a shot", Tubbs answered.

"If they had enough shells to kill all those birds we might get to harvest a decent pecan crop this fall. The balance of nature works on most things but those darn crows don't have a natural enemy around here. It wouldn't hurt to shoot a few hundred to balance things up a little", was the first comment from Uncle John.

"We didn't want to shoot nothing we couldn't eat", Tubbs remarked.

"Son, I've known several adults who eat crow, frequently", grandpaw told the boys as he slapped Tubbs on the shoulder.

The three men laughed but the boys didn't understand.

Jape asked, "Should we shoot a few, then?"

"No, you've had your fun. Now, climb up there and get the cat down and don't be guilty of harrassing the birds, anymore. Tubbs has the right idea, if you don't want to eat it, don't shoot it", Jape's dad instructed.

"Son, by eating crow, I didn't mean literally chewing on the bird."

"How in the world did you boys get that cage up that high?"

"It wasn't easy but it was worth it, I think", Tubbs answered.

Jape looked at his dad, "If I'm not going to get a whippen."

"Not this time, but . . ."

Jape and Tubbs did a 'melonshake', the three men laughed as Grandpaw spoke, "The energy of youth, do you fellows remember being that young?"

"Yes, and I remember," Uncle John said as he turned to point at a large pecan tree about half mile up the creek, "tieing a cat in a crow's nest in that old pecan tree when I was about their age."

"Now, the truth comes out, I remember that." The men laughed and walked over to the tree with the boys. Jape's dad pushed him aside and went up the tree after the cage. Jape could climb a tree but nothing like that, his dad went up fast, got the cage and came down fast with only one hand. On the ground he asked, "Where did you get the cat?"

"Probably the same place he got the cage. Somethings you best not ask a nine year old boy, especially at a time like this."

"It's okay, I know where he got the cat", Uncle John assured him.

"I borrowed the cat and the cage from the store."

"This was meant to be a scientific experiment", Tubbs spoke up.

"And a good one to. I'll admit, you managed to get more crows into this little bottom than I thought existed in the entire state. With you two boys around we have plenty to talk about on the gossip bench at Crossroads. Now, we'll have another topic other than trying to answer the question about entering the war. The last time I talked to you, Jape, you were going fishing, what happened?'', Gramps asked.

Jape, turned to ask his dad, ''Would it be alright for Tubbs and me to go fishing in the river? We would have to stay all night. We'd be back tomorrow.''

"Your grandpaw seems to think it's okay. But stay out of trouble.''

The two boys and Mr. Tips headed up the creek in a run, leaving the men standing with their mouthes open, watching. Remembering a 'few days' ago when they were that age.

Dad shouted, ''Jape, didn't you forget something?''

Jape and Tubbs stopped to look back, Dad was pointing to the cat. The two boys started walking back.

Uncle John spoke up, ''I'm going to the store, if you're only going to return the cat, I can do that.''

Jape shouted, ''Thanks, Uncle John, that's what we would have to do. Tell him thanks. Someone will tell him the cat did a good job.''

"Yep, I'm sure he will hear about it from someone!''

The boys turned to run back up the creek. They were headed out for a two day fishing trip but to those boys it was a two day adventure.

There wasn't any questions about 'what the boys would eat or do you have a sleeping bag,' if the boys were big enough to go fishing they were big enough to take care of themselves. If they didn't catch a fish they would do without food until they got back. They would sleep, if and when they got sleepy, where they were at, either curled up on the creek bank or in a large clump of Johnson grass!

The weather was hot and perfect for fishing. Jape had one fishing hook, the lucky hook and the top cord. Both boys were thinking the same thing, they needed more hooks, if they were going to fish the river.

Jape remarked to Tubbs, ''Let's get that other dozen eggs at Grandmaw's house. Then we can buy more fishing hooks. We can't fish with only one hook.''

"I got a dime, I can buy a hook and cord'', Tubbs whispered to Jape.

"With the eggs, I can get a dime, too . . .'', Jape looked around the continued to speak, ''What you whispering for?''

"I don't know. What'd you do with all your money?''

"Gave it to my mother and she ordered my shoes for school this fall.''

"Yea, me too. I'm going to get new shoes but I may have to wear my old clothes from last year. Mom, well, she's not working much."

"Dad says he won't know about money until after harvest time this fall. Right now, he ain't got no money, either."

"Wonder what it's like being rich? You know with good clothes to wear, fancy furniture . . ."

"Flush toilets right inside the house and a car to drive."

"Right now, I would be pleased with half a dozen catfish hooks and a few yards of cord."

"What do you want to be when you get big?", Jape changed the subject.

"Don't do no good to wish. We can never be anything great like a mailman, doctor, banker or anything like that", Tubbs advised.

"Why not? . . . Cause we're poor?", Jape questioned.

"Sure, you see how the people in town look at us and treat us?"

"Nope, I never paid much attention. I always looked at it from the other side. The city folks are the ones in trouble, no cows or chickens, wonder how they get anything to eat? They must have friends or family in the country to bring them food. They can't all be rich and buy everything they eat out of the store. It's like playing marbles, nothing those city boys can do that I can't do better!"

"I don't know, guess we gotta lot to learn. What you going to be?"

"A big game hunter, or an engineer on the railroad. Might go up north and hunt like, like, Jack London. Have you read?", Jape said.

"Jack London ain't no hunter he's a writer. He may be a city boy!"

"He can't write about things he ain't done, could he?"

"We better cut across here if we're going to get those eggs without being seen. Your Grandmaw does know what goes on around there you know."

"Yea, and we need something to carry them in, too. There's an old rusty bucket in there, too, we'll use that."

They ran to the car body, Jape picked up the rusty bucket, turned it upside down and knocked out some of the dirt, then held the bucket as Tubbs very carefully put the eggs inside. The two boys headed for town to sell the eggs and buy fishhooks.

The boys didn't turn south at the cemetary like Gramps suggested because they had to go into town to get fishhooks. They didn't walk past the bank for fear the fat man might be there and see Mr. Tips or remember the boys. They walked up Charley's street but didn't see him, either. They were three blocks form the store, Charley came out walking toward the boys with a small paper sack.

He smiled while greeting the boys, "Hi, what you boys doing in town today. You don't have any watermelons I see."

"Nope, we're selling eggs so we can buy fishhooks", Jape said.

"You boys going fishing?", Charley asked in passing the time of day.

"Yes sir, we're going to fish the river", Tubbs boasted.

Charley looked into the dirty, rusty bucket the boys were carrying the eggs in, "Where did you boys get the bucket and the eggs?" Then he answered his own question but with another question, "You boys find a hen's nest? You wouldn't sell rotten eggs to these city folks, now would you?"

"We didn't break them open. We only got a dozen."

Charley reached down to examine the bucket and the eggs, "Boys, boys, if you want to sell these eggs to the store, you will have to make them look a little fresher from the outside. First, this rusty bucket, they'll run you out of the store without looking at the eggs. Once they look at the eggs, you're in trouble again, most of them are rotten; however, you may be able to get away with it if you put them in a new looking sack. Now wonder where we could get a new looking sack?"

Charley was always looking for a good laugh. This could have been the only man in town that would help sell rotten eggs. He lowered himself down to a squatting position, placing the bucket of eggs out in front to examine. Opening his sack, he took out a can of pipe tobacco, a plug of Days Work and a lamp wick. He very carefully took the eggs out of the bucket, placing them on the ground. After shaking each egg, he put those that rattled in the bottom of the sack, the rest he placed on top. When all twelve eggs were in the sack, he very carefully folded the paper sack across the top. The paper folds made a very good carrying handle.

He tossed the dirty bucket to one side, looked at the boys and winked, "You may get away with that, if you tell them I did this, I'll lie like the good Christian that I am and deny that I ever saw either of you boys."

All three laughed and Charley gave them a parting bit of wisdom. "Mrs. Wilson sells eggs in there all the time. She sometimes brings in a dozen or two in a sack. They are used to buying her eggs. If you tell them or say something like, "Mrs. Wilson asked me to drop these eggs off", You may be able to pull this off, if not come by the house, I may have a hook or two I could loan you boys."

"Yes sir, and thank you very much, sir."

Charley went on down the street and the boys to the store. The boys looked at each other then laughed as Jape spoke, "He said they were rotten?"

"Well, it has been about two weeks since we found the nest."

"Should we sell them bad eggs?", Jape asked.

"The question, will they buy bad eggs? Charley seemed to think so?"

"Remember he's the one who rolled with laughter when the cat messed all over you. He may be hiding up the street to laugh again."

"It's only a dime, could be some of the eggs are good."

"Wonder what he shook them for?"

"Real old rotten eggs will rattle and I heard some of ours rattle."

"It's only a dime. They will sell the eggs to a rich city person for a lot more than a dime and the rich guy is the loser. Let's give it a try."

The two boys walked into the store, to hear a bell ring when the door opened. A nice lady smiled real big and said, "Good afternoon, boys, may I help you with something?"

The boys smiled as Jape put the sack of eggs on the counter asking, "Do you have fishhooks?"

The lady walked over to a high shelf, then turned to ask, "Catfish hooks, what size?"

Jape pulled out his snuff can, opened it, and took out his lucky hook, "About this size."

The lady looked at the hook, returned it to Jape and took out a small paper box of hooks, "This box is fifteen cents."

"We did some work for Mrs. Wilson this morning. She paid us with a dozen eggs. We only have a dime. We need hooks and some cord too."

"So you boys are going fishing?"

"Yes, ma'am."

"We have some new fishing line. You can get this entire roll for a dime. The cheapest hooks I have are in bulk and they are one cent each. You can take as many as you want."

"I have a dime. If you buy the line with the egg money, I'll buy six hooks, two penny candy bars and two cents worth of those corks. Tubbs pointed to a cardboard box of corks, used for bobbers.

"Now there is a young man that knows the price of eggs and what he wants." She went about getting their hooks, line, candy and corks in a sack as Tubbs laid his dime on the counter. She rang the dime up on the register, turning to place the sack of eggs inside a large case of eggs, she said, "Thanks, boys, and good luck on your fishing trip."

The boys took that as an invitation to exit the crime scene. They walked out the door, then ran down the street.

They turned the corner as quickly as they could and found themselves running down the main street. A cafe was directly in front of them. A large sign read, "Hamburgers 5 Cents, Large bowl Chili 10 Cents." The boys read the sign as they walked, Jape asked, "You ever eat a hamburger?"

"Nope, you?", Tubbs answered.

"Nope, what is it?"

"Mom says its some kind of sandwich, like biscuit and meat only a lot bigger. The meat is not pork or hog meat, its made out of beef. Instead of grinding up meat for sausage, they grind up beef for hamburger."

"Ain't either, they wouldn't call it 'hamburger' if it wasn't made out of ham and even I know ham is from a hog, ground up cow and call it hamburger. You do talk like a city boy. Something sure does smell good."

"Yes, I'm hungry, too."

"Let's go up to the school", Jape suggested. The boys turned to walk back to the school.

"What you going to the school for?", Tubbs asked.

"Let's make a dime playing marbles and get a hamburger."

As always there were several boys playing around the school but no one playing marbles. When Jape and Tubbs arrived, several boys recognized them and ran over to talk. Jape asked about a marble game but no one wanted to play.

He pulled out a handful of steelie's, turning to Tubbs, "Here's your steel marbles. Sorry, I forgot to give them to you."

He counted them out to Tubbs and immediately several boys wanted to buy one.

"They're five cents each. How many you want?", Jape told them.

Three boys spoke up but two had to run home to get the nickel. The one that paid wanted to play a game of keeps shortly after a few practice shots with the steel marble. Within five minutes they had a marble game going. By the time the other two boys returned with their nickel to buy a steelie Jape had won a pocketful of marbles. He sold another boy forty for a nickel and they left the marble game with twenty cents. Now, they could have a hamburger and each have a nickel to spend on something else.

They ran down the street with the money burning their pocket. They had been inside a diner only once before and that was in Wichita, Kansas. They were excited about the thought of going inside a cafe and ordering like the big boys must do all the time. At the door, Tubbs opened the screen door and Jape walked in first. There weren't any tables, only tall stools next to a counter. He didn't see any place to wash up before eating. There was a hat rack next to the door. Both boys hung their hat up as a balding old man with large round bulging eyes, wearing what should have been a white apron if it had been clean, asked, "What you boys up to?"

"We want to eat a hamburger!"

"A hamburger is five cents. You got five cents?"

"Yes, sir."

"Let me see the color of your money and I'll start cooking!"

Jape laid a nickel on the counter and Tubbs followed with his nickel. The man raked the two nickels off the counter, "Two hamburgers coming right up. You boys have a seat and I'll go to work."

He disappeared from view and shouted back at the boys, "You fellows want a pop to wash these down with?"

"How much does a pop cost?"

"Only a nickel."

"Nope, we don't have that much money. Does water cost anything?"

The man chuckled, "No, water is free."

"Could I ask you a question?", Jape inquired.

"Certainly, what about?"

"What is a HAM-Burger made out of?"

"Do you want me to name all the ingredients or do you want to know what kind of meat is used?"

"What kind of meat. He thinks it is pork because of the name."

"No, it's not pork, its good ground beef. I grind my own and its good meat. It will be the best hamburger you boys ever ate. After you finish, you boys be honest with me and tell me what you think."

"There ain't no question about that. It will be the best one we ever ate 'cause we never ate one before."

The man poked his head around the corner, "You boys are pulling my leg. You never had a hamburger before?"

"No, sir, and we never had a milkshake until a few days ago. We are going fishing in the river, too", Tubbs boasted.

"You must eat at home all the time. Where you boys from?"

"We live out at Crossroads", Jape informed the cook.

That old bugeyed, baldheaded man may HAVE made the best hamburgers in the world. The bun was at least seven inches in diameter, with a half pound of meat, two la wrge slices of sweet onion, two large slices of garden ripe tomatoes, several slices of pickle and two pieces of lettuce. The boys felt much better after stuffing that burger into their face. They smiled and thanked the man. It was only a few miles to the river and they knew exactly where that other nickel would be spent tomorrow.

As they walked out the door, the man said, "You boys come back to see me."

At the same time Mr. Tips ran up smelling all the good odors on the boys. He could tell they had been eating something good.

Jape turned to the man, "My dog didn't have anything to eat today. Do you have some scraps that."

"Yes, I do. Just a moment boys." He came back with a double handful of scraps, both meat and bread. Mr. Tips was very thankful.

They walked away from the cafe with all three feeling great, their tummies were full, they had money in their pocket and going fishing. As the boys walked past the store a woman was heard shouting from inside, "That's them, that's them, there they go now! Catch those two boys!"

It didn't take any encouragement for those two to make tracks. When they turned the corner, they were running as fast as they could, Jape knew his foot was as good as new. On looking back, they saw a policeman running out of the store, the same cop that chased them the last time. There wasn't time for conversation, they ran through alleys, across lots and disappeared into the ditch made by Owl creek. They headed down the creek toward the river. The boys were small and the gully kept them hidden from view. They followed the creek for about a mile. When they were out of sight of the highway they walked out of the creek bed, continuing in a more direct line to the river, never giving another thought to the cop chasing them.

In the brush separating the boys from the river, several cottontails jumped up but Mr. Tips was trained not to chase rabbits. When one jumped up, the dog walked around behind Jape, cocked his head looking at the boy for instructions or a compliment for doing the right thing. The boy finally woke up to the fact they might get hungry before dark, told the dog to get the rabbit. A few seconds later, the dog had a rabbit treed in a hollow tree. This was their favorite way of getting a rabbit for dinner. Jape cut a long green stick, by pushing the stick into the hollow he could determine how far up inside the tree the rabbit was. At that point, the stick was cut to the right length to reach the rabbit without a bend in the stick. If the limb had a little fork on one end, it was perfect; however, finding a perfect limb wasn't always possible. And this was the case today, Jape had to make a fork by splitting the small end of the stick. A small piece of wood was pushed into the split, creating a fork at the end of the stick. This fork was pushed up inside the hollow tree until it touched the rabbit. Jape turned the stick causing the fork to tangle in the rabbits fur. He twisted and twisted the stick until it was very tight in the fur, by pulling down and continuing to twist the rabbit was pulled down the hollow until Jape could reach the rabbit with his hand, they had their supper, and their fishbait!

Before they reached the river, they found six long slender rocks to use for fishing weights. At the river, Jape cut six willow poles, one for each hook and a ten foot piece of line for each pole. Once the hook was tied to the line he used his pocketknife to beat or hammer small notches in the middle of the long slender rocks. This was so the line could be tied securely around the rock. Once he got a rock tied on each line, it was Tubbs's turn to go to work. Tubbs put rabbit intestines on each hook for bait, tossed the rock and the baited hook out into the river, stuck the pole into the river bank and went to the next pole — they were fishing for catfish in the Washita River!

Once all six poles were in the water, the two boys sat on the bank to watch for a bite, Tubbs asked, "Do you know what we forgot?"

"I didn't forget, I'm not using my lucky hook."

"Why not?"

"I don't know, six is enough. I don't know."

"Not that, we forgot something else. Six is enough."

"Did we forget to tell the lady the eggs were rotten?"

Both boys broke out laughing to roll back on the red river bank the boys didn't care about the dirt. They were going to enjoy their first fishing trip to the river and a melonshake was in order.

"Yea, that too. We forgot to use the corks."

"Thats okay, we don't need them here. The current is too swift. The corks will come in handy when we're fishing in the creek for Perch."

They continued to watch the poles in silence for a long time. Mr Tips explored the area and came back to watch the boys from time to time. He was licking at Jape's face when Tubbs spoke, "We didn't have to sell those rotten eggs!"

"If, . . . if, . . . if we knew those boys would pay a nickel each for those steel marbles and . . . if . . . we had known right off the eggs was rotten. Well, its too late now, unless we went back tomorrow and . . ."

"That's what I was thinking too. We better go give her the dime back."

"That will be difficult, to give her our last nickel when . . ."

"They sell hamburgers right across the street for a nickel. Yep, and by the time we get back over there tomorrow we'll be ready to ea . . ."

He jumped for one of the poles, "I got a bite, I got a bite." He yanked on the pole pulling out a catfish about fourteen inches long.

The boys continued to fish and talk until nearly dark. Jape cut and carried Johnson grass, making a large pile next to the ten foot river bank. The small cliff was about ten feet behind a large tree trunk. Jape built a fire between the tree and the cliff where he placed the pile of grass. The weather was warm and the fire wasn't necessary for heat but he wanted to cook the rabbit. This way they could sit or lie in the grass, watch both the rabbit and their fishing lines. No way for the fire to get out of control. There wasn't anything but red top soil in every direction.

After several large limbs had burned into coals Jape stuck two green limbs into the ground. Each limb had a fork on the top end. He ran another green willow limb through the rabbit, using the forked sticks to support the rabbit while it roasted over the fire. They had two catfish about the same size. Jape took them to the river, cleaned both fish but left the head and wrapped them in red clay. The clay was taken from the bottom of a little creek bed running into the river. The top soil was twenty to thirty feet deep in most places but some spots the creek washed the soil away exposing red clay. This clay was packed around the fish about an inch thick. Once it was packed tightly, the fish was tossed onto the fire. Once in the fire Jape raked more coals on top of the large mud balls.

The boys knew catfish bite better at night and planned to fish all night. The nice thing about fishing for catfish, they didn't have to keep a watchful eye on the pole. The fish would, generally, swallow the hook and never get off. In their own good time, the boys could take the fish off and put new bait on the hook. They talked and laughed and as they watched, the moon came up.

When the rabbit appeared to be exactly right, Jape took one forked stick and Tubbs the other one. The two sticks were pulled out of the ground, leaving the rabbit still on the stick and between the two boys. They walked a few feet and pushed the two sticks back into the ground. This way, the rabbit was off the fire, it could cool without the boys burning their hands or mouth and they didn't drop it in the dirt. They had eaten roasted rabbit before. With a long stick Jape raked the two balls of baked clay out of the fire. It would be a few minutes before the fish would be cool enough to peel and eat. They knew that attempting to eat it hot would only lead to disaster. Catfish have a very tough hide, the hide will peel off with the clay leaving delicious clean meat to eat. The only problem is attempting to eat it before the fish is cool enough to hold on to. The hamburger tided their appetite until the boys smelled the aroma of the roasted rabbit, although their mouths were watering they waited until the fish and the rabbit were exactly right. The rabbit was cooked to a turn, it was perfect and the fish was very good. The boys wished they had thought to bring some salt, next time!

Jape made a fish stringer from a willow limb. A six foot limb with a fork was cut. One branch of the fork was only four inches long, the other a full six feet. The long fork was pushed through the gills of each fish, the four inch branch acted as a holder, the fish was dropped back into the water and the end of the long limb stuck into the river bank to hold the fish. The fish remained alive but could not swim away with the limb through his gills.

By mid-night, the boys had several fish on the stringer. They slowed down in both their talking and their fishing. Both boys rolled over in the soft pile of grass and went to sleep. Mr. Tips was asleep at the edge of the grass. A few hours went by without incident. Shortly before daylight, the dog was awakened by water splashing and a sloshing sound of rushing water. The dog jumped up, whining, to run in a circle, he didn't understand where all the water had come from. There wasn't anyplace to run to for safety, water was everywhere. The dog barked, the boys sat up just in time to be swept away by a four foot wall of rising water on a river that had risen six feet while they were asleep. They didn't have a chance to escape. The bank behind them was ten feet straight up and the water was swirling all around them. They didn't have any choice, it was swim or drown. Their fish and fishing poles were already gone. Each boy instinctively grabbed his straw hat. At that moment, they were wiped off their feet by the water. They tried to swim to the bank but were swept out into the current. Tubbs was shouting for Jape and Jape shouting to Tubbs and both boys trying to talk to Mr. Tips.

Moments later, the boys were separated, large chunks of wood were mistaken for the other boy or the dog. Each one was working hard to stay alive. No energy or precious breath was wasted on shouting as they were swept from one side of the river to the other. They were rolling along with large limbs, trees, stumps and river debris for about one mile. The water seemed to pick up speed with every foot. As the frontal wall of water rushed on past, they seemed to rise into deeper and deeper water and slowly, slowly their speed began to slacken.

Neither boy had any idea about the fate of the other. They went under one bridge in a twisting and whirling of water and debris. In what seemed like an eternity they went under another bridge, it was getting light and the water was much deeper and they had slowed down. Jape grabbed hold of a limb on a large cottonwood tree that came by, at the same time someone from the bridge shouted, "There's a boy on that log!" Then more shouting from the bridge. Jape couldn't be bothered with people on the road, he had to hang on to something or drown. His strength was nearly gone. By holding on to the tree he could relax and get his breath back. His fight for life had drained all the strength from his eighty-five pound frame. A few minutes of deep breathing, he was feeling better and immediately started looking for Tubbs. He could see in both directions for several hundred yards, nothing that looked like a person or even Mr. Tips.

Jape gathered all his strength and shouted at the top of his lungs, "TUBBS".

Instantly from across the tree trunk Tubbs answered, "You don't have to shout. There's nothing wrong with my hearing. It's my swimming I'm having trouble with."

Jape looked over the tree trunk to see Tubbs hanging onto another limb directly across from him.

"Hello, brother, how about a 'melonshake'."

"If we get out of the water. I'm never going swimming again."

"Or take a bath. Wonder where Mr. Tips is?"

"He's a good swimmer, probably out already."

"We better think seriously about getting out or we'll be in New Orleans by noon, and that is too far to walk back."

"I'm not worried about going down the river. I'm worried about going under and not coming up. Let's figure out how to get out of here."

Jape looked down the river. It was getting light enough so they could see the current and the path the tree would follow. Where the tree would go close to the edge the river bank was straight up. Around the next bend, there were trees sticking out and water had backed up into the little creek but their tree wasn't headed in the right direction.

Jape told Tubbs, "This may be a good spot. Let's climb on the tree and jump out toward those trees and swim hard. We should be able to catch some of those limbs as we go by."

"We can't stay here, we have to go for it sooner or later."

Both boys climbed upon the large tree. They ran down the trunk, their weight didn't seem to have any influence on the bouyancy of the tree. They waited until the right moment, Jape said, "Let's go."

Both boys jumped into the raging water as two men ran up to the point with a rope. Too late, the boys were in the water swimming for their lives again. The men could not get into a position to toss the boys the rope. They watched as the two struggled with the swift current in their effort to reach the tree limbs. As they approached the overhanging tree limbs, it was obvious Tubbs wasn't going to make it. At the last possible second, Jape reached back behind him to grab Tubbs with one hand and groped for a limb with the other. Some how he managed to catch both. The water whipped the boys around into the limbs, exactly where they wanted to be. They heard a cheer go up from the bank. They were safe and it would have taken a tornado to pull the boys loose from those limbs. They splashed around in the water, grappling with the trees in their effort to climb out onto good firm dirt.

Two young men or older boys ran down to the edge of the water and gave the boys a hand up the bank and out onto solid ground of a farmers field. One of the boys asked, "How did you boys fall in?"

"We didn't fall in. We were fishing and got washed away", Tubbs said.

"Anyone else in the water or just the two of you?", someone asked.

The boys looked at each other and ran to look down into the river as they shouted, "Yes, Mr. Tips is in there."

"Oh, my God, he could be a goner. You boys are just plain lucky."

"Oh, Mr. Tips will be okay, he's a good swimmer."

"NO, NO, Mr. Tips is the name of his dog. There isn't anyone."

"Oh, thank goodness, you had me worried", the man replied.

"Well, my dog is important too, look, look there is Mr. Tips." He ran to the bank and big as life, there was Mr. Tips standing on a large tree trunk floating along the edge of the river.

Jape shouted, "Tips, Tips."

The dog looked up, wagged its tail and jumped into the water. He was a better swimmer than the boys. He came out above the spot the boys did and ran up the bank to shake himself, slinging water on everyone.

The little group walked up the river to the bridge. From underneath, the boys didn't recognize the bridge but from ground level they knew it was the east bridge out of Pauls Valley on the highway to Stratford and Ada. A group of people had gathered to watch the rising water.

Tubbs asked, "How in the world, it hasn't rained a drop and the river is nearly bank to bank and still rising looks like."

"That it is, my boy, that it is. No, we didn't have any rain but I guess it came a gullywasher from the Panhandle down through Clinton, Ft.

Cobb and Hobart. That part of the state really got soaked yesterday afternoon and last evening. It was too much, they had a big run off that got here early this morning. And that was what caught you boys. Where were you fishing at, this side or the other side of the north bridge."

"The other side of the bridge."

Another man stepped up, "Are you the boys that got washed down river?"

"Yep, these two boys and their dog got washed all the way down from above the north bridge. What is that about five miles?"

"It's a long way. I'm a reporter, could I get your names, please."

The boys answered all the reporter's questions and posed for a picture. He used a lot of big words in asking them what happened. They told their tall tale before a group of men who had watched the boys get out of the rising water. The reporter asked questions with a hint of disbelief that anyone could live through such an ordeal.

"You're telling me you were washed away, caught in your sleep." He pointed to a river that had risen another five feet since the boys got out. "In that raging river for five miles and you still have your hat on. You boys are as bad as Gene Autry, he can fight for two hours and never lose his hat, but Gene is a paid actor."

The reporter was stopped by one of the men, "Let me tell you something, mister, I saw those boys come around the curve up there. I saw one of them get knocked under by a log and, yes, he did come up with his hat in his hand. He put the hat back on and swam to catch a large tree. Both boys were holding on to the same tree when they went under the bridge."

Jape spoke up, "My hat cost a quarter and if I lose it my Dad'll whip my butt 'cause quarters don't grow on trees."

"The boy's right, the only time you lose your hat is right before you lose your life. I'll admit they were close to losing both but . . ."

"Okay, okay, so they aren't pulling my leg. Where are your parents? Who was with you for supervision?"

"I have been fishing on this river since I was their age by myself. Only a few times in history has this happened. This is usually the safest time of year to fish the river. Those boys are old enough to fish by themselves. And they proved it by getting out alive."

After the reporter finished with all the questions, they were asked to squat with Mr. Tips in the middle, in his effort to get a picture of the two boys and the dog. He said the picture would be in the next day's paper.

The reporter got the story and left. The boys looked around and they were left alone on the bridge. The reporter went back to town without offering them a ride. The boys had a short talk about the problem of getting home. They only had one option open, walk. In that area they had two choices, back across the east bridge, it was seven miles home and ten to Paoli and the other way about the same or a little further.

"Did you lose anything out of your pocket?", Tubbs asked.

Jape pulled out the nickel and patted his Barlow and the snuff can. "Nope."

"We still going to give the dime back to the lady at the store?"

"Yes, I feel bad about cheating her. She was so nice but she didn't sound nice when she was sending the cop after us, did she?"

"If someone sold you a dozen rotten eggs, wouldn't you be upset, too?"

Jape laughed, "Yep, I sure would. So let's walk around to the north bridge and give her the dime back. We can have another hamburger."

"Yea, with what?", Tubbs wanted to know.

"Sell two more of your steel marbles," Jape jibbed.

"Sell two of yours."

"I don't have another one with me."

"We can try. We're in for one long walk. We'll be exhausted by the time we get home."

"Let's hitchhike, stick out your thumb", Jape told Tubbs.

"No one'll let us ride with Mr. Tips." A pickup stopped and backed up. The boys ran to catch up with the stopping vehicle.

Jape grinned from ear to ear, "No one'll let us ride, huh?"

At the truck, the passenger's door opened and Tubbs jumped in as Jape slapped the back of the pickup and Mr. Tips jumped in. Jape started to get into the cab when Tubbs shouted, "Get out of here, its the brush arbor guy."

Before Tubbs could move the man had him by the arm, "I didn't think I would ever see you little cheaters again. I got you now, where is my five bucks?"

Tubbs was screaming, "I never had it, I never had it."

Jape refused to run with the guy holding Tubbs. "I have your money, mister. We were going to return it to you. I didn't want my legs broken but we never saw you again."

"Okay, hand it over and you can go."

"I gave it to a man in Paoli to hold for me."

"What man?"

"Old Charley, the man who did the singing at the meeting."

"Charley, has the money, good, I'll go see him and get it."

"He won't give it to you. I told him to hold it for me, not you."

"You didn't tell him it was my money?"

"I don't know who you are, . . . I told him to hold it . . ." He stopped Jape, "Get in, we'll drive over there and see about this."

The exact move Jape was hoping for, he grinned as he jumped in.

They drove through Pauls Valley and out the highway to Paoli, in silence. The man finally broke the silence by saying, "If you are lying to me, I'll do worse than break both your legs."

"What would be worse than two broken legs?", Jape asked.

"Three broken legs, two of yours and one of mine!", Tubbs answered.

"Now, you're getting the idea", the big guy told them.

"I don't know what you are so excited about. I told you Charley had the money. You know Charley's a fine man, a good Christian, like you . . ."

Man looked over to give Jape a dirty look, "He had better have the money, good guy, Christian or no Christain."

"If he don't, . . . Maud will have it."

"What do you mean, Maud? Who is maud?", the fellow shouted at Jape.

"Maud is the lady who played the piano at the meeting. She rode with Charley to the meeting. He may have asked her to keep the money for me. You see she likes me and . . ."

"I don't give a damn who has the money. I want it back TODAY."

"It's only a little farther. I think you should give us a dime for not spending the five bucks and getting it back for you. That would be fair."

"Fair, . . . you boys are, . . . hell, yes, I would give a dime to get my five bucks back. What you want a dime for?"

"We want to buy a pop down at the ice house on the way home."

"You get me the five bucks and I'll give you a dime."

"You got a deal, mister." He stuck out his skinny little hand and the large paw of the man shook it.

"You turn on the next street to get to Charley's house", Tubbs spoke.

The man slowed the Ford pickup and turned, they traveled slowly and Tubbs gave more directions, until he parked directly in front of Charley's house.

Jape jumped out saying, "Wait here, I'll get Charley for you." He ran upon the porch and knocked on the door.

Charley shouted, "Come on in, I'm on the phone."

"There is a man out here, a friend of Reverend Gibbs that wants a cat. Will you take him over to Maud's and get him a cat?", Jape lied to Charley.

"Sure, tell him to come on in."

"Would you please step to the door and ask him in. And please tell him you'll get it for him. Just shout to'im, . . . 'I'll get it for ya'."

Charley stepped to the door and shouted, "Come on in, I'm on the telephone. Let me finish talking and I'll get it for you."

Jape ran out the door and into the street as Charley went back to the telephone.

Jape asked, "Okay, now the dime and we'll leave you alone."

The man knew Charley was a solid citizen. He reached into his pocket, pulled out two nickels, "Will two nickels do?"

Jape took the nickels, turned to give Tubbs one, smiled at the man, "Now don't you feel ashamed of yourself for thinking bad things about us"

He grinned, "Does make me feel a little bad but there are some of those city boys about your size that can lie as well as you boys tell the truth."

He smiled as he slapped Jape on the back and walked toward the house. The two boys ran down the street toward the ice house. Around the first corner they cut back toward the cafe.

"What did you tell Charley?"

Jape whistled for Mr. Tips, "We have to find a place to hide for a few minutes. I told Charley the guy wanted one of Maud's cats."

Tubbs burst out laughing, "Serves Charley right, for laughing at us."

They ran to the store and burst inside startling the lady. Before she could say a word, Jape laid the dime on the table. "I'm sorry about the eggs. It was a joke or something like that. Here is your dime and we won't do it again."

The lady was in a state of shock, "Okay, thanks, I was going to have your little lying hides for selling me those rotten eggs. If it was only a joke, I'll forgive you boys this time, especially since you gave the money back."

The boys walked across the street and behind the cafe. Jape pointed to a nice shade for Mr. Tips under an oak tree, "Lay down and don't move, stay, stay." The boys walked around front and went inside the cafe. Before they could hang up their hats the Ford truck went speeding past, heading toward the ice house. They ordered a hamburger and paid for it in advance. The ford truck went up and down the street at least fifteen times before their burger was ready to eat. As the cook brought the two hamburgers out the truck went out of town headed south toward Pauls Valley at a high rate of speed.

The cook wiped his hands on the same apron he had on yesterday, "Well, boys, how was the fishing trip?"

Chapter 7
The Skinning Room

The next day, Crossroads was buzzing. The picture was on the front page of the paper. The headlines read, "TWO YOUNG FISHERMEN CHEAT DEATH". The story started out, "Western Oklahoma flood waters awakened the sleepy Washita River from its usual lazy calm into a raging torrent of violence. The vicious current swept two nine-year old boys from the river bank while they slept." The article went on to tell their story and gave their names and addresses. This made the boys more of a celebrity than catching the big fish. Everyone wanted to know, "What Happened?" The boys hung around the store talking for hours. They were enjoying their new found popularity. It was nice! The old guys offered to buy them pop and candy bars. Some of the fellows that never had the time of day for the boys were smiling and patting them on the back.

Generally, Jape's dad had a direct approach to any situation. This was the first time, Jape had ever seen his father at a loss for words of wisdom. Usually there was a direct right or wrong involved, his father would apply a strap to the seat of Jape's pants correcting the wrong. On those few occasions when Jape did something right, he would mumble "good" or pat Jape on the head and smile. This was something completely out of the realm of human control, the flood was an act of God. Jape's mother cried, holding Jape as if he had been killed in the ordeal.

She could have drowned him with her tears but dad stepped in to say, "The kid is big enough to fish the river, he's big enough to take care of himself. Cut the aporn strings, Maw, let the boy go. In no time he'll be a man, better sooner than later."

Mom between sniffles, "But he's only a baby, he's only nine years old!"

Dad looked at Jape, "You better go find Tubbs and go hunting or something while you can. We'll start picking cotton in a few weeks and your playtime will be over, better enjoy some free time while you can."

"There is a letter on the stand from that fur company in St. Louis. I know your grandfather was wanting that more than you were. You might cut across the field and show it to him on your way to see Tubbs."

"Yes, ma'am, I will."

He picked up the long brown envelope and ran out of the house shouting for Mr. Tips to come along. He seldom left the house without the dog.

Jape tore the letter open to find ten shipping tags, a fur price list and a nice letter. According to their letter, Tayor Fur Company would pay top price for any and all pelts caught after November 1 and before March 1. The price list included opossums and all the better furbearing animals. There were lots of opossums and skunks in the area. The farmers had difficulty keeping them out of their chicken house. Any of the neighbors would welcome a trap line for the purpose of catching opossums. The price of an opossum hide was from fifty cents to two dollars. His grandpaw was elated about the price list. He would help Jape with his trap line and had a few traps Jape could use. The price of fur was very good for the difficult times. Gramps felt Jape would be able to make enough money trapping and selling pelts to buy school clothes and have extra money for Christmas. In their long conversation Gramps asked Jape, "Did you know the opossum is our only marsupial?"

"The opossum is a what?"

"A marsupial, like a kangaroo, it has a pocket for the babies. You've skinned a possum before, you know what I mean?"

"Sure, but I didn't know that big word."

"These animals do well for themselves. They eat nearly anything and they are especially fond of eggs. The chickens will hide a nest outside the chicken house but seldom will they get to hatch because some old opossum will come along and eat'em."

"How many babies do they have a year?"

"They have a lot, sometimes as many as 10 or 15 at a time and some will have two or three litters a year. They multiply rapidly, another reason I want you to start catching a few around here. I was watching a nest in that old carbody, and as I suspected, they disappeared."

It was suddenly time for Jape to go see Tubbs, but as he was leaving Gramps chuckled as he shouted, "Jape, you try to stay cool and sleep on higher ground!"

The boy waved and ran down the road with Mr. Tips. Before he reached the road, Mr. Tips was jumping around sniffing at something. Jape went over to investigate and found a horned toad. These little lizards are fairly fast but not difficult for a nine-year old boy to catch. The species appear to be something held over from the ages of the dinosaur. The little animal has spikes or horns on its head. It's face is that of a weird creature, dragon or monster of some type. It has four legs, a body like a small frog, with a tail like a lizard. Jape and Tubbs used it on many occasions to chase the girls with at school. It always worked, the girls would scream and run like a tiger was after them. One evening, he smeared firefly tails on one's horns, giving it headlights like a car, then turned it loose. With the fireflies 'headlights', it could run away, but it couldn't hide. The two boys played hide and seek with the horned toad. They would turn it loose in the yard, run around the house, hide their eyes and count to ten. Then they would run back around the house and try to find the horned toad with headlights. Of course, they played that game last year when they were only eight.

Jape put the toad in his pocket and continued on toward Tubb's house. Several times the toad got out of his pocket but each time he managed to catch and put it back. When he arrived, Tubb's mother wasn't impressed with the toad. Before throwing Jape and his horned toad out of the house, she gave both him and Tubbs a short lecture about fishing at the river. The boys had to promise never to go fishing at the river without her permission. She was adamant about that promise! Both boys got the feeling she would frown on any future request to go fishing in the river. The boys made the promise because they were not all that enthusiastic themselves. One thing for sure, they would never go to sleep on a river bank again. They finally left the house with the understanding they were to go hunting and Jape wasn't to bring any more lizards or horned toads into the house.

Jape reminded Tubbs of four watermelons they had stashed near his house. The problem, they were about to get overly ripe and Jape could not bring one home without Tubbs because they were supposed to come from his patch. Jape wanted to take one to his mother, one to his grandmother and one home to Tubbs mother. This would get them back into good standing again. The picture in the paper was great with the men at the store but mom's are very funny about near death situations.

Tubbs remarked, "We still have all four melons; one for your mother, one for my mother and one for your grandmother. That is only three melons, what about the fourth?"

"You're dumber than a doorknob. I'm going to eat the fourth."

"I get the fifth one. Is that it?"

"Nope, you get to watch me eat the fourth, ain't no fifth."

"This way we can tell mom, your's or mine, that we want them to have the entire melon for themselves. They will say, 'WHAT A SWEET BOY!'"

"Now you're thinking, that's what I keep you around for."

"Lets get this done before it gets hot, it's going to be hot today. The boys started off following Mr. Tips down the road.

"Let me carry the horned toad for awhile."

"No, you might squish'im. He's becoming attached to me. He don't like you. He likes to be stroked on the head with loving care." Jape was rubbing the back of the toad's head, laughing at Tubbs.

Tubbs says, "Okay, I'll bet I can out shoot you and if I do, can I carry the toad."

He knew Jape could not pass up the chance to be competitive at anything.

"Okay, what you going to shoot at?"

Tubbs shouted, "Kill a Blue-Jay flying."

At the same time he made that statement, he fired the slingshot at a Blue-Jay that happened to be flying across the road. The candybead rock blew straight into the path of the bird and it fell dead as a doornail in the road. The boys ran up the road to pick the dead bird up.

Tubbs looked at the bird, then boasted, "See I hit him right in the head and on the fly, . . . your turn."

"I'll never hear the last of this," he gave Tubbs the toad, "your luck from living through the ride on the river is still holding. I can't beat luck. Here you take'im."

"You keep calling this toad a "he", why do you do that? You can't tell if it's a male or female."

"I don't know, call it what you want, name it Sue if you want to. I'll call it Henry and you can call it Abigale. But now, YOU have to eat a dead Blue-Jay, remember, you don't shoot anything you can't eat."

"That's okay, I'll give it to your grandmaw's cat, she'll love it."

"We don't have to make points with grandmaw's cat, too."

"Can't hurt, remember when she gave you the biscuits for Mr. Tips how good that made you feel. She'll feel good about us when we are good to her cat. See, when I think, we don't get into trouble."

"Then you better start thinking a lot more."

"Yep, and I think it's time to set this toad free 'fore we go get the melons."

The boys walked across the pasture to where they had the watermelons stashed. They took turns toting the first melon to Jape's mom. She was very impressed and for a few moments they thought their good works were going to backfire. She wanted them to stay and help her eat the melon. The boys insisted she eat it alone or share it with dad. It wasn't an easy task but they finally got out of the house.

It was midafternoon before they got both the melons delivered, of course, they took time out at the creek to eat their melon and chase frogs. A large butterfly came along and Jape followed it for nearly a half mile across the pasture before giving up the chase. They weren't in the mood to go hunting and the memories of their last fishing experience weren't enticing them to go again so soon. It wasn't in their makeup to sit and watch the grass grow but they didn't know exactly how to waste the remainder to the day. They decided to walk to Paoli and wait for the 4:17 train, they would walk two miles in and two miles back just to get to wave to the man in the caboose.

A half mile past Yoakum's corner, Jape seeing the telephone pole with the three insulators just hanging there ready to fall out, decided to climb up the pole and get all three. This would save the time of waiting for them to fall to the ground. Tubbs stood close to the pole, holding on to the pole with both arms as Jape climbed up to stand on his shoulders. At that point, Jape had to shinny up the pole a few inches at a time. He had been climbing trees for years and could do this very well. The first two insulators came out easy, they were dropped down to Tubbs. Jape was trying to get the third one loose when a car came down the road. The car slowed to a stop right in front of the boys, it was the Sheriff and the fat man. Jape was halfway up the telephone pole and Tubbs was standing there with his mouth open holding two insulators in his hands.

The fat man jumped out of the car, pointing at first one then the other boy as he screamed, "Look, look, would you look at the little thieves. They are stealing my insulators! See! See! Right there, right now!"

He pointed to Tubbs, then up the pole to Jape, "See, see, see, we caught'em red handed. I can't give you better evidence than this, now you will believe what I've been trying to tell you for weeks. These boys are a menace to the community and have to be put away."

The banker was right, the boys were caught. Neither boy had been caught for anything by anyone other than their parents or Mrs. Auld. This was the real elected sheriff, the one with the big white hat, the same one that posed for his picture at the buried treasure hole. Jape held on to the pole, instead of sliding down, he started shinnying up higher. He managed to get above the insulator and by stepping on it he pulled himself up to the top of the pole and sat down.

The fat man screamed more, "Look, look, he isn't coming down like any normal boy would. These dirty thieving little rats are only retarded hooligans. Make that kid come down from that pole. I don't have all day to waste on some sharecroppers idiot kids."

The sheriff spoke for the first time. He looked at Tubbs, "Which one of you is Jape. I remember meeting you boys after the funeral."

Tubbs pointed up the pole, "That's Jape, I'm Tubbs."

"What you doing with the insulators?", the Sheriff asked.

Jape spoke up, "They make good fishing weights. The cord can be tied through the hole and won't slip. The lines are down, no one has a telephone and we thought."

"You thought you would steal them. They don't belong to you and when you take something that don't belong to you, that's stealing," the banker said, turning to the sheriff, he screamed, "I demand you take these boys in. Now, I want paid for all the insulators they have stolen as well as the bearings."

"Boys, I don't have much choice. The banker has a valid point. You will have to go with me to get this matter cleared up. Come down from the pole so we can get this over with."

Jape had been trained to say "Yes, sir, and no, sir", along with the other common courtesy's to all adults and this included, obeying. During his tender nine years he had never talked back or knowingly defied any adult. He always walked into the cloakroom with Mrs. Auld and took his paddling when caught talking in class or throwing paperwads. Once, he stuck a girl's pig-tail into the ink well and got spanked both at school and at home but he never displayed any type of disrespect to the adults responsible for his punishment. While sitting on top of the telephone pole, Jape felt a deep disrespect for the banker. This was a sixth sense or something inbred, like a dog will bite some people and not others. Jape's innerself was working overtime to understand his feelings toward this greedy, rude pig of a man. The sheriff was known as a good man and a good sheriff. On the one hand, he wanted to come down and talk, as his dad and most of the people in the community had supported the sheriff in the last election. On the other hand, most of the people hated the banker but they had to do business with him because his was the only bank in town. Jape's dad and most of his relatives owed money to the bank. Of course, Jape wouldn't know about financial matters but the banker always had the upper hand when engaging in money transactions.

The three people on the ground were looking up at Jape, who burst out laughing to say, "Now I know how a squirrel feels. You going to shoot me off the pole, Sheriff?"

Tubbs had built up some tension, Jape's words caused him to take the opportunity to laugh but the banker and the sheriff didn't find his words that funny.

The banker spoke first, "Not a bad idea."

"No, of course not, but if you don't come down, I will climb up there and bring you down. You will not get the same treatment, if I have to."

"Okay, so I come down. What do we do then?"

"I'll take you boys to town to talk with the judge, that's all."

"We talk to the judge and you'll bring us back?", Tubbs asked.

"I'll do whatever the judge tell's me to do."

"I hope he locks you up and throws away the key. We have to put a stop to you thieving little rats, sooner or later. If we don't stop you now in a year or two you'll be walking into my bank with a gun to rob it."

"To use your own words, . . . sir, . . . NOT A BAD IDEA!"

"Don't be disrespectful of your elders, boy, you're in enough trouble."

"What about my dog?"

"What about your dog?"

"If you take me, how will he get home? Will you give him a ride?"

"No, the dog will go home on his own."

"If he goes home without me, my mother will worry. Will you go by and tell her where I'm at?"

"We'll get word to your mother."

"I'll come down if you let Tubbs go home. He didn't have anything to do with taking these insulators. It was my idea, he was only helping because I asked him to do me a favor. The bearings, well, he tried to talk me out of that. He didn't do anything, it's all my fault, so let him go on home."

"You can add lying to all the other charges. See what I mean these kids are a bad lot. They, they, both of'em need a good skinning."

"I can't let Tubbs go home any more than I can let you go home. You had best come on down or you may never get to see your home again. You are beginning to try my patience", the sheriff was getting impatient.

"Give it up, Jape, let's go and get it over with", Tubbs suggested.

Jape looking down at Tubbs, "The sheriff ain't going to climb this pole with his good clothes on. He'll have to go get a saw to cut the pole down, while he's gone I'll climb down and that fat man can't catch me in a million years."

"You've gone too far, but you're right, I don't want to climb that pole but when I leave to get a saw I'll take Tubbs and your dog with me. How about that, young man?"

"It's much too hot to be standing out here in this heat. Get that damn kid down from there, do your job, Sheriff, do your job."

"Come on down, Jape, if we get into more trouble it will only hurt my mom more. I will be grounded forever the way it is now."

Jape turned on the pole and slid to the ground. He whistled for Mr. Tips, patted the dog on the head and pointed toward the house to say, "Go home, boy, go home."

The dog looked at the boy, whined, trotted a little way and looked back, Jape shouted, "Good dog, go on home."

The boys got into the back seat of the police car.

They rode in silence all the way into Paoli where the sheriff stopped across the street and down the block from the ice house and directly in front of the red brick bank building to let the banker out.

The fat man was all smiles as he spoke on exiting the vehicle, "Thanks, Sheriff, I appreciate your help in getting these little bandits off the streets. Keep up the good work and I'll support you again in the next election and do try to stay cool."

The Sheriff waved but didn't give the banker any spoken reply.

Halfway to Pauls Valley, the county seat, Tubbs spoke,"Do you have a siren?"

"Yes, you want to hear it?"

Before Tubbs could say, "yes", the sound of the siren was blasting so loudly both boys covered their ears.

"It is loud, isn't it. If it wasn't loud, it wouldn't do the job."

"How did you do that? I didn't see you", Jape didn't see the switch.

"I hit a button with my foot. We can't drive with both hands and hold a button with one hand. It's better to have a foot-controlled switch."

"Do you catch a lot of bad guys?", Tubbs asked the sheriff.

"A few, but we don't have many bad guys come through here."

"You caught us, but you know we're not bad. We have been picking the insulators up off the ground. The last crew working on the telephone line were throwing those insulators away. They were being replaced with the big ones like at the top of the poles. We didn't mean to steal anything they wanted to use", Jape tried to explain.

"What about the bankers wheel bearing? Why did you take those?"

"That thing has steel marbles in it, they make good taws. I sell forty marbles for a nickel and they pay a nickel each for the steel marbles."

"You stole the bearings to sell?"

"No, sir, I bought the bearing from another boy for a nickel. After I got the steel marbles out of it a boy offered to buy one for a nickel and after one boy paid a nickel, well, others wanted one too."

"What about the peaches?" The two boys looked at each other.

"What peaches?"

"The ones you boys sold in Paoli."

"Mr. Webster gave us those."

"You telling me you never stole any peaches from Webster?"

"No, sir, I'm telling you, I never stole THOSE peaches."

"Then you do admit to stealing peaches from Webster."

"I wasn't wanting to admit to anything. I was trying to be truthful. I didn't want to cross my fingers when talking with a lawman."

"What about stealing from the collection plate at the revival."

Tubbs butted in, "That sir, isn't true. We never stole any money."

"We never attended the revival meeting. We went once but my folks went home after the singing. We never stayed long enough to see the collection plate being passed around. I often wondered if anyone ever took out money rather than put some in!"

"You never took any money? Wonder why they would come to my office madder than a wet hen to falsely accuse you two boys and make up a story about you taking five dollars from the collection plate?"

Jape started to answer but Tubbs pinched him on the leg to say, "That, sir, you should ask him. I'm sure you'll be talking with our parents. We were with Jape's folks at the meeting. They will tell you exactly what we were doing all the time we were there."

"And I suppose you didn't let the air out of the preacher's tires?"

"No, sir, but we can tell you who did", Tubbs informed the sheriff.

"Only if you make us, we aren't tattle-tales, you know", Jape added.

"No, I understand, but who did let the air out of the tires?"

"The preacher's own kid and three or four of the boys from Paoli."

"What about the sprinkler system going off?", the sheriff continued.

"We were sitting in the springseat of my dad's wagon when that . . ."

"Why are your fingers crossed on both hands?", the sheriff grinned.

The Sheriff was extremely nice to the boys all the way to the court house. He escorted the boys into a large cool room with high ceilings. A man with a city type suit was sitting behind a large desk talking with a uniformed police officer who was holding a man by the arm.

The man behind the desk spoke rather loudly as they walked away, "Bring him back after five days, if he has the same attitude, we'll give him thirty days."

This same man turned to look at the sheriff and the two boys, "What's the story, Sheriff?"

The Sheriff spoke, "This is really a hot one today, Judge, but, of course, you don't have a problem in here. This is Jape and Tubbs, the two boys the banker signed the complaint against."

He turned to direct the judge's attention to the boys. There stood two nine-year old boys, straw hat in hand, each wearing a pair of over-alls and barefooted. They fit the newspaper's photograph, as little fisher-men; however, if that courtroom had been a crossword puzzle those two boys would never fit into that picture. They were certainly out of place and they felt the pressure.

It would have been obvious to most any adult that the Judge and the banker had this all cut and dried. They were using the Sheriff to do their dirty work. The two boys had the misfortune of being caught in the act of stealing insulators, on top of all the other petty crimes they were charged with. The judge looked at the boys and back to the Sheriff, "Once more, what's the story, Sheriff, any merit to the Banker's charges?"

"Apparently most of his claims are true. When we went out to pick them up this morning we caught them in the act of stealing insulators from the telephone poles. This, Your Honor, is a new charge. The banker didn't know they were stealing the insulators until we caught them in the act. Since he is the president and the largest stockholder in "The Telephone Co-op of Paoli" he does want to file a formal complaint. He said to tell you he will be in later to sign another complaint."

The judge leaned back in his chair to survey the two dirty little farm boys, "So you are the criminals of tomorrow, a scroungy lot, I must say. You may as well learn now as later that we are not going to put up with your kind around here," turning back to the Sheriff, he added, "Take them out to the reform school. I'll send commitment papers out later."

The judge turned to busy himself at the desk as the Sheriff walked out and motioned for the two boys to follow him.

The sense of authority surrounding the judge and the courtroom was so overwhelming the boys could almost smell their own fear.

Both boy's knees were knocking together and they nearly fainted when they heard the judge say, "Take them out to the reform school."

Something about the courtroom and the man acting as if HE was God didn't fit with their family values and teachings. The boys didn't say anything because they had been caught in the act and knew they would and should accept their punishment.

The three walked in silence to the Sheriff's car when Jape looked at Tubbs, "Shooting that Blue-Jay was your last piece of good luck. Wish you had saved it till now."

"Are you going to put us in a reform school?", Tubbs asked.

"I don't have any choice, the judge is the boss. The school is only a short distance south of town, your parents can come see you."

Tubbs was trying to control his emotions but tears were starting to well up in his eyes. He was feeling sorry for himself and Jape was feeling hate rather than disrespect for the banker.

Jape reached over to pat Tubbs on the leg, "It's okay, they won't keep us long." He tried to laugh and make a joke, "With any luck, they'll let us go right after dad gets the last bale of cotton picked and hauled to the gin."

The Sheriff's car made a left turn across highway 77 to travel down a gravel road about two hundred yards to a large two-story red brick building. On the front of the building were the words, "Oklahoma School For Boys." The Sheriff walked up the front steps and into the building with the boys. Inside the front door a large woman met them, she smiled and bid the Sheriff good bye. She turned to the boys, "Okay, follow me." She walked down a long hall to her office. The boys were made to stand in front of her desk while she went over their papers. She knew their full names and all their personal information without asking them a single question. She apparently wanted to verify all the information on the paper. Once that was finished, she gave them a lecture about living at the school. They had school twelve months out of the year and the boys would be enrolled immediately. She informed them they would be in class, on time, clean and dressed properly, adding that they would be issued new clothing which included shirts and shoes. They could not go barebooted anywhere outside their bedroom and then only during sleeping hours. At all times they would be properly dressed and groomed. She gave each boy a list of rules and regulations as she pushed a button on the side of the wall.

She continued to talk as she fanned herself with a packet of papers, "I'm buzzing for Mr. Wilson, you will be living in dormitory three. Mr. Wilson is in charge and you will get to know him real well. If you boys follow orders and do as you are told, your stay here can be a learning experience. If you choose to cause problems, you will create a hell for yourself right here on earth." She leaned back in her chair to look at the boys and continue to wave the paper fan, without speaking. The boys were too scared to say a word. After a few moments, she spoke, "I guess looks can be deceiving. You boys certainly don't look like little criminals to me. Did you really do all the . . ."

The lady was interrupted when a man walked into the room. He was a short man, with a slight frame, with a large mustache. He was wearing a red ball cap, a blue short-sleeved shirt and blue pants. The boys learned later this was the uniform for all male employees. He didn't say a word nor did he look at the boys.

The woman spoke, "Here are the two boys I was telling you about. They are local boys from Paoli. Get their clothing and have them in class tomorrow."

He turned as she spoke to the boys, "You boys follow Mr. Wilson."

They walked out the door across a small yard without any grass to another building. They went inside where they could hear laughter and shouts of boys to their right. Wilson turned left and walked down the hall until he came to a door with a sign, "The Skinning Room" over the door. There he stopped, took a ring of keys off his belt and unlocked the door. He held the door open, nodded his head and the two boys walked past him into the room. This was a small room, about twelve feet by twelve feet, no chairs and two men were standing with their arms folded against the opposite wall. The man locked the door behind them and the door closed with a type of suction sound Jape nor Tubbs had never heard before, it was an airtight, soundproof room.

At this point, Wilson spoke for the first time as he waved to the two men, He looked at the boys, "Give me your hats."

He took their hats and laid them on the floor by the door, turned to the men, "Lock'em up."

Each man walked over to take a boy by the suspenders, then tied each boy's hands with a leather strap attached to a large wooden scaffold or frame. Each boy was tied so his arms were spread wide apart, not unlike the old flogging blocks during the slave days.

Jape shouted, "What are you going to do to us?"

"You're going to get a taste of the Donkey Hide, my boy, a little taste of the Donkey Hide. This will get your attention, the rules around here will be obeyed or you will be spending a lot of time in this little room on a full diet of nothing but Donkey Hide", Wilson told the two boys.

"We're going to get a whippin'"?

"It could be called that, yes, it can be called that", Wilson agreed.

"This is all my fault. Tubbs hasn't ever had a whippin' and I'll take his whippin'. Don't give him a whippin', he didn't do nothing wrong."

"I'm glad to hear that but we also have rules to go by. Since this is your introduction to the Donkey Hide I can only give you three slices each. I'll try to make them as sweet as I can. Hope you enjoy this as much as I do. It's too damn hot to be working today, anyway", Wilson stated.

Wilson turned to take a handle off the wall. The handle was attached to a long strip of leather or rawhide about three inches wide. He laced the strap across the floor two or three times causing the leather to pop like a shotgun blast each time it hit the floor.

He stepped over to one side and without any additional warning hit Jape across the back to shout, "One", he retrieved the strap and swung again, "two", bringing the strap back and lashing out with all his might, "three". Jape was trying to keep from crying, the leather strap dug into the flesh so hard that it caused the blood to pop to the surface of the skin. In the spots where the leather hit in the same place all three times, blood was running down his back. Jape took a deep breath and continued to bite his lip. The hurt from the Donkey Hide was not so deep or painful as the scream he heard from Tubbs. The boy had never been hit or spanked and the Donkey Hide was designed for truly bad boys and this lad was a tender nine-year old. Wilson shouted, "One", as Jape screamed, "Bite your lip and it won't hurt so much."

The strap lashed out against the bare skin of Tubbs back, "Two" and the second scream was even louder.

Wilson laughed, "This one does appreciate the value of the Donkey Hide."

A crooked grin crossed his face as he gave the boy the last lick, "Three."

Tubbs held the scream inside but could not contain all the pain as the strap of leather jerked a strip of hide from his back, he groaned and bit a hole through his bottom lip.

Wilson stepped back, tossed the Donkey Hide to one of the men, turned to the other one, "Don't just stand there, rub'em down."

The larger of the two men walked to an old file type cabinet, opened the top drawer, from which he took a gallon coffee can. He walked over to Jape and took a handful of something from the can and rubbed it on his cuts. "It's only salt, boy, it's only salt, it won't kill you but it will make you wish you were dead."

He laughed as he left Jape biting his bottom lip while tears rolled down his face. He continued to rub salt into the bloody stripes across Tubbs back. It hurt so bad Tubbs didn't need to cry anymore.

"You have to dry out for a few minutes. I'll be back in a little while."

He unlocked the door and as they walked out one of the other men asked, "Do you think they'll wait?"

All three men laughed as the door was jerked closed and the boys were alone in their pain.

Jape spoke to Tubbs almost immediately, "Are you all right?"

"Hell, no, I ain't alright." He spoke through clenched teeth. "The salt is killing me and your idea of biting my lip, well, now, half my lip is gone."

"I didn't tell you to bite your lip off. I was trying to keep you alive. I thought he was going to kill you."

"They did, I'm dead or good as dead. They're going to kill us in here, sooner or later. I'll bet they don't tell our parents where we're at. Our parents will think we went fishing and got washed away. No one will ever see us again. I wish I was home right now listening to my mom bitch."

He was building up a self-pity committee of one.

"Think about those hamburgers we ate the other day. That train ride was worth the, Now, I know what that sign over the door means, "The Skinning Room". We're in good shape yet, I've got lots of hide left, only about half my back's gone. I've had more than a few good lickings in my time but never got strapped like that across the back. It does smart, I'd just as soon die from infection than suffer like this with the salt. I remember dad used to put rubbing alcohol on his legs when they were galled, you know, raw between the legs. He would run around shouting for a few minutes in terrible pain while I laughed. He said it sure did feel good when it quit hurting. I didn't realize the pain he was talking about until one day I was raw between the legs. We had been chopping cotton all day and the pain was terrible. I had to walk spraddle-legged, if I didn't my legs touched and it was worse than getting the donkey hide. According to dad, the only cure was rubbing alcohol. Dad talked me into using rubbing alcohol as he had. He told me how to take a handful of alcohol and rub it on the galled area very fast. I did exactly as he told me to do and two seconds later; I was in pain, I thought my legs were going to burn off. I jumped and ran in circles exactly like dad had done. And while I was running and jumping, dad was rolling around on the floor laughing. He managed to tell me that it would feel good when it quit hurting. And he was right, not only did the pain from the alcohol go away but the alcohol burned out the galled area. The next day, I felt fine. This pain is something like that, I'm sure it will feel good when it quits hurting and we'll be okay tomorrow'', Jape was babbling to relieve the pain and tension.

''If I don't die from the pain you're going to talk me to death. That salt feels like a million maggots eating into my flesh or ten zillion little beetles ripping and gnawing on my wounds. You must not be hurting.''

''Hurting!, hell, you have the advantage of me. I never had a maggot, not even one, eat on me and I never had a beetle ripping around on me, either. This is the first time in my life that my hands have been tied so I can't scratch my itch. I know now why horses roll around on the ground.''

''Wouldn't it be nice to be out on the river bank right now. I would jump into the water and wash this all off'', Tubbs said through clenched teeth.

''Now you're talking, whoowee, that would be good. In here, we will never get to go fishing or swimming again.''

''I don't care, I just want to get out of this room. I'm never coming back. The only way they'll get me back in here is to drag me kicking and screaming'', Tubbs declared.

The door was unlocked and Wilson heard his last remark.

''Yes, my boy, that is the way most of'em get back here the second time. You will be back because all criminals, young and old, are exactly alike. You can't obey rules, you don't respect anyone or anything. Oh, yeh, boy, you will be back but you're right, we'll drag you kicking and screaming, only next time you'll either get five or more stripes. The three is only a get acquainted offer. Now that you're familiar with the Donkey Hide, I'll take you to the dormitory where you can read the rules and regulations. If you're one of the few that CAN follow instructions, you may be able to avoid a trip to The Skinning Room in the immediate future.'' He unbuckled Tubbs' hands and turned to take Jape loose.

Tubbs went to work immediately in his effort to get the salt off, asking, "Can we take a bath?"

"That is the next item on the list. You'll shower and get other clothes and then I'll take you to your bunk."

Jape didn't try to get the salt off his wounds, instead he walked up beside Mr. Wilson as they walked down the hall, "How long have you worked here, Mr. Wilson. This must be a well paying position."

The man looked down at the boy who was smiling back at him. Wilson looked ahead and picked up the pace a little but Jape kept up. Wilson looked back at him for a doubletake.

The boy was sincere in his question or Wilson thought so. "This is my sixteenth year, with the state, but not all here at Pauls Valley, and, yes, it is a good job. Today, any job is a good job. Around here it's best to be quiet and speak only when spoken to, you understand?"

"Yes, sir." Jape dropped back but the boys interest brought a frown across Wilson's face as he looked at the boy for a third time.

On entering the shower room the man pointed to a bench, "There is stack of clothing for each of you. You will use soap, wash all the salt and blood off your back. You can wash each others back, if you want."

He turned to point at a shelf next to the entrance to the shower, "That red salve will help heal up the donkey tracks, I'd suggest you rub that on each other, also. You'll wear all your clothes, including shorts. I'll be back in about five minutes. Take the shower and get dressed. You goof off and you'll be back getting more stripes to wash off. It's too hot today, so don't be messing around."

"Yes sir, Mr. Wilson, we'll hurry. What do we do with our clothes?"

"Leave them on the bench where the clean ones are."

He walked out the door and Tubbs started on Jape, "Yes, sir, Mr. Wilson, how long have you worked here, Mr. Wilson, yes, sir, Mr. Wilson. You're pathetic."

"I haven't read the rules yet but without reading them I'm sure you would be in violation of something just for thinking what you would like to call the guy."

"Yes, I'm sure you're right but why be nice to a real rat", Tubbs asked.

"Think, think, do you like the banker?", Jape was using the banker as a fine example for making his point.

"No, no, and HELL no", was Tubbs quick reply.

"That's my point. Do you like Mr. Webster?"

"Sure, he's a nice man."

"He caught us stealing but we like him. The banker caught us stealing and, I for one, hate him. Okay, I'm going to try the Webster treatment on this guy Wilson. If he's human, it'll work, what can I lose?"

"A trip to The Skinning Room", Tubbs shot back.

"I see your point. You want to wash my back first or do I wash yours?"

Five minutes later, the boys were fully dressed for the first time in weeks. The red salve did relieve most of the pain from the strap. They were uncomfortable, hot from the weather and unaccustomed to wearing anything but overalls, the shirt and pants with a belt didn't feel right. Their feet hadn't been inside a shoe in three months. The type, kind or size would not matter, any shoe would have been uncomfortable; however, they were dressed and ready to go with Wilson when he arrived.

He said, "Follow me."

Jape smiled and said, "Yes, sir."

Wilson looked back at the boys, "You boys look like two different boys, all cleaned up with your hair combed."

Tubbs winked at Jape then said, "Thank you, sir."

Wilson looked back at the boys, talking as he walked, "You boys are from around here? Did she say you were from Paoli?"

"Yes sir, we really live at Crossroads."

"Crossroads, I have many good friends at Crossroads. One of my dad's old friends passed away a few weeks ago."

"That was my great grandfather."

Wilson's mouth dropped open, he stopped and turned white as a sheet, "Your great grandfather, your great grandfather, they said you're a bastard."

"That's me, I'm a bastard, Jape has a father."

"No, sir, Tubbs and I both are bastards even though I have a father and a mother. Tubbs and I are bastard brothers by blood."

Wilson wasn't listening to the boy, "You are too polite, you boys aren't like the other boys here. Somebody has made a mistake and I'm not going to go down the tube for someone else's screw up." Wilson started on down the hall talking to himself as if the boys were not following. He walked into a large room with small bunk beds on both sides of the room.

Only three or four boys were in the area when Wilson shouted, "Jack, front and center, Jack." They waited.

A door slammed and a young man ran into the room, "Yes, sir, Mr. Wilson."

Wilson turned to look at Jape and Tubbs, "These are two new students. You will see to it that they read the rules, if they can't read, you will read the rules and regulations to them. If I get a call to The Skinning Room because they don't know a rule, it won't be the boys getting the Donkey Hide. See that these boys get a bunk and no funny stuff." He turned to walk away then turned back, "After you assign them their bunk, come see me."

"Yes sir, I'll be right down", Jack answered.

Wilson walked out of the room and Jack took charge. He walked around the two boys as if he were a rooster cock strutting around two young pullets. "So you're the two thieving little tarts that has been harrassing the entire community around Wayne and Paoli. You don't look like too much to me. Okay, can you read?"

"No, we never been to school", Tubbs lied.

"I know part of my ABC's." He smiled real big and continued, "Want me to say them for you, a - b - c -", Jape tried to be serious with Jack.

"No, I don't want to hear the alphabet. I want to hear you read the rules and regulations", Jack said, pointing to the paper containing the rules.

Tubbs pulled out the sheet of paper they were given at the main office, looked up at Jack to ask, "You mean these?"

Jack answered, "Right", then took them over to a pair of bunks.

He pointed, "These bunks will be your new homes. You will keep the area clean at all times. You will make the bunk each morning, exactly as it is now. You will get up when the bell rings at six and you will be showered and dressed in fifteen minutes. When I shout front and center, you will stand in front of your bunks, I'll come by for inspection and then we go eat. Do I make myself clear?"

"Yes sir, I understand", was Jape answer.

Jack looked up and down the room, "Kid, you don't have to call me sir, my name is Jack and everyone calls me Jack."

"Thank you, sir, but I was taught to call all adults, sir."

"You don't even know me, how do you know I rate a sir or not?"

"I was taught that saying sir elevated the speaker not the one being spoken to. A true gentlemen with a mark of class will call everyone sir."

"You're a real smartass, aren't you. Stay close to those bunks, I'll be back in a few minutes", Jack shot back as he walked out of the room.

"Jack, will you read to us when you get back?", Tubbs shouted.

Jack turned to give Tubbs a dirty look as he walked out of the room.

"Getting cute before we read the rules ain't smart. That one, Jack, ain't nothing but trouble. He's too young to be bossin' us around and he ain't smart enough, we're going to get into all kinds of trouble here."

The old residents of the dormitory came in a few at a time until all 21 of the boys were present. Some of the boys spoke, said "Hi" or smiled as they walked by. Only a few were friendly, each seemed to have problems of his own or else caught up in their own thoughts without time to consider someone else.

One boy immediately walked over to say, "Welcome, if that is the right word. I'll try to straighten that up by saying, I'm sorry to see you here but now that you're here, if I can be of any help, let me know. My name is George."

Tubbs told him their names and they talked for several minutes. George's advice was to keep quiet and not to get caught up in the games some of the boys would try to play.

Shortly after George left a smartmouthed redheaded boy walked over to ask Tubbs, "What grade you in?"

"I'm in the fifth", Tubbs advised.

"I'm in the sixth. What'cha got in you're pockets, they let you in with anything good? Let's see", the jerk jumped forward trying to grab Tubbs. He pushed Tubbs off the bunk and started to feel of his pockets. Tubbs resisted and the boy hit Tubbs in the mouth.

Jape jumped off his bunk to say, "Leave him alone, we've had enough trouble for one day."

"Shutup, punk, or I'll give you some of it", the jerk snarled back as he grabbed Tubbs by the leg in what appeared an effort to jerk him off the bed.

Jape stepped in to push the kid back out of the way. "I said leave him alone."

The boy hit Jape in the face about five times before Jape could even get his hands up. The blows hurt but were not hard enough to break the skin or do much damage. Jape grabbed the boy and they fell to the floor. Several boys started shouting and Jack came storming out of another room.

Jape shouted at Tubbs from the floor, "Get back on the bunk, Tubbs."

Jack pulled the kid off Jape and in the same motion started walking toward the door holding an arm of each boy.

"Where you taking us?", Jape asked.

"To the Skinning Room."

"Like hell, I didn't do anything."

"No, you little misfits never are guilty of anything."

Wilson stuck his head out the door to ask, "What's going on?"

"These two were fighting", Jack informed Wilson.

"Fred again, why is it you get into a fight with every new kid that comes in if he's close to your age?"

"He wants to steal what we have in our pockets", Jape said.

Wilson turned to snap at Jape, "When I speak to you I'll expect an answer and not until."

Wilson turned to Jack, "How did it start?"

"I didn't see it, I."

"No, you didn't see it because you were off reading someplace. You had better start watching these boys. If they get into any more trouble and you aren't there to stop it before it happens, Jack, jobs are hard to find."

"Want me to take them to The Skinning Room?"

"Fred, can you stay close to your bunk for a few days if I forget the Skinning Room this time?", Wilson asked Fred point blank.

"Yea, I guess so", Fred mumbled.

"What?", Wilson raised his voice to get a firm answer from Fred.

Fred looked up and raised his voice to say, "Yes, sir."

"Take'em back, I get off in fifteen minutes. Jack, I don't want any more problems to develop from this unit tonight, is that clear?"

"Yes, Mr. Wilson."

Jape and Tubbs lay on the steel bunk beds, Jape was on the top bunk and Tubbs on the bottom. They whispered and giggled about how neat it was, they actually liked the place. All they had to do was walk down the hall to get to the toilet while at home they had to go outside and walk a hundred yards. They could take a shower every morning and at home they either washed while going swimming or in a washtub on Saturday morning. They watched the other boys, some working at cleaning their area while others were sleeping or lying in the bed staring out into space. A couple times George came by, he was the only bright spot in the whole building.

The last time, he stopped to say, "We'll go eat in a few minutes." He lowered his voice as he leaned down to speak softly to Tubbs, "You guys follow me and do as I do, don't say anything to anyone about anything and by all means don't make some dumb remark about the food. It will be disgusting, but accept it with a smile and you can stay out of trouble. I'll tell you what happened to me one of these days when we can get outside."

Jack walked back into the room and George walked on down to his bunk. Apparently, the bunk was each boy's home. There was a shelf on the wall between the bunks with several hooks or nails on which to hang clothing. The bunks on each side of Jape and Tubbs were both empty. The row of bunks across the room had a boy in every bed. The new boys didn't attract as much attention as Jape thought they would. Although Jape and Tubbs thought everyone was looking at them, the other boys didn't pay that much attention. Each one had personal problems of his own to worry about. The two boys were getting bored with nothing to do when Jack walked into the room, blew a blast on a whistle, like in a basketball game, "Line up for chow." Every boy jumped up and stood in front of the bunk.

Tubbs pushed Jape over to the right side of the bunks, "Didn't you read the rules? The boy in the top bunk stands on the right."

Jack walked down the line looking at the boys, telling first one then another to button his shirt sleeve, tie your shoe, you missed a loop with your belt or some other little grooming chore. At the other end of the line he blew the whistle again, then turned to walk out of the room. The boys ran to follow in a single line but not in any specific order. George didn't say anything, he waited, stepping in front of Jape to provide them with the chance to follow him through the chow line.

The dining room was a large room with long wooden tables and benches the same length on each side. The room, the table and everything in it was painted the same color, grey. George followed the line directly into the dining room. The room could seat a hundred but less than twenty were eating. They followed George down the line which slowed to a halt shortly after walking into the dining room. No one was talking, the only sounds was that of silverware hitting the metal trays and the kitchen workers banging large spoons on trays. Jape looked back at Tubbs and whispered, "Why isn't anyone talking?"

"You didn't read the rules, be quiet or we get skinned."

George turned around to put his finger over his lips as he gritted his teeth. Jape shrugged his shoulders, to shuffle along with the line. They finally reached a counter or steam table, George took a tray and a spoon. Jape picked up his tray, looking for a knife and fork. George looked back to shake his head, pointing to the spoons. Jape took a spoon as there weren't any knives or forks. Each boy walked down the line passing in front of the food. Whatever George did, they did, the server slapped a glob of mashed potatoes on the tray, the next server slopped a spoonful of cabbage next to the spuds, at the end of the line they took a large hard bun or glob of bread that was supposed to be a biscuit. George picked up an empty tin cup and the boys did the same. They followed George around the tables to where Jack was standing pointing to the table where they were to eat, again nothing was said. A large metal pitcher of water sat on one end of the table. Once everyone was seated the boy next to the pitcher poured his cup and passed it down to the next boy. The pitcher made it around the table to end up at the same spot it started from. A few minutes later, a server came by and took the pitcher, refilled it and brought it back.

Jape tried to take a bite out of the biscuit, it was too hard to bite. George looked at Jape as he pulled his head back in a 'watch me' motion. He took the biscuit in both hands and by twisting the bread he broke it in half, one half he sopped around in the cabbage juice, mixed in some of the mashed potatoes and took a bite, then winked at Jape. Jape and Tubbs did the same thing, the bread was hard to break but they managed. Jape was thinking that the bread would make a good softball, they could play catch with it and never hurt it at all. He got the bread soaked up in the juice and took a bite. It was not like mama made at home. The cabbage had been boiled and it was cooked well; however, the food didn't have seasoning. It was completely bland, no salt, pepper or anything to enhance the flavor. Tubbs pushed his food back and folded his arms in a defiant action. Jape was attempting to mix his up and eat some of it.

George finally caught Tubbs's eye, pointing to his tray and mouthed the words without making a sound, "Eat it all gone."

Tubbs shook his head "NO" and George shrugged, "Skinning Room" Tubbs, unfolded his arms, picked up his spoon as George smiled and shook his head up and down. George soaked the last half of the bread in his tin cup as all the other boys were doing, then used the semisoft bread to mop up the last of the potatoes and cabbage juice. Jape and Tubbs had to force down the last few bites but they were finished shortly after George. Once everyone was finished the boy on the front held up his hand. Jack walked back to give each boy's tray a visual inspection, they were all empty of food. He looked under the table, straightened up to slap the table top, all eight boys rose taking their tray with them. Near the door, they dropped the metal cup into one tub, the spoon into another and placed their empty trays on a stack of more dirty trays. Once out the door, George turned to hold his finger over his lips for continued silence, then turned to walk briskly back to their dormitory.

Inside the door, George smiled and said, "Now you can talk. Didn't Jack tell you about the silent treatment during meals?"

"No, I never saw anything so stupid. Why can't we talk?", Jape asked.

"I don't know, some think it's to keep down problems. When they talk, they don't eat, they want'em to eat and get out. Now, what do you think of the chow?", George asked as he chuckled.

"What is Chow? I never heard that before?", Jape admitted.

"I guess it's a reform school word for eating or food. I never heard it before I came here", George said as he shrugged his shoulders.

"Do we have to eat all that stuff?", Tubbs asked.

"Yep, you're lucky today, the food was good. If you let'em put it on your tray, you eat it or a trip to The Skinning Room. If something don't look good, don't hold your tray close enough so they can reach it. Sometimes those servers will reach way over to put something on that they know you can't eat, just to see you get the Donkey Hide."

He turned to Jape, "Fred's a little stupid. He's always in trouble, best to stay clear of him."

"We didn't bother him, he came over to take things out of my pockets."

"If you have anything of value, you should give it to Wilson to keep for you. Sometimes that works and sometimes it'll disappear from the office, too. If you have family, and they come to see you, you should give them anything you want to keep. The big boys here will hold you down and take anything you have", George told the boys.

"They take our stuff and don't get into trouble?", Jape asked.

"Only if they get caught. If you rat on'em, you know tattle-tale, they'll break your head with a board, when you're outside playing. For some reason they hurt people who rat."

"When do they turn out the lights?"

"About ten, Jack is always goofing off. He is replaced during the night by an older fellow who's always out here. If you wake up during the night and need to go to the toilet you should . . ."

"Where is the toilet at?"

George pointed down the hall, "The first door, the boy just went into, that's the toilet. Another thing, watch who is in there when you go. If Fred is in there, stay out, or go ask Jack for permission. Sometimes they have fights in the toilet when Jack is on duty. He don't watch what is going on. That's where the big boys usually catch you and take your stuff. They know Jack is goofing off and they won't get caught."

"What will we do tomorrow?"

"You get up at six, shower and make the bed. Oh, yea, always keep the bed made other than in the evening like this. If your bed is messed up you get another skinning. We eat around seven and our first class is at eight. Are you both in the fifth?" The two boys shook their heads and he continued, "We can go to class together."

"Is school here like any other school?"

"Yea, we even have a woman teacher. She's nice and she treats us exactly like in school in Arkansas. I'm from Arkansas or did I tell you?"

"Do you get spanked in school?"

"Nope, I never have but the teacher don't do the spanking. If you get her goat, she calls Wilson and they take you to The Skinning Room. She don't have any problems with the boys. That Skinning Room does the trick."

At that moment Fred screamed and jumped off his bunk pulling the blanket and mattress off at the same time a large bull snake flew out on the floor. "Who is the wiseguy that put a snake in my bed."

With that remark and the look on his face, several boys burst out laughing, giving hoots and shouts of derision.

George said, "Don't leave your bunk." He ran a few steps to his area and jumped into his bed. Jape jumped onto his bunk, rolled over on his stomach to watch the action. The snake was about five feet long and trying to get back under the blanket that had fallen onto the floor. Fred had his shoes off, running around cursing everyone.

Jack burst into the room shouting, "Okay, okay, what's going on here?"

Fred shouting even louder, "Some wiseguy put a snake in my bed."

"Snake, what snake, where?"

"It's under the blanket." He walked around to the other end of the blanket and pulled the blanket off the snake and instantly the snake coiled."

"What kind of snake is it? Is it a poison snake?", Jack shouted.

"I don't know, I don't play with those ugly things", Fred answered.

"It's a harmless snake, a bull snake, it won't hurt you", a boy from the other end of the room shouted at Jack.

"How do you know that? If it won't hurt you, come pick it up." No one moved to do anything. Several of the boys on the other side of the room broke out laughing.

Jape spoke, "Do you really want someone to get it, sir?"

"Yes, yes, someone take it outside", Jack pleaded.

Jape jumped off the bed, ran over to grab the snake. The snake struck, extending its body, before the snake could recoil, Jape caught it behind the head to pick it up. He turned with the snake wrapped around his arm, "Where do I put'im?"

"Take the thing outside, follow me", Jack advised as he walked out.

He went down the hall in the opposite direction from the toilet, made a left turn to an outside door.

He opened the screen door to say, "Throw the thing out. I don't see how you can bear to touch it. Will it go away on its own?"

"It ain't a bad snake, they eat rats, mice and gophers and things that are bad. Some snakes do good an some do bad. This is a good snake, sir."

"Okay, thanks, now get back to your bunk, it's about time for lights out", Jack told Jape as he pointed back toward the bunks.

The building had electricity and electric lights was something new for these two boys. The lights were bright but when Jack shouted, "Lights out.", and turned the switch off it got dark in a hurry. Some of the larger boys didn't pay much attention to Jack, they continued to talk after lights out.

Tubbs whispered to Jape, "Did you read all the rules?"

"Yea, but that don't mean that I remember them all."

"Jack didn't even try to find out how that snake got into his bed. It seems like the meaner the boy the less one gets punished around here. That Fred isn't a nice person but putting a snake in his bed . . ."

About that time Jape whispered, "Look, Fred is climbing out the window! What's he doing?" Fred disappeared for a few minutes and returned with something in his pillow slip.

Tubbs asked, "What's he doing?"

"I don't know, your guess is as good as mine. That kid is crazy?"

The two boys rolled over in an effort to try to sleep.

Suddenly Fred started screaming at the top of his lungs, "No – NO – DON'T THROW IT ON ME, PLEASE DON'T THROW IT ON ME – GOD OH GOD, PLEASE, I'M AFRAID OF SNAKES."

There was a loud crash as Fred's bunk tumbled over. At the same time the lights came on and Jack ran into the room screaming, "What in the hell is wrong with you now? Oh, my God!" He ran to get the bull snake off Fred. Fred was lying with the snake across his chest, putting on a pretty good act.

"How did that thing get back in here?"

"Your little snake pet, over there," pointing directly at Jape, "threw it on me. He knew I was afraid of snakes and tried to kill me with it."

Jack turned to Jape, "How did you get the snake back so fast?"

"I didn't get the snake."

"Yes, he did, he climbed out the window and came back in with it."

"That's not true and you know it."

"You didn't throw the snake on him?" He turned to look at Fred who was getting his bunk straightened up. The kid in the next bunk wasn't saying a word. He pulled the blanket over his head and kept his mouth shut.

Jack walked over to pull the blanket from the boy's face to ask, "Did you see who threw the snake on Fred?"

"No sir, I was nearly asleep and didn't see anything", the kid lied. Tubbs spoke up, "I saw."

"I suppose you are going to tell me your friend didn't do it. It won't do any good for you to lie for him. Fred has no reason to lie about . . ."

"Yes, he does, I saw Fred climb out the window and come back in with the snake in his pillow slip. He is deliberately trying to get these new boys in trouble. All you have to do is look at Fred's feet and then look at Jape's feet, Fred ran around the house barefooted", George shouted across the room.

He pointed across the room at Fred's sheet, "Look at the dirt on his sheet and look at the tracks by his window. He's a lying tub of salt, always causing trouble."

Fred screamed, "You bastard, you bastard, I'll get you for this." Tubbs whispered to Jape, "I knew there was a reason why I liked George. He may truly be a blood brother."

"You'll be on report tomorrow, Fred."

Chapter 8
The Fight

The boys slept well their first night in reform school and were still sleeping soundly when the bell rang at six the next morning. Getting out of bed appeared difficult for some of the boys. An old man had been watching the boys sleep. The old gent came on duty at midnight when Jack left. He pulled a soft bottom chair out into the middle of the hall so he could see everything that went on. After the bell, he put the chair back into the first room and returned to walk down the aisle between the two row's of bunks, apparently checking to see if the boys were rolling out of bed. He never said a word to anyone, no need, they were all working at making their bed.

George walked down to say, "Follow me and I'll show you the ropes about taking a shower and stuff."

The two boys weren't too eager for a shower but the "stuff" sure did sound good. It would be different, not having to run a hundred yards to get to the toilet.

Jape told George, "Thanks a lot for last night. Hope it won't get you into trouble."

"Oh, it probably will, but around here, I've learned that trying to avoid the Donkey Hide is sometimes worse than getting it. It seems the ones who try the hardest to do right get it more than those like Fred."

"Will Fred get the Donkey Hide for last night?", Jape asked.

"Either Fred or George and I hope it's not George", George grinned.

"What about me, will I get it,too?", Jape was concerned and rightly so.

"I don't know, but more than likely it will be Fred. He is one of the regular screwups. He's about due for the Donkey Hide again. If he don't get it regular, well, once he tried to burn the place down, he's just dumb. I mean real dumb, or stupid. I'm not sure which is the right word."

The shower felt good but drying was a little difficult. Jape took a little extra time to pat the water from Tubb's back, the towel was rough and hurt him to drag across the wounds. The Donkey Hide marks were still very sore. Tubbs had long blue stripes mixed with a little purple, while Jape's were long red and raw looking. With George's help, they were dressed and ready for breakfast with time to spare.

Jape walked up to George's bunk to ask, "What'll we have to eat?"

"Oh, don't get your hopes up, it won't be good. Sometimes we get grits, rice or pancakes, and no, they will not be like mama used to make. Even if they look good and you're hungry don't take much. Sometimes the best looking food is terrible and hard to swallow. The way I figure, it's better to go away a little hungry than to get the Donkey Hide."

They walked to the dining room exactly as they did last evening with the old man leading the way and the boys following. The breakfast smelled of burnt sugar or syrup. A million questions ran through both Jape and Tubb's young inquisitive minds but they had to remain silent. Once more they watched George go through the line. Each boy taking a cup, spoon and a metal tray. This morning they had a choice, boiled white rice which was served with a large spoon, the glob of white rice hit the tray like a wet snowball. It hit with a thud but didn't splatter or run. The only other choice was something that looked like a pancake. No sugar, syrup was used to sweeten the rice or pancakes. George pushed his tray out for rice and Jape did the same but Tubbs must have liked the looks of the pancakes. The server slapped two pancakes on his tray.

Once seated, Jape and George mixed the syrup with the rice by stirring with the spoon. Tubbs cut off a hunk of the pancake and tried to eat it. He chewed it and couldn't swallow without washing it down with water. Jape didn't pay much attention to Tubbs as he was trying to get enough syrup on the gummy rice to get it down. The syrup appeared to be a mixture of old white Karo and a homemade variety of water and sugar.

Suddenly, Tubbs stood up without saying a word. The old man walked over to their table, knocked on the table with his right knuckles, then raised his right hand to wiggle his forefinger for Tubbs to come out. Tubbs started to walk out without his tray, the man pointed back to the tray, Tubbs returned to pick up the tray and walked out the door with the old man right behind him.

Jape and George sat there with their mouths open. Immediately other boys around the room started standing with their tray in their hand. Not a word had been spoken. Moments later, the man returned with Tubbs but this time the man was carrying Tubbs' tray. He pointed to the line which was down to only three boys. Jape and George watched as Tubbs got a new tray and went through the line to get a spoonful of rice and syrup.

While Tubbs was going through the line the old man came back to check on and send all the boys with pancakes back through the line. George and Jape continued to munch at the rice and watch in awe. As soon as Tubbs returned, he winked at Jape and started to eat the rice and syrup. Five minutes later the dining room was back to normal. Everyone was eating quietly at their table while boys from other tables were being dismissed. Jape's young mind was recalling the good breakfast he could be having at home.

He was reliving the recent past in his mind, the train ride and the last few weeks with Tubbs and Mr. Tips-Mr. Tips, he turned to Tubbs and blurted out, "I wonder if Mr. Tips made it home all right?"

The sound of his voice echoed as it rattled around the silent dining room like a marble in a tin can.

One thing about breaking the code of silence in the dining room, Jape didn't have to worry about eating all the rice or carrying out his tray. Two large men instantly lifted him from the table, one man on each of Jape's arms to carry him out the door. On exiting the dining room, one of the men stopped to push a button, then they continued down the hall to The Skinning Room. The old man stood watching the remainder of the boys without blinking his eyes.

Wilson met them at The Skinning Room door, the purpose of the buzzer, he unlocked the door and held it open saying, "Lock him into the position and go on back to the dining room, I can handle this."

The men buckled Jape into position once more and left the room. Wilson was still standing by the open door waiting for the men to leave.

The men left and Wilson closed and locked the door, walked across the room to get the Donkey Hide as he asked, "Didn't you read the rules?"

"Yes, sir, I did."

"You knew about the code of silence in the dining room?"

"Yes, sir."

"You talked anyway."

"May I explain, sir?"

"Do you think you can?"

"Yessir, I can explain."

"Okay, give me your story."

"When the sheriff picked us up yesterday."

"By us, you mean the other boy that came in with you?"

"Yessir, Tubbs and I, well, we were about two miles from home when the sheriff brought us here. I've been so caught up in my own problems I forgot about Mr. Tips. I don't know if he made it home or not."

"Who is Mr. Tips and why wasn't he named in your report?"

"Mr. Tips is my dog, his name is Mr. Tips. He has a white tip on."

"Your dog, you're worried about your dog. Yea, stands to reason, your great grandpappy loved his dogs, it would be in your blood. Jape, I don't have any choice about giving you five lashes with the Donkey Hide. I could lose my job. It's a rule, break the silence in the dining room once and you get five, the next time ten. This is your first time."

Wilson folded the Donkey Hide and hit Jape lightly across the butt, "one" and hit him again lightly "two" continuing through "five".

Tubbs had hit him harder while playing. Wilson hung the Donkey Hide back on the wall and unbuckled the straps. Wilson didn't smile as he spoke, "I have great respect for your family and don't believe you belong here. Hopefully, you will prove me right. I feel I owe your grandfather one so if you feel you got a break prove it by obeying the rules. From now on you will be treated as any other boy in this institution. Do we understand each other?"

"Yessir, and, thank you, sir."

"This should be our secret."

"I've heard my grandpaw say many a good thing about the Wilson's but they never lived around Crossroads. He always said they were good people."

Wilson looked at Jape with a questioning eye, he didn't know if he was being conned or if the kid was for real. Jape, on the other hand, didn't know the meaning of "con" but was doing his best to use the "Webster" treatment on this guy. He had just dodged the bullet and didn't really know why.

Wilson opened the door, "Go to the bathroom and wash you face, don't go back to the dining room. After you wash your face, don't matter if it needs it or not return to your bunk, remember, you've just returned from The Skinning Room, don't run back in there laughing or the jig is up."

Jape turned to look at Wilson, "I'm just ugly, Mr. Wilson, not stupid."

Jape returned to his bunk to find Tubbs with tears streaming down his face. He was crying for the pain Jape didn't have. Instead of climbing up into his own bunk, Jape flopped down on the Bunk to sit beside Tubbs and put his arm around Tubbs and asked, "What's wrong, why so sad?"

"Did I cause you to talk by standing up in the dining room?"

"No, but how did you get away with that?"

"Jape, you didn't read the rules, did you? The rules are clear about the behavior in the dining room. If they serve us something that really isn't fit to eat, we can, at the risk of going straight to The Skinning Room, stand up. After the food is examined, we either get a new tray or we go straight to the Skinning Room. Those pancakes were so salty no one could eat'em. Well, I took a chance and stood up. It was get the Donkey Hide for not eating the pancakes one way or the other. I remembered the rule and didn't want to get you in trouble, too."

"All right, so that's why everyone else with pancakes stood up after you got a new tray. Each boy was waiting for someone to have the guts to be first."

"The man told me out in the hall that I did the right thing. He also told me never to say anything until spoken to out in the hall. He even winked at me and told me to 'hang in there'. He seems to be smarter than Jack. But why did you blurt out loud a question about Mr. Tips when we could talk about that anytime, like now. Is your back bleeding? Do you want me to go with you and put some salve on it?"

"Wilson is alright, he gave me, you'll never believe this and don't say a word about this to anyone, but Wilson only gave me five soft little taps on the butt."

"It didn't hurt?"

"No, not at all, but I'm not supposed to talk about it."

Tubbs pushed Jape out in the floor as George came by, saying, "It's time to go to class, you ready to go, Jape?" George was speaking with a lot of human compassion in his voice because he knew the Donkey Hide very well!

On the way to class, Jape asked George, "Why did they put you in here?"

"That is a short story that I was going to tell you." They had to walk across to another building and George continued to talk, "I was born in Arkansas, lived there all my life. My uncle lives here in Pauls Valley. There wasn't anyone my age in the family, so my uncle dropped me off at the Sun Theatre. I was alone on the front row. There was a purse on the floor about two seats over. No one was sitting close and I opened the purse. It had one dollar and thirteen cents in it."

"Was there a name or . . .?"

"No, nothing or nothing like that. There was a handkerchief, fingernail file and stuff like that. I took the money, what can I say, I did. It was more money than I have ever seen. I went to the front office and asked if anyone had reported losing a purse. The lady said, 'no' and that is when I took the money. I walked back into the theatre, put the purse back on the seat and walked out the door with the money. I didn't get a block from the theatre when a police car pulled up. The lady at the theatre was with the policeman, she pointed to me shouting, 'That's him, that's the boy'. Well, that purse belonged to the judge's daughter and the rest is history. They called me a thief and stuck me in here. My folks had to go home without me."

"We got acquainted with that same judge but we were guilty."

"What did you do that was so bad to get you in here?", George asked.

"We were stealing insulators", Tubbs answered.

"Insulators, what's that and why would you steal that for?"

"We were kinda like you, we were stealing but then again we didn't mean to be stealing anything. My uncle said they were not being used, they were being replaced. The workers took the old insulators off and threw them on the ground. My uncle said he would trade us a .22 shell for each insulator we could find. Oh, an insulator is those glass things that hold the telephone wire on the poles."

"You got a .22?", George inquired.

"Tubbs does, but a lot of good it will do us now."

"How long are they going to keep you in here?"

"They didn't tell us nothing, just hauled us in."

"Did you go to court, you know talk to the judge?"

"Yea, we talked to the judge, or the sheriff did. We didn't get to say anything. He didn't act like we had any say in the matter."

"I only got one year, and I get out in a few days." They walked into the classroom and the conversation stopped.

The teacher was a large woman with a pleasant but gruff disposition. Like Mrs. Auld, she was older, about 35, and was all business. She gave the boys their books: spelling, arithmetic, geography and a reader. The only difference, they would not have any homework as all their work would be done in class. Across the room on the front row sat Fred. At first Jape didn't notice him but when he did he giggled out loud and immediately clapped his hand over his own mouth as the teacher asked, "What is so funny? Please share it with the rest of the class so we can all have a laugh."

Jape obliged, "Yes, ma'am, yesterday Fred," Jape pointed across the room at Fred then continued, "told me he was in the sixth grade. I just saw him and was surprised and for some reason thought it was funny."

With Jape's sincerity and obviously truthful answer several of the boys laughed.

"That's enough, it may be funny to you but to Fred it isn't funny. The real sad part about that statement is that the rest of you will be in the sixth grade next year. The way it looks now, Fred will still be in the fifth grade next year. You should learn a lesson from this and settle down to your studies instead of creating problems."

At recess the teacher went outside with the boys. George and another boy carried the five bats, one softball, two gloves and a catcher's mask. The catcher and the first baseman would be the ones lucky enough to use gloves. They played work up and the teacher was the umpire. Jape and Tubbs enjoyed the game as all the boys got along well excepting Fred. He seemed to have problems with everyone. Once when Jape was playing first base, George caught a ground ball Fred had hit and threw Fred out. Jape caught the ball about two steps ahead of Fred. It wasn't close, the teacher shouted, "You're out." Fred stopped and stood on the bag for a few moments telling Jape the next time he didn't drop the ball he was going to punch his lights out. He had several other mean nasty things to say but he said them too low for anyone else to hear. Jape tossed the glove to the next player and "worked up" to pitcher, leaving Fred standing on first base talking to himself.

The sun was hot and the boys were allowed to get a drink of water before returning to the classroom. The teacher was supervising the boys as they drank. The boys walked down the hall toward the classroom as she went into the room marked "Employees" which contained a toilet for the female employees. Fred ran over, pushed Jape from behind causing him to fall into George.

Fred said, "You dirty, ugly baboon." He swung at Jape with his fist but Jape dodged and Fred missed. Jape pushed him backward. Fred hit the wall and rushed back at Jape swinging wildly. Jape punched at Fred a couple time and the two boys started slugging it out. Without exception every boy there was shouting for Jape.

Several of the boys jumped around asking, "What's the new boy's name."

Tubbs shouted, "Jape, Jape, get'im, Jape."

All the boys started in, "Get'im, Jape — Get'im, Jape."

Fred grew up on the streets getting knocked around all his life but Jape had never had a fight. Fred was getting the better of the fight but Fred wasn't too sure about that. The teacher ran out about the same time as two men came from the other direction. All the boys went back to class except Jape and Fred, they were off to The Skinning Room.

George and Tubbs looked at each other with total understanding. They were hurting for Jape. The teacher gave them a five minute lecture on rules and the reason for rules. She tried to explain to the boys that there was a good reason for all the rules. They had to enforce discipline at the institution. Fighting was against the rules.

Tubbs asked, "Why don't they ask who started the fight and punish the boy that caused the trouble?"

"Sometimes, especially here, boys will lie or a bigger or stronger boy or boys as a group will frame up on an innocent boy to get him punished. When they punish both boys, everytime, without exception, the guilty boy does get punished. Yes, the innocent boy gets his licks, too, but when you learn that fighting doesn't accomplish anything you will not fight back. If you get hit, turn the other cheek and you will not get punished."

The teacher continued, "This is the period for silent studying but under the circumstances we will do something different today, let's have a spelling bee."

She divided the boys into two groups, one group lined up on one side of the room and the other against the opposite wall. She picked up the speller, explaining they would spell only those words they learned during this summer term and the same words Mrs. Auld had taught last fall at Crossroads. When a boy misspelled a word he had to sit down. The boys did surprisingly well. She went down the line twice before a boy had to sit down. Three boys sat down on "accept", two for the other team and one on Tubbs and George's team. The very next word was "accomplish" and another boy on the opposing team sat down but George spelled it correctly. The next word was "empathy" which put every boy down until Tubbs spelled it correctly and the boys shouted their appreciation.

The entire class was cheering for Tubbs when Jape and Fred were returned to the class room. Immediately, the jubilant atmosphere switched, and as the teacher watched their expressions change, she spoke, "Most of you didn't know how to spell the word 'empathy' but your expression as a class, right now, is a fine example of the true meaning of the word. We will discontinue the spelling and get back to reading. Please start reading on page 47 and read until the bell rings for recess. That chapter will be a topic for the class to discuss when we return.''

Jape turned to page 47 but he could not concentrate on the words. His back burned, and pain throbbed from five spots on the inside of his ribs where the end of the Donkey Hide snapped around his body jerking a piece of flesh out each time. The area across his back where the leather had hit blistered the hide but that pain had nearly disappeared. Several minutes had passed and Jape was still looking at page number forty seven. His eyes could see the words but his mind could not comprehend. The day was getting hot. Jape wasn't sweating but something hot was running down his right side. He ran his left hand through the front of his shirt to feel the wounds under his arm. He pulled his hand out to see blood on his fingertips and on hearing Tubbs groan, realized he had also seen the blood. At that moment the bell rang and everyone got up to leave the room for recess.

The teacher offered the red salve to Fred but he shook his head and ran out the door, nearly knocking George down in getting through the door. She approached Tubbs, ''You boys should take a break.'' She gave Tubbs some of the red salve for Jape's wounds and continued to speak, ''Go to the lavatory, take care of his back, then come on out to the ballfield. Will you do that?''

Tubbs answered, ''Yes, ma,am.''

The boys went into the lavatory, Jape was taking the shirt off before the door closed. Tubbs was gritting his teeth because he knew the pain Jape was suffering. Tubbs rubbed his back with the red salve and put a large glob on the nasty cuts on the inside of his right rib cage where the end of the Donkey Hide jerked the hide off. Jape was feeling a little better as he put his shirt back on to go pay softball.

Suddenly, the door burst open and in walked Fred and a big boy about fourteen.

Fred spoke through clenched teeth, ''That's them, the two I was telling you about. That one,'' pointing to Jape, ''caused me to get the Donkey Hide just now. Let's kill'em both.''

He headed for Jape as the big boy hit Tubbs in the nose. The blow knocked Tubbs back against the wall causing blood to gush from his nose. The lad slid down the wall crashing to the floor in a daze. He could see but he couldn't move.

Jape was paralyzed by fear when he saw the blood streaming from Tubbs face. While Jape stood frozen, Fred hit Jape and they crashed together to the floor. They rolled around on the floor with Jape trying to get loose until the big boy grabbed Jape, pulled him away from Fred to hit him in the face and knocked him against the wall. Jape's mouth and nose bled profusely, his mind was reeling but his body wasn't feeling any pain.

Fred's words snapped in his mind, "Let's kill'em both."

Jape thought he was going to die, they were trying to kill him. His mind and body came together in a rush of adrenaline. Instead of trying to get away, he ran at the big boy, tackled him around the waist and knocked him back against the wall. Jape was screaming at the top of his lungs, like a tiger possessed. He moved up the boy's body biting, scratching, clawing while screaming like a wild animal. His teeth lashed out at the boy's chest like Mr. Tips shaking a snake. Only the shirt kept him from pulling the flesh from the body. The larger boy tried to get away but Jape's fingers were clawing at his eyes as his strong sharp teeth sank into the boy's neck ripping the tender flesh away. In a frenzy of rage, he bit half the boy's right ear off and spit it back into his face. The big boy was in extreme pain, he had never seen or heard of anyone fighting like a wild animal, his lungs nearly burst from screaming for Fred to, "Pull'im off, pull'im off, pull'im off." Fred responded to the boys pleas for help and jumped in to pull Jape off. As Jape's teeth slashed at the boy's face and neck, Fred managed to pull him loose but Jape's fury did not calm, it was only transferred, he ran at Fred with the same inferno of violence grabbing him by the right arm with both hands, Jape spun to whipslam Fred back against the wall then tackled him as he bounced off the wall. They crashed to the floor with Jape on top, acting like a wolf or Mr. Tips, he started biting, slicing and jerking chunks from Fred's face, neck and ear with his teeth. The big boy had blood all over him when he jumped up still screaming, he shoved Jape aside, grabbed Fred by the arm to pull him away from Jape and dragged him out the door.

The fight was over and Jape and Tubbs were alone in the restroom. Jape, half-crazed from fear and exhaustion, stood gasping for breath in the middle of the room staring at the battered face of Tubbs.

Tubbs broke the silence, "You told me you could do anything those city boys could do, only better, NOW I believe you. We better wash our faces and get cleaned up. We're both on the way to The Skinning Room now."

"You're bleeding, are you okay?", Jape asked.

"No, I'm not okay, but I'll live. You got blood all over the front of your shirt and you look like hell. Is that your blood? Are you sure you're okay?"

"Let's wash our face and see if we'll live", Jape suggested.

They washed and neither boy had a scratch showing. Both boys had a smashed nose. Tubbs's felt as if it was broken and Jape had a bruised cheek and nose. Most of the blood was from Fred and the big boy.

"Why don't you wash the blood out of your shirt right quick?"

Jape pulled the shirt off, stuffing it into the sink and turning the cold water on when a man stepped into the room, "What are you two doing in here?"

"The teacher said we could come in here and put some salve on these."

Jape turned to show the man the marks made by the Donkey Hide. The fellow who was one of those that watched the boy get the skinning, continued to ask, "What are you doing with your shirt in the sink?"

Jape turned to show him the bloody marks on his right rib cage. "I got blood on my shirt and didn't want to ruin the shirt."

"Did you hear anyone screaming up here?" The boys looked at each other and the man continued, "You just left The Skinning Room, you surely don't want to go back this quick?"

He was interrupted by a second man who stuck his head into the room, "I found'em, come on. It's Fred and his big brother. They've been fighting each other again. You gotta see this, looks like they ate each other up."

The boys could hear the two men laughing as they walked down the hall. The boys burst out laughing, butted heads and did a 'melonshake'.

Right in the middle of the handshake George stuck his head in the door to see the two boy's secret shake.

He asked, "What are you doing?"

They continued to laugh, they had just pulled the caper of the year and beat the 'Grim Reaper' out of a skinning. This was a good reason to laugh but they really didn't understand exactly why they were laughing. They felt good and everything happening was funny.

"The teacher sent me in to check on you guys. We heard screams, but the teacher couldn't hear them. You guys know anything about that?"

"We'll tell you about that later. Tell her we'll be right out, I'm washing the blood out of my shirt."

"Okay, but hurry or she's going to call recess off for all of us."

Jape wrung most of the water from his shirt and put it on wet. Some of the bloodstains were gone, those remaining were not obvious. They ran out to the ballfield smiling from ear to ear. Any other time, Jape would have been crying from the pain with wounds like that on his back, at that moment he felt good about himself. Without Fred around the game was going very well. The boys were enjoying themselves. Jape caught a flyball and traded places with the batter. He was waiting his turn to bat when a fowl ball went flying over the back stop into a little ditch.

Another boy went after the ball and Jape asked the teacher, "Where's Fred?"

The teacher put her finger over her lips and whispered, "He asked permission to go see the doctor. He must be hurting from the Donkey Hide." She looked around to see if any other boys could hear and in the same low tone asked, "How are you feeling?"

Jape smiled, "I've been better, but I'm all right."

George was up next and he hit a long foul ball back behind the back stop. Jape ran after it, dashing across an open area with mowed grass then some tall grass between the school ground and a creek. Across the creek was a two strand barbed wire fence and then a cornfield. Jape ran up the creek and nearly stepped on a cottonmouth, he jumped sideways giving out with a little shout, "Look out, you devil, you.", and continued on to get the softball and toss it back into the game. Everyone was watching him as they only had the one ball. When he got back it was his turn to bat. He got a hit and George knocked him home.

While waiting for someone to chase down George's long hit, the teacher asked Jape, "What did you see out there that caused you to jump and shout."

Jape replied, "A snake, a cottonmouth."

"A Cottonmouth Water Moccasin, are you sure it was a Water Moccasin this close to the school?"

"Yes, ma,am, I've seen lots of cottonmouths", Jape told her.

"After recess, would you show it to me."

"Haven't you ever seen one?"

"No, and I would like to be able to recognize one, if I saw it."

"Don't worry, teacher, if you ever see one you'll know its bad by the way it looks. It is deadly, it looks deadly and you'll know it, too."

"That bad, huh?", the teacher shivered at the thought of the snake.

"I'll go get it and bring it over here", Jape volunteered.

"No, no, no, don't you touch such a deadly thing."

The bell rang and the teacher blew her whistle waving all the boys over to the backstop, "Boys, how many of you know what a deadly snake looks like?"

About half the boys held up their hands as she continued, "The rest of you may be able to learn something in a few minutes. Jape just saw a deadly poisonous snake, A Cottonmouth Water Moccasin, over by the creek. You follow me. Please stay on the trail, Jape will find the snake and point it out to us. Do not, and I repeat, do not get close to the snake."

They walked across the little creek into the tall grass with Jape about ten yards out in front.

A few steps up the creek, Jape stopped and pointed to a small Willow bush, "Look at the bottom of that Willow."

A snake was stretched out on a dead limb at the base of the bush. Jape walked a little farther, picked up a stick and poked at the snake which prompted the teacher to say:

"Jape, leave it alone, it might run this way."

"I wanted you to see it's head."

The snake coiled and raised its head.

"Oh, my, I see what you mean. They do look nasty, let's get out of here. You boys head for the classroom."

They had one more hour of class before lunch. The teacher was a nice lady who made learning fun. All the boys were enjoying the class with Fred gone. No one had said anything, but as they walked from the classroom back to their living area, George did,

"It was a pleasure to have a class without that stupid Fred. He's such a pain in the butt, wonder what happened to him?"

Tubbs burst out laughing, "You will never believe this but Jape went crazy and whipped both Fred and his big brother. He ate'em up."

"I was wondering what happened to me. I was so scared, I guess I WAS crazy. I thought that big guy was going to kill and eat me."

"What are you talking about, what happened?"

Tubbs told him the story and asked, "Will Fred get the Donkey Hide again?"

"Not likely, they'll put him in lockup. They have a room or two in first building, I never been there, but when the Donkey Hide don't work they lock them away from the rest of us. A few days in there, without anyone to talk with, well, I understand they usually change their mind to get out."

"Like jail", Jape asked.

"I guess so, I never been in jail", George answered.

"What, we are all in jail right now", Tubbs informed both boys.

"No, we're not. This is a boy's school", Jape said hopefully.

"Well, I guess, you're both right. We're in jail but they can't lock us kids away like they do the adults. They call it a "school", sounds better."

Jape changing the subject, "What do we do now?"

"In a few minutes we go to eat lunch, if you want to. At lunch time you can stay in your bunk if you want but you have to go through the line at breakfast and supper."

"Do we get to play outside?", Jape asked as he liked to be outdoors.

"Yea, we can go outside for two hours each afternoon. There's not much to do but play ball."

"I'd rather be outside, anything other than being inside all time."

"Sometimes I take a library book and lie in the shade and read."

"You read Jack London's books?"

"He wrote 'Call of The Wild', didn't he, yea, I like his books."

"Yea, he makes reading fun."

"Speaking of fun, will lunch be any fun?", Tubbs asked.

"Not if Jape don't keep his mouth shut."

All three boys laughed and they walked on into the living area in silence.

They washed up and waited for lunch. Jack was back on duty and as usual he was sitting in the room reading a dime store novel. All of the boys in the room seemed a little more relaxed without Fred being in the room. George told one or two what had happened, the word got around that Jape had whipped him good.

Jape and Tubbs were lying on their bunks, Jape being in the top one was looking at the ceiling, said, "Wonder why flies walk on the ceiling upside down?"

"Because they don't have legs on their back, you dummy. They are so light that gravity don't bother them."

"Not either, if they turned loose they would fall off. I'll bet they have little hands and hold on to the ceiling. They got so many legs that they can walk upside down. I seen a boy walk on his hands once."

"Out on the creek we can sit around and watch the grass growing or the creek flow. In here we don't have anything to do but watch the flies crawl around on the ceiling. We are really in trouble", Tubbs exclaimed.

Jape shouted, "There's a dead skunk lying in the road, I one'it."

Tubbs answered, "I two'it."

"I three'it."

George butted in, "I four'it."

"I five'it", Tubbs said.

Jape, "I six'it."

George, "I seven'it."

"I jumped over it and Jape ate it. Jape ate the old dead skunk."

"Darn you, George, you jumped in too quick."

Jack ran around the corner blowing on the whistle, it was time for lunch. Lunch was a bowl of what could be called "vegetable soup" and a chunk of hard bread. It was nourishing and filling but one bowl wasn't enough to fill up an active nine year old. The boys would make do until supper.

On returning to their bunks, Jape asked George, "What do we do now?"

"Everyone goes outside for two hours."

"We have to go outside?", Tubbs asked.

"Yep, they lock the building and you have to go play, read or do whatever you want to. As Tubbs said, you can sit and watch the grass grow."

"Good, wonder how long we have to be in this stupid place. They told you but they didn't tell us anything", Jape griped.

"Wonder when my mom will come see me? She may disown me and never come see me. I won't blame her if she does."

"Yea, seems odd that my dad didn't come down here madder than an old wet hen. Without me, he'll have to milk all three cows by himself and turn the cream separator. Yep, he'll be down here and then I'll really catch it. Now, I can't go home, I'll be the disgrace of the neighborhood."

"Well, there is another way to look at it. When you get back home, if you ever do, I'll bet you can boast about having been someplace none of your friends or relatives have ever been", George commented.

"Yea, but who would boast about being in reform school?",Tubbs asked.

"It was just a thought, just a thought", George laughed.

"We can do that anyway. We've been to Witch-a-paw, Kansas."

"It's Wichita, and we can't talk about that, either", Tubbs explained.

"How did you go to Wichita?", George wanted to know.

George and several of the boys walked over to listen to Jape and Tubbs tell about their train ride. For the first time, they could tell someone else about their trip to Wichita. The story, amidst much bragging and boasting on the part of Tubbs and Jape, was finished under a shade tree immediately after the two hour recess started. Several of the boys followed the three boys outside to get to hear the remainder of the story. When the story was finished the boys continued to talk but nothing to talk about as exciting as the train ride to Wichita.

The afternoon was getting hot, the south breeze was nice but the boys were bored nearly to the point of tears.

Jape asked, "No way to sneak off and go swimming, I suppose?"

"Well, most of us feel a swim isn't worth the Donkey Hide. The river is too far to get to and the only pond isn't all that great to swim in. Some of the boys have sneaked off to explore and made it back without getting caught. When Jack is on duty, we can do nearly anything, if we're careful. When his relief is on duty, we don't dare. That guy counts heads about every thirty minutes. The Donkey Hide ain't worth it", George explained.

"Do you guys ever get to eat a watermelon?", Jape asked.

"Nope, you kidding, I haven't had a melon in four years", a boy said.

"There's a large patch about half mile from here", George pointed in the general direction of the watermelon patch.

Which prompted Jape to ask, "Which direction?"

George pointed to the cornfield behind the ballfield, "Over that way, but it ain't worth it to me. My hide don't look good with stripes. Only a skunk or a leopard looks good with stripes."

"Leopard's have spots not stripes", one of the boys corrected.

"Some have stripes, but I'll change it to zebra, okay?"

"Yea, zebra is fine, they got stripes." "If I told you how you could eat watermelon without getting the Donkey Hide, would you be interested?"

"Sure, only an idiot wouldn't be", George answered.

"You're going to get it again, Jape, what're you thinkin?", Tubbs reminded.

Jape looked at George and asked as he pointed to an old building in back of the playground, "What is that building?"

"A tractor and tools are in there, it's nothing. Well, it's what we hide behind when we sneak out into the corn field. They watch it pretty good but Jack don't watch anything."

"The little creek runs right behind that building and the corn field?"

He made a statement but it was a question for George, who answered, "Yes, that's right, but it isn't much of a creek. There is a spring up by the ball field where you found the cottonmouth. This time of year the water is about all gone by the time it gets down to the building, the soil is only a little wet. Why do you ask about that?"

"Okay, that's perfect", Jape stated.

He looked around at the boys seated on the ground next to him.

"I'll run the risk of the Donkey Hide but wouldn't ask you guys to take a chance. Is there anyone here that feels they could go into the cornfield and get back on the playground with getting caught?"

Every boy there held up their hand except Tubbs, who was grinning and shaking his head.

Then Jape continued, "Okay, would any one of you be willing to go with me to the watermelon patch. You know that would be a bigger risk than just going into the cornfield. The only reward would be getting to eat your fill of watermelon."

"But how will that help the rest of us get some melon?"

"I have a plan to bring some back but we can't all go. Even Jack would miss half of us but he might not notice two or us being gone", Jape told him.

"Okay, I haven't had the Donkey Hide in awhile, I'll go", George agreed.

At the same time three more boys volunteered to go but Jape told them they could take part in the plan once they got back. As they started to leave one other boy put up a howl to go with them. He didn't care about the Donkey Hide, he wanted to get away for some melon. The boy was a rather quiet lad, built strong and Jape felt he could pack a pretty good-sized melon.

"Okay, but you have to follow my lead and don't do anything stupid."

Tubbs butted in, "Yea, like leave the playground to steal melons." All the boys laughed and Jape continued, "Okay Tubbs, it'll be your job to keep an eye out for Jack while we're gone. If he comes out asking about either one of us, tell him we went to play ball, to the toilet or anything. If we're missed while we're gone, you stand up and stay standing up. If he don't come out, you remain seated in the shade. This way we'll know how we stand when we get back to the cornfield."

"For once, I do agree, you have a good thought there", Tubbs admitted.

"Remember, you guys will get melon without any risk", Jape told them.

He turned to George and continued, "Will anyone see us if we just walk over to the shed."

"Unlikely, Jack is supposed to be watching us but he's inside."

"Hope, hope , hope, well, here goes, brother." He slapped Tubbs on the shoulder and the three boys walked off toward the shed.

Fred had been a troublemaker since he came into Jack's unit. The best news Jack had had in a long time was learning that Fred was in lockup. With that bit of information, he knew he could relax and enjoy an afternoon of reading and relaxation. The twenty boys under his direct supervision were not a problem when Fred was gone. The supervision Jack provided was one trip to look out the door and twice he stood up to look out the window at the boys playing softball. This was more of an effort to stretch his legs and rest his eyes at the end of a chapter rather than any sincere concern for the well-being of his charges.

The three boys ran down the long rows that led out of the cornfield into a pasture. They could see the melon patch down the hill below the pasture. The watermelon patch was a big one covering at least two acres. George and the other boy pulled two from the vine.

Jape stopped them. "No, NO, don't pull them from the vine. Here, let me show you."

He walked around looking for a couple of big ones close together. When he found them he shouted, "I'll show you what we're going to do." He dug around the roots and pulled the large vines out by the roots. The soil was sandy and loose, making that task very easy.

Then Jape said, "Now, we carry the vine and all the melons on the vine. Let's see how many is on this one? We're going to have our very own watermelon patch, right there at school."

He pulled the vine free and the runners were ten feet long. "Great, this one has nice long runners and two large melons."

"We going to carry the vine, too?", George wanted to know.

"Yep, looks like two vines may be enough to get us four melons and that should be enough for a nice feed for everyone. Of course, we'll have to eat all the meat, not just the heart, like Tubbs and I usually do."

The boys made their first trip across the cornfield with two melons in such good time that they returned for the second and third. On looking at the playground, Tubbs was still seated in the shade.

Jape laughed, "Okay, let's get them behind the shed."

"Let's eat one first", George suggested.

The other boy, "Yea, let's eat one."

Jape opened one that was already off the vine. They sat down in the hot cornfield and ate it. It was a large sweet melon, the boys giggled and grabbed handfuls of heart. In fifteen minutes, they had eaten their fill of melon. They carried the three huge vines to the edge of the field before crossing the opening to the shed. On crossing the opening they were at risk. All three boys were necessary to carry two large melons attached to a vine with four or five runners with small melons attached. Three trips and a few minutes later all three vines were behind the shed.

"Now, it's time to make our watermelon patch." He told George to dig a hole in one place, the other boy at another damp stop and Jape dug the third hole for transplanting the roots. The melon plants would stay green for a little while but their root system would not realistically survive such a transplant. Jape's idea was to fool Jack long enough to feed all the boys some melon. The fact that they would be eating stolen watermelon in the reform school enhanced the flavor. The boys extended the green vines through and around some tall Johnson grass, laying the watermelons in a natural position. Jape backed up and did a visual inspection, he had seen numerous watermelon patches in his young life and these three vines did look real. The melons and the vines were so laid out that they would provide the immediate appearance that they grew there to anyone just walking by. Jack being a city boy, would not be that hard to fool. Jape only wanted four melons but the plan worked so well they ended up with six big ones.

Jape checked the area between the shed and the cornfield, the ground was so hard they didn't leave any tracks. The job was accomplished, they had their own watermelon patch. The three boys ran across the field from the shed to the shade where Tubbs was still seated.

Jape asked, "Did you see Jack while we were gone?"

"Nope, haven't see anyone. Where's ours, I see you have juice all over your clothes. You guys cheated, you ate one in the patch, didn't you?"

"Sure, but we did the work, too. Now, it's time for you guys to do your part. Which one of you wants to go tell Jack about planting seeds to grow these things?" He turned to look at George, "Is there a rule about planting watermelon seeds?"

"Don't know, I've read all the rules and never saw one."

"I'll tell him I did it, how did I do it? What does a watermelon seed look like?", one of the boys inquired.

"Anyone of you guys ever plant a garden, pumpkins or watermelons?"

"No wonder you're in here, you never had to work in your life."

"I'm not stupid, I ate watermelon and spit the seeds out. Do you simply plant the seed and the plant comes up?", another boy volunteered.

"You got it, you got it, here is our farmer. Don't volunteer any information. Go in there and tell Jack you planted some seeds last spring and forgot about it."

"When did I plant the seeds?"

"He won't ask but if he does, last spring."

"Where did I get the seed?"

"You found them in a garbage can. It don't matter, he won't ask you anything. You go in there shouting that "we", us bad boys, have found your melon patch and are eating your melons. Jack'll come storming out with you and when you show'm your patch, he'll let everyone eat one and probably join us in doing so."

"Yea, tell him he can have one, too", George told him as he walked off.

Tubbs joined the other three boys to run behind the shed. Tubbs was very impressed with the watermelon patch. They took the melon not attached to a vine and returned to the shade. On walking across the yard with the huge melon they were spotted by the boys playing softball and needless to say the sight of a large watermelon broke up the softball game. There wasn't time to cut the melon, Jape dropped it on purpose causing it to burst open. Several boys grabbed pieces and started stuffing their faces. Jape looked at Tubbs, who grinned as both boys leaned forward to butt heads and do their 'melonshake'. The other boys didn't pay much attention, it was their first watermelon in a long time and two crazy boys wasn't uncommon.

The boys were swallowing their first bite of melon as Jack and the 'watermelon planter' ran out the door barely missed colliding with the boys coming from the softball field. This started Jack to screaming and his shouts slowed the boys down to a fast walk.

Jack got to the shade where they were eating watermelon to say, "Okay, the six of you are in trouble."

"Jack, I don't mind them eating one. I have plenty for all of us."

"Where did you grow this thing?", Jack wanted to know.

"Follow me",the farmer boy said as he turned to walk toward the shed.

The boy walked away with Jack following and fifteen boys on Jack's heels. When they arrived at the shed the boy stopped. He wasn't sure if Jack would know what a watermelon vine looked like or even how they grew. He pointed to the watermelon patch. "See, I have some real good ones but since those guys found them it ain't fair if we don't get to eat some, too. I did so want to surprise you."

"Well, well, those do look like good melons. You picked a good spot to plant them. This is good sandy soil and with all the moisture, a perfect place to grow melons. There's nothing in the rules that says we can't grow our own watermelons. You boys grab those big ones and lets go join the other boys. For once, it looks like you fellows did something right."

Jack picked up one of the larger melons and walked toward the building. He turned to shout over his shoulder, "You boys divide those up and put the rind in the garbage." He didn't bother to say what he was going to do with the one he was taking inside. Someone suggested he was going to share with some of the other employees but for some reason George and Jape had their doubts about that.

Jape and George were full of watermelon and volunteered to carry the rinds to the garbage. It didn't take long for seventeen boys to eat five watermelons. On the second trip to the garbage can Jape spotted a red anthill.

Jape took a small coffee can and dug out a large hole in the soft ant-hill. In the hole he buried a gallon can so the top of the can was level with the top of the ground. An ant would walk off into the can but could not get out. He left the can and the boys went on back to play.

George asked, "What are you catching those ants for?"

"Oh, its better than watching the flies walk on the ceiling. I don't know but with your help we'll come up with something."

"Another way to get the Donkey Hide."

"Is it against the rule to play on an ant hill?"

George laughed as they ran back for the last load of rinds for the garbage. The bell rang. "Nope, never saw such a rule but I don't think they ever planned on having such a boy as you in here either."

Chapter 9
The Snake Bite

The boys had to go inside for the remainder of the day. Some were assigned to work details or given chores to do. Two days a week they were allowed to go to the library where they could read, write or do other things. Two or three boys had coloring books but only four crayons. There wasn't much else to do but lie on the bunk and worry about growing up without ever going swimming again, which was exactly what Jape and Tubbs were doing. They had been placed on a roster for work but the school had too many boys for the jobs available. Without exception, none of the new boys wanted to work, and only after getting into serious trouble or crying day after day from boredom did they accept the responsibility of working. These two boys didn't mind the work, they were accustomed to working at home. For the first time in their lives, they were awakened to the realization of the wonderful things at home. Things which they had largely taken for granted and never once stopped to think of as beautiful. The two boys, Jape and Tubbs, were now suffering the first pangs of homesickness.

They had been lying on the bunk staring into space for a few minutes when Tubbs spoke, "Wonder if we are bad boys?"

"How could you, well yes, I guess some people might think that."

"Look at us, we are lying without crossing our fingers. We say and hear dirty words without considering it wrong."

"We never been in a place like this either."

"Yep, I'm hungry all the time. Wouldn't it be nice to hear your mom shout at you. You know, I would enjoy hearing mine scream at me for any reason. It'd just be nice! I would like to see my mom, how about you?''

''I wouldn't gripe about having to milk and do all the chores if I could sleep in my own bed and eat my mom's breakfast again. Ooooh, to get some of her hot biscuits, butter and a tall glass of milk. I would even let dad sleep in and do all the chores.''

''I'll bet you would run instead of 'dragging butt' as your dad is always screaming at you. Yep, if I ever get a chance to hug my mom again, it will be with a completely different feeling, you know what I mean?''

''And to think I used to complain when mom told me to wait for supper or get a glass of milk, a biscuit and piece of bacon when I came in hungry after school. Boy, oh, boy, wouldn't I love to get into grandmaw's biscuits and bacon right now!''

''How about some of those frog legs?''

''Or chicken fried squirrel, hot biscuits and cream gravy?''

''I could enjoy a cold biscuit and sausage like your aunt gave us!''

''I guess our thrashing dinners are gone for this year. I didn't realize I liked milk so much, wonder why they don't get a cow here.''

''Thrasher dinners, you're making my mouth water. I remember those, we better quit thinking about eating or my saliva glands will drown me.''

There was a long silence as the summer's events, both good and bad, were relived in their mind. Each boy went over every detail in his own way.

Jape spoke, ''This isn't right, I'm going home. My dad won't let them keep me in here and treat us like this. I never thought about it before. They can't do this to us.''

''What do you mean they can't, they are, we're here aren't we?''

''Yep, and as my grandpaw used to say when the cold north wind blew in a blizzard, 'there's nothing between us and the North Pole but a barbed wire fence'. The same is true here but in our case the only thing between us and home is a two-wire fence. A barbed wire fence can't stop a blizzard from getting down here from the North Pole and a two-wire fence ain't gonna keep me away from my folks, either'', Jape was adamant in his thoughts and feelings at that moment.

''That would only get your dad in trouble. They would put him in jail too, but I still don't understand why my mom hasn't come to see me.''

''That is strange, my dad should be furious. If nothing else because I'm not home to do the milking. I thought he would tear the doors off this building to give me a spanking, if nothing else.''

''You think they're so disappointed they've disowned us?''

"My folks might disown me as a son but never as a worker. I'm too good at milking the cows and doing chores, they need me and right now I need them. I don't understand why and that leaves only one thing for me to do."

"What are you going to do?"

"I don't know how, but I'm going home. THAT I do know."

"How we going, just walk out and go home?"

"It was very plain in the rules. If we walk away, it's the Donkey Hide. Do you want to take a chance? I can go home and get dad and come back after you", Jape didn't like the thought of Tubbs getting the Donkey Hide.

"We came in together and we should go out together. We should have a plan, good planning is the key to success", Tubbs reminded Jape.

"I'm not sure how to get back to town from here. If we got lost we'll always end up at the river. All we have to do is follow the river to the bridge and then we know the way home."

"How do we avoid getting caught?"

"We could leave at night and no one could see us walking at night. The next day we'd be across the river and we can walk up the creeks without being seen."

"If we're spotted or caught, we get the hell beat out of us again."

"Or put into lockup with Fred."

"Oh, God, that isn't a good thought."

"Why don't we think of a way to get them to take us home! They drove us out here, let them drive us back."

"I like that idea, but how?"

"That, Sir Tubbs, is the question. Give it some thought."

The afternoon was getting hot and some of the windows were not open all the way. One of the boys shouted for Jape to open the windows on his side of the building. The boys made some noise raising the windows causing Jack to come out of the office to see what was going on. He stood in the middle of the hallway for a moment then walked over to ask Tubbs, "Your parents didn't know you were brought in here?"

"I don't know. What do you mean?", Tubbs asked.

"Didn't your parents go to court with you when . . .?"

"Nope, the sheriff picked us up on the road. They were to tell my mom but I don't know if they ever did", was Tubbs reply.

Jape jumped into the conversation, "What did you say?"

"I was concerned about your parents not knowing where you are."

"What d'ya mean?", Jape wanted to know.

"When you live so close, usually, the parents come by to visit."

"My mother would come by, too, if she knew, unless . . ."

"He thinks she's disowned'im", Jape told Jack.

"How many months do you boys have to stay?"

"They didn't tell us anything and we were afraid to ask. We were thinking about asking you", Tubbs continued the conversation.

"I don't have those records. That would be kept in the main office. Most of the boys here don't have a home. We have very few in here with a family on the outside. You two and George are a little different. From what I heard, the three of you are in here for engaging in criminal activity." That statement brought about a long moment of silence as Jack walked back into his little office.

What the boys didn't know would fill another book. The sheriff's office didn't inform their parents. Uncle John lived between Jape's home and the place where the boys were picked up by the sheriff. Mr. Tips chose to stop at Uncle John's rather than go on home without Jape. Uncle John thought the boys would be by in a day or two to get the dog. Each boy's parents thought their son was staying at the other boy's house.

Jape's thinking was about right, his dad didn't like the idea of Jape shirking his work on the farm. Milking and doing all Jape's chores one night wasn't a capitol offence but two days without his coming home was criminal. His dad raved for an hour about the punishment. He checked the Castor Oil, with plans of making Jape take a big dose before grounding him to bed for twenty-four hours. He laid out six months of chores to have him do before he could go hunting again. Finally, when Jape didn't show, he saddled the horse and rode off to look for the boys. He planned to send Tubbs home, give his son a sound spanking for disobeying the rules, then ground him for the rest of the summer and put him to work. When Dad rode past Uncle John's place Mr. Tips ran out toward the road. As the boys and the dog were always together, he rode into the yard expecting to find the two boys. After a short visit with Uncle John he left riding hard toward Tubbs' place, something was very wrong!

Jape's father and Tubbs's mother contacted everyone in the neighborhood but no one had seen the boys. The parents were relieved to learn the boys did not have the .22, it was still in Tubb's room. The parents feared the two boys may have returned to the river and either drowned, been kidnapped, or had met with foul play of some kind. All the terrible things that could have happened to Jape and Tubbs were considered as a possibility. As a last resort, they went to Paoli and called the sheriff's office. The sheriff's office took the information and advised them a report would be filed but could shed no light on the missing boys. No one at the sheriff's office knew anything. The sheriff was out of town for a Sheriff's conference in Oklahoma City and would not be back for two more days.

When the boys could not be found, it was apparent they had met with disaster or foul play and were lost and gone forever. The parents were slow to give up all hope of finding the boys alive. Uncle John contacted the newspaper for help and the two mothers turned to God. They asked everyone in the neighborhood to meet with them at the Crossroads school house for an all night prayer vigil. Charley and Maud came over from Paoli to lead the singing between prayers. Jape's dad didn't go to church very often and said a prayer even less frequently; however, he sat quietly on the back row with a glint of moisture in his eyes. His feelings WERE that the boys had BETTER be dead, if they showed up in GOOD health he WOULD kill them both.

Jape and Tubbs didn't have any idea what was going on at home. All they could do was make the best of a curve that life had tossed their way. The tedium was killing Jape, he finally got George and two other boys into a game of mumblety-peg. The knife would not stick into the wood floor as easily as the dirt but it worked very well. The boys had to throw the knife a little harder to get it to stick into the wood. They played for nearly an hour before Jack came out to investigate the unusual laughter. Once he saw them sticking the knife into the floor he made them discontinue the game, telling them it would ruin the floor.

Jape flopped back onto his bed as the other boys returned to their bunks. "The more I think about it, the better I like the idea", Tubbs whispered. "What's that?", Jape asked. "While you've been goofing off, I put together a plan of escape from this hellhole of starvation."

"Tell me about it and let's see how good it is."

"Your idea of walking all the way home is better than staying here and doing nothing. I don't like all the 'if's' involved with that. IF, we get caught, we get the Donkey Hide. There are so many ways of getting caught that our chances are not even fifty-fifty. Then, if we get home, the sheriff will probably come get us and put our parents in jail, too."

"Stop, stop, stop, don't tell me all that stuff. What is your plan?"

"I don't like the idea of walking. They drove out and picked us up, let's entice them to drive us back home. If they take us home, no one will come get us again. What do you think of that?"

"I like the idea but that's no plan. We're no better off than with my idea. The thing is figuring out how to do that."

"I know that, I'm not stupid. I have a plan!"

"Can't prove that by me and if you have a plan why didn't you tell me about the plan twenty minutes ago?"

"Relax, you're not going anywhere and I know you aren't taking medicine. We'll not rush into this and we can ride all the way home."

"I'm waiting, I'm waiting."

"We get bit by a cottonmouth and they take us home to die!"

"You've lost your mind, I'd rather be here than dead. I may get bit by one of those things someday but never in any lifetime will I volunteer to let one of those slimy things bite me."

"That's right. No one else would either. We don't really get bit, we make them think we were bit and they agree to take us home to die."

There was a long silence as Jape let that statement sink in. He sat up in bed, slapped his hands together and shouted, "You did it, you did it!"

His voice was so loud Jack came storming out of the office to shout, "What are you screaming about? Keep the noise down, we have a place for boys who like to shout. Unless you want to be locked in a padded, sound-proof room, hold your voice down to a whisper."

Jape crawled into the bunk, lying next to Tubbs so they could whisper. The old saying, "two heads are better than one" was never so true. Tubbs's idea was bisected and trisected as they tore it apart and rebuilt it time and time again. Finally they reached an agreement, and a tactical plan of action was adopted. They would find a snake at recess while chasing a foul ball, later the snake would be captured and held in a bucket until the afternoon break. The boys would let two red ants bite them on the leg, each bite about the same distance apart as the snake's fangs. They would use Jape's fish hook to puncture the center of the ant bite to provide the appearance of the snake's fangs. This, of course would be done immediately after lunch and before going out to play. Once the snake was killed all the boys had to do was start screaming and have George run to get Jack. He would see the dead snake and the boys would be taken to the doctor.

The idea appeared sound and they felt good about themselves. It was only a few minutes before they were to line up for chow when

Jape came up with what he thought was an improvement. Jape felt it would be better to get the snake bite in the presence of the teacher and all the students. "How you going to do that?", was the question presented by Tubbs.

"We get the ants to bite us before we go to class. I'm sure that snake is still in the area. I'll kick the snake and jump back sceaming and you will run by and grab your leg. They will see it all right there and we're home free, all we have to do is a little acting."

"Okay, and if that don't work we can follow up after lunch. That's good, we now have plan A and B. Now we make sure there ain't no flaws."

Jack blew the whistle for chow.

They had all they could eat for supper but it wasn't exactly what they were hoping for. What they got was boiled cauliflower, a large boiled potato with the peeling on and some green onions. George smiled and pointed to a large salt shaker, they could put some salt on the potato, no butter, but most of the food was cooked without seasoning, very bland. The salt made the large potato easier to swallow. The salt and the green onion were treats. They were so hungry the meal was almost good, they used the green onion to sop up the salt and ate it with the bread and potato. At home they would have fed everything but the onion and salt to the hogs.

The food would sustain life and was probably more than adequate for good health. These two boys missed more than the good taste and quality of the meals at home. There was something else lacking that they never talked about, either in the institution or at home. It was that thing no one can see but if it is there you know it. When it is really there, nothing needs to be said but it has a way of surfacing in everything that is said or done. Jape's parents were a fine example of the typical family, they seemed to make a point of never using the word but everything indicated that it was there. Jape's dad was a fine example, at meal time he didn't say much. He would look across the table at his son to ask little pointed questions, like, "How did you get that cut on your finger?"

Tubbs had taken the opportunity to explain how Jape stuck his finger in the turtle's mouth. That one question promoted a few minutes conversation as everyone laughed at Jape's expense. His mom would always come to his rescue by reaching over to wipe his hair out of his eyes or pat him on the shoulder. Even when they were scolding him for screwing up, or getting a spanking, never for a moment did he doubt that it wasn't there. This institution was not the same, just the opposite, they knew it wasn't there. It was "Love". A word Jape had heard in some old country songs but never from his parents. It was something he knew at home and was starving for now. It wasn't the lack of food they were hungry for, it was that thing called love. Jape pushed the last of bread and green onion in his mouth and looked over to see if Tubbs had finished. Tears were running down Tubbs's cheeks. The boys were so close that when tears ran down Tubbs face, Jape could also feel his anquish and a large lump developed in his throat. He couldn't talk but he could get Tubbs's mind off whatever it was that was causing the tears. Jape pushed his tray and bowl back and in an effort to place his spoon into the bowl it slipped from his hand, he juggled it as the spoon fell behind him on the floor. Jape fell off the bench in his effort to catch the spoon. There were several "loud" grins but nothing said as he got up and very sheepishly sat back down. At this time their table was released to leave the room, "the man" shook his finger at Jape who shrugged his shoulders in a helpless gesture.

Jape was anxious to get back to the room before Jack finished with his kitchen duties. The boys wandered back from chow without supervision. Jape immediately went into a game of leap frog to get Tubbs mind back on track, then he went to work. He ran out the back door and around the building with plans to get a few ants from the trap on the ant hill. They would need them tomorrow to carry out their escape attempt. He put a few ants into his tool box then changed his mind. He startled himself by laughing, looked around to see if anyone was around to hear him. He dumped the ants out of the tool box back into the gallon can and put the tool box back in his pocket. Instead of taking a few ants, he pulled the entire can of ants from the ant hill and ran back into the building. Inside Jack's office, he placed a book over the top of the can so the ants could not get out.

Jape was working as fast as he could, he took out his pocket knife, opened the extra sharp blade and cut a large deep notch on the inside of the back legs just below the seat of Jack's large chair. Enough wood was left to hold a person's weight if simply sitting down without moving around; however, if anyone tried to lean back in the chair, both back legs would break off. Once the notch was cut into each leg he moved the chair back where it was and cleaned up the wood chips. He noticed that Jack had half the watermelon sitting behind the door. Once more Jape chuckled to himself as he emptied the can of ants directly on top of the watermelon. Jape checked the room out, hiding the ant can in Jack's wastebasket and making sure all would be well later, then rushed out to jump into his bunk.

Jack came sauntering into the room smiling and even spoke to George. As he approached his office he saw the ants on the floor. He slowed to look down at thousands of ants covering the hall floor. He could not walk into the office without stepping on ants. Each step he took crushed about a hundred ants, the sound was that of someone walking on cracker crumbs.

Jack mumbled something, all that the boys could hear was, "Oh, my God, I didn't know red ants liked watermelon. I didn't know ants liked, darn I'm in trouble now, darn, how will I ever get'em out of here." A couple seconds later Jack went flying down the hallway. They thought he was gone when he reappeared to shout, "You guys stay in your bunk." Then he was gone again to reappear a short time later with the two men who had assisted with the Donkey Hide. One man had a bucket and the other a mop. The three men stopped to stand at Jack's door looking at the mess.

One of the men said, "We can't mop up ants." pulling the door open, while looking across at Jack he continued, "Where'd you get the water-melon?"

Jack answered, "Never mind, just clean up the ants."

The other man picked up the melon, wiped the ants off, winked at the other guy as he nodded his head for him to follow. They walked out the back door with the last half of Jack's watermelon.

Jack screamed, "Okay, okay, one of these days you guys will need a favor, I'll remember, I'll remember." Jack tried to sweep the ants up with a broom and a dust pan but the ants were crawling up the broom handle and stinging him on the arms before he could get the pan full of ants outside. The boys giggled when they heard one of the men, who obviously had a mouthful of watermelon tell Jack, "You better get those ants out of there, if Wilson comes by for a surprise inspection tonight he might decide to give you the Donkey Hide."

The other man followed up by saying, "You realize that eating watermelon on the school grounds is against the rules, unless it's on the menu for the boys."

The two men continued to give Jack a hard time and laugh at him until they finished eating the melon, then they left Jack with the ants. Jack used the broom to sweep them out the door but after three hours of sweeping it wasn't difficult to find an ant. Jape felt confident they would be able to find a few tomorrow morning for their snake bite routine.

Jape had passed the word along about the chair. The boys didn't want to miss out on getting the opportunity to see the crash. Usually most everyone was asleep when Jack's relief came on at midnight but without exception they were all wide awake tonight. They were lying in bed playing possum, looking and waiting and listening to every word they could hear, noting that Jack never bothered to mention anything about the ants in the office. Once Jack was gone, the old gent didn't change his routine, he pulled the chair out and sat down. When he sat down all the boys raised up a little but nothing happened. The old boy sat there for a few moments, crossed his legs and appeared to relax. Some of the boys were drifting off to sleep when the guard uncrossed his legs, leaned back in the chair as was his custom every night. Leaning back, he placed all his weight on the back legs of the chair, his arms outstretched in a deep satisfying yawn as both back legs snapped off the chair. The chair and the man went over backwards, he actually flipped over and slid a few feet down the hallway.

The quiet of the night was shattered by loud laughter. Every boy in the room was up on his elbow laughing. The old man didn't think the incident was all that funny. He jumped to his feet, brushing the dust from his clothing and for the first time noticed several ants on his clothing. He tried to put the chair back together by setting it up and putting the legs back in place, then he noticed that the legs had been cut. He threw the legs and the chair into the corner, blew his whistle to shout, "Fall out and line up. I'll give you something to laugh about. Get in line, get in line, and I mean NOW. I'll see to it that someone get's the Donkey Hide for this."

Jape and Tubbs tried to wipe the grin off as they jumped out of bed and stood in line in front of their bunk.

The old guy shouted, "Anyone want to tell me who did this?"

Jape spoke up, "I'd like to help if I can."

There were moans and sighs all up and down the line. Several of the boys thought Jape was going to confess and Tubbs thought he was crazy.

"You going to admit to doing this?", the old guard asked.

"No sir, but you asked if anyone knew what happened?."

"Yes, do you know who did it?"

"No one did it, sir, the ants came in to get the watermelon that Jack had in his office. Earlier tonight three of them worked for a long time but they couldn't get them out either."

"What are you talking about, what has a watermelon got to do with my chair legs being cut off?", the old gentlemen blurted.

"I'm sorry, sir, I thought you were talking about the ants."

"Watermelon, watermelon, who had a watermelon?"

"Jack had one in the office and the ants were attracted to it, I guess."

"Okay, that's enough of that, who cut the legs off my chair?"

"You should ask Jack, I only saw Jack and two other men in there."

"I don't buy that, one of you boys did this. Who has a pocketknife? I know one of you has a pocketknife." No one said a word as the old boy stormed up and down the room as if he thought someone would confess.

"Okay, no one is going to admit to owning a pocketknife, I'll find it and then you're in for big trouble."

He started searching their pockets, boy after boy, until he came to Jape. Tubbs's heart jumped into his mouth, he knew Jape was going to get the Donkey Hide again. Tears were about to flow when he glanced over to see Jape grin and wink. He didn't understand but the man searched everything and didn't find Jape's tool box. The old boy wasn't satisfied, he spent another hour tearing up their bunks, looking into the hollow legs of the metal beds. He shook out the blankets and sheets, checked the mattress and finally gave up.

"Sir, don't some of the fellows, you know guys that work here, play jokes on each other from time to time?", Jape asked with more than a little knowledge of expression on his face.

The fellow turned around to glare at the boy before he answered, "They're not supposed to, do you know something you're not telling me?"

"Sir, you work nights, we're asleep or in school most of the time when you're here. Jack and the other fellows are around all day. We hear them talk a lot but they also have more of an opportunity to give us the Donkey Hide. "Don't you see, we couldn't tell you if we did know something."

The man looked at the boy for several seconds with large question marks in the pupils of both eyes, turned to walk away mumbling, "You may be right, how stupid of me. I'll get even with those guys." He stopped to shout at the boys, "Get your bunks in shape and go to sleep," continuing to talk to himself, "I'll get even with Jack and those guys if it's the last thing I do." He walked down the hall to get an old folding chair to sit on. "These darn ants are crawling all over everything."

The boys worked at getting their beds made so they could go to sleep while the old boy was gone to get the chair.

Tubbs asked, "What happened to the Barlow?"

"I hid it, you dummy."

"That much I figured out, but where did you hide it?"

Jape stood up and smiled, "In a drawer in their office."

"You hid it in their office?"

"Sure, I figured they would search us but I didn't think he would go through the blankets and sheets. Dad used to say, 'when looking for something it will always be in the last place you look'."

"You dummy, when you find anything it is always in the last place you look, that's a joke."

"Oh, well, I didn't think they would search themselves and I was right."

"Okay, now, how are you going to get it back?"

"The same way I hid it, after breakfast tomar."

The hassle with the old man cost the boys a few hours sleep. Six came early the next morning, the boys dragged a little getting out of bed and their bunks made; however, they made it to chow with no problems. Breakfast always had been one of Jape's favorite meals and any meal had always been a good time for Tubbs. Breakfast on the farm was designed for the man of the house who worked from sun up to sun down, like Jape's dad. A man cannot work at hard physical labor for sixteen hours without plenty of good healthy food. Jape was accustomed to eating a hearty breakfast which generally included meat, eggs, and all the milk he could drink. The institution didn't serve any of those items, meat, eggs or milk. This was something he could not understand, the basic foods on the farm were not available here. The boys thought it was part of their punishment, when, in fact, the State of Oklahoma didn't have adequate funding to purchase expensive food items. The taxpayers were backed against the wall in those days, the average citizen didn't have the money to eat like those living on the farm who raised their own meat and grew their own vegetables. The two boys thought they were poor because money for shoes and over-alls were difficult to get. From conversations with other boys in the institution they learned that they were much better off than many who had shoes and clothing to wear.

Immediately after breakfast, Jape retrieved his possessions from the office. The boys all laughed while watching Jape and Tubbs do their 'melon shake'. Most of their mischievous deeds were played out in the open for all the boys to enjoy; however, their plan to escape was not. The two boys went into a huddle, Jape used a pencil taken from the office to make two dots on Tubbs's leg. Each dot would be the exact spot where the snake's fangs would hit. Jape had examined so many cottonmouth snakes that he had a fair idea of the distance between the fangs. Once the dots were made on each boys leg, ants were caught, and there were plenty of ants still lost and roaming about the room. Tubbs had the privilege of letting the ant sting Jape first. The red ant sting isn't something to be taken lightly, it hurts terribly and to some people it can be fatal. Tubbs gritted his teeth and held the ant on Jape's leg so the ant's stinger went directly into each dot, then Jape did the same for Tubbs. The ant sting started hurting and swelling immediately and this wasn't the end, they had to pierce the middle of the sting with the fish hook. The hook was pushed into the swollen flesh just deep enough to make it bleed. They didn't complete their project any too quickly as George came by to ask:

"What's going on, fellows?"

It was more difficult to talk while in pain than Jape thought but he managed to speak, "Not much George, not much."

Tubbs spoke up, "We want to get to the ballfield. That will take our mind off this place. We haven't got used to it like you have."

"No, that's where you're wrong. I'm not used to it either. I don't think anyone could get used to it", George told him.

That first hour in class was like a lifetime, the boys' legs were swelling horribly. The poison from the ant stings was running through and infecting their somewhat rundown system causing them to feel nauseous. This was not good as they had to keep up a good front until after recess. They lucked out as the teacher didn't call on either boy to recite. Several other boys made some big errors in their effort to read and the class had some good laughs while Jape and Tubbs could only manage a smile. After what seemed an eternity, the time arrived for recess. While all the boys raced to see who would be first batter, Tubbs held back and Jape joined in only because that was his nature. He didn't feel up to running, he just wanted to find the snake and get the show on the road.

Jape and Tubbs played outfield, not a single ball was hit toward the snake. They worked up to bat twice before a ball was hit in that direction. George hit a long foul right where they were wanting the ball to go and their hopes rose only to be deflated when another boy ran out and threw the ball back before they could give chase. The next boy hit a fly ball, it was caught, they changed places and George was up again. He hit another foul ball that went into the "snake pit". Both Tubbs and Jape immediately gave chase. Jape ran into the water and back out again looking for the snake, not the ball, when Tubbs started screaming.

"There's a snake on your leg, there's a snake on your leg."

Jape looked down to see a cottonmouth attached to his trousers by the fangs. He jerked the snake loose and threw it away shouting,

"It got me! It got me!"

Tubbs ran over looking at him, in all seriousness, thinking that he truly had been snake bit until Jape winked at him and lowered his voice for only Tubbs to hear:

"Now is the time for acting, scream and run out there."

And Tubbs did exactly that, he jumped up and backward screaming, "Don't come out here, there are snakes everywhere, it GOT me, too! Oooooooh, oooh, Oh, my God, I'm going to die, Oh, my God, I'm going to die!"

All the boys stopped next to the tall grass waiting for Jape and Tubbs to hobble out. Jape and Tubbs walked out to the mown grass and lay down on the ground holding their snake bite. The teacher took a little longer to get to the boys but she had seen the snake attached to Jape's trousers and knew he had gotten bit. The boys could not have staged their show with any more reality with a "prop" on a movie set. She knelt to examine each boy's leg:

"Oh my, oh my, those are ugly fang marks. Can you reach the wound to suck the poison out?"

Jape pulled his leg up to his mouth but the wound was on the outside of the leg and he could't get it to his mouth.

Tubbs volunteered, "I'll suck the poison out of your's and you suck the poison out of mine." The teacher sent one of the boys after Mr. Wilson as she continued to express sincere concern for the two boys. The charade was a total and complete success when Tubbs sucked a mouthful of blood from Jape's leg and spat it out onto the ground. Of course, as the saying goes a little blood goes a long way, most of what he spit out was saliva with a little blood for color; however, Jape was not to be outdone, he returned the favor by sucking a mouthful from Tubbs's leg. At that point, Jape complained of being too sick at his stomach to assist any more and Tubbs followed Jape's acting role.

A few minutes, later Mr. Wilson and his two goons arrived with a stretcher. They put a boy on each end and carried them into the building. Each boy relaxed and enjoyed the ride. Inside the main building they were taken to a small room not unlike a doctor's office only no doctor and no equipment. There was one small bed on each side of the little room and it had the odor of alcohol or iodine. A table sat against one wall, there were some tongue depressers in a glass container and some metal gadgets laying half covered by a newspaper.

Jape noticed everything in the room immediately including his picture on the front page of the paper. It was the picture from the time they were washed away by the flood. When Jape first saw the paper he thought it was the same old paper but as they turned to put him on the bed, he did a double take. The headlines read, "Two Young Fishermen Missing." His heart raced faster, that was the reason his folks had not been to see him. The sheriff had never told his dad about picking them up. Tubbs hadn't seen the paper as he was on the other end of the stretcher. After getting both the boys off the stretcher, the two helpers left the room and Wilson saw the paper for the first time. He folded the paper together instantly and walked out of the room, nodding to the teacher to follow him. The teacher spoke to the boys first, "They have a doctor on the way. You boys be still and don't move or get excited. The doctor will be here in a few minutes." Then she left the room. The boys were afraid to attempt any verbal communication. Jape looked over at Tubbs who winked and Jape waved his hand with the thumb and forefinger forming a circle.

Both boys laid back to wait for the next act.

The teacher returned to stay with the boys until the doctor got there. She was a nice lady who sincerely thought the boys had been snake bit. The boys were taking full advantage of the situation.

Jape asked, "Are we going to die?

"I don't know, let's hope not. The doctor will be here soon."

"Sure, we're going to die, no one has ever lived after . . ." He covered his face with the blanket she had placed over each boy. The teacher thought Tubbs was crying.

"It won't do any good to cry, Tubbs. If we die, we die, there isn't anything we can do about that now", Jape was attempting to console Tubbs.

"Yes, but I wanted to see my mother again before I die", Tubbs sniveled.

"Wonder how long before we die?" Jape looked up at the teacher and with a helpless gesture continued, "Has our folks disowned us, you know they haven't come to see us since we got here." He knew she had seen the morning paper and he wanted to take advantage of her maternal instincts. He continued, "Tubbs feels his mother has disowned him. Now, he is going to die without ever seeing his mother again."

The teacher stopped him by putting her fingers over her lips to sound out the, "Sssssssh, don't talk like that. You boys aren't going to die, we hope!"

"Sure we are, we are going to die in here. We shouldn't have to die in here", Tubbs cried out and the real hurt for his mother was in his voice.

Jape tried to look at the teacher who was attempting to wipe tears from her eyes when someone out in the hall shouted, "Down here, doctor." The teacher jumped up, then looked back to say, "Relax, the doctor must be here."

The doctor and the teacher talked just outside in the hall. The doctor asked the teacher, "Are you sure?"

"Yes, doctor I saw the snake, it's fangs were hung in one of the boy's leg. I saw it with my own eyes, it was terrible."

"And it was a Cottonmouth Water Moccasin?"

"Yes, oh yes. They are such ugly things."

"How long ago, as close as you can figure, did they get bitten?"

The teacher looked at a watch on her wrist and said, "To a minute, sir, it was one hour and seventeen minutes ago."

"I was afraid of that", the doctor sounded fearful.

"Why, what's wrong, Doctor?", the teacher was looking for some hope.

The doctor lowered his voice to ask, "Are the boys in there?"

The teacher must have nodded her head in reply because the boys didn't hear her answer.

The doctor continued, "There's nothing I can do, it's too late."

The teacher also lowered her voice to a whisper but it was easy for the young ears of the boys to pick up, "What do you mean TOO LATE. You haven't even looked at them?"

"No need, I've seen snake bites before. There's nothing I can do for a water moccasin bite. Once in a great while, a person will survive on his own but not because of something a doctor does."

The boys could hear the teacher gasp and the doctor continue, "Are you the boy's kin or something?"

"Oh no, it's just that they are such little boys. The sad part, Doctor, their parents don't know they are in here. Did you see the paper?"

"Oh yea, those two missing boys are in here, how in the world did that happen?"

"I haven't read their file. They seem to be nice boys."

"They come from good families but there is a black sheep in nearly every flock, don't get too involved emotionally, it'll be over before night!"

"You mean they will . . ., they will go today?"

"It's a miracle they aren't dead already."

"What can we do?"

"First thing someone better do is tell their parents. There is going to be hell to pay, even if they were in good health. I would say, pamper them a little and try to make their last moments as pleasant as possible. More than likely they will be gone by noon."

"Wouldn't you please talk to them and do something to make them feel like we're trying. I told them the doctor was coming, it would . . ."

"Oh, well, okay", the doctor turned to walk into the room.

A tall grey haired man with a genteel appearance walked into the room. He smiled at each boy and said, "Good Morning". The boys moaned a "Good morning" each one trying to appear as near death as possible. The doctor held each boy's hand taking his pulse, felt their foreheads and said,

"Well, you boys are going to be sick. Wish there was more I could do, these pills may be of some assistance." He laid two white pills down on the table, they looked like plain aspirin tablets to Jape. The good doctor didn't take the time to look at the snake bite. He walked out the door and the teacher walked out with him.

Tubbs looked out the door and whispered, "I can see them from here, that snake nearly got you. That really did look good, now, how's my idea doing so far?" Tubbs stiffened up in bed and brushed his hair back in a boasting attitude, then continued, "I told you they would give us a ride home."

Jape moaned and groaned then mumbled, "For you, Tubbs, it's acting but the snake really did bite me, I'm a goner, I'm a goner."

Any other time, Tubbs might have bought his act but not this time, throwing a pillow at him, he said, "Don't give me that crap, what the teacher didn't notice, the real snake had ahold of your right trousers leg and your bite is on the left. So, save the acting for them and do a better job."

Jape giggled and said, "Our pictures are in the morning paper, our parents have reported us missing. See, I told you they didn't know where we're at!"

Tubbs laid back down to moan as the teacher came back.

She asked, "How are you boys doing?"

"It's so hot in here, sooooo awful hot, could you get us a fan?"

Tubbs smacked his mouth a few times, "It must be the fever, could we have something cold?"

Mr. Wilson and three other people arrived at this moment Wilson asked, "Anything we can do?"

"Do we have a fan in the institution?"

"The only one I know about is in the superintendant's office."

"Fever, they need it."

Wilson turned to one of the men and nodded, the man left in a run. "We heard part of what the doctor said. I know I'm going to die but we would like to have one more milkshake before we go", was Japes request.

The teacher turned to Wilson who nodded to another man giving the okay for the milkshake. The man left in a run to get the boy's their shakes.

Jape curled up in the bed, "Oh, oh, oh it's so cold in here, could I have another blanket, another blanket, please." And his teeth began to chatter.

Mr. Wilson left to get a blanket as another man returned with the fan. The teacher said, "We won't need that now."

"It's so hot, it's so hot," Tubbs moaned as he tossed and turned.

The teacher plugged the fan into the only electrical outlet and set the fan on the table so it ran on Tubbs.

A few minutes later, Jape asked, "May I get in bed with Tubbs. I want to die with him, may I, please?"

The teacher walked over to his bed and helped him hobble over, to lie next to his friend. They lay there in total comfort with the fan rotating back and forth across the bed. This was the closest thing to air conditioning that money could buy in 1939. Shortly, Mr. Wilson showed up with several blankets.

The teacher told Wilson, "The fever works like that, they will be hot and cold. I wonder if we should call the doctor about giving them food?"

Wilson stepped outside the room and waved with his right forefinger for her to come out to talk. They thought the boys were in so much stress that they could not or would not hear.

"Didn't the doctor say they were going to die. A little food, if they can eat it won't hurt anything. From what they have been eating, I can see where they might like something. Even the criminals in the big house get a choice for their last meal", Wilson may have been attempting to make up for his deeds with the Donkey Hide in his verbal effort to assist in making the boys last meal a good one.

"He also said that some people survive on their own. I wouldn't want to be a party to doing something to hasten their departure", the teacher told Wilson as she walked back and forth seriously considering their thoughts.

"How much time they got?", Wilson asked.

"From what the doctor said, they are living on borrowed time now!"

"Okay, stay with them and if you need anything, I'll be in my office."

The boys lay quietly, watching the teacher out of the corners of their eyes. She left once to go to the toilet and the boys whispered a little. She returned about the same time as the man with two large chocolate shakes. The boys took the glasses in weak trembling hands as they groaned in their effort to sit up.

Jape drank some of his and held out his hand, "No, no I can't get sick now. This is so good. Would you say a silent prayer for me and Tubbs. Ask the Lord to let us finish these before we go."

The teacher lowered her head in a serious prayer and the boys winked at each other and continued to drink the shake as it was meant to be done. Their teacher got to talking with the Lord about the boys and decided to tell him some of her own problems which took much more time on her knees than she expected.

The milkshake was a giant one, large and delicious, the boys were full, content and with the fan blowing across them, something happened that they never counted on, they went sound to sleep.

The teacher rose from her knees to see the boys lying so peaceful and still, she thought they were dead. She pulled the blanket up over their faces and walked out of the room. A short time later, Wilson and his two helpers came into the room. One of the men pulled the blanket back, looked at the two boys still sound asleep, and not noticing the rhythmic breathing of a natural sleep he immediately threw the blanket back over their faces to say, "Too bad that two misfit river-rats like these could cause all of us to get fired, just don't seem fittin."

"Not likely you men will get canned. Only those in authority are in jeopardy, but who knows, they may decide to clean house."

"If those boys escaped and were bitten down by the river. If they found their bodies on the river, we would be home free."

"We could take their bodies down there and dump them off. No one would ever know but us", the third man suggested.

"The doctor was here and all the boys in the dorm . . .", Wilson reminded them as he looked at the man and continued, "You better forget that idea."

"We didn't have any problems at Tucker Farms and we buried 'em nearly every night, right there on the farm. They've been doing it now for years."

After this statement was made, Jape bumped Tubbs with his elbow causing Tubbs to moan as he awakened to yawn and stretch.

The two men jumped outside as one screamed, "Oh mah Gawd, oh mah Gawd, the dead has risen."

"What's wrong with him?", Tubbs moaned.

"Your teacher thought you boys died", Wilson shot back.

Tubbs looked over at Jape and said, "He always smells that way."

Jape realizing that statement was a goof, "I guess we went to sleep, I don't feel so sick but my head is floating, I'm dizzy and I feel like I'm going to pass out." He turned to look at Tubbs, "Are you feeling better?

"Nooooo, oooooh I wish I was dead, I'm sick, dizzy and hungry."

"If you boys think you could eat something. I was told to get you anything you wanted to eat", Wilson said with some sorrow in his tone.

"Is it lunch time yet?", Jape weakly mumbled.

"No, but that doesn't matter, what would you like?"

At that exact moment the teacher and the lady from the front desk walked up. The one that thought they were dead and had covered their face.

The two ladies walked in just in time to hear Jape say, "I would like to have some fried chicken." One woman fainted dead away.

Tubbs's weak voice strained to get it out, "I . . . would like . . . some too . . ."

Lady speaking to Wilson, "Go down town and get some fried chicken."

"But, if they . . . but what if . . .?"

Lady smiling at the boys, "If they change their minds and decide not to eat the fried chicken, I'll bet every bite of it gets eaten, go man go, what are you waiting for, can't you see these boys are hungry?"

Jape spoke again, "A pop would be good with fried chicken."

The lady shouted, "Get some pop for the boys also."

Wilson could be heard in the distance cursing, "Why don't I bring the cafe back with me?"

The women pulled the bed out from the wall so one could sit on each side of the bed. Each lady was stroking a boy's forehead, rubbing the hair back. The boys had never had it so good.

Jape spoke in a weak trembly voice, "My mother used to sing to me, she held me like this lots of times, can you sing?"

"What did she sing to you?"

"'May I sleep in Your Barn Tonight, Mister' and 'Little Joe the Wrangler' were my favorites. Her favorite song was 'The Letter Edged in Black' but I guess the only ones fitten now would be, 'Oh Bury Me Not on The Lone Prairie', or 'When The Works All Done This Fall'."

The lady squeezed Jape up close to ask, "You seem to like cowboy songs, I'm not much for singing but I hum along with the church choir on Sundays." She rocked Jape and hummed a few Christian hymns.

"May I ask for one more favor?"

"Anything, sweetheart, anything."

"Could Tubbs and I change into our old overalls and have our straw hats back that we came in with. If we're going to die, we would feel more comfortable meeting, you know, him, in our regular clothes?"

She patted Jape on the head and left the room crying. The teacher patted Tubbs on the head, "I'll see that she gets your's too."

Almost immediately the two ladies were back with the boys clothing. The trousers had been washed and were ready to wear. The ladies closed the door as the boys changed clothes. A few minutes later they came back into the room to return to their task of consoling the boys until Wilson returned with the fried chicken to find the two women holding the boys in their arms and tears running down their cheeks.

The teacher couldn't believe her eyes at the way those two boys dug into the chicken. She finally made a comment, "We better call the doctor about these two boys. It isn't natural for anyone in their condition to eat like that." The teacher quietly left the room to make the call.

The aroma of the chicken was tantalizing their taste buds and as they had had no meat since arriving at the institution their appetites overcame their caution in this little drama. They ate gustily, smacking and wiping their mouthes on their sleeves. Wilson and the office lady stood there gaping at the boys dumbfoundedly as only moments before they were at death's door and now were eating like little pigs. Jape guzzled down half the pop and winked at Wilson. "Thank you, sir, this is delicious."

Tubbs wiped his mouth, "It couldn't be better if I cooked it myself."

The teacher returned about the same time the boys finished off half a chicken each. She said:

"The doctor is on his way back. He can't believe it either, says they should be dead but if they can eat and keep it down it will be good for them. The snake may not have injected them with enough poison to be fatal. He wants to examine the boys this time. This, he says, is one for the medical journal, he really got excited when I told him the boys were still alive. He indicated he would be here in a few minutes."

"I'll be in my office", Wilson said as he turned to walk out of view.

"I'll bet both you ladies were talking with God, weren't you?"

The women looked at each other and back at the boy, nodding their heads.

"With two wonderful people like you making a plea for mercy, I don't feel it's a miracle that we are feeling better, do you Tubbs?"

"Nope, but I do have a lot of pain in my leg and when I try to move I get dizzy. If I don't move, I seem to feel fine."

Someone shouted for the teacher to come to the telephone and in the same instant the other lady stood up, "Okay, boys, since you are feeling better, I'll leave you alone for a few moments. The doctor will be here shortly."

She walked out of the room and Jape jumped up, shouting, "Tubbs, we have to get out of here now. When that doctor gets here he'll get us the Donkey Hide for sure. Plan or no plan, we have to run right now before they get back."

"Yep, I agree with you again. First hide these Prison Clothes." They poked the clothes under the bed then straightened and folded the blankets. The two boys walked out the front door, dressed in overalls and the straw hats. When they got outside they ran down the main driveway to the highway, where they turned north toward town.

Neither boy had ever hitchhiked but there is always the first time for everything. Jape stuck out his thumb, waving his straw hat and the first car stopped. The man smiled to say, "I'll bet I know where you boys are going."

Jape thought he had recognized them from the picture in the paper and tried to speak but all he could do was gulp and the man said, "You are going to see Robert Wadlow, the tallest man in the world, aren't you. We drove all the way from Wynnewood. We are to meet our grandsons and take them to see him, too. Did you ever dream you would get to see the tallest man in the world?"

"Nope, . . . his name is Robert Wadlow, . . . is that right?"

"When will he be here?", Tubbs asked.

"This afternoon, well, in a few minutes now. You can't miss him, he'll be right on main street. I'll take you boys right downtown, if I can find a place to park. Pauls Valley is growing so, one can't find a place to park short of wayout behind the square. When I drive out there the car spooks some of the horses tied up on the square, so, I try to find a place downtown."

"What kind of car is this?", Tubbs changed the subject.

"Chevrolet, a 1934 Chevy, the best car on the road today. I don't like the Ford, my brother-in-law is a Ford man, now there IS a character. Rarely has a job but when he does, every dime goes into his old junker, he'll get smart some day. Yep, get smart and trade that Ford for a Chevy."

Jape punched Tubbs in the ribs then asked, "Doubt if that will ever happen, no one is dumb enough to trade a Chevy for a Ford, are they?"

"Got a good point, son, a real good point but with a little boot, meby."

The man had to detour because main street was blocked off so the people could stand in the street, look and talk with the tallest man in the world. They walked up the street to mingle with the crowd. The red brick streets were so hot to their feet, they didn't stand in the sun for very long. The shady areas were much cooler. A large crowd gathered around but it wasn't difficult to tell who Robert Wadlow was. He was TALL, in fact, someone talking on a loud speaker offered a dollar bill to anyone who could reach to take it off his head without jumping. Several men over six feet tried but none could reach any higher than Wadlow's ear, the buck was safe. The tall fellow asked for a ''Coke'' and someone gave him a six-ounce bottle of ''Coke''. The boys laughed at the size of his hands, the top and the bottom of the bottle were the only parts of the bottle that were visible. He turned the little bottle up and drank it in two gulps and asked for another one. The boys watched in awe for several minutes.

They were standing in the shade next to the building watching all the excitement when a lady walked up to ask them, ''Didn't I see you boys picture on the front page of the paper this morning?''

Chapter 10

The Banker Lost His Marbles

At the all night prayer meeting, Charley told Uncle John that the boys may have been picked up by Claude. Everyone called the sheriff by his first name. He had been sheriff for so long, it was understood about whom they were talking. Charley tried to telephone the sheriff before coming to the meeting, Claude had not returned from the conference in the City. Uncle John didn't want Jape's dad to hear what Charley told him until he had time to check on a few things. He asked Charley and others to keep it quiet until tomorrow after he had had time to talk with a few people.

After the prayer meeting Jape's father and mother left in the wagon headed home. Uncle John got into his big black car and drove into Paoli to park in front of the banker's house. It was sometime between midnight and daylight but John didn't care. He rapped so loudly the side of the house shook. The banker shouted down in his squeeky voice, "Who is it?"

"It's me, John, and you better get down here quick."

The banker took the time to grab a housecoat, something of a luxury around Paoli in 1939. Most of the citizens had difficulty buying longjohns and his robe may have been the only one in town. When the door opened John shouted, "Where the hell is my nephew?"

"What on earth are you talking about?"

"You know what I'm talking about. You and your buddy, the judge, cooked up something and put Jape and Tubbs in the reform school. You want to tell me about it or shall I go tell Jape's dad. In case you don't know it, he'll kill you with his bare hands. He won't bother to knock on the door, he'll tear the damn thing down. There isn't twelve people in this county that would ask him to do a single day in jail for strangling the likes of you. Have you gone mad or so crazed with greed that you have lost all your marbles."

John stopped to glare at the banker, "I'm waiting, say something!"

The banker stammered and stuttered then said, "Those boys are bad, bad, I tell you. I did the community a favor by getting them off the streets."

"What are you talking about?"

"When Claude picked them up we caught them in the act of stealing insulators from the telephone poles, caught them in the act."

"Stealing hell, I told those boys to get those insulators. If you recall I took the loss for the company on the salvage value of those insulators and told everyone on the board that I could use some of them on my electric fence. You idiot, I paid those boys to get them for me, they weren't stealing."

"I didn't know about that. They stole the bearings off my car, what about that, now, that's stealing and directly from me.

"Your car seems to be running, how did those little boys get a wheel off your car to steal the bearings."

"No, no, my car, that is parked on the vacant lot."

"You mean that old 'Star' that Ralph Williams stripped and left on that lot before he died. It was still there when you foreclosed and took the property. If we check the records, I'll bet that car isn't named on the deed to the property or in foreclosure proceedings. Legally, that car still belongs to the widow Williams. She's such a fine lady, I'll bet she'd give the entire car to the boys, including the bearings. Now, give me some reason those two boys should be locked up, come on, come on. Man, you have lost your marbles. Why, Why, Why, would you do such a thing?"

"Kids come around taking, taking, stealing from that car all the time and I'm fed up with those dirty little alley rats."

"Jape and Tubbs spend most of their time hunting or fishing. I'm sure there are other boys around who look at that old car too. Why didn't you get every boy in town and toss them in the reform school. As much money as the judge owes your bank I'm sure you could twist his arm and get him to do anything you ask."

"No, no, no, it's not like that at all. These boys are really bad, they were stealing peaches and watermelons along with my bearings."

"Christ man, they are terrible if they were stealing something to eat. If we hung every man in this county that had stolen a watermelon or a peach we would only have one yellow banker left. No doubt you never stole anything in your life because you didn't have the guts. I wouldn't give two hoots in hell for a nine-year old boy that wouldn't steal a peach or a watermelon. Let me tell you something, BANKER, those watermelons they stole were mine. I had to hide and wait for over an hour while they covered their wheelbarrow tracks getting out of my watermelon patch. That's half the fun in life, you wait, next winter Jape will catch me at the store and brag about stealing my watermelons. To add to his glory, I told him I didn't have a patch. He thinks I'm hiding the patch from everyone. I told old Charley to buy the melons from the boys and I would give him the money back. Those boys worked harder at stealing those melons and selling them to Charley than they ever have on a thrashing crew or doing chores on the farm."

"How am I supposed to know all that. I caught them stealing and they ran, the sheriff even had difficulty catching'em."

"You really are an idiot, a good boy is exactly like a good dog. If you run at a boy or a dog both will run away. If you hold out a helping hand and speak kind words, they will obey and follow you anywhere. Hell yes, they ran but obviously they couldn't run fast enough, what I can't understand how they got locked up without someone having the decency to tell their parents."

"Claude was supposed to do that, anyway your nephew or not, we got those two alley rats off the street, now you come here in the middle of the night trying to make me look bad."

"You better look in the mirror, you do look bad. My visit may save your life because you'll look worse lying in a casket. Mr. banker, that's exactly where you'll be if Jape's dad learns the truth before they find'im."

"If he comes over here then I'll shoot'im or have him arrested and locked up. This is 1939, not Indian Territory any more, we have laws to live by. A sharecropper like him can't tell me what to do. I'll —."

"You're right, we do have laws and the laws are here to protect us from bankers like you same as angry sharecroppers. It's a shame that you didn't think about the law when locking Jape and Tubbs up. What about their rights, little boys don't have any rights and especially the son of a sharecropper and they couldn't have had a fair trial, hell man, their parents don't even know where they're at."

"That ain't my problem, if he has a problem, he can take me to court."

"Take you to court, take you to court, wouldn't that be another kettle of fish. He would file suit and appear before the only judge in Garvin County, your brother-in-law. First, he don't have money to hire an attorney. He only made fifteen cents on his broomcorn crop and the cotton don't look good. He'll be lucky to sell enough to pay off the mortgage, if he hires an attorney he can't pay the mortgage and he'll lose the –. You greedy louse, you greedy, greedy, louse that was the plan all the time. You and your buddy, the judge, knowing he loves his son more than life itself – you, you, were going to force him into court where he would win his son but lose everything he owns including that corn crop. Yep, you heard about the corn he's growing on that new ground. If you would go to this much trouble to cheat a share-cropper out of a few head of livestock and a corn crop, what wouldn't you do for my two oil wells? You are a louse, a real louse but let me give you another perspective. You, Mr. Banker, have until sunup to make up your mind. I'm going to get a few of my friends who have a little money and a lot of clout in this community. We'll be meeting at my store at Crossroads, if you want to own and operate a bank in Paoli and your friend, the judge, wants to remain in office you better show up at our little meeting with the idea of providing full and complete cooperation in a sincere effort to get Jape and Tubbs released the first thing this morning. There's one more thing, you also better pray that nothing has happened to those two boys or I'll head a vigilante committee of one to hang you myself." John turned and stormed back to his car and drove off in a cloud of dust, leaving the banker standing in the door with his mouth hanging wide open.

The banker didn't get rich and fat during the depression by being stupid all the time. He made several telephone calls, getting the judge and Claude out of bed. Within the hour the three men met at the banker's home in Paoli. Claude was an honest sheriff and wouldn't have any part of going outside the law in the performance of his duties. His office had goofed or there was a breakdown in communications by not informing the boys parents. This was not uncommon when dealing with a sharecropper. Money has been the chief ruler in the rural community, same as in the cities of America since the pilgrims landed. Of course the banker kept Claude and the Judge in the dark about the real reason of his complaint. This way he didn't have to grease their palms with any part of the money from the foreclosure. Claude had to admit he made a mistake in not notifying the parents, the banker had to admit he was mistaken about what the boys had stolen. The Judge informed the two men that it didn't matter, the boys that age didn't have any legal rights and wasn't entitled to a trial, anyway. As the Judge, he had the authority to lock them up, if and when he saw fit, without a trial. He locked the boys up with a court order and could release them with another one. The Judge returned to the Courthouse in Pauls Valley as Claude and the banker drove out to the Crossroads store.

By daylight, Uncle John had gathered only half dozen men at the store but these were the ones who pulled the strings in the community. He explained the problem and they agreed to follow his lead. They agreed to wait an hour after sunup for the banker, if he didn't show they were going to talk with all the bank's depositors and open another bank in Paoli and at the same time start impeachment proceedings against the Judge. They felt the banker was too smart NOT to follow up after being confronted by John and their thinking was correct. The banker and the sheriff showed up right on time to shake hands all around. Everyone agreed a terrible mistake had been made and the right thing to do was correct it.

Uncle John and Claude would drive to the courthouse, where a court order would be waiting, then to the reform school, get the boys and bring them home. Since he had a car, the operator of the store agreed to go tell both boys parents that the boys had been located. John asked him to simply say the boys were all right and he would bring them home later.

Claude rode with John back to Paoli where the sheriff picked up his car, then John followed the sheriff back to the courthouse. The judge just happened to be in conference when the two men arrived to pick up the release papers. The secretary gave the sheriff the papers, he thanked her and the two men left the building.

"The secretary is a nice looking gal. She looks like . . ."

"Yea, she's the banker's niece."

"Oh yea, ain't it a small world", John grinned as he looked at Claude.

"Have you met the Superintendent at the reform school?"

"Nope, not to my knowledge, have I missed something?", John asked.

"Not really, the banker's younger brother. The job's an appointed position, the Judge makes the appointment. Of course after the appointment he does answer to the County Commissioners."

"Yes, well, live and learn, live and learn. Garvin County's tax dollars are well looked after by the Paoli banker. How many of his relatives do you have on your staff, Sheriff?"

"None, but I do have two of his good friends, of course we do our banking in Paoli, to appease the court", the sheriff admitted.

"I hope those boys are all right after a few days in that place, I wonder what they do with the boys in there?", John pondered.

"I understand they go to school all year long", Claude tried to cover up.

They pulled into the driveway at the reform school as John continued, "If I really want to know, I guess Jape will be glad to give me a first hand report. More than likely he'll give me the report, if I want it or not."

The two men got out and went inside the building. Claude introduced John to the Superintendent as he gave him the release papers.

Claude asked, "Would you get both boys right away, please."

"Yes, I wish I could, the Judge telephoned earlier."

"What do you mean, they're here arn't they?", John asked.

"They were here, they escaped yesterday", the superintendent said as he looked at the floor and shuffled his feet.

"What do you mean they escaped?", Claude raised his voice to ask.

"Well, yesterday morning they got snake bit and . . ."

John burst out, "Whatta ya mean, snake bit?"

"Yes, snake bit by a cottonmouth", the superintendent informed them.

"Which boy got bit?", Claude asked.

"Both boys, they were playing ball an . . ."

"Both boys got snake bitten, then they're dead, you threw them in the river to cover up. I've heard about things like this happening in Arkansas but never thought I would lose my own flesh and blood to a . . ."

"Hold it, hold it, the boys aren't dead, they got to feeling better after drinking a milkshake and eating fried chicken they ran away."

"Wait a minute, after getting snake bit, they were able to drink a milkshake and eat fried chicken? Is that the story?", John commented.

"That's what I was told", the superintendent shrugged his shoulders.

All three men laughed as John spoke, "Those two little con-artists, sounds like they were doing the same thing you and your brother have been doing, working the system for all they could get. They should be easy to spot dressed in reform school clothes."

"Nope, wrong again, they talked two of the ladies into giving them their overalls and strawhats, you know to die in. Our staff, including the doctor thought the boys were dying. Those boys did a good job with their snake bite routine. They walked out of here dressed in the same clothes they came in with."

"Had the snake bite been true, you were going to let them die without notifying their parents?" John shook his head looking at Claude then back to the Superintendent as both men broke eye contact to look at the floor. John continued to speak, "You say they left yesterday, what time?"

"Around noon, someone called in, they were seen at the Robert Wadlow show down town."

"They should be home by now, they know the way home", John added.

"Nope, two of our men and a city police officer chased them most of the night. They were seen running from behind a feed store only about an hour ago. Our people are attempting to catch them even as we speak. I didn't know about the release until a few minutes ago or I would have called the hunt off. We don't want the rest of the boys to get the idea there is any chance of getting away from here."

The telephone rang and the superintendent answered, after a brief conversation he looked up to speak, "They've found the boys."

"Great, where're they at? I'll go pick'em up", John told the two men.

The Superintendent raised his hand for John to wait a moment. The telephone conversation continued for a few moments, then he said, "They're at the hospital, one of the boys is in a coma."

"Which boy?"

"I don't know, the doctor's examining him now. Seems they were running across the street when one of the boys collapsed. He wasn't hit, in fact, our people were on the other side of town, the boys gave them the slip two hours ago. A store owner saw the boy fall, when he didn't get up he walked out to see what was wrong, of course, he called for help and eventually hauled the two boys to the hospital, that's where they're at now."

John jumped up running to the door with Claude following a few steps behind, "Come on, Claude, we're going to the hospital, now."

The receptionist was polite and courteous to the men but was firm in her refusal to allow them admittance into the examining room. She told the two men to wait a few minutes, pointing to a small waiting room off to one side of the entrance. The Sheriff and John walked into the room to see Tubbs seated on the far side of the room with a long look on his face, it was obvious the boy had been crying.

At the sight of Uncle John, he burst out, "He won't wake up, he won't wake up, we didn't do anything."

John walked across the room to console the boy. After putting his arm around the child he asked, "What happened?"

"Uncle John, you won't believe me if I told you", Tubbs cried.

"Try me on a little of it, okay?"

Tubbs looked the sheriff right in the eye, "He put us, Jape and me, in the reform school. Said we were bad and . . ."

"I know about that, tell me the part about Jape. What's wrong with him. What happened that he won't wake up?"

"I don't know, we were trying to get away. They chased us all over town nearly all night. We found a place in a feed store and hid but didn't get much sleep. This morning we were trying to get out and one of the guys from the school saw us and the race was on again. We got away and were going across the street and Jape just fell over, he just fell over and never woke up. I don't know what is wrong with him, I don't, I don't."

John pulled the boy up to keep the tears from flowing and saw large marks on the boy's back, which prompted his question:

"My God, son, how did you get those marks on your back?"

"That's nothing you should see Jape's. Those are what the boys at the school call Donkey Tracks, it's the marks left by the Donkey Hide"

"Donkey Hide, what in the world is the Donkey Hide?"

"It is the leather strap they whip us with."

"They use a smaller strap in the reform school than in the big house but the term "Donkey Hide" is common around all criminal institutions" the sheriff informed John.

John turned to Tubbs as he checked his back, "They whipped you?"

Tubbs shrugged his shoulders, "Sure felt like it to me."

John was furious but controlled his rage as he purposely changed the subject back to Jape, "You don't know what is wrong with Jape?"

"No, sir, no, I don't know. He fell down, like he went to sleep."

John hugged the boy again, "I know you don't know, that's what the doctor will tell us. He'll be finished with the exam in few minutes, then we'll know what's wrong. It can't be serious!"

John pushed the boy back a little so he could look into his eyes, "Tubbs, did he get snake bit, could this have anything to do with that snake bite?"

"No sir, we didn't get snake bit. Unless he's allergic to a red ant bite because that was all a, well, it was all a lie. We were trying to get out of that place, that's no place to live. I'm sorry for those boys in there."

"I don't know, I'm sure Jape has been stung a million times by a red ant, we have so many of them around here. This could be a delayed reaction of some kind to the ant sting. You boys fooled them at the reform school into thinking a red ant sting was a cottonmouth bite?''

Tubbs' face lit up in a radiant smile, ''Well, there was a lot of good acting along the way, but yes sir, that's what we did.''

''A cottonmouth leaves two fang marks and an ant . . .''

''We used two ants and pierced the center of the sting with Jape's fish hook. It did look good, and the way it went down, made it even better.''

The doctor came in at this moment without a smile. He looked the little group over and assuming that Uncle John was Jape's dad proceeded to explain his findings,

''Gentlemen, this isn't good news. The boy has all the symptoms of Spinal Meninjitis and as you know the disease is fatal. Not only fatal to that boy lying in there in a coma but it is highly contagious.'' He turned to point to Tubbs, ''This lad has been exposed and will probably come down with a fever in a few hours and lapse into a unconsciousness. We'll have to put the two boys into isolation. Since they have been together for the last several days, it will save time and space if we put them into the same room here at the hospital.''

He looked at the sheriff, ''These boys, I understand, have been residing at the school outside of town?'' The sheriff nodded his head without speaking and the doctor continued, ''The entire population will have to be quarantined, no one will come or go from that school. The employees on the job will remain on the job. If this disease gets out of there and it may be already, we could lose hundreds.''

''Are you sure the boy has Spinal Meninjitis?'', the sheriff asked.

''No, I'm not, but all the symptoms are there, he's in a coma, the temperature is high, he has swelling of the knees and, well, I have asked two more doctors to come by and give their opinion. They have dropped all their patients to race over here and examine the boy within the hour. This, I assure you, isn't a small matter.''

Turning again to John, thinking he was the father, the doctor said, ''I'm sorry you have to learn about your son like this but death is a fact of life. I can only ask you to pray that my opinion is wrong. I hope you have other sons.''

''I'm not his father but I love him just as much. I'll go get his father and mother, they best get the news from me.''

The doctor pointed to Tubbs, ''I want to check you over right away. Son, you best come into the room with your friend. If you were going to be infected, you are all ready. You won't mind waiting with your friend, will you?''

"No sir, I'd rather be with'im."

Tubbs asked John, "Will you tell my mother where I'm at?" he paused to add, "Telling her I'm at the hospital will sound a lot better than, telling her you know, where I've been!"

"Yes, Tubbs, someone is on their way to see your mother now. If she hasn't all ready left, I will bring her back with Jape's parents."

Uncle John returned to the hospital with all three parents, arriving shortly before noon. The receptionist asked them to wait, explaining that the doctor had left word with a nurse who would be in to speak with them. The nurse arrived before they were seated in the waiting room.

Jape's dad asked, "Can I see my boy?"

"Certainly, first I want to tell you that the boy is in a coma. You can see him but only through a glass window. At this point, the doctor has diagnosed his condition as Spinal Meninjitis. This disease is highly contagious and those coming in close contact can also be exposed." She looked at those waiting and spoke to Tubbs' mother, "You are Tubbs's mother, your son is feeling and looking well. He must remain with Jape for awhile as he has been exposed and if we don't keep him under quarantine there is too much danger of an epidemic. We don't want hundreds to come down with this disease, you understand?"

Tears were streaming down mom's face, "Let us go see him now."

Without another word the nurse turned and they followed her out of the room. A nurse with a mask over her face rolled the bed over to a large glass window which was like looking through a nursery window.

The nurse explained, "This is our old nursery, we use it for this purpose occasionally but, thank goodness, we rarely have any contagious diseases. We had to move a few patients out, but, this way we are safer."

They saw another bed across the room and someone was asleep in it.

Tubbs' mom asked, "Is that my boy in the other bed?"

"Yes, please excuse me." She rapped on the glass and waved for the nurse to come over to the glass. The she raised her voice, "Please get the other boy, his mother is here to see him."

Tubbs jumped out of bed, ran out the door and into his mother's arms before the nurse could stop him. Both mother and son had tears of joy streaming down their faces. His mom said, "You best go back inside. The nurse will get into trouble if you don't. You will be fine."

The nurse grabbed him by the arm pulling him back inside the room saying, "Sorry, sorry, but I need a job, they won't let me out of this room for fourteen days, unless Jape wakes up. You best go say a prayer, we'll do everything humanly possible here." Tubbs ran to the window to wave at everyone as they took one last look at Jape lying in the bed sleeping.

Uncle John drove everyone home in silence. Dad finally spoke, "I'll need to talk with you, John, after the women folk are out of the car."

"I know, after they are out of the car."

"I have to know now, did Jape do something bad?"

"No, that I assure you, he never did anything bad. In fact, what he did was, well, it was my fault. I agreed to trade him one insulator for one .22 shell and he picked up the insulators the telephone crew threw away."

"You mean he traded you one insulator for one .22 shell, yes, he told us about that. We thought you were one of the owners of the Paoli Telephone Company and didn't see anything wrong with that", mom told him.

"You're right, I'm one of the stockholders but the banker is the Chairman of the Board, he has forty-percent of the stock and I only have twenty. The rest of the stock is owned by friends of mine and yours. When we had to replace the insulators with the larger ones, I paid the company ten dollars salvage value for the old ones. The insulators are mine."

"Do you know how he contracted the disease?", mom asked.

"No, but before this is over we'll find out."

John let Jape's mom out to stay with Tubbs' mother so the two men could go for a drive and talk. The two men drove to the Crossroads store while they talked. John made Dad promise to listen to reason before taking any action on his own and with that promise he told the story of how the banker got Claude and the Judge to lock the two boys up. Of course, John didn't have any proof but anyone knowing the banker knew he never did anything without sound financial planning. Dad agreed not to kill the banker until after the boy's funeral.

The banker was right, this wasn't Indian territory any more and there were laws to live by but those in power or with financial influence controlled the laws and those enforcing them. The written law was only enforced on the poor, like the sharecropper. The powerful, like the banker could do as he pleased, financially raping the public without fear of prosecution. If some poor soul had the guts and the money to file proceedings in court, the Judge, was either a relative or bought and paid for. The poor man didn't have a prayer with the written law.

One thing and one thing only kept the rich and powerful living close to the words of the written law, ''FEAR'' of the unwritten law of the poor. If and when the rich no longer faced that ''FEAR'' the banker would expand his greed to others and John's two oil wells could be next, if not this banker, a bigger and fatter one from the City. When there is no remedy within the court system, justice will be found by other means — and it hasn't changed!

Everyone in the community felt the banker, in this case, signed his own death warrant when he appointed himself a vigilante committee of one and signed the complaint against those two boys in his deliberate effort to get them railroaded into the reform school. Although their deaths may or may not have been directly caused by the acts of the banker, he was a solid choice to pay the price as the villain in that community. John and Dad shook hands and agreed not to take any action until after the boys' funeral or, if it was God's will, the boys recovered.

Uncle John's car was used as transportation to and from the hospital. Dad tried to buy gas but John refused to accept his money. John agreed to let dad bring his team over and disc one section of his broomcorn field. Dad insisted on paying his way. When John refused to accept money for gas dad decided to walk to and from town, and at that point, John agreed to let him disc the field. In those days, accepting something for nothing was considered a disgrace. No man accepted a handout if he was able to work and dad was very strong. Once the field was disced he could accept the ride with pride while maintaining his dignity.

The paper splashed the story about the outbreak of the terrible disease on the front page of the paper. Due to the fatal nature of the disease they didn't make the boys out to be terrible as Tubbs was afraid they would. The entire community around Paoli and Crossroads prayed for the two boys, all but one man.

The old doctor in Paoli, the man who brought Uncle John, Jape and most everyone else in the community into the world didn't sit on his butt, cross his fingers or pray. He got into his motel 'A' roadster and drove to the hospital. Everyone there knew him, he asked to see the doctor in charge but the doctor wasn't in. The two mothers had been there most of the night as they had every night since the boys were admitted. The old doctor asked them if it would be all right to talk with Tubbs and look at Jape. The women were proud to have his opinion in the matter and gave their permission.

The doctor went right into the room with Jape and Tubbs without any fear of contacting any disease. He checked Jape over as Tubbs watched. then asked Tubbs to be seated and the two started talking.

"Tubbs, what were you boys doing the night before this happened?"

Tubbs looked around as if checking to see if someone was watching, then he asked, "Do you know we were in the reform school?"

"Don't worry about that but, yes, I read the paper."

"I was afraid of that. Everyone will know, Jape isn't a bad boy. If he dies, they'll remember him as an escaped convict, won't they?"

"Well, if you will forget about him dying for a moment we might be able to save his life. Please talk to me, young man."

"I am talking to you doctor, I am talking."

"Yes, you are, but I'm not asking the right questions, I guess. Did you boys fall, run into anything or get hurt the night before Jape went to sleep. You know what I'm asking, did Jape get hit on the head?"

"No one hit him, they never caught us. They were never close enough to hit us on the head. Oh, oh, Jape ran into an old clothes line, it was about knee high, it tripped him and he banged the back of his head on a rock. He rolled around on the ground for a few minutes and complained about being dizzy but we had to get out of there. A little while later we . . ."

"That's what I thought, come here." The doctor walked over to pull back the covers exposing Japes legs. He asked Tubbs, "The clothes line hit Jape about right there?" he pointed to swelling across both Jape's knees.

Tubbs answered, "Yea, I guess so, that's about right. He didn't complain about the knees he rolled around rubbing the back of his head and didn't get up right away."

The doctor raised Japes head and turned it to one side to feel the back of his head then reached over to feel the back of Tubbs head. He winked at Tubbs as he pulled the cover back over Jape's legs. "You boys do a lot of swimming this time of year, don't you?"

"Yes, sir, we used to."

"You boys will be back swimming again in a few days."

Both mothers had been watching the doctor through the glass. They were waiting for what they feared would be a fourth fatal opinion. The doctor spoke first, "Ladies, ladies, I'm not the greatest doctor in the world but if you will give me permission as your family doctor to try to change my learned colleagues opinions from a fatal disease to a minor injury, I'll take over the treatment; however, I must have your consent because I'm not the most popular doctor in this hospital. Treating another doctor's patient is highly frowned on but I'd rather be frowned on than watch while your son dies." He turned to Tubbs's mother, "There's nothing wrong with your son. No reason in the world he can't go home with you today."

Jape's mom nearly shouted, "What's wrong with Jape?"

"Jape has a simple concussion but if he isn't treated soon, he could die. The brain has swollen from a bump on the back of his head. Don't be upset at the other doctor's findings, all of the signs or symptoms were present in Jape for their diagnoses but an error has been made and should be corrected immediately. Will you give your permission to start treatment for a concussion?"

"Yes, certainly, sure go ahead and please do what it takes." She burst out crying and the two women embraced each other and openly wept. They pulled away from each other to laugh in relief as hard as they had been crying.

Both women, speaking at the same time, stated, "It's God's blessings."

The doctor was walking into the boys' room when he heard that remark, he smiled at Tubbs, "I do the work and the Lord gets the credit." he then told Tubbs, "Get dressed and get out of here, go see your mother. Jape will be up and around in a couple days."

Tubbs ran out the door right into the arms of his mother. At the same time the director of the hospital stormed into the hallway shouting at the doctor. "You can't come in here and take over another doctor's patients, those boys are quarantined and I'll see to it that you never practice medicine again."

The good doctor smiled and called the director by his first name, "Son, you are about to give yourself a coronary. Relax, if it will make you feel better, get in touch with the medical board. I'm president and I'll write you a very nasty letter right back. In the meantime you can forget about the quarantine." He pointed his finger at the director, "Now, you will call the reform school and give them the word and let those good folks go home. There isn't any disease and never was."

"If there is any problem . . .", the director shouted.

"If there is any problem, I'll take full responsibility for everything, I'm telling you. You see, I'm a doctor, a real doctor, I realize you don't get the opportunity to come in contact with one very often."

"But, but, this is highly irregular!", the director sniveled.

"Yes, yes, I know, that boy in there has been my patient since I delivered him nine years ago. He has a simple concussion, I'm not going to stand around and argue or worry about protocol while he dies. I have started treatment and will come back in a couple hours to check on him." The doctor walked a few feet toward the two women, turned his back on the director and continued speaking, "Jape should be able to leave the hospital by morning. There's nothing wrong with Tubbs, he'll be going home with his mother right now." He winked at the two women and spoke over his shoulder to the director in a rather loud voice, "When you tell my colleagues about this you don't have to spell my name right, just say that old quack from Paoli, they know me!"

Knowing Jape's parents would be sitting in the little waiting room all night, the doctor showed up around midnight to sit with them after having given Jape another treatment. They were still covering the local gossip and had not gotten to the war in Europe when the nurse came in grinning from ear to ear, "He opened his eyes and asked for Mr. Tips, is he here?"

Dad smiled and told the doctor, "That's his dog, Mr. Tips is his dog." He reached out to shake the doctor's hand saying, "Thanks, thanks and I'll be coming in to see you. I'll settle up with you . . ."

"Forget it, don't bother, it was nothing. You don't owe me a dime."

They walked rapidly to the room to find Jape looking around and as they walked in he exclaimed, "Whooo, whooo, am I glad to see you guys. Am I back, did they catch me?"

"You're in the hospital son, you gave us quite a scare."

"I'm in a regular hospital, not in the . . ."

Jape's mom had tears streaming down her face and couldn't speak. She was holding on to the boy's arm, squeezing his hand as Dad did the talking.

"How do you feel, any sore spots?", the doctor asked.

"I feel hungry, I could drink a gallon of milk." He looked up at his mom to add, "Oh, I would love some of your hot biscuits and gravy."

"That didn't answer my question but I found out what I wanted to know. Let him remain in here tonight, I'll have the nurses bring him lots of good food. After he eats, he will go back to sleep but it will be a normal sleep. He will wake up hungry again, feed him and take him home."

"When we get him home what do I . . .?", mom was concerned.

"Now that he is going to live . . .", the doctor spoke but was interrupted.

"I'm not too sure about that, I may kill'im when I get'im home", Jape's dad told them in a matter of fact voice but everyone knew he was joking.

"That was what I was going to ask you not to do, it is doctor's orders, 'take one young boy, give two doses of love from two loving parents daily and spank firmly on a regular basis', that will nearly always guarantee good health, but do not kill, it is too difficult to raise them up this far to lose one."

They shook the doctor's hand again before he left the hospital.

Jape left the hospital the next morning. Uncle John was there with his car and it should have been a happy time; however, only Mom was happy. She was smiling, giving the Lord credit for saving her son. Dad felt the old doctor was responsible for bringing his son back from sure death and for that he was thankful but only to the doctor. The ride home should have been a happy one; however, no one was talking except Jape and his Mom. John and Dad had seen the marks on Jape's back and rib cage. Jape's dad had used the check lines on Jape several times, leaving marks on the kid's butt, the marks of a spanking. The marks on Jape and Tubbs were on their backs, that was a beating, not a spanking. The school teacher, Mrs. Auld, gave the children a spanking now and then and without exception they needed it. Without the spanking, the boys would be telling the teacher how to run the school. This was different, something was wrong and neither John or Dad could figure out exactly what it was. Each person, man woman and child in that entire community had been spanked a few times. This went beyond spanking, they didn't know on whom to vent their anger.

John drove directly up to the front door of the banker's house. He told Dad to stay in the car but dragged Jape out of the front seat by the arm and walked briskly to the front door. Before John could ring or knock, the door opened and the two men glared at each other for a several seconds. The banker stood framed in the doorway with his hands on his hips as he was KING of his castle and standing firm on his home court. John was equally determined to make a point, shouted, "Look, look." John spun Jape around so the fat man could see the large lash marks made by the Donkey Hide.

John continued, "That's what they give the boys at the reform school, guilty or not on being admitted, it's the school policy. Look, look."

Jape stood there like a monkey in a cage as John turned him first one way then the other. As always, the boy didn't have a shirt on, the whip marks across his back were only too obvious. The banker's mouth dropped open, his hands dropped off his hips and his head began to shake from side to side as he slowly spoke, "They don't, they didn't, ooooooh my God, what did I do?"

John pushed Jape toward the car and on leaving said, "You're asking for help in the right place. If God can't help you, you're outta luck."

Jape looked back to see a totally different man, that fat man standing in the door way looked helpless, he had what appeared to be real tears in his eyes. Jape had to look back a second time, the man WAS human after all.

They drove away from the bankers house as Dad asked, "Don't you think that was a waste of time. He would steal the nickels off his dead mother's eyes. More than likely it's too late to do any talking with him."

"Forget the banker, let's get on with our own lives. Jape and Tubbs are fine. In a few days everything will be back to normal. It's time to live and let live, everyone makes mistakes", mom suggested.

"Could we go by and see Tubbs?", Jape asked.

"A good idea, let's go see Tubbs", Uncle John agreed.

They parked at Tubbs' house, Jape and his mother went inside. Jape was feeling good but weak and didn't feel like walking far. While they were inside the two men talked.

"Does the fact that Jape didn't die make a difference?", dad asked.

"No, shouldn't, the man is guilty as hell and should have to pay for his misdeeds but the law, at this point, is on his side", John advised.

"You mean in his pocket, one way or the other."

"We must think about this a little while. The boys are alive, we can take our time, get more input before doing something we could regret."

"Look at those whip lashes on those boys' backs, I couldn't do anything that I would ever regret as much as I regret what's happened to Jape, I'm hoping not to live to regret not doing something. What about the man who actually used the whip on the boys. How does he fit into this?"

"I don't know, hard to believe that a man would do something like that for money. These are hard times and men will do strange things in their effort to feed their family."

"The banker is an easy target, I'm trying awfully hard to look at this and keep an open mind, from where we're coming from, is that possible?"

"Don't know, let's sit on it for a few days. We can do a few hard day's work and clear our minds. We'll both think better and we'll talk again."

Three days later John dropped by to talk with Dad one evening telling him to ride up to the store around noon the next day and bring Jape. He didn't say anything else as he didn't have time to talk.

Dad stopped him, "You were right, a few days hard work did a world of good. John, you better take the time to listen. I cannot live with

myself if I do nothing. I can't sleep, I can't eat and I'll feel better after
I get my hands around that fat bas . . ."

"Hold it, I'm having the same problem and I do know how you feel.
You realize that either boy, Jape or Tubbs could probably whip that
fat man. It would'nt be any physical challenge or accomplishment.
An old friend of Dad's is driving down from the City tomorrow, he
asked me to wait until after the meeting tomorrow. I gave him my word,
so get a good night's sleep and if we don't get satisfaction, I'll personally help you hang'im."

The next morning Jape milked the three cows while laughing at and
talking to all the animals. For some strange reason he did the chores,
ran to get the wood or carry water without being told and mom didn't
hear any whining or complaining from him when he was asked to wash
the dishes, something Jape hated to do. Once he kissed his mom as
he rushed past to get to the dirty dishes. When asked to get the shovel
Jape said, "Yes sir," and took off in a dead run and came back the
same way. Dad thought, 'from the ashes of every fire' wondering if
the scars on his spirit were as visible as those on his back. He watched
the boy with a totally new outlook.

While saddling up the horse to ride to the store, Jape asked, "They
are going to talk about Tubbs and me, aren't they?"

"Something like that, I guess."

"Well, I, uh, who's going to, do I have to, . . . oh, forget it",
Jape mumbled.

"Don't worry, everyone at the store will be in your corner for a
change", dad told his son.

"I'm not worried about my corner. George and the others need help."

"Who is George?"

"One of the boys, just a boy from Arkansas, nobody, nobody."

"Let's listen to what they have to say and don't worry."

They arrived on horseback immediately after Uncle John drove up with
Tubbs. The two boys were in fine spirits, they raced at each other and
instantly stopped to butt heads and do the 'melonshake'. At that time
someone asked, "What are you boys going to do with that danged fish."

Jape shouted, "We're going to have a feast one of these days."

The longest and biggest car in the world drove up and a gigantic
man stepped from the vehicle. Jape exclamed, "It's Sam Houston."

The big man turned to point at Jape, "I like that lad, the greatest
compliment I have ever had in my life would have to come from a
little boy. That boy has read his history book. Sam and I have one
thing in common, we are both six foot six."

Everyone there was standing around in awe of the well dressed big guy. John walked out of the store to say, "Hi." and shook hands with the big fellow who continued to talk,

"Hello John, it's been awhile since we played 'Red-Rover' across the street, huh?"

"Yep, a lotta water under the bridge."

The big guy took control as he raised his voice, "Well, folks, my name is McCrimmins. I'm not exactly your neighbor but I own a little pasture land over there," nodding his head toward where Jape and Tubbs caught the fish. Then he continued, "I went to school with John right here at Crossroads. To make matters worse, I'm also an attorney and I'm running for the State Senate. So you see, I'm here for several reasons. Since I grew up here, I know how hard you folks work and how difficult it is for working people to find justice in the court system. I have a friend in the car, who can help you, if you will take the time to listen."

"Who is it?", John asked.

"Don't matter, will you give me your word to listen", McCrimmins asked, "Then, I have another speech for you. Okay, is it a deal?"

John looked around then asked, "Won't hurt to listen, will it?"

Everyone seemed to have nodded their approval.

"Okay, John, I now have everyone's word. You will let him have his say without any nasty remarks, okay, John." McCrimmins shouted, "Come on out, it's safe." The banker came crawling out of the car to the "boo's" of nearly everyone.

"Let him have his say. If God had made mankind without greed you would probably like the banker. So for a few moments blame God for the man's greed!", McCrimmins shouted.

The banker walked over to the crowd, he knew everyone and had on more than one occasion talked with all of them about financial matters in his bank. He started slowly attempting to control his emotions and words, when McCrimmins said, "What do you need, a soap box?"

"Your words were true, my entire life has been consumed by greed. Yes, my own greed. It's time for me to change. I can't speak for any of you, I can change myself. I started the moment h I saw those stripes on Jape's back. First, I want to apologize to those two boys and their parents. Yea, yea, I know you have heard that old "I'm sorry" routine before. Y'all all know me and I know you, you know that words come easily for me but these words come hard. You know me and I'm sure that most of you have said things like, 'He'd steal the nickel's from his dead mother's eyes', about me and I've heard some of you say much worse. I'm willing to put my money where my mouth is. I mailed a check to the hospital, I paid the boys' hospital bill and told all the doctors to send me their bill, I'll take care of them too. I cannot pay for the pain I've caused those boys to suffer but I . . . want . . . you . . . good . . . people to . . . know that . . . I really do care." Tears were streaming down his face and he couldn't continue talking.

McCrimmins spoke for him, "What we would like to do is hold court out here at the store. If we went to town, to the Courthouse, the boys, am I correct, their names are Jape and Tubbs?" Someone nodded and he continued, "the boys would not have any rights. Here in our court they will have THE say. Well, what do you say?" He looked straight at John for an answer.

John asked, "What are you talking about?"

"I'm an attorney, I'm sure the parents would like to see the banker hanged, shot or burned at the stake. Well, we are here to offer him up for judgment, sentencing, and punishment."

"You're joking?", was John's reply.

"No joke, we do have a condition, one or both of the boys must be the Judge and no death penalty."

"This sounds silly, like kid stuff", John shot back.

"John, look around you, life is kid stuff. I can see those boys backs from here. You think a homestyle court would be a charade, you should sit in on the real juvenile hearing. Children aren't even entitled to a trial, all they get is a hearing. Ask the boys about the trial they got before being locked up and subjected to the Donkey Hide. Gentlemen, children don't have any rights, think about it, this is 1939, we are well into the twentieth century. We have a trancontinential railroad, airmail coast to coast, radio and electricity will soon be available to everyone. In the immediate future you, yes you, will be driving your own automobile. Men, it is time to provide some rights for our children. If you are thinking, McCrimmins has a motive to his madness, yes, you are thinking right. The point I hope to make is that something is wrong. When you hear it from the likes of me your memory fades rapidly but when you hear it from one of your own and especially from a child you will never forget. What I want is for your boys, the victims of the system, to have their say. This is their only chance, they can talk to each of you as an individual but you and I know that won't happen. The parents don't have a remedy through the courts, remember, I'm an attorney. I can file a law suit for the parents, to have another Judge throw it out of court. Children, gentlemen, do not have any rights. I'm trying to tell you it is high time to change the law. If you will appease me, we will enter a plea of guilty at this point. The boys will have their say and provide the penalty." He looked directly at Jape to continue, "You boys get together and tell us which one or if both of you want to be the judge." He hesitated for a few moments then told John, "John, you pick three people as assistants. Your voice will act as the Supreme Court, you can overrule the boys, if you choose to do so. When you feel the decision is fair, the banker will live with it."

"You are serious, if these boys decide the banker should pay two thousand dollars for his short comings?", John asked.

"If the banker doesn't write the check on the spot, I will."

Everyone looked to John to talk for them. Dad sat quietly on the bench whittling, his mind was made up, if the wrong wasn't corrected, he would in his own quiet way handle it, everyone, including the banker knew that too. McCrimmins knew if something wasn't done the banker would be a cadaver within the next few months, and the county would have one more unsolved murder on the books.

John looked around to ask, "Do I need to tell you the names of . . .?"

McCrimmins stopped him, "Nope, don't have to."

"Why don't we ask the boys?", John suggested.

"Great idea, what about it, fellows?", McCrimmins asked.

The two boys looked at each other and shrugged their shoulders. Jape spoke, "We don't need any more trouble. The banker was mean and hateful but I never heard of a boy gettin' to punish a banker. Is that what you are asking?"

"Exactly, at this point but the issue I hope to make will be a much broader one after I get the opportunity to show everyone the big picture, but yes, you will have a say in punishing the banker."

Both boys grinned and nodded as Jape said, "Yea, I could handle that."

"Which one wants to be the Judge?"

"What will the other boy do?", Jape asked.

"Be the attorney, like me, a spokesperson, tell everyone about how you were wronged."

"Tubbs will be the Judge and I'll be the attorney."

"Yes, and it will be fitting and proper for the boys to get the opportunity to tell their story. We want to hold this meeting in the schoolhouse so everyone can hear what we have to say."

Jape butted in, "People will think Tubbs and I are bad just because we've been in the reform school and that ain't good. We aren't bad and a lot of those boys inside aren't bad either. If the banker is going to spend some money, let him throw a feed for everyone in this community. While everyone eats we will have the, whatever you call it. Can we do it that way?''

''Out of the mouthes of babe's, that is the best idea since old Eli Whitney did the gin'', McCrimmins shouted in full agreement with the boy.

The banker interrupted with a broad greedy smile, ''We can hold it on a Sunday, invite Charley and Maud then sell tickets at the door.''

A round of loud boo's greeted this remark while everyone laughed shaking their heads.

''Old habits do die hard, that man is greedy, he can smell a dollar from half a mile. The man is so cheap, I was visiting his farm last week, we were across the back forty when he got sick to his stomach. That chinchy fellow ran across forty acres to puke in the hog trough.'' Everyone laughed with a few hoots for applause, as McCrimmins continued, ''I'll hold the banker in check, there will not be any admission charged. That, my boy, is a fine idea. The banker will be happy to foot the bill for a public picnic dinner.''

''That's not all'', Jape shouted.

Total silence descended upon the men as they turned to look at the boy.

''We want Mr. Wilson to bring the rack and the Donkey Hide out to the school and demonstrate it. We want everyone to see how the boys in the reform school are punished, you know, what happened to us!'' That request caused eyes to drop and feet to shuffle.

McCrimmins took over. ''This young man will do well for himself; however, he is cutting into my glory now. I am campaigning on prison reform and this topic is my area of expertise. I accept this as a wonderful opportunity, I have the urge to unload my speech on you gentlemen but . . .''

''Spare us, please, spare us the speech'', John shouted as he laughed in unison with most everyone else.

''It is difficult to put icing on the boys request but I'll try, but just who is Wilson?,'' McCrimmins asked, turning to the banker for the answer.

''He is one of my brother's supervisors at the reform school.''

''He's the one that know's how to use the Donkey Hide'', Jape added.

Dad was gritting his teeth and having difficulty keeping silent.

''Yes, no reason we can't get Wilson and some of the equipment from the school, which goes along with the regular program I am taking across the state in my campaign. We have officers from the men's prison at McCallister who demonstrate similar equipment. I will take this rare opportunity to combine the two, and after discussing every detail with these two boys, attempt to enlighten the community on our prison system."

"And reform school", Jape cut in.

"Yes, including the reform school. The only thing left to do is set a date, two weeks from Sunday, okay?", McCrimmins asked.

"Can't be any later, everyone will start picking cotton around that time, best make sure it goes off on schedule."

"Okay, I'll take full responsibility for everything except the boys. Jape will have his speech for the prosecution ready, and Tubbs will have some idea of what punishment the banker should endure. I will have people here from both the prison and the reform school. The banker will write the check after I order the food for the occasion. Oh, how many people can we expect?"

"For free food, everyone will show, two hundred", John guessed.

The banker moaned as McCrimmins, "Sounds as if interest rates just went up at the Paoli bank, I'll keep an eye on that for you also."

The two weeks flew by because Jape and Tubbs were getting back into the swing of home life. They went hunting at least three times a week and swimming almost every day. Mr. Tips was nearly as happy to see the boys as they were to see him. Jape thought he barked treed in a happier voice than before they left. Mama's chicken fried squirrel and cream gravy sure beat unseasoned cabbage and potatoes. Every time they sat down to a home cooked meal and lowered their head for grace, for the first time in their young lives they were truly thankful. The thought of George and the boys forcing down that terrible rice or breaking a glob of baked dough they called bread, brought a different meaning to home and mama's cooking. If only they could invite George to dinner!

The boys spent most of the two weeks together, 'the Judge and the attorney' for the prosecution, openly discussed the case, not unlike the real Judge's and attorney's do today on the golf course. These boys were trying to do the right thing, wouldn't it be nice if all the conversation on the golf course today was directed along their line of thinking. Before the two weeks passed they had arrived at a mutual understanding of what they wanted but they didn't know the words they would use to get their point across. Jape liked Mr. McCrimmins, even if he was a politician, he was a good man. Jape would say what he had to say and felt McCrimmins would understand if no one else did. Both boys agreed on their plan and went on with another hunting adventure.

During the two weeks, Jape's parents never once brought the matter up. Mom was happy to see Jape's smiling face at the dinner table. She could care less about the stupid games the men were planning. Dad didn't put much stock in the "Kangaroo Court", he would watch and wait. A free meal at the banker's expense he could take or leave. McCrimmins was another story, he didn't know how to take him. No doubt, McCrimmins was trying to grease his own axle but it wasn't so bad to scratch a man's back that would return the favor without a knife in his hand. He was looking at McCrimmins with an eye of caution.

The Sunday finally came. Everyone was decked out in their best duds. Jape and Tubbs had on shirts, their good overalls and their new school shoes. Tubbs' mom had to work and couldn't be there so Tubbs stayed all night with Jape. They rode in back of the wagon with Jape's parents. This was a bigger event than the revival meeting, cars and wagons were everywhere. Dad tied the team up in back of John's store so he and John could walk across the street together. This was a 'noon' feed and everyone arrived about eleven and most started eating immediately. It turned out to be a giant feast, McCrimmins stood around laughing and talking. When someone paid him a compliment on the food he said, "Purchasing this food was a real pleasure, the first time I ever had the opportunity to spend a banker's money. This is your interest on the interest you have been paying for years, so eat hearty."

This was a harvest feast and more, they had 'baloney'. That storeboughten meat was something different, the boys tried it and fell in love with 'baloney'. Every boy there ate at least ten slices, the table was covered with fried chicken, baked turkey, roast beef, a baked pig and many other meat dishes but the banker was in his car racing toward Paoli to get another ten pounds of balogna.

The entire community felt McCrimmins did a fine job of fulfilling his promise to put on a feed for the community. Some felt it was too much, the same thing could have been accomplished for a lot less money. It was McCrimmins who insisted on giving the best to the people at Crossroads. Probably because he went to school there and the main reason, he wanted their votes come election time. Either way, everyone was full when the show started.

Everyone ate outside, then went inside the tworoom building for the program. The school building faced the west with two front doors, one for each room, a room divider was moved opening the building into one large room. The stage was located to the right upon entering the front door or the south end of the building. McCrimmins was well prepared, the stage curtain was closed as he opened the meeting with a few cute and witty comments. He outlined the program, explaining that the last event would be the little court session. After the program was outlined he turned the show over to a Captain from the men's Prison at McCallister and at the same time the curtain was opened to a scene not unlike the day Jape and Tubbs was introduced to the Donkey Hide.

The Captain didn't say a word, he picked up a large wooden handle attached to a strap of leather six inches wide and five feet long. In a quick motion he flipped the leatherstrap into the air, bringing it down hard across the floor. When the leatherstrap hit the floor the noise was equal to a shot gun blast. In three quick motions, the strap was pounded against the floor, each time rocking the room with the sharp blast from each blow. The audience was aghast at the horrible thought of someone getting beaten like that in this time of modernization, THIS was 1939 and there were laws, Oklahoma became a state in 1907. Indian Territory habits were gone, the nation was supposed to be living by the written words of civilized laws.

The captain stopped and turned to the audience, holding up the wide piece of leather as he stated, "This is called the Donkey Hide. It is in use today at the prison, we give every man that comes in five lashes with the Donkey Hide, that is part of the punishment. The institution has rules, exactly like you have laws to live by. Inside the prison, we have a few more rules to live by than you have out here. If convicts do not obey the rules, the Donkey Hide is applied to encourage them to change their ways. It works, to a degree."

The captain continued to explain prison life, bringing out a man dressed in a broad black and white striped prison uniform with a number on the left breast pocket. After several minutes, he introduced Mr. Wilson from the local reform school. Wilson talked for another half hour on the operation of the reform school, which included another demonstration of the smaller version of the Donkey Hide as used on the boys in the reform school. For this demonstration he had the same flogging block from the school right there on stage with a boy strapped in. Then in a surprise move, waved his hand in an effort to get Jape on stage.

Jape walked upon the stage, "I'm not volunteering for more Donkey Tracks."

The audience laughed although they didn't know why. Wilson explained that the Donkey Hide left marks, asking Jape to take his shirt off. The audience gave out with a terrible, "AAaaawwooooo," when they saw the marks on the boy's back. Wilson assisted Jape put his shirt back on, then continued, "When the Donkey Hide is applied to men or boys they leave those kind of stripes, some show more than others but always, marks. At the prison or the reform school these marks are referred to as tracks, Donkey Tracks. I don't have to tell you people these are hard times. I have worked for the fine State of Oklahoma for sixteen years and a little more. It has been my job to put those tracks on the backs of boys for the last seven years. Eating regular and keeping my family eating regular has always been important to me, that is until yesterday. Yesterday, I turned in my resignation. I will no longer be a party to that type punishment. I'm hoping to assist Mr. McCrimmins change the system so boys will not have to wear Donkey Tracks anywhere at anytime and men like me can keep working." He walked off the stage to a loud roar of applause.

The captain came back on stage to unveil a large wooden chair, which all the adults recognized immediately as the "Electric Chair" which was the legal means of providing the death penalty in Oklahoma in 1939. The Captain explained the function of the chair as he strapped one of his assistants in for a demonstration. The demonstration took another twenty minutes but everyone's mind was still on the Donkey Tracks seen on Jape's back.

The demonstration complete, McCrimmins took center stage again. He proceeded to explain what had happened, the entire incident with the boys and the banker. To the boys' surprise, he made them look like purely innocent victims leaving out many of their little crimes. He made the banker look bad but, of course, he was a politician and knew where the votes were. McCrimmins explained what the boys were about to do, to set punishment for his client, the banker. In starting he would say a few words on the behalf of his client.

McCrimmins asked Jape and Tubbs to step upon the stage. One of the assistants produced the teacher's chair for "The Judge" and Tubbs took the seat and Jape sat off to the other side.

McCrimmins, pointing to Jape, "That kid is only an attorney, all he gets is a metal folding chair."

Everyone laughed as McCrimmins continued to speak, "Okay, the stage is set. In a real trial, each attorney would make a closing argument or statement. This is what we're going to do today. I'm going to say a few words for my client, the banker, and Jape is going to say a few words for himself and Tubbs, yes, yes, a little different, but it will work."

Someone shouted from the audience, "Don't you think you're a little outclassed, up against those two?"

Once more the audience laughed.

McCrimmins, "Thank you, thank you sir, I was wondering how to get that point across to you. In a real court, boys or children don't have any rights. At least they are going to be heard in this court. Let me repeat that, children don't have any rights. Do you realize that a judge can take your children by signing his name on a piece of paper. No one can bother the court with facts, there isn't any law on the books. The law does not protect your children in any way; not from a crazed parent, a drunk parent, a crooked Judge or a greedy banker."

Once again he stopped to point at his client, the banker, before continuing. "Ask Jape, I don't have to, I know what happened. Those boys were doomed to the reform school and the Donkey Hide the moment greed popped up in the banker's eyes. Now, in defense of my client, this isn't entirely his problem. This greedy banker didn't pass the law, he took advantage of it. You people elect those who do make the laws. You're going to get the opportunity to vote for someone that will work for change. If you agree that your children and all children should have rights, help me change the law. I will work as hard for you as I am working for the banker today, all you have to do is vote!"

McCrimmins cleared his throat, swallowed and said, "Excuse me, now, would you please answer one question, and be honest. How many of you adults were spanked as children?" He stopped talking to visually survey the audience, then added, "Too many hands to count, let me ask it another way. How many never got a spanking in their life?" He looked around the room searching but there wasn't a hand raised. To get a laugh he shouted, "Put your hand down, my client, the banker, was the only one whose hand I saw. See what your child will turn out to be if you don't apply the firm hand of discipline. Yes, I believe in spanking too. The problem, as voters, we approved spanking as a form of disciplinary punishment, what we get is beatings. Some stupid idiot's interpretation of the law, allowed my client the opportunity to take advantage of these boys. We need someone in office to revise some of the laws and provide new laws to protect the children from tyrannical Judges. Your Judge isn't the only Judge that is on the take, oh yes, that is the proper phrase. A Judge that can be swayed by friendship is equally as guilty as one swayed by money. We have both in every city in this nation. There is something wrong when a Judge can sign his name and take children away from their parents without investigation or a trial. In nearly every case the children are the victims of the legal system. The old saying, no one is above the law, well, I think it's high time we place all children ages ten and younger above the law. Yes, I realize that is impossible, but ladies and gentlemen, it is 1939, don't you believe it's time to take care of our children and jump into the twentieth century. Some of those that will be asking for your vote, don't understand the problem. When you go to the polls, remember, I do understand, and I thank you." He bowed to the people who applauded and he turned back to wave his arms to get them to stop.

"I have one more statement, then, I'll give Jape a chance to talk. It is about time for the Judge to sentence my client. The banker and I will set up a trust fund for these two boys' college education. What about that?"

Once again the audience cheered as McCrimmins waved for them to stop. "Now, I turn the floor over to Jape." He walked over toward Jape to ask, "Do you want to stand up or talk sitting down? Is there anyway that I can help?"

"Yes sir, sit down and let me talk", Jape suggested.

Once again every one laughed as McCrimmins ran over to take Jape's chair.

Jape had recited or read aloud in class a few times, but never stood before a large group of people. He was scared, he looked at Tubbs who grinned. Jape pushed his hands deep into his overall pockets and spoke, "I'm scared to death, but not nearly as scared as the day they tied our hands into that thing." He turned to point at the rack sitting on the back of the stage. "At least today if I goof or say a wrong word, Mrs. Auld, ain't here to correct my English."

He was interrupted by a very polite but firm female voice from the back of the room, "Oh, yes I am young man."

This gave the audience one more chance to break the tension with laughter. Jape turned to look at McCrmmins as he continued, "Tubbs and I were guilty of doing some bad things but not bad enough to, you know, get put in the reform school. We don't want the banker's money for college, if and when we get that far we will find our own way to school. We don't want anything for us, what we want is what Mr. Wilson was talking about. Take the Donkey Hide out of the Reform school and let Mrs. Auld show them how to use the paddle."

Once more the crowd whistled and hooted.

"We didn't belong in reform school and most of the boys in there don't belong in there either. Some of them didn't do nothin', they don't have parents and have to face a life with the Donkey Hide, silence and terrible food."

Jape looked back at McCrimmins and grinned at Tubbs, "I'll admit, I do have more than a little influence on this Judge and I have asked him to have your client change the meals at the reform school. I have agreed to furnish the fish for a big fish fry at the reform school. Of course, the cost of cooking and all the good stuff the city folks eat will be served at your client's expense."

Jape stopped and looked around, shrugged his shoulders and added, "That's all I want or have to say."

The crowd applauded as McCrimmins took the floor shaking his head to say, "And to think, that boy's words of wisdom would not be heard in any court of law in this nation, he doesn't have any rights. Sorry, folks, but I can't pass up another opportunity to keep my mouth shut, VOTE FOR ME AND CHANGE THE LAW." He started to sit down then turned back, "Oh, now is the time for the Judge's decision. I yield to the Judge, the floor is your's, Tubbs."

"Do I stand up or can I sit down?", Tubbs asked.

"Your Honor, you may do as you please", McCrimmins told him.

"Okay, let me drag the chair out toward . . ."

McCrimmins ran over to take the chair, "Your Honor, allow me, where do you want to place the chair."

"Up next to the edge of the stage so I don't have to look at Jape while I talk. He'll make me laugh."

"How about right here?"

"That's perfect."

Tubbs settled down by twisting around in the chair then looked out across the audience, gulped and tried to speak. "Yes, yea, I see right now what Jape was talking about. I did have something to say but I forgot what it was. Oh yea, the banker, we want, oh, as the Judge, I want the banker to work with Jape and Mr. McCrimmins to change things at the reform school. I insist that he put on the fish fry, you know, take Jape's fish and have it cooked."

He turned to McCrimmins, "If you can't find anyone that knows how to cook, you can ask Jape's grandmaw, she is the best cook around."

Once more the crowd hooted in agreement.

"As the Judge, I didn't ask Jape about this next part. This is my idea, the men may not let me do this but I feel Jape should get some reward personally from the banker. The other day I heard one of the men say that he thought the banker had lost his marbles. Well, that got me to thinking. If the banker hasn't lost his marbles, as the judge, I would give him a chance to lose his marbles. I want the banker to play marbles, keeps, with Jape for two hours ever Sunday until it snows. In case the banker don't know how to play, I'll be present to provide the rules and tell each player when the two hours are up. I'm sure the banker don't have any marbles; Rule one, the banker will buy fifty marbles from Jape at a price of one dollar each and should the banker need additional marbles before the two hours are up he will buy those from Jape at the same price. At the end of two hours, the banker will sell all the marbles he has in his possession back to Jape for two dollars each. The banker has a 'chance' of getting excellent interest on his investment. The first game will be held outside immediately after this program.''

The audience was in a state of shock, they didn't understand the childish decision to play a game of marbles. Some were laughing, while others were criticizing the entire charade.

The program had gone so well up to this point, McCrimmins jumped up shouting, ''No problem, the banker should get on his knees more often. Playing marbles could be the right start.''

He looked toward John for some type of response, John answered, ''Tubbs, is the Judge and I don't have a problem with that marble game. I've seen Jape play marbles. I'm the one that thought the banker had already lost them all!''

''Great, but we won't hold the boy to buying the marbles back at two dollars each'', McCrimmins responded.

''There won't be none to buy back, that was only a hook to get the banker interested, anyway'', Tubbs laughed making it clear to McCrimmins.

McCrimmins lowered his head and looked out of the corner of his eye at the Judge, ''Can Jape play marbles?''

Tubbs grinning from ear to ear, ''Can you talk?''

McCrimmins looked across the room at the banker, ''Can you play marbles?''

The banker shrugged his shoulders, ''For a dollar a marble, you can bet I'm going to learn.'' The banker appeared to be taking it all in good stride.

''I like this'', McCrimmins said as he raised his voice, ''For those interested, there will be a marble game on the north side of the building in fifteen minutes.''

The crowd left the building laughing, they had been treated to a wonderful meal, enjoyed a most entertaining and informative show. The banker appeared to be sincere in his effort to correct his mistakes, for many reasons, including the right to live, while establishing a new and more solid foundation of trust with those in the community.

Everyone was sauntering out the door laughing and talking. Jape told Tubbs, "I don't have any marbles with me."

Tubbs, "You always have your taw."

Jape, "Yes, I got the tool box but you said fifty marbles."

Tubbs, "Yep, I furnish the marbles and pick'em up fer half?"

Jape grinned, "You're as bad as the real Judge or the banker."

They walked around the corner and found a large smooth spot on the ground where Tubbs drew a large ring. Immediately after drawing the ring McCrimmins and the banker walked up.

McCrimmins spoke, "We have one minor problem, the banker spent his last few bucks on balogna. Is there some way we could finance this first game?"

"If we loan him the marbles, it would be the same as loaning him the money. What has he got to put up for security?", Tubbs joked.

John piped up, "Attach the car or demand the deed to the bank."

"You can leave the money at the store, next week sometime. We aren't in the banking business, yet!", Tubbs answered seriously.

"I'll see to it that any money he owes will be left at the store. What if the banker wins all Jape's marbles?", McCrimmins asked.

Tubbs lowered his head to cock it sideways, as Mr. Tips always did when the boys were eating sausage, to grin, "He has about the same chance of beating Jape as the widow Williams has of getting her lot back."

Everyone there shouted with laughter, as Dad nudged John's arm, "Can the kid play marbles?"

"You haven't seen Jape shoot marbles? Just watch, watch!"

"I don't know, I never watched him play. He can milk a cow about as fast as anyone I ever saw. I would enter him in a milking contest."

Tubbs looked over at John and winked as he asked, "Anyone have a watch I could borrow to time this contest with?"

John pulled out his pocket watch and gave it to Tubbs.

Tubbs gave the banker fifty marbles, leaving five in his pocket for Jape to stake up in the first game.

Tubbs turned to the banker, "You have to stake five marbles up each game."

After the ten marbles were placed in the ring, Tubbs racked them into a large "V" in the center of the ring, then announced, "Each player will lag to see who shoots first. Anyone deliberately stalling or taking too long to shoot will lose that turn and losing two turns will result in loss of all the marbles in that game. In two minutes, the game will start. He walked out about ten feet and drew a line. Raised his voice to say, "You can lag now to see who shoots first."

Jape threw his taw and it rolled within two inches of the line. The banker tossed one of the marbles, leaving it about a foot away from the line.

Tubbs said, "Okay, Jape shoots first, and it's time to start."

Jape knelt down on the line then stopped to look up at the Judge, "I need to take my shoes off."

Tubbs turned to the banker and grinned, "Looks like he's going to give you first shot." He looked back at Jape to say, "You should have thought about that before. Take your shoes off and forfeit your turn?"

Jape smiled up at the banker, "Go ahead and shoot". Jape untied his shoes and slipped the new shoes off and gave them to his dad, "Don't want to scuff the toes playing marbles."

The banker crawled up to the line and thumped his taw in the general direction of the marbles. The taw hit the ground and bounced over without hitting the pile. It was Jape's turn, he placed his fist that held the marble on the line, aimed and fired, his taw splattered the pile knocking out several marbles. The taw stuck in the middle and he continued to shoot. His taw would hit the marble he was aiming at then spin or roll across or around to the marble for the next shot. When he wanted it to, the taw would spin to the right or to the left or back up after hitting the marble. That taw seemed to dance as if it had eyes. Jape didn't miss until the ring was empty of marbles.

"I didn't get but one shot and lost five bucks", the banker complained.

"The boy forfeited his first shot or you wouldn't have gotten that", McCrimmins reminded the banker as everyone laughed.

"I don't have a chance playing that kid's game!", the banker griped.

"Now you know how we feel walking into your bank!", John shot back.

"What happens if I don't get to shoot?", the banker asked.

"The same thing the widow Williams got when you forclosed!", someone shouted. The game was being accepted as exactly that, "A Game" by most everyone and about half of the men were remaining to watch the game.

"The looser always gets to shoot first in each game. I have a feeling you'll get to shoot in each and every game." Tubbs reminded him as he collected five marbles from each player and racked another "V" in the center of the ring. And again Tubbs reminded the banker, "It's your shot."

The banker dropped to his knees, he placed his hand down on the line in his effort to shoot. Jape watched, then, kneeled down beside the man to say, "Sir, if you will turn your hand over, like this, aim before you shoot, in shooting you thump the taw . . . look at the one you want to hit, with your eye, line it up. You can shoot better if you think about it."

"Like this?" the banker asked as he rearranged his hand and the taw.

"I have a feeling before it snows this winter, this lad is going to teach you a thing or two about the game of LIFE as well as the game of marbles", McCrimmins told the banker but loud enough for all to hear.

"If you think about it seriously, not much difference in the two!", John remarked in all seriousness.

"Look's like I'll either learn to play marbles or he'll own my bank. And, I may have to employ both boys as business managers."

"I have a feeling everyone in the community is going to have a new thought about the banker losing his marbles!", McCrimmins joked.

"These boys have succeeded in doing something every preacher in the community has failed to get accomplished . . .", John teased.

"What's that John?", McCrimmins asked.

"Get the banker on his knees and you know he's going to be praying for snow." He raised his voice an octave or two so the small group of farmers could hear. "Just in case the banker has some pull with the heavenly father, you fellows better get your cotton in, we may have an early snow."